Sequenced: a YA Dystopian Romance

THE SEQUENCING CHRONICLES

ELAYNA R. GALLEA

Copyright © 2021 by Elayna Doucet

First paperback edition December. 2021

Cover by getcovers.com

Map by Daniela Pray

ISBN (ebook): 978-1-7779283-0-8

ISBN (paperback): 978-1-7779283-3-9

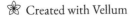 Created with Vellum

To my husband, Aaron.
For always believing in me and being my biggest cheerleader.
I love you.
To Britanny and Jack,
For being my reason every day.

Contents

PART THREE

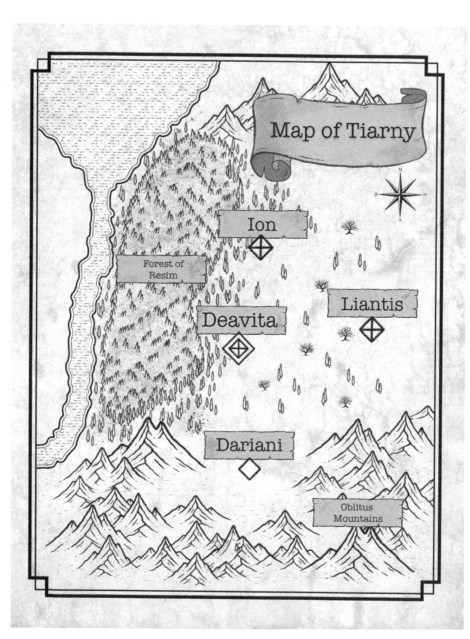

Prologue

53 Years After Inception

5   The storm raged through the night, thunder booming through the skies as bright lightning provided much needed glimpses of the path ahead. Torrential rains fell as the wind whirled around the hooded pair hurrying down the road. The scent of fresh rain flooded their senses as it washed away the sweat and grime that had been crusting their clothing after days on the run.

They ran through the night; the lightning guiding their movements as their black capes billowed in the wind. They moved swiftly; the rain soaked through their cloaks and blood-red tunics, causing never-ending streams of water to run down their bodies. Strands of their hair stuck to their faces as they travelled. They had left the relative safety of the Forest of Resim hours before. There, the blackened trees and ebony leaves had successfully hidden them from their pursuers throughout the day.

Once night had fallen, the time to move had arrived. The couple had packed up their small camp; the male holding his sword and sharpening his daggers while the female slung her bow over her back before she placed the precious bundle in a sling on her chest. No one spoke. The only sounds were the sticks breaking under their feet. Even the birds were silent, as though they too understood the urgency with which they moved. With a quick prayer to the Source, petitioning Her for safety and well-being, they had left the forest the moment the sun slipped beneath the horizon.

Anyone watching from afar would have seen two Royal Protectors patrolling the Queen's Road. Nothing too far out of the ordinary, except for their distance from the capital. It wasn't unheard of for the Queen's Protectors to be safeguarding the trade route, although she hadn't left her castle in years. Most people didn't know that, though. The Officials had made sure that word of the Queen's illness hadn't gotten past the Firsts. There were whispers of speculation that rang through the streets of Deavita, the capital, late at night. Some said that the Queen had gone mad after the Purge. Others argued that disease had eaten away at her mind. Regardless, everyone in Tiarny knew of and respected the Queen. To do anything less would be to invite the Source's wrath.

If anyone got close enough to the Protectors running down the Queen's Road, their distance from the capital wouldn't matter. Prying eyes would know something was wrong when they saw their evident exhaustion, the bags under their eyes, the weight of sleeplessness hanging over them. If the wrong person saw the bundle they carried, it would all be over. This was their only hope. The Prophets often spoke in riddles, but on this, they had been clear. If the Sequenced got their hands on what they were ferrying through the wilderness, they would lose all hope forever.

Hours passed as they ran through the night. They stopped long enough to eat and take care of their basic needs before they continued moving. They had brought precious supplies for themselves and the bundle when they left the Oblitus Mountains, but even these were running low. They ran and ran, constantly going northeast until the sun rose once more over the grassy hills.

"Julian. Wait." The woman spoke for the first time in hours, her voice hoarse from lack of use. They had moved off the Queen's Road, ducking into a forest that lined the trade route. Her warm brown eyes were bleary, her black hair damp and sticking to her sepia skin as she leaned against the trunk of a large evergreen tree. The rising sun loomed above, reaching out with its tendrils, shoving back the darkness they so desperately needed. With every moment that passed, their ability to travel safely was disappearing. "We need to find a place to rest. *It* needs to eat again."

They didn't dare speak out loud the truth of what they were carrying. In Tiarny, it seemed even the trees had ears. The memory of the Purge was fresh in everyone's mind and no one wanted to risk the Queen's ire.

Julian nodded. "You're right, Mari. I don't think we'll make it to Ion today." He sighed and leaned up against a tree, dropping his pack on the soft green grass below. The scent of pine filled the air. Julian crouched down and rifled through the contents before he pulled out a small bottle that he extended to his companion. "Here, take this. There's a grove of trees over there. No matter what happens, stay hidden. Keep *it* safe. I'll find us a place to stay and be back soon."

Exhaustion was apparent on his features as he rubbed his hand over his face. Picking up his pack, he shouldered it once more before he ran deep into the forest.

Mari paced among the trees, worry lining her face. Hours had passed. The heat of the day had come and gone, and Julian still hadn't returned. The threat of their pursuers loomed large over her head. Protectors and Officials had been tracking them since they had escaped from the Oblitus

Mountains, the precious bundle tucked under Mari's cloak. They had gained some distance during the storm last night. The rain had washed away their scent, but Mari knew it wouldn't take their pursuers long to find them now that the weather had cleared.

The bundle was restless, its bottle long since emptied. Soft cries were filling the air and Mari was running out of ways to keep it quiet. She was down to the last few pieces of bread and cheese she had been keeping in her pack. Her water supply was dangerously low. Her heart pounding with worry, she kept peeking out from the trees, glancing to see if Julian was nearby. Every sound, every twig cracking or crunch of leaves caused her to jump as she waited for her partner to return.

Finally, she could wait no more. The sun was setting; the day was coming to a close. In her heart, she knew he wasn't coming back. There was no way he would have left them here alone on purpose. Silent tears tracked down her cheeks as she shouldered her pack and grabbed her bow. She placed the bundle in the sling around her chest, tears falling on its bald head as she hurried. She had to succeed. There was no other option.

Sending prayer after silent prayer to the Source for Julian's soul, Mari took a deep breath and left the grove of trees that had shielded them throughout the day. Her stomach protested her lack of proper sustenance as she once again began to run, her legs pounding on the dirt road. She had to make it to Ion tonight. She had no choice. Mari knew she wouldn't last another day on the road.

Once again, she ran through the night, her muscles crying out in pain with every footfall. The woman was grateful that her movement lulled the bundle to sleep. At least in sleep, it wasn't wailing, threatening to give away their position. There was no storm tonight, no clouds in sight. The stars glittered in the sky, lighting the path ahead of her. Hour after hour, she ran. Her lungs burned with the effort, her limited stores of water had disappeared hours ago.

And still, she ran.

Finally, when the moon was high in the sky, Mari almost cried out in relief as her destination came into view. There was a modest wooden cottage with a thatched roof in the distance, a lantern shining in the window and casting shadows on the garden outside. A few fruit trees surrounded the home, their branches creating eerie shapes in the darkness. Relief poured through her body, coating every nerve and numbing her grief. She had made it.

The Royal Protector let out a silent sob as she ran the final few miles to the cottage. She arrived on the doorstep, her sudden stop waking the bundle once more. Mari saw its eyes grow wide as it threatened to scream. Just then, the door swung open, its hinges groaning their protest into the still night air. A young couple stood in the doorway, their faces tired but alert.

"Quick, come inside." The man said urgently as he held the door open, gesturing for Mari to enter. She gazed upwards to look him in the eyes as he murmured. "We expected you yesterday. Where is your companion?"

His dark eyes searched Mari's as though looking for answers.

She had been expecting this question and had known it would come. Even so, it was too much.

"He didn't make it." Mari choked on the words, forcing them out. "He never came back this morning." Tears began streaming down her face once more, the reality of the situation hitting her.

The sight of Mari's tears stirred the other woman into action. Her white cap bobbed as she moved to the fire, grabbing a kettle that was hanging above it. She poured a cup of piping hot tea and placed it on the table next to Mari.

"Here," she said. "I'm Berta and this is Rolf. Let me help."

Berta sat down and gestured for Mari to hand her the bundle.

Grateful for the offer, the exhausted Protector gently took the baby out of the sling before passing it to Berta. Mari watched as she pulled open her shift and began nursing the child. She immediately relaxed as the babe settled in the woman's arms. With a sigh of relief, she reached around her neck and unclasped the necklace she had been wearing since they fled the Oblitus Mountains. She placed the delicate necklace into Rolf's awaiting palm.

Exhaling, she ran a hand over her face.

She had done it; she had accomplished her mission.

Mari knew she couldn't stay in the small cottage. The presence of a Royal Protector would attract too much attention. She finished the cup of tea and warmed herself by the crackling fire before she stood in the doorway, going over things one last time.

"You know the plan?" Rolf whispered urgently.

Mari nodded. She and Julian had gone over it step by step while they were on the move. They had always known it was possible they wouldn't both make it to Ion. They were willing to sacrifice everything for this baby.

"The baby is the hope for us all." Mari repeated from memory. "You were handpicked because Berta gave birth to your own daughter two weeks ago. You will take in the baby and raise her alongside yours as twins."

As if on cue, a wail came from a crib in the corner. Berta hurried over, placing both babies in the crib. Mari smiled softly before continuing. Her voice lacked emotion as she recited the plan.

"Your cottage is far enough out of town so as not to raise many questions. Your baby hasn't yet been Blessed by the Officials. There is a sympathetic Midwife who will write paperwork for her, legitimizing her presence in the city."

Mari stopped, her voice catching as tears ran down her cheeks. Berta stood up and took over the telling of the plan, having picked up both babies in her arms. "She will grow up in Ion and live with the other children in the city. We're a two-day ride on horseback from the capital and we don't see why the Queen would bother coming out this far. She shouldn't even know *it* exists."

Shouldn't.

That was the key word that all their hopes were relying on. There weren't many Firsts in Ion. It was almost exclusively populated by Seconds. Known for their work with their hands, the Builders and Protectors in Ion were renowned throughout Tiarny. The baby would be safe here. She had to be.

Mari ran her hands through her hair, reciting the rest of the plan to herself as she prepared to leave. The baby would be warded with Rolf and Berta, learn with them, and grow with them. No one would speak of Mari ever again.

As Rolf opened the door, Mari twisted.

"Wait." She said, holding up her hand. "You'll give her the necklace?"

The firelight reflected off Berta's white cap as her head moved up and down. "On the morning of her Sequencing, we will give her the pendant and tell her of her prophecy."

Tears running silently down her cheeks, Mari bowed to the couple as she exited once more into the darkness. Her role was done. There was nothing to do now except wait for the prophecy to be fulfilled.

And so they waited.

Days became weeks, and weeks, years.

Generations passed.

Soon centuries went by.

Part One

Chapter One

wo hundred years later,

It hadn't rained for three years, seven months and twenty-two days.

Not that Nellie had been counting or anything.

Every morning, she went about the same routine. She would wake up and look at the sky, anticipating something different. But it never changed. Everything was always the same.

Today was no different. The early morning sun shone on Nellie as she walked down the dusty street in her sky-blue tunic and leggings. She kept brushing the dust off her clothing, despite the fact that as soon as she wiped some of it away, more appeared. She sighed, throwing her hands in the air before continuing down the dirt path. She felt a pleasant warmth on her tan skin as the rising sun made its promise of heat known to her. Walking along, Nellie gazed upwards as if today, of all days, would be *the* day the rain would come pouring down.

Having woken up at four bells today after sleep had evaded her most of the night, Nellie walked through the city of Liantis. This was a familiar path; one she could have taken blindfolded after making the trek every day for the past fifteen years. She didn't see anyone else, her thoughts her only companion. With each step she took, the dry earth crackled under her feet.

Nellie faltered slightly over the bridge connecting her to the main part of town. Leaning over the wooden railing, she looked down at the Miapith River. She snorted, remembering that one of her Tutors had called it the "greatest river to ever run between Liantis and the capital." Today, the river was anything but great. Nellie watched as a minuscule stream of water ran down the center of the dried-up river bank.

When she was younger, she used to beg Guardian Clarence to take them to the river to watch the fish jump. One time, they had gone and Nellie had seen dozens of fish swimming down the river all at once. She had been so excited; her grip had slipped on the wet railing of the bridge. Screams had filled the air, but before she could hit the water, the powerful hand of her Guardian had pulled her back up.

He had tutted before quickly herding all ten wards off the bridge and back to the warding center. Nellie shook her head as she remembered that day. Disorder and unrest seemed to find her no matter where she turned, following her around as though they were her best friends. The once-raging river had been reduced to a rocky stream. The only fish she saw was the dried-up carcass, long washed ashore and picked apart by carrion. Sighing, she let go of the dry railing and dusted off her hands.

Shadows still covered most of the homes she passed. The burning sun had rendered their small garden plots useless, the brittle and dehydrated ground inhospitable to growth.

Nellie hurried past the Temple, the large black structure imposing against the early morning sky. Long ago, Queen Iphigenia had decreed that the only acceptable material for Temples would be wood taken from the ancient trees found in the Forest of Resim.

Unlike most of the trees in Tiarny, the trees in the forest were impressive in both their sizes and colour. Or rather, their lack of colouring. Every single one was as black as coal. Their bark was as dark as the midnight sky, the sap an inky black that ran down the trunks. The trees grew tall, and the dark leaves shimmered with the light of the stars.

When Nellie had been about six years old, an older ward named Bethany had been looking after all the younger wards while Guardian Clarence had taken Yenna to see the Healer for a cut on her leg. For once, it hadn't been Nellie who had gotten injured, although she remembered feeling sad when Yenna had cried. Being as accident prone as she was, Nellie was on a first-name basis with many of the Healers. One of the kinder Healers, a man named Josef, had told her all about his Healing apprentice in Deavita after she had a nasty fall. Josef had been her favourite Healer, but like the rest of them, he disappeared one day. Guardian Clarence had said they had summoned him back to the capital.

Bethany had ordered the wards to sit in a semi-circle around her, arranging her sky-blue tunic around herself before she had spoken. Eight pairs of eyes stared intently at Bethany, their ears straining to hear her.

"You never want to find yourself lost in the Forest of Resim," Bethany had whispered, eyes wide as she looked each ward in the face. "The leaves of the trees can grant a person eternal life, but the bark of the trees is so dark that if you ever walk into the forest, you will lose all sense of time and place."

The wards had all gasped in unison as Bethany spoke. Shivers had run down Nellie's spine as she listened intently, her eyes never leaving the older girl's face.

"If someone is so unlucky as to get lost in the Forest of Resim, they will *never* be able to see the sky or their surroundings. The enormous trees and their blackened leaves block all the sunlight so that no one can ever find their way out."

A sudden coldness had struck Nellie, and she had pulled her arms around herself, tucking them over her legs. While she was rearranging herself, she saw a raised hand out of the corner of her eye. The boy, an older ward by the name of Elijah, had raised his hand politely before speaking. "Excuse me, Bethany?"

"Yes?" Bethany had replied, her brown eyes sharp with what appeared to be irritation.

"Guardian Clarence said that the Source Herself had planted the Forest of Resim when she first came to Tiarny, bringing the trees with Her as a memento of her home. He said that the trees and the Temples are a constant reminder to the citizens of Tiarny that everything good came from the Source. She came to Tiarny to save the people from themselves."

"Well, yes, that's true," Bethany had replied, but Elijah interjected once more. "Guardian Clarence told me that every time I see the stark black pillars, I should remember that the Source had created the ideal society for me."

Bethany's face contorted and Nellie heard her grumble something about Elijah taking over her story. Tension had filled the air, but at that exact moment, Guardian Clarence had re-entered the warding centre. Soon after, the eighteenth bell had rung and Maude, Nellie's mother, was right on time with the other parents for pickup. The warmth of her mother's arms had brought a smile to Nellie's face. On that day, she remembered fondly, her mother had brought a peach to eat on the walk home.

The memory of the sticky, sweet juices dripping down her chin made Nellie chuckle as she passed the Temple. Bethany had been Sequenced not long after that day, and she hadn't seen the older girl for years. As she tried to remember where Bethany had ended up, the sound of another set of footsteps came from behind Nellie. A warm laugh filled the air as a heavy weight suddenly landed on her back. Wisps of turquoise hair flew into Nellie's face as her best friend Fay's giggles rang in her ear.

"Morning, Nell." The sound warmed Nellie's heart. "I thought I might catch you walking about. Couldn't sleep either?"

"It evaded me all night," Nellie agreed. She walked past the warding center; the building still cast in shadows. She shifted to adjust for the weight on her back. She felt as though she knew the entire building by heart. It was her second home. Nellie could remember the very first time she entered the warding centre like it was yesterday. She had just turned three and her mother had plaited her long blue-black hair for the very first time.

It had been such a strange sensation, having her hair pulled back from her face instead of hanging in loose waves around her shoulders. Nellie had walked into the warding area while clutching her mother's hand when she saw another little girl with bright turquoise hair playing on the ground. As soon as she had seen Fay, she released her mother's hand and ran towards her. Before the sun had set on her first day in the warding centre, they had bonded and started down the path towards a lifelong friendship.

Laughing as she shuffled along, Nellie tickled the back of Fay's knees.

"Can you believe we've been friends for fifteen years?"

"I can't," Fay said as she slid off Nellie's back. As she shifted to walking beside Nellie, she grabbed Nellie's hand and gave it a squeeze. "I'm glad we are being Sequenced at the same time."

"Me too. I can't wait to move on from being a ward, but I'm scared."

Pulling Fay close, Nellie took a moment to enjoy the warmth of her friend's hug. Soon, they were walking once more. Or rather, Nellie was walking and Fay was sauntering down the street. Nellie shook her head in amusement. That was typical Fay. Their personalities meshed together perfectly. Like day and night, they were two parts of the same whole.

The wind ruffled Fay's ringlets as she skipped down the empty road, the sound of her voice echoing off the buildings. "Remember when they were building the Temple? It seems so long ago and now; we're going to be Sequenced there."

"I know," Nellie whispered conspiratorially while tucking her midnight blue hair behind her ear. She glanced down at her friend. "You know, I've been waiting for the change that will come with today for a long time. I'm so tired of being a ward."

"You know what I'm tired of?"

"What?"

"I'm tired of listening to everything Guardian Clarence tells us to do." Dropping her voice, Fay continued, "Fay, do this. Now, do that. Fay, listen to the Tutors." Giggling, she spoke once more in her normal register. "For the Source's sake, he is so boring sometimes!"

"Fay," Nellie hissed, her eyes widening as her friend spoke. "You can't talk about him like that. What if people hear you?"

"Pshhh," Fay said while looking around at the empty streets. "No one will hear us. Do you remember all the boring lessons we had to learn in class with the Tutors?"

"Of course, I remember," Nellie replied, laughing. "I almost always paid attention. You know that."

"What do you think today will be like?"

"I'm not sure, but I'm a little scared to find out. What if..." Nellie ducked her head and whispered. "What if we're Sequenced to be Thirds?"

"Don't be silly. I don't think the Source would ever do that to you." Fay's voice sounded confident, although Nellie saw her glancing around dubiously. The wattle and daub hovels that housed the Servers were a far cry from the beautiful homes of the few Firsts who resided in Liantis. Stacked together, the streets were narrower than the area where Nellie and her mother lived. Brown tunics were hung on lines strung up between the hovels, intermingled with the sky-blue tunics of wards.

"Besides," Fay continued as she picked up a smooth rock and rolled it between her fingers, "you know that as long as everyone fulfills their Sequenced roles, we will want for nothing. The Source has created the perfect place for us to live."

Nellie's lips turned up at her friend's confidence, wishing she could have some of that too. Too soon, the fifth bell tolled, the sound echoing through the city. At the sound of the bells, the girls looked at each other, eyes wide. Nellie clutched Fay's arm before turning toward her home.

"Promise you'll come pick me up for the Sequencing, Fay?" Nellie asked.

"I promise."

Running home, Nellie began passing a few townspeople who were beginning their days. Most of them grimaced in her direction. She wasn't sure if it was because of the unbound midnight blue hair that flowed freely behind her as she ran through the streets or because of the dust she was kicking up with every footfall.

As her feet pounded the dirt, Nellie sent prayer after prayer to the Source.

Oh please, Source. Let it rain. Open up the skies. Let it not be too late for us. The ground is crying out. We need the rain. Provide for us once more, as you promised all those years ago. For herself, she added, *let me remain in Liantis with my mother.*

As her limbs protested the movement, only one prayer remained in her mind, echoing repeatedly. *Oh please, Source. Let it rain.*

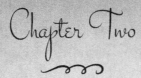

Chapter Two

Lost in thought as she walked to the well in the centre of the courtyard, Nellie didn't hear her mother calling for her right away.

"Eleanor Marie Merrick," Maude's voice cut through the early morning air, echoing across the square. "Come inside this instant. I've been calling you for the last ten minutes." Nellie detected a note of ire in her mother's voice as she continued to yell. "You know this day is too important to be gazing up at the sky. Fill the jug with water and come inside."

Sighing loudly, Nellie turned towards her mother's voice, her porcelain jug dangling precariously from her fingers as it clanged softly against her legs. She had left the cover for the jug back at home, not wanting to have to carry it to the well and back.

"One moment, Mother." Her voice echoed around the courtyard. "I'm filling the jug right now."

As quickly as possible, Nellie shifted the wooden lid off the well and slowly lowered the bucket into the well. As soon as the water started falling over the edges, she pulled it up inch-by-inch. Nellie held her breath as she poured the water into her jug, keeping her eyes trained on the precious liquid. Thank the Source there wasn't anyone else waiting in line behind her, or they might have grown impatient with the time she was taking.

A few days ago, Nellie had overheard a few of the neighbourhood women, a Tutor and a Tailor, gossiping near the well. Her ears had strained as they spoke, their words seemingly ridiculous.

"I'm telling you, Sylvia, it's true." The speaker, a busty woman wearing the indigo tunic of a Tailor, had been speaking loudly while Nellie had been waiting to collect water. "The Firsts in Deavita have magical tubes that deliver water straight to their rooms. I heard it straight from Ronald, who heard it from Wallace, whose sister was Sequenced as a Midwife and works in the capital."

Sylvia, who Nellie recognized as a Tutor that occasionally came by the warding center to teach the wards about geography, had gasped, her hand flying to cover her mouth. She had almost dropped the jug of water she had been carrying. Nellie had watched, wide-eyed, as Sylvia had hugged the jug of water to her chest like a baby.

"You can't be serious, Doreen. How do they ration the water?"

"That's the thing," Doreen replied, her voice dropping to a whisper. Nellie strained to hear the rest of the conversation. "Wallace said that Firsts don't even have water rations. We can only use a jug a day, but they can use whatever they want."

"No," Sylvia had gasped. "That can't be."

Doreen nodded, a look of superiority crossing her face as she relayed the news. "And that's not all. She said that the Thirds only get three cups of water a day, per person. Not even a jug per family."

Nellie had watched as the two women gathered their jugs and walked away from the well. They shuffled along slowly in what Nellie called the "water walk." No one moved quickly with water in their hands. Everything in Tiarny was crying out for it.

Balancing the now-full jug precariously on her hip, she started on her own water walk. She placed one foot after another, her eyes never leaving the colourful cobblestones that covered the ground. Her muscles were firm after years of drawing up water and they never wavered as she followed her ritualistic path home.

The usually bustling square was eerily still, the only sounds coming from Nellie's shoes scuffling on the ground and the occasional meows coming from Olim, the courtyard cat. As he sauntered up to Nellie and started rubbing himself on her leg, she bent down and placed the jug on the ground before rubbing his back. The sound of his purring filled the square, easing some of the tension in Nellie's chest.

As she approached her home, the bright yellow building brought a smile to her face. Her eyes crinkled as she looked over the colour of wheat, sun, and stars. She had chosen this shade when she was only five years old, her mother giving her the chance to pick their new paint colour after Maude had had an especially successful year as a Provider. Up close, Nellie pursed her lips as she took in the peeling paint coming off the front door of her mother's mercantile.

Sighing, she added it to the ever-growing list of chores she kept in her head entitled 'Things to do once I've been Sequenced'. Painting joined things like reading books that Guardian Clarence had told her she couldn't read, fixing her mother's favourite mug she had accidentally broken a few weeks ago, and spending more time with Fay.

The sixth bell rang as Nellie opened the door to the townhouse. The sound was loud, and it echoed through the square. Moments later, Nellie heard the sparking sounds of life. The small townhouse she shared with her mother had paper-thin walls, and the sounds of their neighbours rising from their beds filled her ears.

Nellie watched from the doorway as other children ran silently out to the well, the only sound in the square was the smacking of their shoes on the stones.

As she stood watching the children, she was transported back to the first time she really understood the significance of the Sacred Solstice. She had been ten years old and complaining to Fay about the Sequencing Ceremony that was due to take place the next day. "Why do we have to go?" She had whined. "It's not like wards or parents can even see what happens, since we aren't even allowed to watch." Fay's eyes had kept widening while Nellie spoke, a look of terror entering her eyes. She had poked Nellie, mouthing for her to stop, but it was too late. Nellie turned around to see her Guardian standing right behind her, his arms crossed as he looked down.

Immediately upon hearing her complaints, Guardian Clarence had sat all the children down for an impromptu reminder of the importance of the Sequencing Ceremony. He made Nellie sit front and center, in front of all the other wards. Her cheeks had reddened as she realized she was being singled out. She had ached to move her chair back and sit next to Fay, but she didn't. Her palm had still stung from the last time she disobeyed. Nellie had swallowed hard before staring straight ahead.

Clarence had paced in front of the ten wards, his hands behind his back and his legs spread apart as he loomed over them. Nellie had watched as the mid-day sun had reflected off the window panes, shining in her eyes. It shimmered across the room, lighting up the Guardian's russet skin and giving his yellow tunic the appearance of being flecked with gold. Once the only sound in the room was that of his feet pacing back and forth, he had spoken.

"Every single year," he had intoned, his voice deep and gravelly, "ever since the Year of Inception, Sequencing Ceremonies have taken place all across Tiarny on the Sacred Solstice. Long ago, the Source took it upon Herself to come to this land and gift our people with the Sequencing. Tomorrow, we will attend the Ceremony with all the other wards, standing behind the citizens and those who are about to be warded. It is an honour to be permitted to attend a Sequencing."

He had paused, his gaze hard as he stared at Nellie, before he asked, "Can anyone tell me why we have the Sequencing?"

Seconds ticked by, becoming minutes as silence filled the room. Finally, the rustling of a sleeve came from behind Nellie. The corners of the Guardian's mouth lifted slightly as he motioned for the ward to speak. Nellie had immediately recognized Fay's tiny voice as it rang out in the classroom.

"The Sequencing exists to create order where there was none."

"Very good, Fay." He nodded slightly. "Why do we submit to the Sequencing each year?"

"Because it is the supreme will of the Source."

"Correct. You should all learn from young Fay here. I'm certain the Source will bless her for her studiousness during her own Sequencing. Now, we know that the only reason Tiarny exists today is because of the Source. Every single person in Tiarny is expected to honour Her with their presence at the Sequencing."

Shaking her head free of the fog of distant memory, Nellie pushed the door to the mercantile open with one hand while cradling the jug of water with the other. It creaked as it opened, one side of the door scraping against the floor as it moved.

The downside, her mother always said, of living in a home that was built 143 Years after Inception. Their mercantile might be one of the oldest buildings in Tiarny, but it also meant that it was full of mice, spiders, wobbly flooring and crooked walls. It also meant that history filled the building, which Nellie loved.

The smell of spices wafted towards her, and her stomach rumbled at the idea of eating anything that wasn't a dried bean or quinoa. She dreamt of fresh fruit and vegetables, of dishes that were flavourful and not made of pulses. Her nose was picking up the scent of oat bread, though, so she knew her dreams wouldn't be coming true today.

As her eyes adjusted to the dim lighting, she could hear her mother's apprentice Philip moving around in the storeroom. Philip had been Sequenced as a Provider last year and had immediately undertaken the three-day journey from Deavita to Liantis on horseback. When he had first arrived, he had been shy and withdrawn, barely wanting to speak to Nellie. It took many months of prodding and gentle conversation, but eventually he had opened up to her.

"It's not that I don't want to be a Provider," he confided in her one evening over a cup of tea. "It's just that I miss being in Deavita. I don't even miss being a First, really. I just miss my friends. None of them came to Liantis with me."

Nellie nodded her head in understanding. The very thought of being forced to leave everything she knew behind broke her heart.

"I can't imagine what it must have been like, Philip. I'm sorry, you must miss your family too."

He had grimaced a little before smiling softly at her. "I suppose so... my home life... wasn't amazing. You're lucky that way, you know. You and your mother have something special here. She told me, you know, about your father?"

Nellie had nodded mutely, her hands gripping her mug of tea as she stared at the table. She blinked back tears at the thought of her father. Her mother never spoke of him and she never even knew his name, let alone where he had been Sequenced. All she knew is that there had been a terrible sickness that year that had swept through Tiarny and her father had caught the Violet Death one day and was dead two days later. Every time she asked her mother about her father or the mysterious illness, Maude brushed Nellie off.

"I'm sorry. I know he died when you were just over a year old, but that doesn't make it any better. I'm glad she's able to look after you as a Provider and a mother."

After that first heart-to-heart in the storeroom, the two of them often spoke when the mercantile wasn't too busy. Nellie found Philip's readiness to listen refreshing, and she had confided in him that what she really wanted, more than anything, was to choose. Something. Anything.

Placing her jug of water on the small table her mother kept near the front door, shifting it slightly to ensure the jug wouldn't topple over, Nellie walked into the storeroom to greet her friend. There was a strange pinging sound coming from the backroom that intrigued her. The moment she pulled open the door separating the front from the back, the pinging sound got much louder.

Philip's back was to Nellie as he poured a steady stream of dried beans into an awaiting glass container. Nellie recognized the jars, having accidentally broken quite a few when she was younger before her mother had gently barred her from "helping" in the mercantile. Now, it seemed Maude had relegated the job to Philip. Bags and jars surrounded the man in question.

The aroma in the backroom was intoxicating, strong herbs mixing with the spiciness of dried peppers and the sweetness of sugar in the air. Nellie always loved working in the back of her mothers mercantile and as she inhaled, she felt some of the tension of the impending Sequencing release.

~

As the door swung shut behind Nellie, Philip jumped. He turned around and as his black eyes connected with hers, she saw a smile spread across his face.

"Hello Nellie. Today's the day. Are you excited?"

She plopped down on the only chair in the backroom, sighing as she ran her fingers through her hair.

"Excited? Nervous. I want to be Sequenced as a Provider, like you and Mom, but I'm also nervous. I *really* don't want to be Sequenced to be a Server." She picked at a loose thread on her sky-blue tunic. "What if I get sent to Dariani?"

Dariani was located to the south of the capital and was rumoured to be much warmer than the other cities in Tiarny. It was a five-day ride on horseback or an eight-day walk. Where Ion and Liantis were bustling towns filled with trade and markets, people rarely came and went from Dariani. More precisely, people often left the ramshackle town, but few people came to visit. Almost all citizens living in Dariani were Thirds, with the exceptions of Firsts and Seconds sent from the capital.

His back turned once more, Philip laughed as he kept working.

"I'm serious, Philip." Nellie huffed. "It's already hot in Liantis. I don't think I could handle the desert heat in Dariani. It gets hot enough here. If I had to leave, I'd prefer the cooling temperatures of Deavita or Ion. Not to mention the fact that Thirds have to deal with even more rations and restrictions than Seconds."

Philip tensed, his back straight as the only sound in the room came from the beans.

"If you get Sequenced into a lower class, Nellie, you'll learn to live with it. I did." He whispered, his words wafting over the air as he continued to work in the corner.

Her cheeks reddened at the reminder that just a year ago, Philip had been Sequenced down a class.

"I'm sorry, I didn't mean it."

He sighed, putting the beans down before turning towards her. "I forgive you, Nellie. I'm not angry. Believe me, I know how much this day means to you. Remember, the Source knows best. She created the optimal society in Tiarny so that we can live out our days in perfect peace and harmony."

"You're right, Philip. I know you're right. Whatever happens, she has my best intentions in mind."

Before Nellie could say anything else, she heard a set of footsteps pounding on the stairs above her. Her mother's voice rang down the stairs.

"Philip! If Eleanor is with you, you tell her to come upstairs right now. She needs to get ready."

Philip winked at Nellie, his voice dropping into a whisper. "You'd better grab the water and run up there. You don't want to get thrown into prison for being late to your own Sequencing."

Even though his tone was playful, both of them exchanged a look as they acknowledged that this, most definitely, was not a joke. Missing the Sequencing Ceremony was a crime punishable by a week spent in the dungeons. No matter how boring sitting through a Sequencing might be, nobody wanted to spend even a minute, let alone an entire week, in the dark dungeons located throughout Tiarny.

"You're right, Philip." Nellie replied as she pushed herself off the stool. "I definitely don't want to feed the rats."

Rumours abounded that the rats who lived in the dungeons were so hungry that they would try to take a nibble out of anyone who stepped foot in their domain, even while they were still awake. If a person was exhausted enough to fall asleep in the dungeon, they would inevitably wake up covered in dozens of rat bites- if they woke up at all.

Needless to say, all citizens on the Sacred Solstice were rushing to ensure they made it to the Sequencing on time.

Chapter Three

Cushioning the full jug of water in her arms, Nellie inched up the stairs to the second story that she shared with her mother. She kept her eyes trained on the landing, ignoring the long shelves lined with large burlap sacks of flour, dried beans, quinoa, and oats.

A tear streaked down her cheek as she glanced down at the worn imprints of the old fruit and vegetable barrels that used to be strewn throughout the store. Her stomach grumbled at the memory of fresh produce, her mouth salivating as she thought of the cloyingly sweet smell of overripe peaches. At the memory of her favourite food, Nellie briefly closed her eyes.

That one moment, lost in a daydream, was all it took for her to stumble on the stairs. She tipped over, her grip on the jug of water almost slipping before she caught herself on the railing. She watched in horror as a droplet of water splashed out of the jug and hit the landing. The splash it made echoed in her mind as she went upstairs. Nellie groaned.

Just one day, that's all I need. One day without trouble.

Nellie gingerly climbed the last few rickety steps and entered the living area. The aroma of fresh bread hit her as soon as she walked into the space. Her nose tingled and her fingers itched in anticipating as she placed the water jug on the counter before cutting herself a piece of the delicious bread. The moment the first bite hit her tongue; she knew she was in heaven. A soft moan escaped her as an explosion of flavours hit her tongue. How the Bakers could infuse so much flavour in such a plain piece of food, she would never know.

Once she had eaten her breakfast, Nellie looked around the familiar space. Everything was just as she had left it. The dark wooden kitchen table and chairs sat invitingly in the middle of the space, still adorned with the plates from last night's meal. Nellie picked them up and placed them in the sink, mentally making a note to get to them after her Sequencing.

As she turned from the sink, she saw her mother sitting on the worn settee on the other side of the room. There was a clinking sound that came as Maude placed her teacup on the side table and stood up. Her bones creaked as she ambled across the living room. A frown flitted across Nellie's features as she watched her mother. She had gotten much slower over the past few years and Nellie was beginning to feel concerned.

"Ah, there you are, Eleanor," Maude said, the corners of her eyes crinkling as she looked at her daughter. "I was wondering what you had gotten up to. Today isn't a day for dallying. We need to get you ready for your Sequencing."

Casting the thoughts of her mother's well-being out of her mind for the moment, Nellie quickly pulled Maude in for a hug. The smell of roses filled her senses and for a moment, Nellie was transported back to her youth. She recalled being a young ward of only three years old, being escorted to the warding center for the first time. Her mother had let Nellie use her special rose-scented shampoo on her hair for the occasion, and the smell had given Nellie comfort the entire twelve hours her mother had been gone.

"You're right, Mother." Nellie pulled back just a little and looked down as she tucked a lock of her mother's black hair behind her ear.

"Of course, I'm right. Now, go get ready in your room. I'll be there in a moment."

"Yes, ma'am," she said, giving her mother another hug before walking into her bedroom. She may not have been a young ward who needed to be bossed around any longer, but the Guardians always taught her to show respect to her elders.

The morning of Nellie's third birthday, her mother had explained that disobeying her Guardian would be absolutely, unequivocally, not tolerated. "The Source appointed them, Eleanor." Her mother had explained as she had braided Nellie's long hair. "Disorder and disarray are extremely displeasing to the Source. Make sure you are on your best behaviour."

"I'll do my best, Mother."

She really had. Sometimes, though, Nellie remembered being punished for things that felt completely out of her control.

She was five years old, her long hair braided behind her as she sat silently sobbing at the table. The other wards had long since left, and the only sound in the room was the rain splattering on the roof. Her Guardian loomed over her; his gaze steely as he looked at the untouched plate of food in front of Nellie. Thunder boomed as he spoke. "Eleanor. Are you refusing to eat your food?"

Nellie gulped, her tiny hands fidgeting with her sky-blue tunic as she had stared at the food. "I tried; I really did. My tummy hurts." Tears had streamed down her face, the smell of salt filling the air.

"In that case, you will not eat until lunch tomorrow. Feel free to drink your water." Guardian Clarence had reached down and removed the plate from in front of Nellie, leaving her alone. That day, tears had been her

constant companion. She had wrapped her tiny arms around her legs, sobs wracking her entire body as she cried. The pain in her stomach had been excruciating, the water doing nothing to sate her hunger.

That evening, her friend Elijah had slipped a piece of bread into Nellie's palm with some sleight of hand that had amazed her. He was only three years older than her, but he had always been looking out for her. Late that night, Nellie had devoured the bread in her bed while she had pondered what exactly she had done wrong. Her five-year-old mind just couldn't comprehend why she was being punished for being sick.

The next day at lunchtime, Nellie had scarfed down her food without a word.

Shivering at the memory, Nellie fingered the long, three-inch scar on her arm. Nightmares of that punishment still haunted her to this day.

Yes, she had certainly been taught that she needed to respect her elders.

As soon as she entered her room, Nellie saw a neatly folded outfit lying on top of the quilt her grandmother had made for her. There appeared to be a note resting on the bundle of clothing. She approached the bed, her fingers twitching at her sides as stared at the beautiful material. Just as she was extending a finger towards the clothing, her mother's voice came from the other room.

"Did you find the tunic, Eleanor? The Tailors delivered it while you were at the warding center yesterday and I put it aside for you. What do you think?"

"I think... it's not blue." Nellie grinned as she reached a finger out to touch the snow-white tunic. She gasped as the material enveloped her finger. "It feels like a cloud."

Nellie heard Maude laughing from her bedroom next door, the sound reminding Nellie of the twittering of birds in the early morning.

"I'd be willing to bet, Eleanor, that you'd be happy if you never wore another piece of blue clothing for the rest of your life after having worn it for fifteen years. I know I was so excited to shed the blue tunic of my youth for my Provider's clothing after my Sequencing."

"You've got that right." Nellie muttered as she picked up the note lying on top of the tunic.

For Eleanor Merrick, daughter of Maude Merrick.
Class: Second
City: Liantis.
To be worn on the Sacred Solstice, 749 Years after Inception
In order to receive the Source's Blessing and be Sequenced.

Dropping the note on the bed, she bent down and picked up the tunic. It felt exquisite. She turned it over in her hands, marvelling at the embroidered bands of silver and blue that ran along the hem, twisting back and forth like two streams of a river over the otherwise white material. She recalled a lesson during which Guardian Clarence had explained that the blue thread represented the wards they were, while the silver stood for the citizens they would become.

Underneath the tunic was a pair of crisp, cream-coloured leggings. Shedding her old clothing, Nellie put on her Sequencing attire. She was awed by the way the soft and supple material hugged her curves. She made no secret about loving food and she had always loved her body. As she twisted this way and that, she admired the fit of her new clothing.

The Tailors have really outdone themselves this time. I can't believe they made this in just three moon-cycles.

The leggings were just long enough. Nellie wiggled her feet, admiring

32

the fact that the leggings stretched all the way down to her ankles, the soft material caressing the tan skin of her legs. The clothes even smelled fresh, infusing her small bedroom with the scent of lavender as she spun around in circles.

Soon, Nellie thought as she rotated in place. *Soon, the rest of my life will begin.*

Chapter Four

J ust as Nellie was admiring the fit of her new clothes, she heard a knock on her bedroom door.

"Eleanor, can I come in?"

"Of course."

This was as big of a day for her mother as it was for Nellie. If the Sequencing Ceremony went as Nellie hoped, there would be another Provider living under the roof before nightfall.

At the sound of the door opening, Nellie twisted around to face her mother. Maude stood in the doorway; her soft brown eyes wide as she took in her daughter. They shimmered with unshed tears as she watched her spin around in her new Sequencing outfit, her hand covering her mouth.

"Oh, Eleanor. You look amazing." Maude's voice was thick with emotion. "I can't believe it's finally your Sequencing. Your grandmother would have loved to have seen this day."

"I miss her so much." Nellie wiped a tear from her eye, a vision of her grandmother appearing before her. She had passed to be with the Source six years ago and Nellie still felt the hole her death had created in her heart.

Maude sniffled, her eyes misty as she smiled gently and shuffled over to Nellie. Frowning slightly, Nellie watched as her mother seemed to limp as she moved. Before she could ask her about it, Maude pulled Nellie in for a hug. She squeezed tightly, her fingers wrapped around Nellie's long, wavy hair. "I'm sure your grandmother is with the Source watching you at this very moment."

Tears began streaming down Nellie's face and she wept for a minute into her mother's shoulder. Maude was already wearing her Provider's tunic and Nellie patted at the damp spot on her mother's shoulder.

"Don't worry about it, my dear." Maude pulled on Nellie's arm, her movements stiff as she led Nellie over to the bed before she pulled a small black box out of the pocket of her dark leggings. It was the size of her palm and reflected the sunlight as she held it out. "Eleanor. I have a gift for you."

"A gift?" Nellie echoed her mother's words. "I've never received a gift before."

Maude smiled softly, her eyes never leaving Nellie's. "I know, the Source forbade gift-giving a long time ago. But this one is special."

Tenderness filled her mother's brown eyes as they looked up at Nellie. "Generation upon generation of Merrick women have passed this gift down on their Sequencing Day. My great-grandmother four-times-over received it from her mother, Berta. This is what my mother told me on my Sequencing Day."

Nellie fiddled with the edges of her tunic as she watched her mother intently.

"Long ago, this land used to be home to many types of people. There were Guardians and Builders, Tailors and Scholars, Servers and Protectors, just as there are today. But there was also another group of people. People knew them as Wielders. Wielders were special because they could hold the four elements of the Earth in their hands and manipulate them to their wills. They used this special form of magic as they worked alongside the Source and the Queens. The Wielders helped Tiarny grow into the country it is today."

"Magic?" Nellie sputtered; her eyes wide. She felt her brows raise on her forehead as she stared at her mother.

Nodding, Maude's lips tilted up slightly. "Magic. It used to run wild through the land, but it has been lost for several centuries now."

Nellie's mind started running a million miles a minute. Her eyes grew wide, her face pale as her gaze never left her mother's face.

"No one knows where the Wielders came from or the origin of their powers, but they eventually disappeared out of Tiarny altogether. Or at least, that is what they want us to think. Ultimately, the citizens of Tiarny turned against Wielders. Most Wielders had used their abilities to help crops grow and to bring water into the land. They kept people warm during the resting seasons. However, there were some Wielders who sought greater power than what the Source had Sequenced them into."

Nellie dropped her head into her hands and began breathing deeply. Seeming to notice her discomfort, her mother began rubbing her back in soft circles.

"The Wielders pushed back against the Queen, wanting greater recognition for themselves than other Sequenced citizens. The rebellious Wielders nearly instigated a civil war, which would have destroyed the entire foundation of Tiarny."

Nellie sat in complete silence and stared at her mother, who kept rubbing her back. The feeling reminded her of her childhood and provided a grounding for Nellie as she struggled to remain calm.

Breathe.

Just breathe.

You can't have a panic attack right now.

"I know this is a lot to take in, Eleanor. Just let me finish and then you can ask me questions."

Nellie nodded, but her mind was still reeling. None of this sounded remotely normal.

Maude dropped onto the bed next to Nellie. Her mother's hair was the colour of the night sky and it fell in long waves, curtaining her face.

"The Queen determined that the threat of revolution grew too large. The Wielders were gaining support throughout the classes and were becoming a genuine threat to the monarchy. Queen Francesca and her Royal Protectors headed up the Inquest to rid Tiarny of the Wielders once and for all. She felt they had become too powerful for their own good. The Queen purged the country of Wielders in the year 546 After Inception. Since the Purge, no one dared speak of the Wielders for fear of incurring the wrath of the Source."

Nellie's jaw fell open.

A purge?

Nellie knew she was openly staring at her mother, trying to understand what she'd just heard, but she couldn't stop herself. The more time she had to think, the more questions she had.

"I don't understand." She whispered, her eyes darting around the room before they settled on her mother. "If this is true, how do you know about it? Why do you know? What is the mysterious gift? What is going on?"

Nellie fell back, her head cushioned on the pillow as she shut her eyes and rubbed her temples.

"You kept secrets from me," she said softly, hurt laced through her words. "Ever since Dad died, we've been a team. That's what you always said. And yet, you kept this a secret."

Maude's face reeled at the mention of Nellie's father. "That was a low blow, Eleanor."

Refusing to look at her mother, Nellie's gaze remained firmly on the threads running through the tunic.

"How could you lie to me?" Nellie's breath began coming in short bursts, her palms sweaty as she lost focus.

"Look at me, Eleanor." Her mother said in a slow, calm voice. "Take a deep breath. Concentrate on my voice. That's it."

Nellie listened to her mother talk and focused on her breathing. The last thing she needed was to have a panic attack today.

Breathe in

Who is this woman, and what has she done with my mother?

Breathe out

What is she talking about?

Breathe in

Why did she have to dump this on me today, of all days?

Breathe out

Calm down. Don't panic. Think.

Finding her breathing settled, Nellie turned her gaze to her mother. She scooted backwards on the bed, trying to create some distance between the two of them. A look of hurt flashed across Maude's face.

"I know this is a lot to take in. When your grandmother shared this story with me, I had many of the same questions. We don't have time to answer them all right now, but it's important to know that our family has been keeping the memory of the Wielders alive.

"Hundreds of years ago, there was a prophecy that stated that one day, a Wielder would rise who would be more powerful than all other Wielders combined. It stated she wouldn't arrive until Tiarny was in dire straits and ready to accept a new generation of Wielders. Until that time arrives, we are to keep *this* safe."

Maude gestured to the box in her hands before she continued.

"This has been the Merrick family legacy to pass this down from one generation to the next. My mother told me that long ago, the last Wielder risked everything to have this made."

Maude opened the box, handing it to Nellie. Inside was a silken lining that carefully cradled a beautiful silver pendant. It measured roughly the size of a coin; the sides were so thin they were barely there at all. The pendant shone in the light of the morning sun.

Nellie held her breath as she cautiously extended a finger to touch the pendant. Gently, she pulled it out, dangling it from her fingers. It was lightweight and cool to the touch, the metal as smooth as the river on a still day. It hung on a thin silver chain; each link so small that she had to squint to see them clearly.

"I've never seen anything like this," she murmured. Turning the pendant over in her grasp, she gasped. "Look at this."

Excitement filled her voice, banishing earlier thoughts of panic as she inspected the jewellery. Maude leaned over to see what Nellie was pointing at.

"There's a flame engraved here, burning in front of a solitary tree. There are bits of red and orange embedded in the pendant. It looks like the flame is moving."

Awe filled Nellie's voice. She flipped the pendant around and stopped, her brows furrowing.

"What's this?"

Covering the other side of the pendant were a dozen strange markings that she didn't recognize.

"I don't know, Eleanor. The markings clearly aren't in the common tongue, but they must be important."

Suddenly, Nellie's fingers flew to the scar on her left arm as worry crossed her face.

"Mother, the Protectors... if they saw this..."

Nellie didn't even have to finish the sentence. Her mother swooped in and held her tight. "Don't worry, Eleanor. They won't." She lifted the pendant and tucked it under Nellie's Sequencing tunic. "Keep it safe and hidden, and everything will be fine."

Squeezing her mother, Nellie tried to inhale the scent of roses and banish the fear from her mind. A memory kept playing on repeat. She had been seven years old when she had witnessed the Protectors dragging a young woman away through the streets. Guardian Clarence had smugly informed the wards that they had found her with a small picture in her home.

"Because of the Queen's Decree dating back to 327 Years of Inception," he had said, his gaze piercing, "All Seconds and Thirds are forbidden from owning any form of artwork."

Nellie didn't know what had happened to the young woman, but she had never seen her again.

"You might wonder why I'm giving you this today, of all days?" Maude's voice broke through her reverie. Nellie had been so caught up in her thoughts that it took a moment to hear her mother. She nodded mutely in reply, and her mother continued speaking.

"When my mother gave me the pendant, she said it was extremely important to wear to the Sequencing Ceremony. She didn't know why, only that the prophecy insists we must pass the pendant from mother to daughter on the day of the Sequencing Ceremony. Today, I'm giving it to you. You must wear it, but be sure that no one can see it. We don't want you to catch any unwanted attention from the Committee."

Nellie nodded mutely; her eyes fastened on the empty black box.

"I promise Eleanor, it will be okay."

Nellie sat back against a wooden chair in the living area while her mother brushed and plaited her long, blue-black hair. From her perch, she was looking directly into the solitary mirror hung on the door to her mother's bedroom. Despite the cracked surface and the spots created by age, the reflection took Nellie's breath away. She shifted this way and that, turning her head slightly before her mother admonished her to sit still, admiring the tall, shapely woman she saw in the mirror.

Emerald green eyes that reflected the sunlight stared back at her, her freckled nose standing in contrast to her midnight blue hair. The pendant, though hidden from sight, felt warm as it lay against her skin.

The scent of roses washed over her, calming her nerves and imbuing her with a sense of peacefulness. Nellie's eyelids grew heavy as her mother brushed her hair and eventually, she shut her eyes for a brief reprise. She dozed, basking in the warmth of her mother's affections.

Before Nellie felt ready to leave, the sound of bells rang throughout their home. She jolted awake; the sound pulling her out of her slumber. Every other day of the year, the bells tolled on the hour, every hour. But today, now, they were ringing to signal the impending beginning of the Sequencing.

This was the moment.

This was the beginning.

Chapter Five

Having said her goodbyes to her mother and Philip, Nellie pulled the worn wooden door of the mercantile wide open. She held her hand in front of her eyes as the sounds of footfalls and whispered chatter hit her ears. The sun glistened off windows, sending shards of painful light into Nellie's eyes. She took a moment to lower her gaze before stepping outside. Already the air had warmed up from her walk this morning, and she pulled her tunic away from her arms as she moved.

Dozens of wards streamed past her home, each of them wearing the same ceremonial wear as Nellie. It had been a long time since Nellie had seen clouds, but she thought that the flood of wards heading to the Temple looked like a gigantic cloud floating down the street. A few of the faces were familiar, but many were not. Nellie saw a rainbow of hair colours flying past her.

When she was only three years old, she had asked Guardian Clarence why some people in Tiarny were born with hair the colours of the shades of the rainbow. He had sat down next to her and picked up a paintbrush as he explained, "the Source has Blessed us with colourful hair as a reminder of the many paths of Sequencing. There are as many possible Sequenced paths as there are colours of the rainbow. It is a reminder of Her faithfulness." Guardian Clarence always took his role seriously. He often reminded the wards that it was his duty to instill them with their singular purpose in life: to make it to and experience a successful Sequencing.

As the wards streamed past her position at the mercantile, each adorned in their own ceremonial garb, Nellie's lip turned up as she heard a familiar voice ring out from the crowd.

"Excuse me, excuse me, coming through. Please move, ugh, excuse me."

Sighing in relief at the sound of her best friend's voice, Nellie raised herself up on her tip-toes, her eyes searching over the sea of wards. All that she could see of her boisterous friend was the top of her turquoise hair as the crowd swallowed her whole. Nellie bounced from one foot to the other as she waited for her to get close to the mercantile. She watched as a young male ward stopped in the middle of the street, only to be quickly shoved along by the crowd. She clutched the doorframe of the mercantile, not willing to let go until Fay was with her.

"Nellie! Nellie!" She could hear Fay calling for her through the throng. Eyes wide, she watched as even more people went onto the streets as citizens of all ages began making their way to the Temple.

"I'm here," Nellie yelled, but the continuous tolling of the bells swallowed the sound of her voice. She was straining to hear Fay over the sound of hundreds of footsteps. She waved her hand high above her head as she watched Fay push through the crowd to get to her.

Her turquoise-haired friend was breathless and flushed as sweat dripped down her forehead. Panting, Fay dropped her hands to her knees and breathed deeply, trying to catch her breath. She gasped, droplets of sweat hydrating the parched ground as they fell off her face. "We have to go now. I don't even want to think about what Guardian Clarence might do if we are late to the most important event of our lives."

Having caught her breath, Fay latched onto Nellie's hand and pulled, her grip much stronger than she appeared capable of.

"Come on, Nell." Fay said. "I don't want to get separated before the ceremony."

"You're right. Being late to our own Sequencing Ceremony would really take the cake, wouldn't it?"

At the mention of cake, Fay groaned. "You had to bring up cake, didn't you?"

Both their stomachs grumbled at the distant memory of baked goods. The Officials considered baking to be a waste of water, so cake and all other delicacies were nothing but a distant memory for most of the citizens of Tiarny. The Queen had decreed that no Seconds or Thirds could bake, sell, or eat cakes and other sweets.

Nellie shook her head to clear the memory of the delicious cake before she ran into the street with Fay. Hand in hand, they stayed together and joined the throng of wards heading towards the Temple.

It was time to march to their future.

Walking arm in arm through the throng of people, the friends chatted about the Temple.

"The last time we were at the Temple," Fay said, looking up at Nellie, "I heard one Priestess say that the one in Deavita is twice the size of ours. Can you believe it?"

"I can. Don't you remember how enormous the Temple was when we toured the capital six years ago? I remember the stuffy guide telling us all about the religious ceremonies that took place at the Temple. As if she didn't know that Seconds celebrated things like the yearly Blessing of the Harvest and the Feast of Thanks in Liantis."

Fay snorted in reply. "That's true. Remember the Priestesses in Deavita?" She leaned in close to Nellie to whisper. "My mother says that they don't even have a class. Since the Source hand-picks them to serve Her, they live above the classes."

"That's true, but imagine having to get up at all hours of the night to ring the bells? I think I love to sleep too much for that."

Too soon, the friends came to the edge of the crowd. They waded through the sea of wards, eventually finding a spot about twenty feet from the front of the Temple.

"Nell," Fay whispered urgently, tugging on her friend's sleeve. Even standing on her tip-toes, she barely came to Nellie's shoulders. "I can't see anything. What do you see?"

Keeping her voice low, Nellie described the entire scene to Fay. There was an elevated dais that stood in front of the Temple. It was currently empty, but she was certain it wouldn't be for long. Behind the dais, there were four black pillars that rose from the base of the Temple, supporting its long flat roof.

On each of the four corners of the Temple was a large and detailed Ionian-made statue of a beautiful woman. They were the four Goddesses of Tiarny, daughters of the Source Herself. The Temple artists had sculpted each of the four goddesses with their arms outstretched, reaching towards the sky. Each one looked as though she was seeking an embrace from their Mother.

Fay sighed, clutching her hands to her chest. "It sounds lovely. I bet the statue of the Source looks magnificent today."

"It does. The white marble is shimmering." Even Nellie had to crane her neck to look at the humongous statue. "It's a shame our parents aren't closer to us. I'm sure my mother would have loved this."

"I know. Mine would have loved it too. But the Source was clear. No one but wards may be in the square on the Sacred Solstice. They already had their Sequencing, this one is ours."

"That's true." Nellie sighed, turning her head to look outside the Square. Somewhere in the sea of citizens was her mother. "It must be almost eight bells. I wonder how long we're going to be standing out here?"

"I don't know," Fay whispered. "My dad said his Sequencing lasted for nine hours, but of course, he was Sequenced in Deavita. How long was your mother's?"

"She told me it had lasted five hours, but there weren't many wards waiting to be Sequenced in Ion that year. The most memorable thing that she had shared with me was that it had poured during her Sequencing. A veritable thunderstorm. She said the Master of Ceremonies declared it the most Blessed Sequencing Ceremony since the Sacred Solstice."

Fay's eyes were wide as she stared at Nellie. "A storm?" Wonder filled her voice. "What a Blessing. Your mother must have felt so touched that the Source would bestow such a sign of favour during her Sequencing."

Nellie opened her mouth to reply, but before she could say anything, the bells stopped tolling. Silence suddenly reigned in the square. Raising her hand to shield her eyes from the sun, Nellie looked towards the man who had just marched onto the dais. She immediately recognized him as the highest-ranking Official in Liantis. He presided over all the ceremonies, including the Sequencing.

A few years ago, before the rain had stopped, Guardian Clarence had invited Master Diaxin to come and speak to the group of wards. They had all been sitting in their socks, having discarded their muddy boots at the door when they entered the warding center, when the Official had come

46

into the center. His red hair had been plastered to his face, and he had shed his soaked over-coat the moment he had entered the room.

For the next hour, Master Diaxin had shared about the duties of an Official. He had been Sequenced 721 Years after Inception. He explained that every season; the Queen sent Firsts from the capital to govern the cities in Tiarny. After that visit, Nellie and Fay had made a game of guessing how long various Officials would last in Liantis. None had been in Liantis longer than Master Diaxin, who had come to the city over ten years ago.

The man she now saw standing on the dais looked nothing like the one who had visited the warding center. Instead of his typical Official's tunic, he was wearing a long white robe with billowing sleeves. Rather than being lined with silver and blue like Nellie's, the Tailors had lined Master Diaxin's robe with gold.

Eyes trained on the Official on the dais, Nellie fingered the long scar on her left arm. Remembering the day she had gotten the scar, she felt herself pale despite the heat of the sun. Her gaze never left the Official as she subtly patted her chest, making sure the pendant was safely out of view. She breathed slightly easier, trying to banish the thought of punishments from her mind.

Silence filled the air as everyone observed the Master. As the highest-ranking First in town, his word was the law.

And today, his words were set to push Nellie onto the path of her fate.

Chapter Six

"Ladies and gentlemen. Wards and Guardians. Firsts, Seconds and Thirds. Citizens of Tiarny. Welcome to the seven hundred and forty-ninth Sequencing Ceremony. As you know, this is but one of many Sequencing Ceremonies taking place across Tiarny today. This ceremony marks the day our wards step towards their future. Today, they will experience the Blessing of The Source Herself."

The entire crowd was silent as the Master's voice echoed through the Temple Square.

"Every single one of you standing here before me was born for this moment, your future set apart by the Source. Seven hundred and forty-nine years ago, on the very first Sacred Solstice during the Year of Inception, the Source took it upon herself to save our people. In the time leading up to the Year of Inception, the Source was watching the people of this land when she grew frustrated with their evil ways."

A cool breeze blew through the square, the only sound the ruffling of tunics as all eyes were trained on the dais.

"Taking pity on the people, the Source came to this land and

Sequenced the very first citizens of Tiarny. She imbued the people with purpose. When she came, she took a group of uncivilized, careless people who cared more for making war and honouring men above all else and moulded them into a society of functional citizens. She created a society where every person had a place, no matter their abilities. There is room for everyone in Tiarny. Thank the Source."

At that moment, every single person lifted their right arms and raised them to their hearts, their fists curled as they echoed the Master's words. "Thank the Source."

As the words rang through the square, the red-headed Official returned the gesture before he continued speaking. His voice seemed even louder now than before, his eyes blazing with the fires of passion.

"The Source set about the Sequencing to bring order and structure to the evil people's otherwise dysfunctional lives. After She saw how successful the first Sequencing was in curbing the chaos that had dominated these lands, the Source declared that henceforth, every ward would undergo their own Sequencing the year they turn eighteen. If you were born in the year seven hundred and thirty-one after Inception, you have been Blessed. This is your time."

Master Diaxin paused, and as one, the crowd of wards spoke. "This is our time. Bless the Source."

"The Sequencing allows for each person to be placed wherever they are best suited to serve. Wherever the Source Sequences you, whatever your title, whatever your occupation may be, know that receiving the Source's Blessing and being Sequenced is the highest honour in the land."

The Official expertly ignored the subtle eye rolls and glazed expressions that surrounded Nellie as he continued on with his speech. She knew it was the same one he gave every year. However, the speech seemed to be more powerful, more important than ever since this was now *her* year to be Sequenced.

"You may know this story. You may recognize it from the countless times you have heard it in the past. But realize that today, this story becomes your reality. Every one of you will enter the Temple and stand in front of the Committee. Now it is *your* time. The Source has decreed that each of you will receive your Sequenced positions today. You will walk into the Temple as a ward and emerge as a new, fully Sequenced citizen of Tiarny."

Nellie knew that being a part of the Sequencing Committee was an extremely high honour. Each member of the Committee was a First sent from Deavita and specifically appointed by the Source to ensure that every ward was properly Sequenced. The identities of the Committee members were a highly guarded secret. Even if she wanted to find out who they were, she had no way of doing so.

Anxious after standing for so long in one spot, Nellie shifted under the heat of the sun. The movement shook the pendant loose, and she felt it rub against her skin. The necklace felt warm next to her skin, as though it was emitting a strange type of heat. But that couldn't be right. Nellie brushed it off as an illusion brought on by the warm climate of the growing season.

Lost in thought, she missed part of Master Diaxin's speech. Fay squeezed her hand, subtly bumping her hip into Nellie's. Thankfully, the Official was still speaking when Nellie pulled her head out of the clouds.

"-blessing. You should each be praying to the Source while you are waiting for your Sequencing. We will begin today's Sequencing with Alexea Kiani. Alexea, please proceed inside the Temple."

Just like that, it had begun. The Master bowed to the crowd before he spun around. With a final flourish of his long, billowing robes, the red-haired Official marched inside the Temple. A collective sigh ran through the wards as the Master disappeared from sight.

Nellie watched as Alexea Kiana began moving through the crowd and up the temple stairs. She glided over the steps, her feet barely touching the black marble as she moved. Nellie's eyes tracked Alexea's every movement. She had seen Alexea from time to time around the city, but she never really got the chance to know her. No matter where the Source Sequenced Alexea, Nellie knew she would stand out. Her amber skin and coal-black curls stood out against her ceremonial outfit, creating a striking contrast as she stood above the crowd.

At the top of the steps, silence fell over the crowd as Alexea turned around and faced her fellow wards. Nellie couldn't see her eyes from where she was standing, but she saw a wide grin on the curly-haired beauty's face. She appeared to be thrilled. And why not?

The Sequencing represented the future of every person born in Tiarny.

Alexea's powerful voice rang out through the square.

"In order to honour the Source, I give myself to be Sequenced. Will you have me?"

"We will." The words came from the lips of all the wards, the ceremonial phrases having been instilled in them from a young age.

Guardian Clarence had made Nellie repeat the lines over and over again. When asked why the phrasing was so important, he had huffed. "Together, you are strong. Alone, you are nothing. As a Sequenced unit, you can do anything. The power of the Sequencing is not in the individual but in the collective." He had run his hand through his short black hair before continuing. "This is how the Source saved the people with the First Sequencing, and this is how the Sequencing continued to help Tiarny grow and thrive."

Having completed the ritualistic call and response, Alexea bowed low towards the crowd and turned to enter the Temple. She climbed the black marble steps before the large double doors of the main Temple area swung open to admit her. Soon, she was out of sight. As Alexea disappeared into the Temple, Nellie heard whispers all around her as people speculated where Alexea would be Sequenced.

Every Sequencing was different. Sometimes wards were in the Temple for a minute or two while they received the Source's blessings, while other times they were in the Temple for much longer. Nellie had asked her mother for details about what happens inside the Temple, but she could not tell her.

"It's not that I don't want to tell you, Eleanor." Maude has murmured over dinner one night. "It's that I can't. You'll remember learning about the Oath?"

Nellie had nodded, swallowing her mouthful of lentils before she replied. "Yes, Guardian Clarence told us we will take an Oath that prevents us from speaking of the Sequencing with anyone who had yet to undergo their own Sequencing."

Despite knowing the Oath existed, it hadn't stopped her from asking her mother about her own ceremony repeatedly.

Nellie was picking at a loose thread on her tunic when the large double doors of the Temple swung open with a *boom*. She looked up just as a smiling Alexea marched out of the Temple. She no longer wore her white Sequencing tunic. In its place, the black-haired beauty wore a red tunic with two grey stripes running down the sides. It accented her amber skin beautifully.

Fay nudged Nellie in the side, "She's a Protector, then. I think this is perfect for her. Don't you think?"

Nellie nodded absentmindedly. She thought that Alexea's inherent grace would be well-suited to her new role. Fighting was a lot like dancing.

There was a certain refinement needed to move without sound, to wield a weapon with ease and to protect those around you.

"I think they did a great job," she tipped her head towards Fay, whispering. "Maybe she'll even work in Deavita as a Royal Protector one day."

Fay shivered, wrapping her arms around herself. "I don't know Nell. Royal Protectors kind of scare me. I heard they will go to any lengths to uphold the Queen's law."

At a loss for words, Nellie placed her hand on her friend's shoulder before returning her attention to the Sequencing. One by one, the crowd of wards around them thinned as wards kept entering the Temple. They were mostly run-of-the-mill Sequencings. There were two other Protectors who eventually joined Alexea wearing the red tunic with two grey stripes running down the sides.

One, a boy named Seamus, stood at over six and a half feet tall and looked to weigh as much as a tree. Nellie knew he couldn't be eating fresh fruits or vegetables other than the same beans and peas as everyone else, but she wondered where his bulk came from. He appeared to be someone who spent his entire life working out, his muscles popping as he stood on the dais in his new tunic. Seamus came sauntering out of the Temple grinning ear to ear, wearing his new tunic with pride.

The other newly Sequenced Protector was Penelope. She was Nellie's neighbour and insisted on being called Penny. She was quiet and liked to keep to herself, always armed with a book in hand. Nellie had even seen Penny reading while carrying her empty jug of water to the well. She would have thought Penny would have been Sequenced to be a Tutor or perhaps a Scholar, so it surprised her to see her neighbour emerge from the Temple wearing the red tunic of the Protectors.

Not only were there wards who were Sequenced as Protectors, but there were also new Builders and Tutors, Guardians and Servers, even another Provider, just like her mother. When a young man emerged from the temple wearing the tunic of an Official, there was a collective intake of breath.

"There hasn't been an Official Sequenced from Liantis in over fifteen years." Fay whispered excitedly. "We are witnessing a historical moment."

Raising a brow, Nellie tilted her head. "How do you know all this? We take all the same classes."

"I know these things, Nell, because I've paid attention in classes."

"That's..."

The Temple doors swung open once more, the sound echoing through the square. A young woman emerged from the Temple; her shoulders drooping as she dragged her feet along the onyx marble. Tear marks ran down her pale face. Dampness had gathered on the brown tunic that hung on her frame.

Nellie heard a sharp intake of breath from all around her. Whispers flew as the wards watched the woman descend down the marble stairs.

"Can you believe it?"

"Not Yenna."

"A Server."

"She'll probably have to move to Deavita."

"She's a Third."

Nellie heard the sounds of shock swirling like a cyclone all around her. Before anyone could pinpoint where the whispers were coming from, they all stopped as suddenly as they had begun. A voice called another ward in, and another Sequencing was underway.

As the hours dragged by, the number of wards dwindled and the number of newly Sequenced citizens continued to rise. People began shifting from one foot to another as muscles were discreetly being stretched. Nellie pulled her tunic away from her skin, revelling in the cooling breeze as it touched her skin. Oh, what she wouldn't give for a rain shower right now. Nellie was just about to turn to speak quietly with Fay when she heard her name ring out over the crowd.

"Eleanor Marie Merrick, come forward to be Sequenced."

This was it.

Her Sequencing had arrived.

Chapter Seven

A s soon as Nellie's name rang out over the square, she inhaled sharply. Suddenly, it was hard to catch her breath. Sweat began pouring down her back as she gave Fay's hand a last squeeze and pushed through the crowd. Bodies shifted, creating a path for her as she walked with her head up high.

Nellie felt as though she could hear everything that was happening all around her as she moved towards the looming Temple. The rustle of fabric, the sound of gravel crunching under her feet, and the breath leaving her lungs all left their mark on her as she moved.

The pounding of her heart echoed in her ears as the vital organ began pumping blood faster than it ever had before. Nellie heard its beat in her ear like a drum, encouraging her to keep walking.

She had only heard a drum once before. Artists were a rare sight in Liantis, but when Nellie was ten, she had met a drummer who travelled with a small group of Artists. They had been on their way to Deavita from Ion until a bad windstorm waylaid them.

After meeting the musicians, Nellie had spent the next night curled up beside her mother on the settee. "Why can't Seconds and Thirds always have music?" She had wanted to ask all day and her curiosity finally got the better of her.

Maude had tucked a loose lock behind Nellie's ear, running her thumb down Nellie's tan face before she replied. "Music has the ability to expose the deepest parts of our souls. People's souls and their emotions are inconsistent and volatile. The Source introduced the Sequencing to keep us from straying back into the evil of our past. If enough people were exposed to music, they might rebel against the Sequencing and chaos would reign in the land once more. You see Eleanor, creativity encourages thought, and free thought can be incredibly dangerous."

As Nellie's heart beat faster and faster, she realized that this was one form of music that could never be taken away from them.

Boom-boom

This is it.

Boom-boom

Every step I take is a step closer to my fate.

Boom-boom

Move. This is not the moment for weakness.

Boom-boom

Go. Now.

The view from the large dais was incredible. Standing on the enormous wooden structure, Nellie counted hundreds of heads. The weight of their gaze was heavy as she stood above them all. There were a few large birds flying overhead, the sound of their wings echoing over the crowd as they waited expectantly. The shining sun made it difficult to make out individual faces, but Nellie knew that somewhere in that crowd was her mother. She drew energy from that knowledge, inhaling deeply as she prepared to speak.

"In order to honour the Source, I give myself to be Sequenced. Will you have me?"

Nellie's usually powerful voice was shaking, her fists clammy as she stood perfectly still. Her words echoed out over the square, settling over the crowd. Finally, the words "we will" rang out in unison over her. Her shoulders loosened and her fists unclenched as strength settled into her bones.

Time slowed to a crawl as Nellie crossed the threshold of the Temple. The sunlight vanished as the enormous doors banged shut behind her. A moment passed as her eyes adjusted to the darkness, the scene inside the Temple coming to life before her. It looked different from the last time she had been in here, during the annual Blessing of the Harvest. At that time, there had been a vast space in front of the large, black marble altar dedicated to the Source. The large rectangular windows had been opened and sunlight had been streaming through. Now, though, there were heavy black curtains that hung, blocking out all sights and sounds from outside.

There was a dimly lit table that stretched the length of the room. It was shadowed in darkness, the only light coming from a dozen lit wax candles that adorned the table. The wax dripped down their elongated lengths, settling in odd formations at the base. The flames flickered and danced over the mysterious faces of five formidable Officials who sat at the table. They each wore the same long white robes as Master Diaxin, although somehow, they looked even more formidable than the red-headed Master ever had.

Large, heavy hoods covered the hair of each Official, rendering it nearly impossible to see any of their facial features. They remained in perfect silence, unmoving, with their hands folded in front of them as they watched Nellie. She had been waiting to be Sequenced for her entire life, but right now she couldn't wait to get out of the presence of the

Committee. Her stomach twisted into knots as she stood under their unwavering gaze, wishing the ground would swallow her whole.

Just as Nellie thought she couldn't handle another second of the burdensome silence, one Official began to speak, their piercing voice shaking Nellie free from the pit of her anxiety.

"Eleanor Marie Merrick, please step forward."

Nellie quickly obeyed as she fingered the scar on her left arm. She had grown used to its presence on her arm over the past few years. The memory of the searing pain flashing down her arm served as a reminder that she needed to behave.

Please Source, let them not notice the pendant.

Despite its lightweight appearance, the necklace felt as though it weighed a ton as it hung on a chain around her neck. She fought the urge to hunch her shoulders, forcing her back to remain straight despite the weight. The only things moving were her hands as she kept straightening her tunic, waiting for instructions.

The Committee member seated closest to Nellie spoke, the flames casting eerie shadows on their faces.

"Do you, Eleanor, agree to the absolute power of this committee, as divinely appointed by The Source Herself?" The Official's voice had a musical lilt and Nellie thought this one must be female. Perhaps the same age as her mother?

The response came unbidden to Nellie, although she had never been told what to say during her Sequencing. It was as though her mind had known the words all along, and was now being given the opportunity to say them.

"I do. I give myself to this Committee to be Sequenced." Her voice rang through the chamber, echoing off the walls and marble flooring.

"And do you, Eleanor, agree to follow the path of your Sequencing no matter where you go?"

Another voice arose from the table. This time it was the soft, feathery voice of an elderly woman. Her accent marked her as being born and bred in Deavita, the capital.

"I do." Nellie stood tall, her shoulders tense as she faced the Committee. A surge of emotions flooded her as she stood in the Temple, the moment she had been waiting for finally upon her. "I give myself to this path, no matter where it may lead me."

A third voice addressed Nellie, this one a male. His voice was noticeably different from the other Officials she had heard from so far. The mysterious man spoke quickly, his voice lacking all emotions.

"And finally, do you, Eleanor Marie Merrick, swear to keep the contents of these proceedings secret from this day forward until you meet the Source Herself?"

"I do," Nellie replied. The moment she uttered the final vow, a strange weight settled upon her in the pit of her stomach. It was like nothing she had ever felt before.

"Good," the same Official spoke, his voice a touch lighter than the moment before. "Even if you were foolish enough to try and speak of the events of this room, the Binding Oath you just took will prevent you from doing so."

Nellie's mouth dropped open as her eyes widened in shock. She had heard rumours of Binding Oaths that bound their speakers to The Source, but she had never sworn such an oath herself. Until now. Nellie watched as the Committee members seemed to settle slightly in their seats, their postures relaxing as they looked at one another.

So far, so good. Nellie thought triumphantly. *That must have been the worst of it.*

She was wondering what would happen next when the same soft voice belonging to the Official from Deavita began speaking once more.

"Eleanor Marie Merrick, we have been watching you closely over the years. Your Guardian had shared with us about your strengths and weaknesses, your social behaviour, and the results of your tutelage. He's also shared with us your... unique affinity for disorder."

Unique affinity for disorder? That's a kind way to say "getting into trouble". I hope this doesn't mean they'll move me to the Third class like Yenna. I can't move to Dariani.

Lost in thought, it took Nellie a moment to realize the Official seemed to be waiting for her to say something.

"Umm... yes?" She said sheepishly, blood rushing to her cheeks.

Yes, I seem to cause trouble left and right. No, I don't do it on purpose. Yes, it seems to be a gift of mine.

The Committee member chuckled softly before continuing.

"As I was saying, we have been watching you closely. After consulting with your Guardian, we took your case directly to The Source. As with every single ward who undergoes the Sequencing, we wanted to make sure we placed you on the right path."

The soft-spoken woman stopped speaking and another of the hooded Officials picked up where she left off. Nellie hadn't heard from this one yet, she was certain. His voice, deep and thunderous, directly contrasted with his stark, business-like words. Nellie thought he sounded young, much younger than the other Committee members she's heard from so far.

Of course, it was hard to tell how many seasons someone had been on this planet when they're wearing billowing robes and a large hood. He could be a hundred years old, for all Nellie knew.

"Eleanor Marie Merrick. The Source had decreed that you are to receive Her Blessing. She had declared that your Sequenced path is that of a Healer."

Nellie's eyes bulged at the proclamation. Colour drained from her face and her heart stopped beating all together as she stared at the

Sequencing Committee, struggling to breathe.

There must be some mistake.

The same Official continued, "You will leave for Deavita with the others at daybreak tomorrow. There you will remain for the next four seasons, apprenticing in the Healing Arts in Deavita before you begin your work as a Healer."

Four seasons. That means I'll get to come back to Liantis. Please Source, let me return to my mother. She needs me.

Images of her mother, alone and weeping in the townhouse, ran through Nellie's mind as she stared at the Sequencing Committee.

She tried to force a mask of indifference over her features, but it was surprisingly difficult. Her bewilderment must have been on full display, because the soft-spoken Official began speaking again.

"This must come as a shock to you. It was to us as well. Liantis hadn't produced a Healer during a Sequencing ceremony in... well over two centuries. But The Source was clear in the direction She wishes you to take."

"Annabel." The Official with the deep voice hissed. "That is enough! You know The Source doesn't allow us to divulge anything else."

"Dion, she deserves to know what we know. She's going to have enough trouble adjusting as it is."

Dion.

The name rang through Nellie's mind, as it struck a chord deep inside of her. Something about it made her feel... intrigued.

Wait.

Trouble?

What kind of trouble?

"Trouble? What do you mean?" Nellie's voice wobbled as she still struggled to catch her breath. Her heart had begun beating again, the sound echoing in her ears as she watched the silent group sitting in front of her. Her mind was racing as she tried to wrap her mind around what was happening.

Annabel drew in a deep breath and glanced at Dion before replying.

"As a Healer, your mentors will teach you the ins and outs of your Sequenced occupation. The apprenticeship to be a Healer is difficult. We won't lie to you. It is a monumental task for anyone, but it will be even more difficult for you as there aren't many Healers left. The Source hadn't Sequenced many people to be Healers in recent years. In fact..."

Before Annabel could continue speaking, Dion slammed both hands on the table and stood up.

"That is *enough*."

His deep voice echoed through the vast Temple. The movement had shifted his hood and Nellie saw two obsidian eyes staring at her from behind his hood. The man's face was like chiseled stone. His fingers darted up and pulled his hood forward before he sat down again. Silence dominated the room as the other four Officials glanced at Dion. Nellie watched as each of them shifted, their backs straight as they looked straight ahead. Whoever this man was, he seemed to be powerful enough that everyone obeyed him. Nellie felt invisible under the gaze of the Officials as they all sat motionless, seeming to wait for some signal.

She was feeling more anxious than ever, her breath coming in rapid bursts as she assessed the situation. Having a history of panic attacks that seemed to arise at the worst possible moment, Nellie tried to clear her head and do some of the meditative breathing Guardian Clarence had taught her. She picked a point in the distance, a small silver plaque on the midnight-black altar, and stared at it with all her might. She kept running her hands down her tunic, wiping away imaginary wrinkles. The pendant felt like a thousand-ton stone under her tunic, growing heavier by the second. The Officials continued to look right past her, seemingly engaged in some silent battle of wills. This was certainly not how she had envisioned her Sequencing.

A few more minutes crept by. The Officials began passing a sheet of paper between themselves and occasionally scribbling on it while Nellie stood on, watching. The benefit of the silence was that she had time to think about everything that had just happened. One thought had begun running through her mind on repeat.

New plan: Go to Deavita for my apprenticeship and make it back to Liantis as quickly as humanly possible. Please Source, let me return to Liantis and my mother.

She kept her eyes focused on the altar behind the Sequencing Committee, her breaths becoming steadier as she won the battle against her anxiety.

Finally, the last Official, the one who had yet to speak, stood up.

"Eleanor, we are sure you feel overwhelmed by everything that has happened. Please come with me to receive your new tunic. Your Guide will explain more about your new position tomorrow on the trek to the capital. That is all for today."

Nodding, Nellie followed the Official out of the room. She loomed over him, his head barely coming up to her chest. He led her into a small space off of the primary area of the temple. Not much bigger than her bedroom at her mother's mercantile, shelves and racks of various sizes filled the small chamber.

On one side of the space, there were three overflowing bookshelves. Intrigued, Nellie took a step towards the bookshelves before the Official cleared his throat.

"Ahem. The tunics, Healer Eleanor, are on *this* side of the chamber."

Healer Eleanor.

Nellie jolted upright at the sound of her new title. She had been many things in her life until now. Daughter, ward, friend. And now, the Source had chosen her to be a Healer.

She walked over to the Official in a daze and took the clothing he offered her. Her long fingers brushed his umber ones as she took the material, the warmth in his touch pulling her back to the present. She just stared at the Healer's tunic for a moment, running her fingers down the black tunic. There was a singular white stripe that ran from the tip of the shoulder to the hem of the tunic. The material was some sort of woven cotton, the fabric much softer than her ward's tunic.

A perk of being a First, I suppose.

Holding the piece of clothing in front of her chest, Nellie thanked the nameless Official. She began looking around the small chamber uncomfortably, shifting from one foot to the other, when the Official backed out of the room, dipping his head ever so slightly as he shut the door. "I'll wait outside for you. Please be quick, Healer Eleanor, as we must continue with the Sequencings."

Please be quick. My life had just turned upside down, and he says "please be quick."

For the first time in hours, Nellie was alone. She inhaled deeply, flopping down on the only chair in the room. She ran hands down her braid, tucking in stray hairs as her stomach began protesting its lack of sustenance. It felt as though she had lived a thousand lifetimes during this day, and she hadn't even eaten lunch.

Standing up once more, Nellie's fingers shook as she pulled off her Sequencing tunic and folded it neatly. She placed it on the back of her chair, swapping it out for the new black tunic the Official had handed her. With a quick prayer to the Source that she would get to return to Liantis soon, Nellie slipped the new tunic over her head and pulled her braid out of the neck.

Before she turned the door handle, Nellie remembered the pendant she was wearing around her neck. With a quick movement of her hands, she tucked it out of sight. Thank the Source.

With one last glance at the small chamber that had provided her an unexpected moment of rest, Nellie turned the doorknob and stepped into her future.

Chapter Eight

The next few minutes seemed to pass by in a blur. The nameless Official ushered Nellie out of the Temple. Her retinas burned as she stepped out into the midday sun, the heat of the day hitting her like that of an open oven. Beads of sweat instantly appeared on her brow. As she shifted to accommodate the heat, Nellie heard gasps run through the crowd. The sounds of chatter stopped as everyone stared at her. She shrunk under their gaze, her cheeks ablaze as she was suddenly the center of everyone's attention.

Chin up, Nellie. You can do this.

Inhaling deeply, Nellie pulled her black tunic down and straightened her back before she descended the steps. She held her head high, her gaze fixed on the horizon as she moved. Nellie marched through the crowd of wards, her gaze flitting over faces as she sought a familiar face. She knew Fay had yet to be Sequenced, but she breathed a sigh of relief as her eyes lit upon Penny. Exhaling, Nellie went and stood next to her instead.

The view of the Temple wasn't great from this vantage point. Their

Sequencings completed; the Officials relegated the new citizens to the side of the Temple. They had a front-row view of the side of the Temple, the enormous ebony walls of the Temple looming over them as they waited for the Ceremony to be over. The sun was shining directly above them and all around her, people were shifting about as they sought what little shade there was to be had. Nellie didn't speak to Penny, but pulled her in for a quick hug before they watched the rest of the Sequencing Ceremony unfold.

It seemed to Nellie that all the other Sequencings were going much quicker than hers. There was a steady stream of Providers, Protectors, and Builders who exited the Temple. Alongside them were a few new Guardians, Tutors, and even a new Midwife.

Fay was one of the last wards to be called in for her Sequencing. The moment her name rang out, Nellie stood on her tip-toes to watch her friend ascend the dais. Even from the side of the Temple, she could see that her best friend's bright turquoise hair sparkled in the sunlight. She grinned as Fay climbed the Temple steps. Fay's back was straight as she walked with purpose. From their many childhood adventures, Nellie knew that her best friend didn't have a shy bone in her body. Just yesterday, Fay had expressed to her she felt that the Sequencing was just another adventure to be undertaken.

With bated breath and sweaty palms, she waited for her best friend to exit the Temple. Nellie could hardly stand the wait and was shifting from one foot to the other when the massive Temple doors finally swung open.

Fay had been in the Temple less than a quarter of the time Nellie had spent in front of those five ominous Officials. She practically bounded onto the dais; her white Sequencing tunic having been exchanged for an indigo one with a bright blue stripe running down both her sleeves.

"Penny," Nellie whispered excitedly to her left, "Fay's going to be a Tailor."

"I know, Nellie. I think that's perfect. Remember when she used to make ridiculous braids in my hair when we were wards together?"

Nellie snorted before covering her mouth with her hand. Eyes turned in their direction and both women stared straight ahead with their mouths clamped together.

Just as Fay descended the steps, Nellie whispered, "I do. She's so creative. This is the perfect path for her."

"Nellie! I can't believe it! I mean, I really cannot believe it." Fay pulled Nellie into a quick hug before coming to stand next to her friend. She was out of breath and speaking so quickly that all of her words were flowing together. Nellie didn't even think Fay was breathing as she spoke.

"You are going to be going to Deavita do you remember when we went there with Guardian Clarence and we saw all the Firsts the beautiful buildings the river even the Palace. OhmySource do you think you'll get to visit the Palace?"

"I don't know what I'll get to do in the capital," Nellie mused, careful to keep whispering. "Maybe I will get to see the Palace. It must be beautiful, since the Queen commanded that only Builders from Ion work on it. I don't know though, Fay, I just wish I could stay here. I don't understand."

"Nell." Fay's coal-black eyes grew to the size of saucers as she glanced around quickly. Her friend discreetly picked up Nellie's left arm and rubbed her hand over the scar. "Let's talk about this later."

Nellie's own eyes widened as understanding washed over her. She squeezed Fay's hand, which was still gripping her arm.

"Of course, you're right." She replied, nibbling on her upper lip as she glanced around.

Fay forced out a high-pitched laugh. "Of course, I'm right. Come on, it's almost time for the Final Blessing. Source forbid we miss out on that. My mother would have my head."

Nellie snorted as she nodded her agreement. Fay's mother, Sheena, certainly was a force to be reckoned with. Her head may have only reached Nellie's chest, but she was one of the most forceful people she had ever met in her life. Despite her best efforts, Sheena had never been a fan of Nellie's.

I bet she'll be happy I have to go to the capital, Nellie thought before her green eyes flew open.

I have to go to the capital.

Her lip quivered as she sucked in air like she was starving. Her emotions were running wild, her heart pounding as the reality of her situation became real. She had heard the Officials earlier. But hearing something and knowing it, having it become reality, were two different things.

"Fay, I... I have to leave."

Her voice broke on the last word as salty tears rushed to her eyes. Her vision blurred as they flooded down her cheeks, tracking down her tan skin before they dampened the ground beneath her. The dry, crumbly earth itself seemed to weep alongside Nellie as it darkened, absorbing the moisture generated by her sorrow.

"I know, Nell." Rivulets of tears began running down Fay's cheeks, joining Nellie's in a pool of grief. Their shoulders shook in unison as they stood hunched over, mourning the loss of their future together, saying farewell to what would never have the chance to come true.

She had dreamt that she would have her own children one day and raise them alongside Fay. Even though she had never spoken the dream out loud, the Sequencing had unequivocally changed the direction of her future. *That is the problem with dreams. Sometimes they're stolen from us before we even have the chance to realize them.*

After a time, her tears dried up. The deep well of emotions inside of her was empty and the dark earth beneath her feet the only evidence of her sorrow.

Fay hiccupped as she wiped her cheeks. "Let's get through the Final Blessing, Nellie, and then we can deal with the capital. You're my sister no matter where we are."

Nellie clutched Fay's hand and squeezed it before bending down and whispering in her ear.

"No matter what, Fay, we are soul-bound. Forever."

"Soul-bound."

For a peaceful moment, Nellie remained beside her friend. The knowledge that the Sequencing would tear them asunder come daybreak lay heavy over both of them. But they knew, together, they were strong.

Side by side, they could conquer anything.

When the sun was high in the sky, the final ward, a lanky black-haired boy with terracotta skin named Josiah, went through the Temple and received his Sequencing as a Protector. Murmurs rose through the air as Master Diaxin marched back out onto the dais. He was still wearing the long billowing robes, but he had tied his red hair back with a cord. The few strands that had escaped were plastered to his cheeks as sweat streamed down his face in rivulets.

"Attention," he said. The crowd stilled at his words. Conversations ceased mid-sentence, babies stopped crying, even the sound of the birds faded into nothing. Silence reigned as everyone watched the man on the dais.

"Citizens of Tiarny, as the seven hundred and forty-ninth Sequencing Ceremony comes to a close, let us end by sending a Final Blessing to the Source. Please, bow your heads."

As one, every single person stood in the square bowed their head. The only sound was the faint meowing of a cat in the distance. Even the newborns, too young to be warded, had the good sense to stay quiet during the Blessing so as not to anger the Source.

The Master's voice wasn't exceptionally loud, but it echoed through the silent square as every ear strained to hear him speak.

"To our Eternal Source," he intoned, "thank you for always watching over the people of Tiarny. You came to us when we were uncivilized, leading lives of strife and war, and led us to a place of healing, peace, and calm. We ask you, oh Source, to bless us once more with rain for our parched land."

The Official paused, stretching his arms to the heavens. His voice shook as it rang out over the crowd, slowly increasing in intensity.

"We beseech you, oh great and benevolent Source, to send us clouds laden with rain to nourish our dry ground. Please, bless us once more with bountiful crops. Thank you for the Sequencing, for taking the time to set each citizen on the correct pathway into the future. We ask for your Blessing on these newly Sequenced citizens of Tiarny as they go forth into tomorrow and every day after that. Bless the Source."

As Master Diaxin lowered his arms, the crowd spoke as one. "Amen." Nellie and Fay murmured the words along with the rest of the citizens, their voices raspy.

Having spoken the last words of the Blessing, Master Diaxin walked off the Temple grounds. The bells began tolling once more in celebration of the newly Sequenced members of society.

Suddenly, a boisterous mob took the place of the silent crowd. Bodies began pushing against each other as families sought each other amongst the crowd. Citizens and wards alike flooded the Temple Square. Where there was a sea of white prior to the Sequencing now became a rainbow of different coloured tunics.

Amid the crowd, Nellie stood on her tip-toes, sweat running down her back as her black tunic gave her little relief from the heat. She looked across the Temple Square, her eyes narrowed as she searched for a particular person. A moment later, a triumphant grin spread across her face as she saw the person she was looking for. Grabbing Fay's hand, Nellie looked down.

"Do you trust me, Fay?"

"Always."

With that, Nellie took off and began pulling Fay through the sea of people. Fay's act of trust paid off as they neared the edge of the square. Nellie sagged in relief when she saw her mother standing with Fay's parents under one of the red oak trees that lined the square. Fay's father Arnold was standing tall in his Builder's tunic as he held little Lucien. He was just a year old and too young to be warded.

Late one evening two years ago, long after Nellie had been sent to bed, she had overheard Fay's parents talking with her mother about their recent dealings with the Midwives. Sheena had shared with Maude that they had been on the waiting list to have their birth-control lifted for over a decade, but the Midwives had only recently approved it. Opening her door a crack, Nellie had watched Sheena cradle her swollen belly. She had never seen Fay's mother look as happy as she had that evening.

This wasn't the first time that Nellie had heard about Midwives. The Tutors taught all the wards about human anatomy and the Healers administered a special form of birth control to all wards, male and female, from the moment they turned twelve. Sitting on the stool as she received her first shot, Nellie had asked the Healer all about them. The Healer had explained that they suppressed female cycles and prevented both unwanted pregnancies and the transmittance of sexual disease. Every citizen above the age of twelve received the injections on the first day of every other full moon cycle.

Curious, Nellie had asked what would happen if someone refused the shot. Her question had echoed through the room as all the other wards inhaled sharply, eyes trained on the Healer.

"The Source has wisely decreed that if a person wishes to stop taking birth control, they must receive a special dispensation from the Midwife. It is the Midwife's job to ensure that there is a perfect balance in Tiarny's population."

After that, Nellie hadn't questioned the Healer anymore.

Lucien looked just like Fay, his skin dark and his eyes bright as he waved his fists in the air. The only difference between them was their hair colour. Lucien had dark curls that shone purple in the sunlight. The baby had been quiet during the Sequencing, but now he was making his presence known as he wailed in his father's arms, his limbs thrashing as he struggled to break free.

The moment Nellie's gaze met her mother's, she felt her breath catch in her throat. All the emotions she had been feeling while standing with Fay came flooding back in. Gasping for air, Nellie ran right into her mother's embrace. She breathed in deeply as she revelled in the warmth of Maude's arms. The scent of roses mingled with that of lavender, sweat, and tears. There they stood, mother and daughter, as the rest of the world slowly faded away. The heaviness of the situation settled on Nellie's shoulders, as she suddenly realized that this might be one of the last times in the foreseeable future that she could hug her mother.

"I thought I was out of tears, but I guess not," Nellie whispered as she wiped her nose on the cotton handkerchief her mother offered her.

"Eleanor, my child. Look at me." Maude tucked a stray hair behind Nellie's ear before standing back and admiring her daughter. Pride shimmered in her eyes as she spoke. "It's okay. I'm here now."

Overcome with emotion, Nellie tightened her grip on her mother. She refused to even open her mouth, let alone speak, for fear of opening the floodgates of her tears. She knew that if she cried now, she would not stop until daybreak tomorrow.

"We have much to talk about, Eleanor," her mother said. Maude looked around the group and made eye contact with Fay's parents. They communicated in only a way parents seemed to do, silently but with purpose. She nodded, her voice feathery and quiet upon the hot afternoon air. "We should go."

"But what about Fay?" Nellie asked meekly, still unable to let go of her mother.

At least I'm not crying right now. Focus on not crying.

Maude addressed Fay's parents over Nellie's shoulder as she rubbed her back.

"I'm sure that Fay's parents appreciate that I want to spend as much time as I can with my daughter before tomorrow. Isn't that right?"

Both of Fay's parents nodded, their faces grim with understanding. When the sun rose on the morrow, Nellie was duty-bound to be on her way to the capital. She had no choice. She had to leave with the sunrise.

Gulping back tears, Nellie wiped the remnants of her earlier tears off her cheeks and released her mother. She grabbed Fay, hugging her soul-sister before she gave her a tight squeeze.

"I'll find you tonight. Promise me, you'll be at our spot."

Fay's eyes watered again as she returned Nellie's hug. She squeezed so tightly that Nellie gasped for air.

"Absolutely." Fay's lips tipped upwards. "I wouldn't miss it for the world."

Nellie tore herself away from her best friend and began walking away from the Temple with her mother. Her heart was so heavy as she replayed the events of the day.

Trouble.

Annabel had said Nellie would run into trouble. She just didn't know it would start so soon after the Sequencing Ceremony.

Chapter Nine

Silence filled the air as Nellie and her mother walked home. The crowds on the streets slowly diminished and then disappeared as they neared the mercantile.

Most people were out celebrating their Sequencings with their families. The bulk of newly Sequenced citizens were remaining in Liantis. Most of them had a reason to feel jubilant. Most of them weren't Nellie and Maude. The mother and daughter trudged back to the mercantile, hunched over with their heads bowed low as the weight of the day settled upon them. Nellie hadn't felt so sombre since the day they buried her grandmother Wilhelmina.

Nellie had been very close to her grandmother. When Nellie had only been four years old, her maternal grandmother had moved from Ion to Liantis to live with them. Wilhelmina had been a Tailor but as she grew older, her body had grown frail. Eventually, her fingers weren't able to hold the needle and thread anymore. The Source had blessedly decreed that instead of being Re-Sequenced, she could come and live with her daughter and granddaughter. Wilhelmina had lived with Nellie and Maude for eight years before she had passed away.

As Nellie walked beside her mother, her mind was swirling with so many questions. It took every effort she had to put one foot in front of the other.

Goodbye.

How can one word be so short but so difficult to say? Why do I have to leave the only place I've ever known for my entire life? How can I abandon the only people who truly know me?

Why is the Source asking this of me?

The gravity of what was to come was pressing down so heavily on Nellie's shoulders and she could not seem to find the right words to say goodbye to her mother. They walked in silence all the way home, each one pulling strength from the other.

A half-hour had passed by the time Nellie and Maude had walked up the rickety stairs into their living space. Sighing, Nellie devoured a piece of bread as soon as she entered the home. Her stomach sated, she had sorted through her thoughts and had found the strength to speak.

"Mother, I-"

"Eleanor, wait. I need to say this now." Maude gestured towards one of the kitchen chairs, waiting for her to sit down. "Eleanor Marie Merrick, I am so proud of you." Tears glimmered in Maude's eyes. "I know you can't tell me what happened in that Temple, and I know you're confused. But no matter where you are, no matter what happens to me, know that I love you so much and am so proud of you. Your destiny has always been for great things. Remember that the Source Sequenced you as a Healer for a reason. She knows you will excel in that position."

"Oh Mother, I love you too." Nellie was weeping, silent sobs racking through her body. Her nose was running uncontrollably, and she reached for a handkerchief to clean herself up. She had thought she had run out of tears in the Temple courtyard, but her body continued to betray her by having a seemingly endless supply of tears.

"Eleanor," Maude spoke so softly as she pulled her into her embrace. "My dear, sweet child. It will be alright."

"Do you really think so, Mother? Because I'm not so sure." She did not feel strong at the moment. She felt weak and afraid for the future. Her mother had always been her strength, her source of encouragement, her light. Now? They were being forced apart and separated for the first time in her life.

"I am so worried. What will become of you? Who will take care of you?"

"Silly girl, I'm a Provider. If I can't look after myself, no one can." Maude murmured as she rubbed Nellie's back.

"I know. I promise you, I'm going to come back to Liantis as soon as my apprenticeship is over."

"Eleanor. I need you to know that I will be okay. No matter what happens, know that I have what I need. The Source Sequenced you into your path for a reason and She will look after me."

Nellie nodded. The expression on her mother's face left no room for discussion. This conversation was clearly over, and she didn't have any energy left in her to argue with her mother on her last day at home.

Maude sat on the old, worn settee and patted the spot next to her in invitation.

"Come, Eleanor, sit with me for a while."

Nellie sat down on the familiar piece of furniture and curled up next to Maude, laying her head on her mother's lap. She hadn't lain like this since she was a young ward, but she desperately needed comfort right now. Her mother gently took apart her braid, the scent of roses washing over her as she lay her head in her mother's lap. They sat together in silence as Maude brushed Nellie's hair, smoothing out her long locks.

79

They spent the next twenty minutes enjoying the tranquility and peace that came with having nothing to do as they soaked up every moment of each other's company.

Eventually, though, Nellie sat back up. Time marched on, as it was wont to do. No matter how much a person might want to stop time, that power belongs to no one. Reality had come flooding in as she lay with her head in her mother's lap, reminding her that there was much to do and very little time in which to accomplish it.

When the sun rises tomorrow, I have to leave.

I can't believe how much can change in a day.

"Mother. I have so many things to say to you. I don't even know where to begin." Nellie choked on the words, squeezing her eyes shut and counting to three before she continued. "I'm scared. I'm leaving everything I have ever known to begin down a path that no one from Liantis has been on in over two centuries. My Sequencing-"

Suddenly, Nellie's mouth slammed shut. No matter how hard she tried to tell her mother about what happened in the Temple, she couldn't force her lips to form the words.

Understanding filled Maude's eyes as she squeezed her daughter's hand, rubbing her calloused thumb over the back of Nellie's hand.

"It's okay, Eleanor." Maude's voice was hushed. "You must have taken the Oath; they wouldn't have let you leave the Temple without it. You can't tell me what happened. Just... nod your head. Was it scary?"

Nellie nodded her head, wiping stray tears from her eyes.

"I remember mine was too. Was it... overwhelming?"

Again, she nodded her head.

"Were you surprised, Eleanor? By the path that the Source chose for you?"

"Surprised doesn't even begin to express how I feel about my Sequencing." Nellie's voice was high-pitched, her eyes wide as she babbled. "How could this happen to me? There are so many things I wanted to do. Who will repaint the front door?"

"Well... Philip can do that."

"I suppose. I just... I don't want to leave you. A year seems so long and I'll be so far away. You know they won't let me leave for a visit; I'll be too busy in the capital. I'll miss you."

On the last word, Nellie's voice cracked as she fell headfirst into the well of sorrow inside of her. She wept as her mother pulled a blanket over her and stroked her midnight blue hair, murmuring words of comfort as sobs wracked through her body.

Eventually, Maude sat Nellie up on the settee and stood in front of her with her hands on her hips. It instantly reminded Nellie of the many lectures she had received over the years. She braced herself, but instead of feeling dread, Nellie felt a wave of nostalgia. She sat up, her back straight and her arms resting on her knees as she looked intently at Maude. There wasn't an ounce of trepidation in her body as she watched her mother, waiting in anticipation for the words of wisdom to come out of her mother's mouth.

"Chin up, Eleanor." Maude spoke in a firm voice as she paced back and forth in front of the settee. "I will not tell you that this will be the easiest thing that you've ever done. Far from it, it will almost certainly be one of the hardest. But if we never push ourselves, we will never grow. The Source has laid out a hard path for you so you can grow into the woman I know you will be. She chose you for this, Eleanor. You will thrive. It's in your blood."

Nellie's lips tilted up in a smile as she watched her mother. She catalogued each word and stored them in her heart, to be taken out at a later date and cherished.

∾

Nellie remained in the mercantile with her mother until dusk fell, talking and reminiscing about life, Wilhelmina and Nellie's wardship. They laughed and cried as they shared their favourite memories with each other. Sitting at the small kitchen table, they ate a light meal of oat bread with beans and quinoa. Neither of them was truly hungry as thoughts of the days ahead filled their minds.

When the light dimmed and the sun lay beyond the horizon, Nellie hugged her mother tightly. Shivering as the cool night air banished the earlier warmth, Nellie grabbed her worn indigo coat from the row of hooks on the wall. Healer or not, she didn't have time to be ill.

With her coat over top of her new tunic, Nellie almost felt normal. Almost being the operative word. If she tried hard enough, she could briefly ignore the fact that the Sequencing had permanently changed her life.

As warmth began to course through her veins, Nellie waved goodbye to her mother before bounding down the wooden stairs. Fay had promised she'd be waiting for her at *their* spot, and she didn't want to waste even a moment with her best friend.

When they were younger, the girls would often meet at the well to walk to the warding centre together. As soon as the sixth bell rang, Nellie would run outside and meet Fay, who would leave her home early to be there on time.

Nellie had countless memories of playing with her best friend in the courtyard around the well, dancing in the rain, and even chasing Olim around the yard and feeding him treats.

As soon as she walked out the door, her face broke into a grin. She saw Fay standing at the well, twirling the ends of her scarf around as she waited. For the second time in one day, the pair walked through Liantis. Hours passed by as they reminisced about the past and made plans for the future. As they marched past the Museum of Artifacts, Fay suggested they take a break and sit on the wooden bench stationed outside. The two-story museum sat in a small park that used to be home to dozens of fresh flowers. Despite the gardens being gone, the benches remained. With a glimmer in her eye, Fay pulled a small piece of crystalized ginger from her pocket with a flourish. Nellie's eyes widened at the sight.

"Where did you get that?" She whispered excitedly.

"I've been saving it for us to share. I wish we had something more, but..." Fay shrugged as she looked at her feet. It was too dark to see much, but Nellie grabbed her friend's hand.

"It's perfect, thank you."

She pulled her best friend in for a hug before they split the tiny treat. Flavours of spice and sweetness exploded in Nellie's mouth and she moaned at the first taste. It had been so long since she had tasted anything like this. Too soon, the treat was gone. A comfortable silence filled the air as they sat in front of the ornate building. After a time, Nellie shifted in her seat to look at her best friend.

"I'm going to come back, Fay. I promise."

"How can you promise that?"

"I just know it. They said my apprenticeship is in Deavita, but I'm going to ask them as soon as I get there to be stationed back here in Liantis. I'm a First now, that has to mean something. Besides, I just know that life in the capital won't be for me, Fay. I want to stay here with you."

After looking all around and making sure the area was deserted, Nellie laid her head on Fay's shoulders. Whispering, she shared with Fay all that her mother had told her this morning. When she got to the part about the Wielders, Fay's eyes were as big as saucers. Fay had so many questions, but many of them Nellie wasn't able to answer. There were so many things she still didn't know.

"Thank you for trusting me with this, Nell." Fay chewed on her lip, as though she wanted to add something else.

"Go on, Fay. I'm listening."

"It's just that... Nell, you don't want to share this with just anyone. Everyone knows the Firsts aren't exactly easy going."

Nellie jerked back slightly. Hurt flashed across her face at her friend's tone.

"Fay, I-I'm a First now. You..." A flash of red flickered in the corner of Nellie's eye. She stiffened, lifting a finger to her lips as her eyes tracked the movement. She blew out a breath, realizing it was just a cardinal and not a Protector.

Two years ago, Nellie witnessed the Protectors take a young woman away after someone had reported her for cursing the Source for her infertility. She had never forgotten how the woman had screamed as the Protectors held onto her arms, dragging her through the dusty streets. They pulled her all the way to the Courthouse. Her feet had gouged out the earth, leaving a trail of distress behind her. She had never seen the woman again, and Nellie had no idea what had happened to her.

After that day, Guardian Clarence had explained to the wards that, on very rare occasions, the Source could request that Re-Sequencings take place.

Nellie had thought about the woman from time to time, but she never dared ask about her. Whenever she thought about it, memories of broken glass and a sea of red reminded her that silence was better.

Fingering her scar as she watched the cardinal fly away, Nellie whispered to Fay.

"Did you mean what you said?" Hurt filled her voice as she looked at her friend with wide eyes.

"I mean, yes." Fay said slowly. "Most of the Firsts we know are pompous and full of themselves. But Nell, you're not like them." She placed her hands on Nellie's, the warmth of the connection soothing.

Soon, Nellie relaxed, the tension leaking out of her as she sat in silence with her friend.

"You know, Nell, you're the closest thing I've ever had to a sister. I know you better than I think you might know yourself. I know that you're different from the other Firsts. You're so caring and generous, always looking after the people all around you. You know what it's like to come from less, to live the life of a Second. Even though your mother's a Provider, you still had to give up fresh fruit and vegetables just like the rest of us."

Nellie grimaced at the reminder. She knew Fay spoke the truth. They had lost access to fresh produce, along with everyone else in Liantis. Her mother hadn't even been able to get Nellie's favourite peaches.

Oh, how Nellie loved peaches. It had been so long since she had tasted the succulent fruit, but Nellie knew that even if she never had another peach in her entire life, she would never forget the taste of the sweet juice as it dripped down her throat. Of all the things stolen by the drought, peaches might have been the worst of them all. Even worse than cake, and Nellie had adored eating cake.

"Do you really think so?" Her usually animated voice was barely audible as she whispered.

"I know so, Nell." Fay smiled; her eyes gleaming in the moonlight as she stared up at Nellie. "And besides, I know the next time you see a peach, the juice will be dripping down your chin in two seconds flat."

Nellie laughed. She couldn't help it. Fay was right, and she knew her so well. Every moment that she spent in Fay's presence was a balm to her weary soul. Sitting on that bench, she started a new list in her mind. This one was called 'Reasons to come back to Liantis as soon as possible.' Right at the top of the list were her mother and Fay.

Fay promised Nellie that she would look in on Maude, assuring her repeatedly that she would drop into the mercantile every day and make sure she was alright. As the moon shone down on them, the two friends clung to each other, with only the stars as their witness.

Nellie's Sequencing, her new position as a Healer, her departure, none of it mattered as Nellie stood on the side of the road and hugged her soul-sister tightly to her chest.

Tonight, she would cherish every minute in Liantis because tomorrow, she would say goodbye.

Chapter Ten

The sun rose far too soon the next morning. Nellie had been awake past the midnight bells the night before with her mother. They had discussed anything and everything that came to mind, laughing and crying over cups of tea and a pack of gingersnaps that her mother had saved for Nellie's Sequencing. It had been so long since they had eaten anything so delicious and both women had cried tears of joy the moment the gingersnaps fell apart on their tongues.

After having set what felt like just a few moments ago, the traitorous sun began its daily ascent into the heavens. Nellie had hardly slept, having tossed and turned for most of the night. Her mind had swirled all night, her thoughts a vicious cycle.

Go to the capital.

Finish my apprenticeship.

Come home.

Her pillow had seemed to be made of stone, each adjustment lacking the relief she had so desperately desired. When she finally found a moment's rest, she woke up as soon as the first bright rays of sunlight shone through her windows.

She groaned as she took in the perfectly blue sky and bright sun through the small window beside her bed. Today would have been the perfect day for clouds or even a thunderstorm. Her mood in that moment certainly matched that of a storm. Unfortunately, there wasn't a cloud in sight.

Huffing, Nellie groaned as she stretched out her arms and felt the sleep-induced stiffness in her muscles crack as she moved. Every inch of her body protested her attempts to wake up. Rubbing her eyes, she struggled to keep them open. The comfort of her bed beckoned her like a warm caress.

Nellie ran her fingers through her hair, pulling out tangles that had gathered as she slept.

"What I wouldn't give to wash my hair today," she muttered to herself as she worked through the tangles. The summer humidity seemed to hate Nellie's hair, causing it to become a frizzy mess the moment it was clean. Despite having washed it only two days ago, she felt grease as she rubbed her fingers through her hair.

All the Seconds in Tiarny used the communal baths on their dedicated wash days, which fell on every fourth day. The baths were always busy, but since the feeling of clean hair was one of Nellie's favourites, she put aside her modesty for the sake of cleanliness. The day the Officials had declared that the Queen had decreed that the use of extra water in Liantis was punishable by three days in prison, Nellie had sobbed. It wasn't the worst thing the drought had caused, but this was the decree that had affected her the most.

Nellie contemplated going back to sleep, but the reality set in that she could not afford to lose even another minute, let alone the time it would take to have a decent bath. As she was debating the merits of continuing to sleep, she heard the bells ring out from the Temple.

One, two, three, four... five!

No, no, no. I can't be late today.

Exhaling, she swung her legs out of bed. Her bare feet hit the floor, her toes curling as the morning chill seeped into her skin. Her thin nightgown barely did anything to protect her from the early morning cold.

There's a reason I never get up this early on purpose.

Shivering as the cold hit her, Nellie hurriedly grabbed her favourite worn green housecoat with the frayed edges from the nightstand and slipped it over her shoulders. She knew she had no time to waste, for this day was too important to risk angering her travel companions. Even though she would love nothing more than to stay in bed until ten bells past midnight, she had to get ready. The sun had ignored her pleas and had risen. The day had already begun.

Nellie was learning the hard way that time waited for no one. It was a cruel headteacher, ignoring those who begged it to slow down, continuously marching on despite the desires of the lesser mortals who depended on its existence.

Shaking her head to clear away the traces of sleep, Nellie quickly pulled on her new black tunic and leggings. Sitting beside her tunic was a pristine pair of black, lace-up knee-high boots. Her mother had said a Server had dropped these off the previous night, along with a note for her.

Healer Eleanor,
We require your presence at the well tomorrow at six bells past midnight.
You may only bring one bag of possessions.
Anything else you bring will be left behind.
Don't be late. Your Guide will be waiting.

As she pulled on the new boots, Nellie couldn't help but admire the way they hugged her legs as though the Tailors had made them specifically for her.

A quick glance out the window while she was tugging on the second boot told Nellie that she was likely already late. The sun was rising high in the sky, chasing away the last streaks of darkness.

Great, Nellie thought. *Just what I need. Another day in the sun-baked land. What I wouldn't give for some rain.*

Lost in thought, Nellie launched herself off the bed before she properly tied her shoes. She took a step forward before her left foot caught on the undone lace of her right boot. She stumbled and almost met the mattress with her face before she threw out a hand. Gasping, she finally found purchase on the wall and righted herself.

Phew, she thought as she crouched down, lacing up her boots before double-knotting each side. *Crisis averted.*

Dressed and ready for action, Nellie took one last moment to assess herself. She fingered the pendant under her tunic as she contemplated its importance. She had thought about lifting the chain off her head last night, but something stopped her. Taking it off just didn't feel right. Suddenly struck by the need to see it again, she pulled it out and held it up to the sunlight. The pendant scintillated as she shifted it to and fro before returning it to its resting spot under her tunic. Somehow, it felt *right* as it rested upon her skin.

Had it really only been a day since her mother had given her the necklace? Nellie felt as though she had lived an entire lifetime since yesterday morning.

Pulling a brush through her hair to rid herself of the last of the tangles, she plaited her hair and tied a black piece of leather around the bottom. Having completed her morning ritual, she flung the braid over her right shoulder before glancing around her bedroom. It looked the same as always, but something felt different; Nellie felt different.

Her Sequencing had irrevocably changed her. She could feel it in her core. Nothing would ever be the same.

As she looked around the home she had shared with her mother since birth, Nellie tried to memorize the way everything looked and felt. When she returned in a year, she hoped everything would look the same. Too soon, her mother pulled on her arm and led her out the door.

"We have to go, Eleanor." Maude was out of breath, holding the full jug of water in her hands. A pang of dismay went through Nellie as she looked at her mother with the jug.

I suppose she'll have to do that every day, now that I'm gone.

At her mother's insistence, she grabbed a piece of bread off the counter, stuffing it in her mouth as she strolled through the room one last time.

"Eleanor." Her mother huffed, pulling her arm. "We need to go. It's imperative that we leave now. The fifth bell rang half an hour ago."

Of course, I would run late today, of all days.

Grabbing the small travel bag filled with her meager belongings, Nellie took the stairs two at a time. The ancient wood creaked its disapproval as she ran, but she made it in record time. Having reached the front of the mercantile before her mother, Nellie held open the door before stepping outside and linking arms with Maude.

Arm in arm, mother and daughter marched to the appointed meeting place. Their feet fell in synchrony with each other, the sound of their steps on the worn cobblestones echoing through the air. The irony of the meeting place was not lost on Nellie, the thought sending a pang of sadness through her heart. She and Fay had not said goodbye last night, unwilling to voice last farewells.

There were over a dozen people standing around the well as Nellie and her mother approached. Sounds of casual conversation filled the air, with the occasional laugh rising above the group. About a hundred feet from the well, Nellie stopped and pulled her mother in for a hug.

"I'll miss you, Mother," she whispered, her voice steady despite the tears gathering in her eyes. "I love you so much."

"Eleanor, my darling, remember that no matter what happens, I love you and am proud of you. The Source be with you."

"Oh, Mother," Nellie kissed her mother on both of her cheeks. "I'll be back in a year. I promise." She squeezed her mom one last time before releasing her. Her chest grew cold as the warmth of her mother's body left her. Nellie wiped away tears from her cheeks, filled with the knowledge that no matter what happened, nothing would ever be the same.

As she turned towards the well, she took a deep breath and plastered a smile on her face. The last thing she wanted was for the others to see her as weak.

Chapter Eleven

N ellie wasn't the only newly Sequenced citizen travelling to Deavita. As she neared the well, her lips tilted up when she saw Yenna.

I'm glad I will know someone.

The new day seemed to be doing wonders for the Server. There was a wide smile on her face as she stood at the well and chatted with the others. She was animated, her arms flailing about as she told a story to two Protectors. They appeared completely captivated by the story, their lips agape as Yenna spoke. The Server had pulled her long blond hair back in an intricate braid that now hung over one shoulder. Nellie noticed that along with Yenna's brown tunic and black leggings, she was wearing the same boots as Nellie. In fact, as she turned in a circle, she saw that everyone at the well was wearing the exact same boots.

Nellie had been the last one to arrive at the meeting place. She counted just over a dozen and a half people, including a hooded Official, five other citizens besides herself and Yenna, and twelve armed Protectors. She thought it was strange that they would need Protectors for a simple three-day trip to Deavita, but she couldn't seem to find the right moment to ask why they were necessary.

Maybe they're just for show?

Other than Yenna, Nellie saw one other face she knew. Standing beside the hooded Official and speaking in whispered tones was a man she immediately recognized. The man, who loomed over every other person standing at the well, was one of her oldest friends, Elijah Fletcher.

Despite not having seen him in three years, Nellie would have recognized him anywhere. Besides his distinctive height, the Source had blessed Elijah with a mane of lengthy black curly hair and tawny skin. Paired with the grey tunic that marked him as an Engineer, he was wearing what Nellie was realizing were the signature boots for their outing.

I wonder what he's doing here in Liantis? It's such a long way to travel just to go back to the capital.

Even though Elijah's presence piqued her curiosity, Nellie felt excited to see her old friend. They had a long history together. Like her, he had been under Guardian Clarence's wardship from the year he turned three until his Sequencing three years ago. The Source had Sequenced him as an Engineer and Elijah had gone to Ion for his apprenticeship. Engineers were rare in Tiarny and they all trained under the best Builders in Ion.

When Elijah had left Liantis, he had been a tall but lanky boy. Truly, Nellie hadn't paid him much attention. But now, she found her eyes drawn to him. Whatever had happened to Elijah in the past three years, one thing was certain. He had grown from that scrawny ward into a tall, self-assured man. His face tapered to a point under his chin, his long nose falling in perfect symmetry between his wide-set chestnut eyes.

As Nellie approached the well, Elijah turned from his conversation with the mysterious Official and grinned. His left cheek had a slight dimple that only grew when he spoke.

"Nell-bell," Elijah's rich, gravelly voice boomed across the courtyard.

"And here I was thinking I wouldn't get to see my favourite midnight-blue-haired friend."

Nellie cringed at the sound of her childhood nickname, but a smile tugged at her lips. She had always been the tallest female ward her age, but even she had to crane her neck up to speak to Elijah.

Nell-bell? That's how it is, is it? Well, two can play at that game, she thought, smirking to herself.

"Lijah," she giggled as Elijah's brows drew together at the mention of his own childhood nickname. "It's so nice to see you. When did you get to Liantis?"

His mouth twitched, a smile dancing on his lips. "I got in late last night, Nell-bell. I went straight to my parents. The twenty-third bell had already rung by the time I dropped my horse off at the stables."

Before Nellie could ask any more questions, the mysterious Official stood up straight and clapped their hands. The sound echoed through the square, conversations instantly ceasing as everyone turned to face him. The Official massaged the back of their neck as they looked around the group. Their hood was slipping back and Nellie saw a lock of silky brown hair that fell on their face.

"Alright. We don't have time to waste. The trip to Deavita is long and we need to get started right away."

As soon as the hooded man spoke, Nellie recognized the deep, thunderous voice.

Great, she thought to herself, frowning. *Of course, the Guide is Dion. Can't I catch a break? This guy seems to hate me and I haven't even done anything to him.*

With a quick movement, Dion pulled back his hood and shook out his shoulder-length hair. "Since we're going to be travelling closely together for the next few days, you should know who I am. My name is

Dion Mercer and I'm your Guide for this excursion. If you have questions, ask your neighbours."

For the first time, Nellie got a clear look at Dion's face. The Source had blessed him with strong cheekbones, jet-black eyes that seemed to follow you wherever you went and a full set of lips. His hair was a silky brown that fell in small waves around his face. His mahogany skin only amplified the appeal of his face. A face that was currently glaring at Nellie.

She involuntarily took a step back as Dion's steely black eyes stared at her. Startled, her fingers loosened and before she knew it, her bag had fallen to the ground. Blood rushed to her face, the tips of her ears turning red as the few items she had stored inside rolled out onto the dirt road.

Dion's nostrils flared, his eyes tracking a purple rock rolling on the ground towards him. Time slowed as the rock moved, coming to a stop right in front of the Official's feet. His eyes bored into hers as he bent down to pick it up, his frosty gaze never leaving hers.

Stepping forward, Nellie grabbed the rock out of his hand with a quick "Thanks" before she scrambled to pick up the rest of her belongings. The only sound in the square was that of her knees on the stone as she scrambled to collect her possessions.

Of all the people, it had to be him.

Dion glared at Nellie, his mouth set in a hard line, as he watched her stand upright. She clutched the bag to her chest, her back hunched as she blinked back tears, wishing the ground would swallow her whole.

"Everyone needs to head to the stables to pick up your horse. I'm assuming you all know how to ride?" Dion's voice echoed throughout the square.

Nellie stifled a groan as she noticed everyone else nodding. Her hand shaking, she lifted her right arm into the air.

"Excuse me, sir?" Her voice came out reedy as she shifted from one foot to the other.

Dion sighed deeply. He rolled his eyes heavenwards, rubbing his temples with long, mahogany fingers before answering Nellie.

"Yes, Healer Merrick?"

"I- I don't know how to ride." She avoided his gaze, picking at a thread hanging from the bag. Cobblestones had never been as interesting as they were in that moment. "I've never even been on a horse, sir."

Finally gaining the courage to look up, Nellie saw that Dion's face had turned stony. He gritted his jaw, his eyes narrow as he looked her over.

"Of course, you haven't," The ill-tempered Official sighed, rubbing a hand over his face. "You'll have to ride with me then."

Nellie stifled her groan before it could make it through her lips. She fought to keep her face blank as she nodded her head in acquiescence. She stood perfectly still as he finished his speech, unwilling to move even a muscle. Her grip never faltered on her bag of belongings as she wondered about the maddening Official who clearly had an axe to grind with her.

Having given the orders to head to the stables, Dion didn't speak another word to Nellie until they were standing side by side, looking up at an enormous chestnut-coloured horse. The horse's mane was long and luscious, the deep colour shimmering as the bright light of the sun hit it. Someone had taken care to brush and saddle the beast before the expedition. As Nellie stood next to the horse, she admired the way it stood towering above her. Even next to Dion and Elijah, the horse was enormous. She had never seen a beast so large. It was both terrifying and stunning.

Having never been this close to a horse, Nellie couldn't tear her eyes from its enormous form. Noticing her awe, a Server walked up to Nellie and introduced himself.

"Hello ma'am. My name's Geoff and this is Blaze."

Nellie had raised a brow at that. "Why do you call him that?"

"Well, ma'am. It's just that, once he gets going, there's no stopping him. Blaze is the fastest horse in all of Liantis."

Geoff puffed out his chest, pride beaming on his face as he patted the horse's flank fondly. Geoff looked to be no older than Nellie. He was at least a foot shorter than her and skinny, his brown tunic hanging off his shoulders. The Server had wispy green hair that floated into his face whenever he moved his head. His eyes were a pale grey, which Nellie had thought oddly suited the pale, almost translucent, colour of his skin.

Leaning in, Geoff beckoned Nellie closer as he whispered.

"I even heard, ma'am, that the Official wants to breed Blaze once he gets to the capital. There's good money in it, I heard him say."

"You mean Dion?"

Geoff peered around Nellie's shoulder at the ill-tempered Official before nodding his head.

"Yes, ma'am. That's the one. He was telling me yesterday all about the horses he has back in the capital. Frankly ma'am, I wish I could go with him to see them."

"I had no idea he was interested in animals." Nellie mused as she covertly observed Dion out of the corner of her eye. He was towering over one of the Protectors, engaged in an animated discussion.

"Geoff," Nellie asked, tilting her head, "would you happen to know what happened to the other four Officials who were here for the Sequencing yesterday?"

The Server nodded eagerly, "oh yes, ma'am. They left right after the ceremony yesterday, not wanting to remain in Liantis a moment longer than necessary. I had to rush back to the stables right after the Sequencing to make sure their horses were saddled and ready to go."

Before Nellie could ask Geoff any more questions, he scurried away, explaining that he had to saddle all the other horses. The stables were full of activity, people rushing about as horses whinnied and stamped their feet. When Nellie was younger, she used to see many horses as people rode down the Queen's Road, but in the past few years, horse traffic had all but stopped. Only the few Firsts who travelled to Liantis from Deavita ever had horses. Everyone else travelled on foot.

Nellie could not even fathom the amount of money required to furnish an expedition of this size to the Capital. Just thinking about the amount of gold invested in this trip made her stomach turn. Surely this was the reason they had an Official riding with them. They needed Dion to ensure the Capital's investment in the group was safe.

Mental note: make sure I learn how to ride so I can make the journey back home by myself.

Nellie began looking around the stable, subtly noting exactly how the saddles were placed on horses. Humming, she catalogued all the information, praying to the Source she would have the chance to use it sooner rather than later.

Suddenly, a thought struck her. She beckoned to Yenna, who was busy learning how to saddle a horse from another Server.

"Do you think you could teach me?"

Yenna looked at Nellie blankly, confusion flitting across her face.

"T-Teach you what?"

"Teach me how to saddle a horse. And maybe to ride?" Nellie tried to keep the eagerness from her voice as she spoke, her green eyes wide with excitement.

"I don't know..." Yenna glanced around before taking a step closer to Nellie. "Why do you need to know how to ride a horse? You're a First now and you'll be riding with Dion."

Nellie exhaled loudly and rubbed her temples. "I know, but I just... I want to know how."

"Yenna, come here," a Protector said from the other side of the stable.

"I'm sorry," Yenna shrugged, looking apologetic, before she hurried over to the Protector's side.

Exhaling loudly, Nellie looked back at Blaze. The horse had begun to shift around in his stall, eagerness filling the air. The fact remained that the enormous beast would certainly make it to the capital faster than if she walked. As Nellie looked up and fingered the saddle, she felt grateful that she would ride with Dion. Geoff had assured her that Blaze was gentle, but Nellie could not imagine calling any creature this size "gentle".

Just as Nellie was contemplating how long it would take her to hike to Deavita, Geoff came and grabbed Blaze's reins. He led the horse outside, holding onto the reins as Dion came sauntering out of the stable. Dion had shed his robes and now wore a clock over a silver tunic and breeches. He looked much younger now than he had before.

The corners of Dion's mouth turned up in what Nellie thought was a smile as he rubbed Blaze's flank a few times while murmuring what sounded like words of praise. Nellie's eyes were wide as she witnessed Dion being... kind. She blinked, but before she could say anything, Dion placed his large hand on Blaze's saddle. This close, Nellie saw his hands weren't smooth like she had first thought, but rough and calloused.

"Ready?" Dion lifted a brow as he spoke, his voice low.

"I suppose so," Nellie said, shrugging. "It won't do me any good to wait."

Nellie clutched the reins and held on for her life while Dion grabbed her hips with both hands and lifted her onto the saddle. As soon as her feet lifted off the air, her heart plummeted to the pit of her stomach. She was a bundle of emotions, her nerves flying all over the place. There was a strange feeling where Dion's hands touched her sides. It wasn't alltogether unpleasant, but certainly shocking. She could feel his cal008es through the soft fabric of her tunic and his touch was almost gentle.

Her eyes wide as she looked around, taking in the view from atop the horse, Nellie tightened her grip on the reins. She had never realized just how far away the ground was, or how hard the dry earth appeared to be. She hadn't thought she had a fear of heights before, but this experience might just be changing that for her. Nellie's grip on the reins was so tight that she began losing feeling in her fingers.

Before she could muster up the courage to move even an inch, Dion swung up in the saddle behind her with the practiced ease of a professional horseman. His closeness stunned Nellie, but there wasn't much to be done about it. She needed to get to Deavita, and it was becoming painfully clear she could not get there on her own.

The sooner we get to the capital, the sooner I can come home.

"Eleanor." Dion leaned forward and whispered in her ear; his voice barely audible over the sounds of chatter filling the stable yard. The scent of fresh rain and lush grass filled her nose. It was intoxicating to be around. Nellie's breath caught in her throat, the tips of her ears reddening as she breathed in his scent.

"If you don't hand me the reins, we won't ever leave." He held out a hand expectantly.

He was right.

Nellie knew he was right.

But the knowledge that she needed to let go was a lot different from actually giving up the reins. Her hands didn't seem to want to move right now. In fact, Nellie wasn't sure they would ever move again. She was pretty certain that she would go to meet the Source with Blaze's reins in her hands.

"I don't think I can," Nellie whispered as she tightened her grip on the reins. "I think you'll need to take them."

"If you're sure."

Nellie sucked in a deep breath before nodding slowly. "I am."

Dion leaned forward and reached his arms around Nellie. She froze as she felt his chest against her back, the heat from his body warmer than anything she had ever felt before. Slowly, he pried the reins out of Nellie's hands. His arms closed in around her, caging her in, as he removed the reins from her grip. Dion patted Blaze on the head, stroking the horse's mane before leaning in close to Nellie once more.

"Hold on to the saddle horn, Eleanor, and try to relax." Dion's voice was deep and that, combined with the heat at Nellie's back, made it hard for her to concentrate on anything happening at all.

What is it about this man that makes it so hard to focus?

Before Nellie could get a word in edgewise, Dion kept speaking. "The journey will be hard enough without you being as tense as a board."

Nellie shifted in her seat, grappling with her hand placement on the horse's back. None of this felt natural to her.

"My name isn't Eleanor, it's Nellie. Only my mother calls me Eleanor."

Dion laughed, the sound rumbling through her body, causing her to tense.

"I'll call you whatever I want, Eleanor."

Huffing, Nellie didn't respond to Dion's remarks. Instead, she focused on shifting in the saddle, seeking a comfortable position. "There certainly isn't much room for propriety on this creature, is there?" Nellie mumbled.

"Unfortunately, not." Dion's back stiffened, his thighs tightening around the horse. "I have a feeling this is going to be a long few days. Now, hold on."

Blaze abruptly leapt forward, robbing Nellie of wind as she held on for dear life. The horse dashed down the Queen's Road, his namesake proving true. The sound of dozens of hoofbeats soon filled Nellie's ears as the rest of the entourage raced to join them.

On Blaze's back, Nellie looked behind her one last time and watched as the town she had always known faded into the distance. She could feel her heart cracking as they rode away. Being a ward had been easy. It was simple. There was always someone to tell you what to do, where to go, what to learn. Nothing about Nellie's current situation felt uncomplicated, safe or simple.

She would never have imagined that the day after her Sequencing, she would ride into the wilderness on the back of a horse with a man who most definitely hated her. And yet, here she was. Riding into the unknown with her past growing distant and an unknown future ahead.

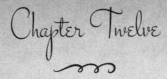

Chapter Twelve

Nellie soon learned that she hated horses with a passion. No, hate may be too light of a word. She despised horses. She loathed horses. Nellie would gladly meet the Source before having to ride another one of these monstrous beasts.

A few hours after they left Liantis, Nellie had lost all feeling in her legs. Every time the horse took another step, her muscles screamed in agony. *There has to be a better way to travel. This is torture. I can't believe I'm going to have to do this again to come home in a year.*

At first, Dion had pointed things out to Nellie as they rode.

"The Queen's Road, as you probably know, was commissioned by the very first Queen in order to connect all of Tiarny."

Nellie nodded. She knew this. Unperturbed, Dion had continued speaking. "It used to be well-traveled, but recently, there aren't many people who take it."

As they rode past field after field of quinoa, beans and wheat, Nellie kept her eyes on her surroundings. They widened as she took in the beauty of the cloudless sky against the yellow shafts of wheat blowing in the wind. Soon though, even that grew tedious. Every once in a while, Nellie would see a few trees that broke up the monotony of the fields. They were nothing like the lush trees she remembered from in her childhood. The trees had red and orange leaves, even though it was the middle of the growing season. Nellie felt shivers running down her back whenever she saw the strange vegetation. Something about the trees just felt odd.

"Who takes care of the fields?" Nellie had muttered after they had passed yet another wheat field, more to herself than anything else, but was pleasantly surprised when Dion answered.

"There are special Farmers who are sent out from Deavita to the farmlands in shifts. They go for a season to care for the fields. They pull the water they need from dug wells to keep the fields properly irrigated. Without the special irrigation system, Tiarny would have already fallen into complete chaos when the rains stopped falling."

"What will happen when the wells run dry?" Nellie had asked.

Dion had tensed, and for a long moment, he didn't reply. Minutes passed. Just as Nellie thought perhaps he hadn't heard her, he said softly, "you don't want to know."

Nellie had shuddered at the ominous tone of Dion's voice. He had stopped talking to her after that, his grip on the reins firm as he led Blaze along.

Riding along in silence with only her thoughts for company, Nellie wondered where they would find water for the horses. She hadn't seen a single river or stream since they had left Liantis. Just as the thirst in her throat was becoming pronounced, the entire convoy pulled over for a rest.

Nellie sighed in relief when she took in the well about two hundred feet away from the Queen's Road. Once she had taken care of her personal needs, she sat down next to Elijah and Dion.

"Where did the wells come from?"

She hadn't directed the question towards Dion, so it had surprised her when he answered.

"There are wells lining the entire Queen's Road all the way to Deavita. If things go as planned, we will follow the route from one well to the other. We should be in the capital by nightfall, three days from now."

"The Protectors will pull up enough water for each of the horses and ourselves so that no one becomes dehydrated, but not much more than that." Elijah said, his gaze thoughtful as he looked across the field. He sighed, looking out. "It'll be nice to have access to water again."

The conversation had soon turned away from the water and Nellie had tuned out the men, instead observing the various Protectors. They had split up as soon as the group had left Liantis, with a pair of Protectors riding at both the front and the back of the convoy, the others spread out between. As soon as they had stopped, they had watered the horses and were now engaged in some sort of swordplay as the creatures rested.

Watching the training, Nellie suddenly realized that she didn't know how to defend herself. If an attack occurred, she would be less than helpful. She wasn't really sure who (or what) the perceived threat was that they were protecting them against, only that it existed.

When she was younger, one of the Tutors had taught the wards all about the wilderness separating Deavita and Liantis.

"The land between has been deserted for many years," the Tutor had intoned in a monotonous voice. "Queen Hannia, who had reigned from the years 620-657 after Inception, declared the wilderness inhabitable in the year 653. There had been very few people who had lived in the wilderness before this declaration, and that number has now essentially diminished to zero."

As she watched the Protectors training on the edge of the Queen's Road, Nellie unbound and shook out her hair before braiding it once more. Her cheeks reddened as she saw how much dust was covering her clothes. After a few minutes of attempting to clean herself off, she sighed as she accepted that her cause was futile. Throwing her hands up in the air, Nellie rubbed temples and watched the other citizens mingling about until Dion made her get back on Blaze.

The novelty of the entire experience had quickly worn off. Every time Nellie dismounted to stretch, her entire body was in more and more pain. Muscles she hadn't even known existed seemed to cry out with each movement. To her dismay, Dion didn't appear to be in any pain at all. He leapt on Blaze's back with ease, his eyes shining with delight every time Nellie looked back at him.

When the road widened enough to allow two horses to ride abreast, Dion began calling Elijah up to the front with them so they could talk. Both men seemed extremely comfortable with each other, and Nellie soon learned they had met two years ago in Ion. Elijah's occupation as an Engineer meant he had met and interacted with many other Firsts through his work for Queen Rosalind. She had recently come into power just over five years ago and was having a new summer Palace built for herself in Ion. Personally, Nellie thought that was a tad extravagant, considering it hasn't rained for almost four years and people were on water rations, but who was she to judge the Source's appointed Queen?

As Dion and Elijah continued to trade stories about their time in Ion and Deavita, Nellie felt smaller and smaller. She had never considered herself to be a mousy person, but hearing these two men talk about their adventures around the country, Nellie felt as though she had lived her life in a hovel. Feeling as though she had little to contribute to the conversation taking place around her, she remained quiet and listened, getting lost in her own thoughts.

No wonder it upset Dion to be stuck with me. I must seem so simple to him, a country girl who doesn't even know how to ride a horse.

She kept most of her thoughts to herself, growing more irritated by the second. Every time she tried to cut into the conversation and add her opinion, the men would reply before quickly steering the conversation back to topics that she either had no interest in or no knowledge of. Her annoyance flared as they made her feel small and insignificant.

Country girl or not, she didn't deserve to be ignored.

If there was one thing that her mother had instilled in her from an early age, it was that she was always worthy of someone's full attention.

Nellie knew that Dion's rude demeanour to her was unfair and directly correlated to his irritation of having to ride with her. To top it all off, he kept insisting on calling her "Eleanor", despite her numerous reminders that, in fact, she preferred Nellie. Even Elijah's jovial "Nell-bell" was more acceptable than "Eleanor". Dion only seemed to respond to Nellie's questions when it suited him, deflecting all other attempts at conversation with a gruff "mhmm".

Fine, Nellie thought grumpily. *I'll just stop talking to him. Let's see how he likes that.*

By the end of the first day, a thick layer of dust covered Nellie's tunic and leggings. Her braid had long since fallen apart and there were wisps of her hair flying all over the place. Unsurprisingly, Dion looked as comfortable as ever. Not a hair on his head was out of place, and each speck of dust somehow lent itself to an air of aloofness. He barely looked as though he had been on the road, let alone riding on the same horse as Nellie.

By the time they dismounted that first evening, Nellie was simmering with anger. She had all but fallen off of Blaze and stumbled into the bushes to relieve herself before coming back to find a place to rest.

Groaning as her muscles protested at even the smallest movement, Nellie silently unrolled her bedroll beside Yenna before falling onto it in a heap. She had scarfed down a simple dinner of bread and goat's cheese before she closed her hands over her chest, hiding the small bump of her pendant. Before she knew it, she had fallen into a restless sleep. The Protectors hadn't allowed them to build a fire, so Nellie lay shivering against the cold, dry ground as she tried to find a comfortable spot to lay her head. In her exhaustion, she hadn't even thought to brush and re-braid her hair, instead leaving it to deal with in the morning.

Laying her head on her small bag of belongings, Nellie had seen a similar look of exhaustion on Yenna's face. The other woman appeared to be as miserable as Nellie as they both shifted on their bedrolls, trying to find a comfortable position well into the night.

At least we aren't getting rained on.

For the first time in many years, Nellie was grateful for the lack of rain. She had always hated getting wet, and the idea of sleeping under the stars while it poured was not appealing. Nellie finally fell into a restless sleep where she dreamt of broken glass and a solitary tree burning in the distance. She tossed and turned all night, waking up every time the Protectors changed their guard.

She pushed the thought of danger out of her mind, convincing herself that they were just acting as guides. She could not afford to dwell on the possibility of peril, for if Nellie thought too long about what might befall them, she feared she would never regain the courage to continue on the Queen's Road.

Chapter Thirteen

After another hard day of riding that went much like the first, Nellie was extremely disappointed to find they would have to sleep under the stars again. She hated "making camp" almost as much as she hated horses.

Camp was a loose word. Just like the day before, early in the evening during the second day, the convoy simply pulled off the road at the nearest well. They watered down the horses and unravelled their bedrolls to lie on the hard, rocky ground. The night brought with it a reprieve from the heat, but unfortunately, it provided little else.

Nellie's resolve to stop talking to Dion had lasted until the second evening. As dusk fell and the fading light painted the sky red and orange, Nellie groaned as Dion helped her dismount. Stretching her sore muscles and wincing at the pain, Nellie surveyed the sparse location and felt frustration bubble up inside of her. As much as she wanted to remain silent, she just could not stop herself from talking. She had so much to say and she spent the past twenty-four hours bottling up all of her thoughts and emotions. Now they were all bubbling up inside of her, eager to be released into the world.

Even on the worst days in the warding centre, Nellie had never gone so long without carrying on a meaningful conversation. Loneliness had been her only companion on the ride, as Dion spent most of the day deep in conversation with Elijah. They spoke about things she didn't understand, bonding over their affinity for horses and people they both knew from the capital. Both men seemed to be natural horsemen, riding their steeds with ease. Nellie, on the other hand, felt like a mess with her sore muscles. Who knew sitting on a horse all day could be so taxing?

After having stretched her muscles, Nellie marched over to watch Dion unsaddle Blaze. She was subtly taking notes, trying to remember how everything worked for when she could finally come back to Liantis. Yenna hadn't yet responded to Nellie's request for help, so Nellie was making sure she was watching everything Dion was doing.

Maybe, just maybe, I'll find a way to get home to Liantis before the year is up.

"So... I'm sure you know what's best for us, but is this really a good place to camp?" Nellie rasped. "I mean... There are just fields and the occasional tree as far as the eye can see. The ground didn't really look that comfortable, and..."

Her voice trailed off as Dion stopped what he was doing to turn and stare straight at Nellie. He lifted a brow, rubbing the back of his neck as his dark eyes observed her every movement.

"Do you see a better place to camp, *Eleanor*?" Dion smirked.

"Don't call me that," she seethed. "My name is Nellie and you know it!"

She stamped her foot, but the ground simply absorbed the sound.

Dion watched her, his dark eyes following her every movement, but he didn't say a word.

She huffed, running her hands down her head. "Why are you like this?" She asked angrily.

"Like what? I'm just trying to figure out what's going on, Eleanor. Do you know of a secret settlement between here and Deavita? If so, I'd love to hear about it."

"Obviously, I don't, Dion. I don't even want to be here. Just let me go home!" Nellie snapped, moving closer to the infuriating man. She stopped a foot from his body, quivering with anger as she stared up at him. Somehow, he still smelled of fresh rain even after two days on the road. The knowledge incensed her. Her pulse throbbed in her neck as she stared at him, fists clenched.

"All I know is three days ago, my life was vastly different. Ever since my Sequencing, which you were a part of, by the way, everything has turned upside down. Is it too much to ask for an actual place to sleep? I'm so tired and muscles I didn't even know existed are aching. Everything hurts, I'm hungry and I'm sore. I miss my mother and I'm worried about her."

Nellie finally stopped talking and dropped wearily to the ground. Holding her head in her hands, she felt the weight of the last few days come crashing down on her. Her heart wrenched as she thought of her mother. She couldn't shake the vision of her mother stiffly walking around the apartment. Nellie just knew there was something wrong, something Maude hadn't told her. And now, it was too late. Nellie was in the middle of the wilderness, surrounded by Dion, of all people. She blinked back tears as she stared straight ahead. The last thing she wanted was to give Dion yet another reason to see her as inadequate.

The effort to remain calm took all of Nellie's energy. She was so preoccupied that she didn't see Dion approaching until he crouched down beside her. He laid his hand on her shoulder, the weight of it was both comforting and confusing.

"Eleanor, look at me."

The soft tone of his voice shocked Nellie. She had never heard him speak this gently before. To be honest, she wasn't even aware he was capable of kindness. Nellie tilted her head toward Dion, her eyes wide, but didn't open her mouth for fear that her tears would break through her flimsy barrier.

"I understand what-"

Before Dion could continue speaking, loud shouts began coming from around the camp.

It was the Protectors. Something was happening.

Startled, Nellie jerked her head up. Immediately, her eyes widened in surprise. At least three dozen ragged-looking people wearing tattered tunics of every colour were surrounding the makeshift camp. There were shouts coming from all over as people realized what was happening.

The attackers had no similar characteristics other than their wild appearance. They were brandishing weapons made of sticks and leather, with only a select few bearing steel weapons. Although they outnumbered the Protectors three to one, they were clearly lacking their rigorous training.

Where did these people come from? Nellie wondered with a jolt. They had at least a day to go before they reached Deavita.

Leaping to his feet, Dion let out a slew of impressive curses. His eyes wide, he glanced around and assessed the situation. Quickly, he slid his left hand into his cloak and pulled out a lengthy silver dagger. Grabbing her hand, he helped her to her feet. Out of the corner of her eye, Nellie saw the other citizens huddled together in a circle as a trio of Protectors fought off any attackers who got too close. They were about two hundred feet from her, though, and a hoard of attackers stood in between them.

"I'm guessing you don't know how to use this Eleanor, is that right?" Nellie's eyes flew back to Dion's face. The Official spoke quickly, the calm tone of his voice betrayed by the rapid movement of his eyes as they darted back and forth. He was scared. A chill went through her as she realized that this, whatever this was, definitely was not the plan.

Nellie nodded. She had no weapons training. She had never had a reason for it. Her face drained of colour as she saw how many people were surrounding the camp. There were shouts coming from all directions as everything fell into utter chaos.

"Take this end." Dion pressed the hilt of the dagger into Nellie's hand. It was heavier than it looked. Her fingers wrapped around it subconsciously, her mind racing to catch up with the situation at hand.

"Eleanor," Dion said, his hand pulling her chin up to look him in the eyes. "Look at me. Concentrate. I need you to go behind that tree. Can you do that?"

"Yes." Nellie's voice was shaky. She gulped and spoke with more force. "Yes. Yes, I can do it."

"Okay, excellent," he said. "Make sure you keep the dagger pointed away from your body. Can you do that?"

Nellie nodded.

"Good. Now go hide. Don't come out until Elijah or I come and get you." Dion's voice was firm as he pushed Nellie towards the large evergreen tree. The sounds of attack were still surrounding them from all sides. "If anything happens, I want you to get on Blaze. Ride as fast as you can to the capital. I realize you don't know the way, but Blaze does. He's been there many times and will get you there. Let him guide you and follow the Queen's Road."

"Don't... don't leave me." Nellie hated the fact that her voice sounded feeble and insecure. She clung to Dion's hand, willing him to remain by her side.

Dion frowned. She could see conflict raging on his face as he decided what to do.

Finally, he sighed. "I'm sorry Eleanor. It's my responsibility to make sure you get to the Capital in one piece. I'm going to do everything in my power to make sure that happens. I need you to hide."

Not for the first time, Nellie wondered just *what* exactly Dion did as an Official. Before she could ask him though, Dion reached inside his cloak again and pulled out a silver broadsword.

Nellie had seen the sword strapped to Blaze as they rode through the wilderness, but she hadn't imagined that they would ever need it.

Listening to the chaos surrounding her now, she felt foolish for ever thinking that the Protectors had been there to guide them. How naïve she had been. The camp was falling into complete pandemonium. Everywhere she looked, there were Protectors fighting for their lives. Though the assailants outnumbered them, the Protectors were better trained. Whoever these attackers were, they didn't have the military precision of the Queen's forces.

Armed with his sword, Dion looked back at Nellie before he ran into the mass of people. Her stomach knotted as she watched him run into the throes of battle. She soon lost sight of him as he disappeared in a throng of red tunics. Ducking low behind the tree trunk, Nellie tucked her head between her knees. Her grip on the dagger was steadfast, her knuckles white with tension. She tried to make herself as small as possible.

There was so much yelling. She heard screaming coming from everywhere behind her. Peaking over her knees, Nellie could see none of the conflict. The fields of wheat blew gently in the wind, the sight at odds with the screams that were filling her ears.

Sounds of pain and anguish were echoing all around the camp. The wounded were already wailing, their song of pain shattering her heart into thousands of tiny pieces. It was unlike anything Nellie had heard before. The tangy scent of blood filled the air, replacing the scent of sweat and grime that had been there.

After a few minutes passed, the sounds of battle lessened. Taking a deep breath and double checking her grip on the dagger, Nellie slowly moved around and peeked over the side of the tree. What she saw shocked her. There were bodies everywhere. A dozen attackers were lying prone on the ground. The dirt, dry and cracked as it was, was turning a deep red. Nellie wanted to throw up. She had never seen so much blood before in her life. Closing her eyes for a moment, Nellie inhaled.

One.

Two.

Three.

Exhaling, she reopened her eyes and began searching for Dion and Elijah.

Nellie could barely make out the bodies of the two men across the camp, but she saw their heads rising above the rest of the Protectors. The sight filled Nellie with relief, the knot in the pit of stomach loosening slightly as she laid eyes on the men. Most of the assailants appeared to have been subdued. Those who hadn't met justice at the end of swords seemed to have fled into the fields. Any attackers who were unfortunate enough to have remained behind were being taken care of by the Protectors.

It was a massacre.

Nellie stood up from her spot behind her tree as she watched Dion go head-to-head with a wild man who was of average height. Compared to Dion, he looked tiny. The man was one of the remaining few assailants still standing. The attacker was wearing a tattered grey tunic that looked remarkably like Elijah's, the wear and tear notwithstanding.

The wild man was wielding a short sword, slightly smaller than Dion's own weapon. Her breath caught in her throat; Nellie couldn't tear her gaze away. Her hands clutched the hilt of the dagger as she stared, entranced by their intricate dance of war. When one thrust, the other spun around. As Dion slashed his sword down on his opponent, the other man brought up his own weapon and blocked his attack. Metal clanged against metal, the sound ringing throughout the camp. The men continued to fight, seeming to pivot in place as they danced a deadly waltz to music only they could hear.

Nellie couldn't breathe. She had never seen anything like this. Every time it appeared Dion would get hurt, he evaded the blow and turned, continuing this deadly dance. She relaxed slightly as Dion gained the upper hand when suddenly; she felt something sharp stab her in the back.

"Don't move." A gruff voice came from behind her. "I won't hesitate to push this in all the way."

Gasping, Nellie dropped the dagger and slowly raised both her hands above her shoulders.

"Please, don't," she whispered. "You have the wrong person."

The voice sniggered, the sound low and sinister in her ear. Before she could react, something large came into contact with her head. An immense pain came rushing in as Nellie crumpled to the ground. Crying out, she could barely see the silhouette of her attacker before she succumbed to the darkness.

Part Two

Chapter Fourteen

Groaning, Nellie gripped her head in her hands as she slowly came to. What happened to her? The last thing she could remember was yelling at Dion. And now... something was wrong. Her head was pounding and there was a stabbing pain gathering behind her eyes.

The last time Nellie felt this out of sorts, she had fallen off a ladder when she was ten years old. She had her sights set on a kitten that had gotten itself stuck on a branch dangling twenty feet in the air when her foot slipped and she had gone careening to the ground. The fall had been one of the two most painful experiences of her life and the resulting broken right arm hadn't helped matters. The break had healed, but even now, Nellie would sometimes feel bursts of pain running through her arm.

Rubbing her temples, Nellie slowly cracked one eye open. Wincing at the bright candlelight that seeped into her vision, she began taking stock of her surroundings. Wherever she was, it certainly didn't seem very welcoming.

The room, barely furnished, was about the size of her bedroom at home. It was windowless, the only light in the space coming from two lit sconces that hung on the wall. The air smelled like the earth with a faint tinge of lavender woven throughout.

Nellie was lying on a thin, rough mattress placed on the dirty wooden floor. Hay protruded from the mattress, sticking into Nellie's limbs. She instinctively itched her arms as she surveyed the room. She didn't see any dirt in the small chamber, but she couldn't stop scratching at her body. Visions of spiders and ants crawling over her flooded her mind. Shuddering, Nellie sat up and crossed her legs, tucking her feet under herself. She leaned over to inspect the only furniture in the room. There was a small white nightstand that stood about two feet high, placed next to the itchy mattress. It was bare, the only decorative piece was an iron knob shaped like a tree.

That's curious. I've never seen a knob like this before.

In Liantis, they made knobs of plain iron. The doorknobs had one use and so the Ionians forged them in simple, usable circles and ovals. Guardian Clarence had always instructed the wards that in Tiarny, functionality was prized over beauty. He reminded the wards time and time again that the Source Herself had decreed that artistry was unnecessary and frivolous. She had outlawed all art forms for Seconds and Thirds.

Nellie couldn't draw her gaze away from the curious tree. Reaching out a hand, she marvelled at the artwork. The knob was cool to the touch, but the ironwork was flawless. Every detail was intricate, as though its maker spent hours perfecting the small piece of hardware. Pulling the knob, Nellie sighed as her gaze met an empty drawer.

Placed in the corner furthest from her perch on the mattress was a modest white chamber pot. It appeared to be made of porcelain, and there was another strange tree etched on the surface of the pot. Nellie didn't waste too much time thinking about the significance of the tree, as her gaze drifted to the only door in the room.

Hope filled her as she jumped to her feet. She wobbled for a moment on unsteady limbs before she caught herself and strode to the door. Taking a deep breath, Nellie grabbed the handle and pulled.

Nothing.

It wouldn't move.

She didn't give up. She wiggled the handle, trying to pull it to the left and then to the right, but the door was bolted in place. Someone had locked her in here, taken the key and left.

Staring at the door, Nellie's thoughts began pulling her down into a whirlpool of self-doubt and anxiety.

Where am I?

Who took me?

Where is Dion?

Nellie's vision blurred as tears rushed to her eyes. Her hopes disintegrated as she stared at the door, her mind swarming with unanswered questions. Her unknown assailants had separated her from everything she had ever known, and she did not know what to do.

She let out a mirthless laugh as she surveyed the situation.

"I could have used a lesson about this, Guardian Clarence. Maybe fewer lessons about the history of Tiarny, a little more about what to do if you're being held captive in a windowless room by a mysterious group of assailants."

The only response to her words was the flickering of the candle flame.

Sighing, Nellie plopped down on the rough mattress. She put her head in her hands, groaning as she considered how she would ever get back to her mother now. Exhaustion weighed on her, her limbs heavy with sleep, when suddenly, she jolted upright. The memory of a lesson she had heard as a ward came flooding back.

She had been only eight years old when Guardian Clarence had taken the wards on a tour of the Museum of Artifacts. The Museum was full of relics left behind by the people who lived before the Year of Inception. Eyes wide, the children had kept their hands to themselves as they had marched two-by-two through the museum. At the end of the tour, the Tutors had talked for hours about the terrible ways people lived before the Source. Of all the lessons they had learned that day, the one that had chilled Nellie's soul had been the way men took advantage of defenceless, vulnerable women. Silent tears had run down her cheeks as she listened, arms wrapped around herself. She hadn't been able to look at any males for the rest of the day.

Sitting in the windowless room, Nellie's heart thrummed as she patted her black tunic and leggings. Her breath went out of her in a *whoosh* as she realized everything appeared to be the same way that she remembered. Her underclothes were still in place, and even though dust and wrinkles covered her clothes, they were still in one piece. Even her boots were still on her feet.

Thank the Source.

She rubbed her arms in an effort to ward off the chill that had crept under her skin. Goosebumps peppered her flesh. She couldn't help but feel relieved. In Tiarny, couples didn't have to remain untouched before their union, but everyone involved in relations must consent. Nellie knew that occasionally, there were people brought before the Protectors because they pushed their partners too far.

How terrible. And what if they had taken off my tunic and discovered my pendant while I was unconscious?

The pendant!

Nellie's hand flew to her chest in alarm, but she let out a sigh of relief as she felt the familiar bump under her tunic. The pendant emitted a strange, but not unpleasant, heat as it lay against her chest.

As she lay her head back against her knees, Nellie realized she had lost the dagger Dion had given her. Despite their less-than-amicable relationship, the thought that she had lost something of his sent a pang through her chest. The Official's irritating smirk flashed through her mind as she imagined his reaction when he found out she had lost his dagger.

Having grasped the impossibility of escape, Nellie became aware of an ache in her throat the likes of which she had never felt before. It felt as though she had been screaming at the top of her lungs for days on end. Although the pain had eased slightly, her headache returned full-force as she ran her tongue over her dry, chapped lips. Just as Nellie thought things couldn't get any worse, her stomach gurgled loudly.

Breathing rapidly as panic overtook her, Nellie walked to the door and called out.

"Hello?" Her throat ached from the effort. "Is anyone there? Hello?"

Nothing. Silence filled the air as Nellie lay her forehead on the door. She began shaking, her voice little more than a whisper, as she continued to call for help.

"Help, someone please, help. I need water."

Nellie took a deep breath and tried to centre her thoughts. Guardian Clarence had taught her some meditative breathing to help with the frequent panic attacks she used to get as a child. They seemed to get worse after she had accidentally gotten locked in a closet for five hours. The panic attacks had decreased with age, but they would still sporadically overtake her.

This is not the time for a panic attack, Nellie. Focus.

Inhale

This is not the end. I need water. I did not leave my home, my mother, and my friends to die trapped in some windowless room after being taken captive.

Exhale

I. Will. Survive.

Inhale

I will get back to Liantis. That is the only thing that matters.

Exhale

New plan.

Inhale

Step 1. Water. That's definitely important.

Exhale

Step 2. Figure out where I am.

Inhale

Step 3. Escape.

Exhale

You've got this.

Emboldened, Nellie grabbed the cover of the empty chamber pot and sat cross-legged on the floor. She slouched, her back against the wall, as she began banging the lid on the door. Someone had to be nearby. Someone had to hear her.

She refused to consider the other possibility.

Several minutes passed as Nellie lifted the lid and hit it against the door.

Bang

Bang

Bang

Finally, she heard the sound of her salvation. Footsteps filled the air, growing louder with each passing second. Hope flooded her as she continued banging on the door.

"Help, please," Nellie cried out as loud as she could. "Help me. I'm trapped in here."

Finally, someone had heard her pleas. There was a shadow on the other side of the door. Nellie heard metal clanking as voices murmured. Scrambling out of the path of the door, Nellie moved too quickly. She tripped and flew backwards, landing awkwardly on the itchy mattress. Just as she clambered to right herself, she heard the beautiful sound of a key turning in the lock.

By the time the door flew open, Nellie was sitting cross-legged on the mattress, looking as put-together as she could manage under the circumstances. She had smoothed down stray hairs and made certain her pendant was lying flat against her skin.

"Well, well, well. What do we have here?" A mellifluous voice resonated from the doorway, drawing Nellie's gaze upwards to its owner. The melodious tone of the woman's voice sounded angelic, not something Nellie would ever have associated with a warrior. She was tall, with dark green hair that reminded Nellie of the evergreens that grew in small clumps around Liantis, with large whiskey eyes. Someone had done her hair in a series of tight braids that fell in intricate knots down her back. She had freckles covering her cheeks and nose, standing out against her copper skin.

Instead of the tattered tunics that Nellie had seen her attackers wearing before she blacked out, this mysterious woman was wearing a long, grey, sleeveless dress with two slits that ran up to her thighs. She wore a strange pair of black leggings under her dress that stopped at her knees, preserving her modesty but allowing her room to move. The dress itself didn't appear to be made of the same coloured cotton usually worn by the Sequenced citizens in Tiarny. Nellie was fairly certain she had never seen the material before, but it appeared very soft.

As the woman moved, Nellie noticed two daggers in holsters strapped to her captor's thighs. Gulping, she wished she still had Dion's dagger on her. Even though she didn't know how to use it, it had made her feel strong. As she worked up the courage to look at her captor's face, she saw hardness in the warrior's eyes.

She stood, her legs thankfully no longer wobbling, as she looked at her captor. The mysterious green-haired woman lifted a brow as she watched Nellie stand.

"W-Who are you?" Nellie asked, her voice shaky.

There was no response from the woman as she stared at her. Minutes passed as she waited for an answer. The woman simply crossed her arms and stared at Nellie. Finally, Nellie grew irritated and tried again. "Can you please tell me why I'm here? What do you want from me?"

The woman just laughed at Nellie, the melodious sound directly at odds with the anger in her eyes.

"Oh, my dear," she smirked, her eyes flashing darkly. "You are in no position to ask questions here. We will tell you what we want when it pleases us to do so. As for right now, our leader has instructed that I bring you them. I'm assuming you won't cause any problems and force these two *friendly* guards to hurt you?"

Gulping, Nellie looked past the woman and saw the two guards flanking her for the first time. She had been so preoccupied with her situation that she never even noticed these guards. Unlike the strange dress worn by the woman, the guards were wearing intricate armour that covered their arms and legs. They each had a hand on their swords as they stood tall, their faces like stone.

"Yes," she said, shivering. "I'll come willingly."

Nellie had nothing to collect from the tiny room, so she simply followed the woman and her guards out of the room. As she walked, she tried to catalogue everything she saw. *The more I know, the easier it will be to escape and return to Liantis.*

The group walked down a long, clean hallway with no end in sight. Nellie kept expecting to see a window, but she never did. They passed door after door; the only lighting came from lit sconces that were roughly ten feet apart on the wall. Each sconce cast long shadows on the walls; the flames flickering as they marched past. Walking behind the warrior, Nellie kept her arms clasped in front of her. Goosebumps covered her flesh.

What I wouldn't give to be arguing with Dion right now. At least in Deavita, I would know what was going on. I need to get out of here.

Spurned on by her thoughts, Nellie noted every door and hallway the woman led her through. Finally, they stopped in front of another door. Unlike all the others she had seen, someone had embellished this door with strange markings on them. Nellie felt certain that she had seen them before, but she couldn't remember where.

"Remember," the mysterious woman said, her hand on the doorknob. "You are not here to ask questions. *She* will ask the questions, Eleanor. Don't make us use force on you, it doesn't bring us pleasure."

Wondering how the strange woman knew her name, Nellie nodded her head once before she felt hands on her back. She was unceremoniously shoved into the room.

As soon as she righted herself, Nellie gasped. Her eyes widened as she took in the surrounding space. This window-less chamber was the opposite of the room she had woken up in. It was lavishly furnished, a large wooden table filling most of the space. Large sconces were spread throughout the room, their light flickering on the walls. There were grand wooden chairs arranged around the table, lending the room an air of authority. Just like the rest of the building, the flooring was a dark-coloured wood. Nellie saw a colourful area rug under the table, blues and golds filling the room with a majestic air.

Someone had decorated this room with an assortment of paintings. There had to be a half a dozen pieces of artwork scattered throughout the room, including a large tapestry that took up an entire wall. It was a masterpiece. The artwork called to her in a way that nothing ever had before. She stood unmoving as she drank in the piece of art.

The artist had perfectly depicted a forest in the middle of the harvesting season, the burnt oranges and bright reds of the leaves seeming to leap off the woven piece of art. In the middle of the forest was a large fire, the flames so lifelike that they seemed to flicker as Nellie looked at it. Just as she took a step towards the tapestry, a thin voice began speaking.

Chapter Fifteen

"Come forward, Eleanor Marie Merrick."

The voice, old and withered but imbued with a strange sense of strength, came from the far end of the table facing the tapestry. Nellie had been so preoccupied with the artwork that she had missed the shrivelled elderly woman sitting across from it.

Nellie took a few steps forward and stopped, not wanting to anger the green-haired warrior and her guards who had brought her here. Wringing her hands together, she looked at the small woman, unsure of what to do. She didn't want to sit without invitation, so she ended up just watching the old woman, waiting for directions. Everyone in the room seemed to defer to her, waiting for her direction. It was clear she was their leader. The idea of a woman being in charge wasn't shocking to Nellie, as there were many powerful women in Tiarny. The Source Herself was a woman.

What shocked Nellie wasn't the woman's leadership position, but her age. Nellie had rarely seen people who looked as old as the one currently sitting in front of her. In Liantis, people rarely made it to their sixth decade of life. Once Sequenced, Seconds and Thirds worked seven days of the week, only taking breaks on the twelve feast days that were scattered throughout the year. Studying the shriveled old woman who sat in front of her, Nellie thought she must have been at least eighty years old.

The aged woman sat tall in her seat. Her long white hair was held back from her face in a series of tight braids that ran down the length of her back. There were ribbons woven through the ends, standing in bright contrast to the shocking whiteness of the hair itself. Deep lines and wrinkles that spoke of the many years that she had lived on the planet covered the elderly woman's face and hands.

The leader wore three large silver rings in each ear and had what appeared to be a heavy golden necklace hanging off her neck. She was wearing a long, navy blue robe with billowing sleeves that brushed the table as she moved her arms. The woman, seemingly content to let Nellie study her, picked up a mug of what appeared to be tea and took a long sip. Her eyes shifted around the room the entire time she drank, not staying in one place for more than a few seconds.

The leader's robes covered her arms, but there were strange markings tattooed on her hands. Nellie saw swirls and whorls that ran from the tips of the leader's fingers and disappeared under the sleeves of her robe. They were similar to the markings that were on the door, although the woman's tattoos were much more intricate.

Suddenly, Nellie shifted backwards as she realized the old woman was completely blind. A thick film covered her mocha eyes as they roamed the room, unfocused.

"Come here, child," the leader commanded.

Once again, the strength of the woman's voice surprised Nellie. By all appearances, she would be frail and weak, but she was not. Motioning for Nellie to sit in the chair to her right, the leader sat quietly. Not wanting to anger the woman or the guards at the door, Nellie hurried over to her side and sat down. The chair creaked as she sat; the sound filling the otherwise silent room. As soon as Nellie was seated, the elderly woman picked up her mug and sipped before speaking again.

"How are you, Eleanor?"

Nellie blinked back her surprise. No one had asked her how she felt in, well.... forever. As a young ward, she had been taught to obey her Guardian. She carried a scar on her arm as a reminder of that. Fingering the scar on her left arm, Nellie shuddered before replying.

"I'm... well, I'm quite thirsty." Nellie spoke quietly, her voice still raspy. Her headache had receded during the walk, but the ache in her throat was stronger than ever.

Nellie's admission seemed to take the old woman by surprise. Her mouth opened in shock and a look of anger crossed her wrinkled face. The elderly woman craned her neck towards the door and glared in the general direction of Nellie's escort. The old woman had barely moved, but in those few moments, her leadership skills were clear. Her back straightened and her smile fell off her face, her visage taking on a grim expression before she spoke.

"Bronywyn," the old woman barked, her grip on the mug tightening. "This child is parched. Have you not taken care of her?"

Bronywyn? That must be the name of the mysterious green-haired woman who had brought her here. Nellie glanced at her escort in the strange, grey dress and saw her looking at the floor.

"Well..." Bronywyn drew out the word as she grimaced, her feet shuffling on the floor. "No Mother, I didn't. We put her on the third level when she got here. I didn't think it would be safe to let her roam about."

"Safe? Bronywyn, don't be ridiculous," the leader said, her voice filled with anger. "Eleanor is our guest. You will get her some food and water right now."

Did she say guest? I certainly don't feel much like a guest right now. If this is how they treat a guest, I'd hate to see how these people treat their enemies.

"Now?" Bronywyn scowled, her eyes flashing with anger. "But Mother, what if-"

"Bronywyn, you will do as I say *now*." the old woman's voice reverberated through the room. "It is not your place to question the wisdom of your leader."

The blind woman shifted in her seat, her unseeing eyes seeming to know exactly where Bronywyn stood. If looks could kill, Nellie was certain the green-haired warrior would be dead by now.

"Don't make me regret asking you to help with our guest." the leader said.

"Yes, Mother." Bronywyn said before sending Nellie a frosty look. The warrior bowed to the leader before she spun on her feet and whispered to the two guards.

"I'll go right away." Bronywyn said.

Nellie watched as the warrior bowed to the leader once more and backed out of the room, not turning her back on the leader for a single moment. As soon as Bronywyn exited the chamber, Nellie's stomach rumbled loudly. Heat crept into her cheeks as she stared at the table. Thankfully, the guards stared straight ahead, seemingly content to continue ignoring Nellie.

"I'm sorry, Eleanor, that you haven't received proper treatment," the old woman continued. "I will ensure you are comfortable for the duration of your stay here. I will make sure Bronywyn knows you are to be looked after."

Nellie couldn't bite her tongue any longer.

"I'm sorry, ma'am, but who *are* you?" Nellie winced at the tone of her voice. It was sharper than she had intended. "How do you know my name?"

The leader gave a half-smile, her thin lips opening to reveal a mouthful of straight, white teeth, before responding.

"You are just as feisty as your ancestors. I'm glad to see there's so much life in you. Fight to keep it Eleanor, for you'll need that energy for the battle to come."

"I'm sorry, but a battle?" Nellie's eyebrows rose as she looked at the elderly woman. "I'm afraid you have the wrong person. I'm not who you think I am. I'm not a Protector. I don't know how to fight at all. The first, and hopefully, last time I ever held a dagger was about ten minutes before *your* men attacked me."

The Guardians had always taught Nellie to be respectful towards her elders, but she was having trouble keeping her voice calm after all the things that had been happening to her since her Sequencing. Her life had been turned upside down in the past few days and nothing had gone as planned. Now to find out she's been the victim of some sort of mistaken-identity kidnapping? That was the straw that broke the camel's back.

As Nellie pushed back the chair, intending to storm out of the room and find her way back to Liantis, the older woman reached out and grabbed Nellie's arm. Her touch was soft, her skin reflecting her age, but her grip was firm and full of authority. With a jolt, Nellie realized the old woman smelled like roses, just like her mother.

"Who am I?" the woman replied, tilting her head. "I have had many names over the years, but Eleanor, you may call me Jacinta Blackwater."

What a beautiful name. Nellie had never met anybody named Jacinta before. The tattoos on the older woman's hands and the opulent jewellery the leader wore entranced Nellie. She had never seen anyone wear so many beautiful things all at once. Unfortunately, no matter how fascinating Jacinta appeared, all signs pointed to her having orchestrated Nellie's kidnapping.

"Thank you, Jacinta. Can you tell me why I'm here?"

Sighing, Jacinta brought her mug to her lips and took a sip of her drink before replying.

"I'm not sure how much you're ready to hear yet. For now, I'll just tell you we brought you here for your own good. Deavita is a dangerous place, especially for a newly Sequenced Healer. We couldn't risk you being brought to the capital. You could have been harmed, or even killed. The only way we could safely extract you was on the route to Deavita."

"Why would someone want to harm me?" Nellie paled at the thought of someone purposely attacking her.

"Eleanor, how much do you know of the history of Healers in Tiarny?"

"Well... I...." Nellie thought for a moment. Truly, she didn't really know much about Healers. The Tutors always encouraged knowledge and learning, but Nellie could barely remember receiving any education on Healers outside of recognizing them as a Sequenced occupation. Most of her knowledge of Healers came from first-hand experience brought on by her many mishaps. Rubbing her temples, she replied, "I only know the Source chooses specific people to be Healers during the Sequencing. That's it."

Jacinta's mouth fell into a firm line as she clenched her jaw. Minutes passed in silence, and Nellie was wondering what exactly she had said that was wrong.

"There's much you don't know." Jacinta said gruffly.

Nellie leaned back in the chair, trying to create space between herself and the older woman. Sighing, Jacinta rubbed her forehead before continuing. "It's not you, child. It's just that it has been a long time since anyone spoke of a Sequencing in this room. I don't think we have time to go into that specific history today. For now, let me just share that Healers in Tiarny, especially in recent years, are an endangered species. As soon as word reached us that there would be a Healer being Sequenced in Liantis for the first time in over two hundred years, we knew we needed to act to save you. Your life is in more danger than you know."

It was becoming evident that there were many things that Nellie didn't know.

"Who is this *we* you speak of?" Nellie asked, her head in her hands.

Before Jacinta could answer her question, the door swung open. It slammed against the wall, the resounding bang echoing through the room. Nellie looked up to see Bronywyn standing in the doorway. Her cheeks were flushed and her eyes were sparkling with anger. However, the moment she stepped into the room, her face underwent an amazing transformation. Nellie watched in awe as Bronywyn carefully changed her expression, pulling a mask of cool indifference on her face before she walked over to the table.

The warrior was holding a large wooden tray that was overflowing with food. At the sight of sustenance, Nellie's stomach began reminding everyone of its presence once more. She leaned over, glimpsing the tray as Bronywyn placed it on the table in front of her. Nellie's lips tilted up as she saw the tray held a jug of water, a dozen large pieces of flatbread, and a massive wooden bowl filled with what smelled like deliciously spiced lentils.

Once she had set the tray down on the table, Bronywyn looked to Jacinta for direction. Not missing a beat, Jacinta cocked her head before patting the seat to her left in invitation. The moment the green-haired warrior sat down; Jacinta bowed her head and led the trio in a blessing.

"We come to you today, Oh Source, to thank you for the delicious food you have provided for us. We pray you would continue to strengthen us for our tasks ahead and give us courage for what comes next. Oh Source, let your wisdom hold strong. Please, allow this food to strengthen our bodies. Thank you for all your provisions."

Nellie cocked her head at Jacinta's blessing, the words echoing in her mind as she looked at the elderly woman. Her hunger won out over her curiosity, however, and she quickly picked up a plate and ate the food Bronywyn offered her. The moment the food hit her tongue; Nellie moaned. Whoever these people were, they knew how to cook. She had never eaten lentils like these, cooked with garlic, onions and tomatoes and heavily spiced, but she thought they were amazing. The food she had eaten for the past few years in Tiarny was more for sustenance than taste, and she was extremely pleased to be presented with something both delicious and filling.

Once she had eaten, she felt more satisfied than she had in a long time. Delicious food had an amazing way of clearing one's mind, and after having indulged in both food and water, Nellie felt more at ease than she had since before her Sequencing. She still needed to learn about the group who kidnapped her, but she was feeling more like herself after having revelled in a delicious meal.

Having eaten her fill, Nellie sat up. She was eager to learn more about where she was.

The sooner I find out, the sooner I can leave.

Jacinta shifted in her chair, her unseeing eyes looking at Nellie before she set her now-empty mug down on the table. The elderly woman signalled to Bronywyn to fill it as she steepled her fingers on the table.

"You asked me how we knew your name, Eleanor," Jacinta said. "We know everything about you. It's time you knew who we are."

Chapter Sixteen

L eaning back in her chair, Jacinta was the picture of ease at the head of the table. Nellie didn't move her eyes from the woman, absorbing every word.

"You have asked who we are. To answer that Eleanor, let me tell you what we do. We are a collective formed by individuals who have broken away from the rest of Tiarny, or the Sequenced, as we prefer to refer to them. I'm going to assume you've never heard of us before. Is that correct?"

Nellie nodded her head in agreement before she remembered the elderly leader could not see her. She mumbled, "Yes, that's right."

"Many of our members were born into the group," Jacinta said. "However, we have several members who have defected from the Sequenced society."

She paused, taking a long drag of her tea before she rubbed her temples.

Defected.

The word bounced around in Nellie's mind. It was all she could do to sit back and listen in disbelief as Jacinta spoke. With every word that came out of the blind woman's mouth, it became more and more clear that Nellie had somehow found herself in the middle of a very dangerous situation. Whoever this woman was, she was insane.

People who broke away from Tiarny. Nellie's green eyes never left the woman as she mulled her words over. *I've never heard of such a thing. How is this even possible?*

Clearing her throat, Jacinta spoke once more. "You may have already surmised that I am the leader of this group."

Nellie found her voice and replied, her voice sharper than she had intended as she replied, "Yes, it appears that way to me."

Jacinta's lips turned up at Nellie's bluntness. Nellie knew she should show more respect to the elderly woman, but as exhaustion and irritation warred with her, she could not bring herself to care.

After taking another slow drink from her mug, the old woman let out a long breath.

"As a collective," Jacinta said, "we all share a mutual goal. We have one reason for existing. We spend every day of our lives trying to save the Sequenced and those the system of Sequencing crushes. Each person who is part of this group has their own story, their own reason for being a part of this movement. Their stories aren't mine to tell. However, if you were to ask anyone why they are part of this group, they will undoubtedly tell you they want to release Tiarny from the confines of the Sequencing."

Nellie rubbed her temples as Jacinta spoke, the woman's words confusing her more by the second.

This poor old lady has lost her mind. Old age must have addled her brain. She speaks of the Sequencing as though it were a prison?

Jacinta was still talking, ignorant to the fact that Nellie was staring at her with eyes as wide as saucers. "-liberate the citizens from this oppressive regime currently holding them hostage."

At that, Nellie snorted a mirthless laugh.

"I'm sorry, oppressive regime?" Nellie shook her head, slamming her hand down on the table. Jacinta's mug rattled. "How is the Sequencing oppressive? They never did anything to me. You kidnapped me."

The register of Nellie's voice was climbing higher and higher as she tried to contain her panic.

How did I always end up in situations like this? This would never happen to Fay. She always knew what to do.

"Yes, you speak the truth, Eleanor." Jacinta folded her hands over themselves. Frowning, she furrowed her brows. "We kidnapped you and I'm sorry about that. If I could change the way you got here, I would."

Stunned, Nellie found herself at a loss for words. She certainly hadn't expected to hear the older woman admit to having kidnapped her.

Bronywyn, who had been lounging back in her chair and simply watching the exchange between Jacinta and Nellie, sat straight up at that admission. She pushed her intricate braid over one shoulder as she sneered at Nellie. When reclined, the woman almost seemed... normal. Now that she sat with her back straight, her nose wrinkled as her eyes shot sparks, Nellie remembered that this woman was certainly not her friend. She was a warrior through and through.

Nellie gulped, realizing once again that she was once again defenseless if someone tried to hurt her. She knew no self-defence, no weaponry skills. For the Source's sake, she didn't even know how to cook more than a basic meal! For all the preparations the Guardians had done, all the lessons Tutors had instilled upon her, all the hours she spent in the warding centre, Nellie felt completely useless in the face of imminent danger.

"Well Eleanor, I'm not sorry." Bronywyn stood up and paced, her hands furled. Nellie was grateful for the table separating her from the intimidating woman.

The green-haired warrior spoke as she moved, her gray dress flowing out from behind her. "The means we used may have been rough, but we took you for your own good. If you had made it to the capital, Source knows what would have happened to you before we could save you."

"Why does everyone think the capital is so dangerous for me?" Nellie asked, her voice rising, her eyes wide as she glared back at Bronywyn. "I don't even want to go to the capital. Just take me back to Liantis. My mother needs me."

Somewhere in the recesses of Nellie's mind, she knew she couldn't go back to Liantis just now. If she didn't report to Deavita for training, the punishments would be unimaginable.

When Nellie had been eleven years old, she and Fay had been playing outside the warding centre kicking around a ball made of rags when Nellie had accidentally tripped and fallen through one of the large windows separating the warding centre from the yard. The glass had shattered, raining down all around her as she fell. She remembered looking down and seeing a shard of glass about three inches long sticking out of her arm. Nellie hadn't screamed, only clinically assessed the situation as she waited for help. She had felt as though she saw herself through someone else's eyes, just sitting surrounded by shards of glass. Blood had streamed down her arm, her face growing paler by the second.

One of the other wards had fetched Guardian Clarence, and he had come running with a Healer. Somehow, they were able to pull the glass from Nellie's arm and stitch the long laceration closed. The Healer kept muttering something about the Source watching over Nellie, as hundreds of pieces of glass had surrounded her, but the cut on her arm was the worst injury. Guardian Clarence had told the Healer to make sure it would scar. With tears in her eyes, Nellie had looked up at the large man.

"Why?" A moan had escaped her lips as she cried, the pain of the sutures too strong to ignore.

"Nellie, I know this isn't easy. But you need a reminder to be careful.

The next time you get hurt, you might not get off so lucky. The Source has been watching out for you, but you don't want to anger Her. One day, she might retract Her blessing. If she does, where will you be? Tiarny can only operate if everyone works together. How many accidents have you gotten into over the years, Eleanor?"

Nellie had shaken her head, "I don't know," she had whispered. "They're not on purpose, sir."

Guardian Clarence had sighed. "I know. But sometimes things we don't do on purpose can still bring about pain. This scar will forever be a reminder to you that the next time, the punishment might be worse than a cut on your arm."

That had been that. The Guardian had left Nellie in the Healer's hands and walked away. Every time Nellie looked at the rough patch of skin on her arm, she heard Guardian Clarence's words. *The punishment might be worse.*

No, she couldn't go back to Liantis without fulfilling her duties in Deavita first. But every second she spent *here*, with these people, was taking her away from her mother.

Taking a few deep breaths, Nellie tried to ground herself. Her palms became slick with sweat and anxiety swirled around her as she tried to focus on her breathing.

Inhale, exhale, repeat.

Sighing loudly, Bronywyn stopped her pacing and walked over to Jacinta, touching her arm before leaning over to whisper in her ear. Nellie couldn't hear what they said, but they spoke for a few minutes before pulling apart. Jacinta squeezed Bronywyn's hand before nodding.

"Go ahead." The elderly woman murmured.

Go ahead? Go ahead, what? Why won't anyone ever fill me in on what's going on.

Nellie rubbed her hands over her face as she sat in the chair, a wave of exhaustion over taking her. Her eyes were blurry with fatigue as she wearily watched Bronywyn bow low towards Jacinta. Despite her blindness, Jacinta smiled and waved a hand dismissively towards the green-haired warrior.

"Have a good evening, Mother," Bronywyn said.

Turning towards Nellie, the warrior gestured towards her. Her voice was firm and unwavering. "Eleanor. You want to know why we think the capital is so dangerous for Healers? You'll have to come with me to find out."

Bronywyn walked towards the door without a second glance backwards. She held a taper in her hands, which she quickly lit from a sconce by the door before disappearing into the corridor.

Nellie quickly bid Jacinta goodbye before she hurried after Bronywyn. This time, she was paying attention and noticed the two guards who fell into step right behind her. She wouldn't be missing their presence again. Their swords clanked lightly against their armor as they moved, filling the air with the soft sound of metal. For a moment, Nellie felt as though she was back in Liantis, listening to the sounds of the Protectors walking down the street on their rounds. It was a comforting sound, but the relief it brought with it soon dissipated as she remembered she was the victim of a kidnapping by a consortium aiming to take apart the Sequencing.

Bronywyn walked quickly, her legs making quick strides of the halls as Nellie hurried after her. They went through dark hallways and down a flight of stairs for what seemed to be a few minutes. The earthy smell grew stronger as they moved through the passageways, mixing with the scent of various oils that were burning throughout the corridors.

Nellie didn't know how much time was passing, for she was having trouble keeping track of time in the windowless building. The sconces were still the only source of light, other than the taper Bronywyn held in her hand. Nellie's eyes were adjusting to the dim lighting, but she missed the endless blue sky. The sun had provided constant sunlight and they rarely needed to use candles in Liantis.

Finally, Bronywyn stopped in front of yet another door. She didn't appear to be out of breath at all, even though Nellie felt as though her lungs were burning. Before Bronywyn pulled the door open, she turned towards Nellie and held up a finger. Her whiskey eyes were steely as they bored into Nellie's.

"What you're about to witness will be extremely difficult to see, but it is necessary for you to understand why we believe you to be in danger."

"I understand," Nellie said, crossing her arms in front of her chest. "I'm here, aren't I?"

Bronywyn shook her head slightly as she held the door open and gestured for Nellie to enter. Hoping she wasn't walking into a trap, Nellie pushed back her shoulders and walked through the door. As soon as her eyes had adjusted to the darkened room, Nellie inadvertently let out a soft gasp.

They were standing in a small room that looked just like the one that Nellie had woken up in a scant few hours ago. There were, of course, no windows in this room. The lack of direct sunlight appeared to be a trademark of the mysterious building.

It took Nellie's eyes a moment to adjust to the dim lighting in the room. The gloomy space was sparsely furnished with a cot and a nightstand. In contrast to Nellie's earlier quarters, there were also five small lit candles scattered throughout the room. Their tiny, yellow flames were flickering and casting their shadows over the solitary occupant.

Nellie's eyes widened as she took in the sight of an extremely emaciated boy sitting on a thin mattress. Her mind went blank as she stared. He was so thin that she could see every single bone in his frail upper body. The child's sepia-coloured skin stretched thin over his weak frame.

Even when the rains had stopped falling and fresh fruits and vegetables became a thing of the past, Nellie had never seen a person in such awful shape as the boy sitting in front of her.

He looked as though he hadn't eaten in weeks.

Nellie couldn't tear her eyes from the child sitting on the cot. He was wearing a long black tunic, not unlike the clothes that Nellie herself had on. In contrast to the Tailor-made clothing the Officials had given her at her Sequencing, the boy's clothes were hanging off of him. It was as though they could not find purchase on his too-thin form. His wide, black eyes stared blankly towards the door. The child's hair hung limp around him as he sat staring, seeming to look right through the women as he studied some unknown point in the distance.

Inching closer to the boy, Nellie saw his lower body was wrapped in a thick, gray blanket. The child was shivering profusely, despite the heat in the building. His teeth were clattering together and Nellie could see that his tiny frame was struggling to remain upright as chills afflicted him.

How is he cold? The building is so warm.

Nellie was sweating, and she was wearing a cotton tunic. She could not imagine how hot the boy must have been under the blanket. Standing there, in front of the emaciated child, she could feel her face contorting to reflect the horror she felt. Pressing her hands to her cheeks, Nellie turned towards Bronywyn. Her mouth fell open, but no words came out.

"Eleanor, this is Axel." Bronywyn's voice was soft; pity lining her usually hard eyes. "We rescued him a week and a half ago from the Sequenced in Deavita. He was desperate for help."

Nellie looked back to the form huddled on the cot. Someone had wrapped his left arm in a thick white bandage. There was a slight discoloration around the edge of the bandage, betraying an infection hidden under all the material. Nellie had seen infections before, usually from scrapes and run-ins with rusty nails, but she had never seen anything as bad at this. Whatever happened to him, he must have suffered some great injury.

"Bronywyn, what..." Tears filled her eyes as she struggled to find words to express her horror at the situation she was witnessing. If she hadn't seen it with her own two eyes, she would never have believed it. "What happened to this boy?"

"Boy?" Bronywyn let out a mirthless laugh. "Axel is no boy. He is older than you are, Eleanor."

Nellie's jaw dropped open, the colour draining from her face.

"What... why... How is this possible? What happened to him?"

"Deavita happened to him." Bronywyn's voice was hard, her eyes sharp in the darkness. "Axel's Sequencing took place five years ago, and he had been working in the capital ever since. He worked under one of the oldest Healers in Deavita and had been a Healer in the House of Restoration."

The House of Restoration. Nellie vaguely remembered learning about this place. The Firsts used it to remain youthful, while the Seconds and Thirds aged as the Source intended. The only one in the entire country was in the capital. Since they barred Seconds and Thirds from using it, Nellie's education surrounding the mysterious building had been slim.

Bronywyn continued talking as she poured Axel some water from a brown clay jug that sat on the nightstand. The boy- no, the man- reached for the cup with his too thin hand and brought it to his lips. He grimaced as the movement jostled his injured arm.

"A few months ago, the Royal Protectors decided Axel would be better off being imprisoned than following his Sequenced path as a Healer."

Nellie was having trouble thinking straight. What was happening? A Healer, just like her, imprisoned in the capital? And by the Queen's own Protectors?

The Royal Protectors were an elite force of warriors that were hand-selected by the Queen to serve her. It was one of the highest honours in Tiarny to be chosen to serve as a Royal Protector. How could the Queen's own Protectors have done this? Axel looked as though they had tortured, starved, and beaten him within an inch of his life.

Was this the fate waiting for Nellie in the capital, the future that the Source had set out for Nellie? The one that Dion had been taking her towards?

Even though Nellie knew Dion didn't like her much, she hated to believe that he would have willingly escorted her to a fate like this.

Standing in the small room, staring at a man who suffered a fate worse than Nellie had ever imagined was possible, her heart began pounding in her chest. It was so similar to the way Blaze's hoofs had pounded the dirt as they had traveled from Liantis. Her lungs felt like they were on fire as she struggled to breathe. Hot tears began streaming down her cheeks as she shook. Each breath felt like shards of glass in her lungs, each one not enough to sate her need for air. Her hands were clammy and sweat began pouring down her face.

Too late, she realized what was happening. She grabbed onto Brony-wyn's arm for support before the panic attack overtook her completely. As Nellie fell to the floor, she let out a strangled cry for help before everything went dark.

Chapter Seventeen

F or the second time in two days, Nellie woke up with a pounding headache in a room she didn't recognize. She must have blacked out after the panic attack. Taking in a deep breath, Nellie forced open her eyes. She looked around, surprised that she found herself in yet another new room.

Well, at least this is an upgrade.

This new room was a suite fit for a queen. The air smelled like peppermint; the aroma pulling her out of her slumber. There still weren't any windows, but Nellie's lips turned up as she felt the blanket that was laying over top her. It was the thickest, fluffiest comforter she had ever seen. She ran her fingers over the material, admiring the tiny trees and flowers embroidered all over the soft material. It was beautiful, but more importantly, it was warm. The blanket was covering an enormous four-poster bed that filled most of the space.

The room was lit with the same sconces that Nellie had seen around the windowless building. The lights flickered, casting eerie shadows upon the walls of the large room. She noticed an unlit candle in a holder hanging near the headboard. Grabbing the candle, Nellie sat up and lit it, using the flame from a sconce hanging on the wall near the bed.

Holding the candle up high so as not to cause any disasters, Nellie inspected her surroundings. The first thing she noticed was that they had paired the enormous bed with an equally enormous headboard. Once again, it appeared as though someone had carved some strange symbols into the woodwork. Upon closer inspection, she thought the carvings were old, much older than the Common Tongue. There were intricate shapes and swirling glyphs that formed complex patterns on the wood. Nellie did not know how to make heads or tails out of the strange inscription. Whatever they meant, she would have to find out later.

Having lain down for Source-knew how many hours, Nellie felt a sudden urge to move. She hopped off the bed and stood on the plush carpet adorning the wooden floor. It was blood red, the same color as the tunics of the Royal Protectors. Making a mental note to investigate the carvings on the headboard later, Nellie explored the rest of the room. She still felt slightly sore, but it was nothing like her first night on the Queen's Road with Dion.

There was a pair of black nightstands flanking the enormous bed, each one double the size of her own nightstands at home. On one nightstand, she found a brown clay jug filled with water and an empty cup ready for her use. Nellie gulped a cup of water before continuing her explorations. Even though she wasn't remarkably thirsty, if there was one thing she had learned over the past three years, it was to have a drink of water whenever one was available. You never know when a plentiful resource might become scarce.

On the other nightstand, Nellie pulled open the drawer to find a small book. She broke into a grin.

Finally, something familiar.

With the tender reverence of a person who appreciated the delicate beauty of the written word, Nellie reached out and touched the small tome. The book was thin with a navy-blue cover. Beautiful golden writing lining its edges. It looked ancient, its fraying edges and cracked spine testifying to its age. When she picked it up, she noticed that there was an interesting image of a tree embossed on the leather cover. Tucking this piece of information into her mind to ponder further, Nellie picked up the ancient book gingerly and carried it over to the bed.

Carefully holding the candle away from the book to not set the text ablaze, Nellie leafed through its pages with care. She marveled at the scent of the pages, their aroma reminding her of the library in Liantis. She felt a quick pang of homesickness as she thought of her hometown and renewed her vow to return as soon as possible.

I'm coming, Mother. Just hold on.

The pages themselves were yellowed and stained with age, the black ribbon being used as a bookmark frayed at the edge. Much of the ink had faded with time, but Nellie could still make out a few of the words that remained on the pages. Too many words were gone for the story to make much sense, but Nellie loved a mystery. Folding her legs underneath her and sitting up against the headboard, she continued perusing the book until she heard a series of loud knocks at the door. Each knock reverberated through the room, echoing off the walls.

"Eleanor, are you awake?" Nellie knew the voice on the other side of the door belonged to Bronywyn.

If I wasn't already awake, I would be now. Nellie groaned, mumbling some nonsensical words towards the door as she untangled her legs, careful not to bring her candle too close to the book as she moved. A small *thump* rang through the room as she placed the book back on the nightstand before hopping off the bed and walked over to the door. Nellie experimentally put her hand on the doorknob and twisted. Her eyebrow raised as the knob turned easily in her hand.

Her jaw fell open as the door swung open in her grasp. When she pulled the door open and saw Bronywyn, the enigmatic woman was chuckling softly to herself. In the short time Nellie had known the green-haired woman, she had seen her as a warrior, a compassionate woman and an indifferent onlooker. This time, as the hint of a smile graced her lips, Bronywyn's face softened. She almost looked like a different person.

"Mother has decreed you are to be treated as an honoured guest, Eleanor. We do not lock guests in rooms. I... apologize for the way we treated you when you first arrived."

Even though Bronywyn seemed to choke on the word 'apologize', she got it out. Nellie hadn't been expecting an apology from anyone, certainly not from the warrior who admitted to kidnapping her.

"I-I accept your apology." Her brows drew together as she remembered something she had wanted to ask about. "Jacinta, she is your mother?"

"She is," Bronywyn said, her face softening further. Her lips slipped into a full smile, her eyes crinkling as she spoke of the elderly woman. The transformation was truly shocking. With her severe expressions, Nellie thought Bronywyn looked fierce. Now Nellie thought the warrior was truly stunning. Her eyes glowed and her nose crinkled. The movement of her lips softened her strong cheekbones. Nellie had thought the woman to be at least four decades old, but now, she could see that Bronywyn was no older than three decades.

"You should do that more often," Nellie said. "Smile, I mean."

She surprised herself with her comment. She hadn't meant to speak out loud, but the compliment slipped out before she could stop it. Bronywyn didn't seem like the woman to take kindly to people speaking out of turn, even if the speaking was complementary. Luckily for Nellie, Bronywyn seemed to take her comment in stride.

"Thank you." The warrior sighed as her brows drew together. "My birth parents were killed when I was an infant, and Jacinta raised me as her own. She has given me everything I ever needed. Because of my mother's age, I take care of most of the physical duties of the leader. She used to do a lot more, but over the past few years, her body has shown signs of deterioration. Now she is the voice of the leader and I act as her body."

Nellie felt a strange pull on her heart as a connection formed between herself and her captor.

"I'm sorry to hear that," Nellie whispered. "My father died when I was a baby, too. It's a group I wish no one was a part of. My mother is all alone now, that's why it's so important for me to get back to Liantis."

No longer wearing the intricate braid she had been sporting earlier, Bronywyn's dark green hair was now falling in waves that framed her face. Her hair fell to the small of her back, giving her face a softer appearance than before. At the mention of Nellie's mother, Bronywyn's lips tilted down.

"I'm sorry for your loss. But it's not safe for you to go to the capital right now." Walking into the hallway, Bronywyn gestured for Nellie to follow her. Sighing, Nellie glanced back at the mysterious book before heading into the dark corridor.

"Everyone keeps saying that, but you have your family here. I don't have mine," Nellie said as her eyes filled with tears. "I-I really miss my mother. You are so lucky to have yours with you."

A wave of homesickness that was unlike anything Nellie had ever experienced before suddenly struck her. She ducked her head and hugged her hands around herself, trying to bring up positive memories of her mother. Her smile, the way she saved gingersnap cookies for Nellie, her laugh. Gulping down her tears, Nellie followed Bronywyn down the halls. Stopping at yet another door, the warrior emerged from a room bearing some food and four canteens of water.

"I thought you might be hungry, Eleanor. You slept for fourteen hours after we saw Axel yesterday."

"Thank you." She replied, dipping her head towards the strange woman. "I am hungry."

"We'll eat as we walk. I have someone who wants to see you."

Intrigued, she followed the woman, the guards constantly at her back. She had so many questions.

Who would want to see her? It wasn't as though she had many friends, or even one, among her abductors. Nellie didn't consider Bronywyn or Jacinta friends, although they seemed to be warming up to her. Even with their recent acts of kindness, Nellie knew she wouldn't be forgetting their roles in her abduction.

The women walked in silence for a few more minutes down the dark passageways, turning left before the hallway came to an abrupt end. There was yet another mysterious door. Bronywyn pulled the knob and pushed the door open, waiting for it to swing wide before she crossed the threshold.

As Nellie followed Bronywyn, her brows lifted in surprise as her eyes took in the long, winding staircase that appeared to climb up high to the sky.

The small group stood on a wooden landing that was about five feet in diameter. Nellie jumped as the door slammed shut behind the guards, blackness instantly engulfing them. This stairwell took darkness to a whole new level. It was completely dark except for the flickering candle-light provided by tall, white candles that were hanging every few feet up the length of the stairs. Nellie heard dripping sounds coming from all around her, along with the occasional scuffle of small feet.

Breathing in deeply, she coughed as dust filled her lungs. The air in the stairwell was chilly, smelling of dirt and musk with a tinge of sulfur. To call the air unpleasant would have been an understatement. The stairwell

154

was damp and Nellie could see and hear evidence of the multitude of critters who called this place their home. She inadvertently drew her limbs closer to herself as she tried to avoid touching any of the walls.

"Well Eleanor, answers await you on the other end of this staircase. Shall we?" Bronywyn said.

Relieved to get out of the tight space, Nellie nodded enthusiastically. "Let's do this."

Nellie wanted answers more than anything. If nothing else, she had learned over the past few days just how much she valued information. She had also learned just how little she knew. What had felt like a copious amount of education and training before her Sequencing was now small and inadequate.

Everyone felt as though they knew what was best for Nellie, but no one was asking her to make an informed decision about what was best for herself.

What I want is to go home to my mother. She needs me. Perhaps this will lead me closer to her.

Excited by the possibility of information, Nellie bounded up the stairs after Bronywyn. The guards followed them, trailing a few steps behind Nellie.

I suppose being the leader's daughter has its advantages, including a personal guard.

Although Nellie had begun climbing the stairs with enthusiasm, her eagerness soon faded. They never seemed to end. The dripping sounds continued as the group climbed, and Nellie's labored breaths soon echoed throughout the stairwell. No one spoke, their footfalls the only evidence of their presence. Every once in a while, Nellie heard something running on the wall beside her and she pulled her arms in closer. There was a symphony of sounds surrounding her.

On and on they went, up the seemingly endless spiral staircase. As they continued their ascent, the sconces on the wall lessened in frequency until they disappeared all together. The lack of lighting worried Nellie, but before she could say anything, Bronywyn pulled a taper from her pack and lit it using the last remaining sconce. The light from the torch blazed ahead and Nellie hurried up the stairs to remain in step with the fierce warrior. Having climbed what seemed to be hundreds of steps, the realization struck her that they must have been deep underground. No wonder there were so many sconces everywhere. There was literally no other light source available.

She hadn't even known there were any underground buildings anywhere in Tiarny.

After it seemed as though an eternity had passed, the group finally reached the top of the stairwell. Nellie was out of breath, her lungs burning as she gasped for air. The musky scent of the stairwell had faded and now the air smelled crisp, like grass mixed with dew. A few feet above where they were currently standing, there was a large hatch with a handle the size of Nellie's head. Bronywyn handed the torch to Nellie with a word of warning to keep it held high. Before Nellie could say anything, the green-haired warrior reached out and tapped her hand on the metal hatch.

Tap-tap-tap

The women waited for a moment before the groaning sound of metal on metal filled the stairwell. Nellie winced as blazing sunlight filled her vision, blinding her momentarily. Bronywyn and her guards ascended first, leaving Nellie alone for a moment before she reached for the final rungs of the ladder and pulled herself out of the hatch. Shielding her eyes, she stood, her back aching from the climb.

After a minute or two had passed, Nellie inched her hand off of her eyes. The warmth of the sun warmed her skin and she discovered she was standing in a grove of extremely tall trees. The bright blue sky was barely visible through the cover of green leaves. Of course, there wasn't a single cloud in sight.

There was lush, blue green grass that covered the hatch that they had emerged from. The grass under her feet was tall and tickled her kneecaps. She felt the tips of the grass through her long leggings. Nellie was grateful that she was still wearing her black boots, so her feet were protected from the danger of venomous snakes.

In the distance, Nellie heard four voices speaking as she looked around. One was definitely Bronywyn's, while the other three were male. She assumed that two of the voices belonged to the straight-faced guards who followed Bronywyn everywhere. The fourth voice was a mystery to Nellie. It was rich and gravelly, the sound pleasing to Nellie's ears. The male's voice sounded vaguely familiar to her, in the way that a dream can sometimes haunt your reality after you wake up.

Bronywyn and her mysterious companions were talking in the distance. Nellie could see their forms through the trees, but they were little more than shadows at this point. As she looked around, she realized that, for the first time; she was alone and unguarded. This was her chance, her opportunity to get away. She inhaled deeply, spinning in a circle. Nothing. There was no one. The only sounds other than her breathing came from the leaves rustling in the wind.

This was it.

This was her moment.

She could return to Liantis, to her mother.

Not willing to spare another moment's thought, Nellie decided. She had to do it. Fingering the scar on her arm, she breathed in deeply.

Please, oh Source, keep me safe. Let me get away from these people and back to my mother.

Branches cracked as she moved. She could have sworn she saw something moving in the distance. Nellie shifted her direction, her feet pounding through the forest as she moved.

Look where you're going, Nellie.

Keeping her gaze trained on the horizon, Nellie ran quickly through the trees, avoiding vines that dangled from up high and logs that were on the ground. Too soon, she felt her lungs burning. She stopped for a moment, ducking under a large pine tree, her hands on her knees as she struggled to catch her breath. Panting, she was standing under the tree when a cracking sound came from behind her.

Her face paled at the sound. Eyes wide, she straightened and slowly peeked around the tree trunk. There, in front of her, was a pale blue snake with bands of yellow and green alternating stripes that ran down its long, thin body. It was at least ten feet long, its body curled up around itself as it stared at her. Nellie felt the breath leave her body as she found herself face-to-face with a *mianos* snake.

Guardian Clarence had warned all the wards of walking through long grass, explaining that Tiarny's most venomous snake almost always hid between the blades of grass. A mianos snake could grow up to thirteen feet long, and its enormous jaw could open to encompass a person's entire arm.

Oh Source.

Nellie stared at the snake's golden eyes, the venomous creature hissing as its tongue slipped in and out of its mouth. With her hands in the air, eyes never leaving the snake's gaze, she backed away from the tree. She slowly moved, twigs and leaves crunching under her feet as she shuffled backwards. Guardian Clarence's words were playing on repeat in her mind.

"If you ever come across a mianos, never, ever, touch it. You do not want to anger the reptile. Within moments of being bitten by a mianos snake, you will lose all feeling in your body. Once the mianos snake has incapacitated you, it will drag you off to devour you bit by bit."

Ten feet separated her from the mianos.

Then twenty.

Thirty.

The snake never moved. It watched her every movement, a terrifying statue in the forest.

When she could barely see the glimmer of the mianos's golden eyes, she turned and ran as fast as she could. The sun pounded down on her, the shade from the trees not doing much to mitigate the heat of the day. Sweat poured down her body as she moved swiftly. She was careful to lift her feet, not wanting to accidentally fall into a pit of mianos snakes as she ran. Her legs burned as she pushed and pushed, jumping over roots and running around broken logs.

Soon, Nellie came upon a rushing stream running through the forest. Looking around her, she was satisfied there weren't any snakes around. Sighing with relief, Nellie crouched at the edge of the water. There were stones and sand marking where a large river had once flowed through the forest, but the life-giving resource was still present. Multi-coloured rocks filled the stream, the water clear as it ran by. She cupped her hands, drinking her fill of the water. It tasted sweet; the liquid refreshing as it ran down her throat. Filling her hands once more, Nellie let the cool water fall over her face, dampening her hair and wetting the collar of her tunic around her neck.

Refreshed, she got up and continued to race through the forest.

Just a bit further, Nellie. The Queen's Road has to be around here somewhere. Find the Road, follow it home.

Nellie kept her eyes trained on the horizon as she looked ahead, her feet pounding the ground. Too late, she saw a fallen tree directly in her path. She tried to leap over it, but her aim was off. Gasping, she fell, her right ankle twisting at a terrible angle as it fell into the rotting log.

"No." She cried out, yanking on her leg to pull it free. Tears streamed down her face from the effort. "No, no, no. Please. I need to get back to my mother."

Hobbling, Nellie stood up and nearly collapsed. The pain from her foot was excruciating.

This can't be happening. I can't stay here. Who knows what other creatures live in these forests?

Gasping, Nellie clenched her fists as she stood on wobbly legs. Her legs shook, but she managed to stand. Nellie swallowed a cry of pain as she held onto the tree for balance. Glancing around, she saw a long branch lying on the ground nearby. After a series of painful shuffles and hobbles, she finally reached it. Biting her lip to keep from crying out, Nellie pulled herself upright, using the branch as a crutch, and inched her way through the forest.

One foot in front of the other.

The pain soon became unbearable. Groaning, Nellie slumped against the ground, moss providing a comfortable seat, as she pulled off her boot. Her eyes widened as they took in the purple and black bruises that mottled her foot. It was unrecognizable. Her foot swelled even as she rubbed it, tears running down her face as she assessed the damage.

Too late, she heard a branch crack behind her.

"What were you trying to accomplish?"

Chapter Eighteen

Nellie screamed, her back arching in surprise, as a hand fell on her shoulder. She looked up and immediately wished she hadn't. Bronywyn stood above her, her jaw set in a hard line as she stared at Nellie. One of Bronywyn's personal guards was standing a few feet behind her.

"I suppose you didn't hear me, so I'll ask again. What. Were. You. Trying. To. Accomplish?"

Nellie stared at the green-haired warrior; her eyes wide as she tried to form words.

"I-I was going home. I told you, my mother needs me."

"You foolish girl," Bronywyn sneered as she glared at Nellie. "You can't go back. It's not safe." Bronywyn inclined her head towards the guard. "Ulric, come here."

The guard instantly stepped forward, his hands hovering near his sword. Nellie flinched as his gaze landed on her.

"Carry her back with us."

Ulric nodded and picked Nellie up, carefully avoiding her injured foot as he cradled her against his chest. She wasn't small, but he carried her like she was made of air. Nellie struggled to get loose, but his grip on her only tightened as he walked.

"I'm surprised," Bronywyn said almost conversationally as she picked her way through the forest behind the guard. "I didn't think you had it in you to escape. You got further than I thought you would."

"I will get back to Liantis." Nellie swore through gritted teeth. "I need to."

"You keep saying that," Bronywyn said, "but maybe our mutual friend will be able to dissuade you from this train of thought."

With that, Bronywyn stopped talking. Despite herself, Nellie soon shut her eyes as Ulric carried her through the forest. Her ankle was throbbing, and the pain ran like lightning through her entire body. Sleep was a welcome reprieve.

Nellie woke up as her body hit soft grass, the impact jarring her ankle and causing her to cry out. She opened her eyes and moaned. A single tear ran down her cheek as she realized they had brought her back to the same clearing as before. Nellie pulled herself up into a sitting position, her back against a tree, as she looked about. Bronywyn muttered something to Ulric, who nodded before he hurried off into a patch of trees. Nellie watched him warily, her shoulders tensing as he returned a minute later carrying a large pack. It dropped on the grass with a thump as Ulric backed away. Bronywyn approached Nellie warily, hands extended as she held out a drink of some kind.

"Eleanor, drink this."

"What is it?" Nellie asked.

"It will help with the pain. It's part of the emergency healing kit we brought with us."

Grimacing, Nellie sipped the drink. It was cloyingly sweet, but it seemed to numb her lower half almost instantly. She gulped it down quickly, her brows furrowing as the drink slipped down her throat.

"Good. Now, let me see your foot." Bronywyn took the drink from Nellie.

Nellie balked. "What? Why?"

"Why? So that we can treat it. It doesn't look broken, but it is definitely sprained. You're lucky, it could have been a lot worse."

"I don't feel lucky." Nellie wiped her cheeks, her hands coming away damp. The guards both stood at the edge of the clearing, their gaze trained on her. Her shoulders slumped as she realized they wouldn't be letting her out of their sight. "Go ahead, I won't stop you."

Despair filled Nellie's mind as Bronywyn wrapped her ankle in a white bandage. Every movement sent shards of pain running through her leg despite her best to keep still. Tears streamed down Nellie's face as she wept.

This was my one shot to get to my mother, and I lost it.

Nellie cried until she was out of tears. Shuddering, she wiped her eyes as she looked around the clearing. There was a strange purple flower that she had never seen before sitting near her fingertips. Reaching out, Nellie grabbed it and ran it through her fingers. The petals were soft and velvety.

"I don't remember you caring much for flowers when we were younger, Nell-bell."

Nellie jerked, her brows drawing together as Elijah's enormous frame walked towards her from the trees.

Did I hit my head as well as turn my ankle? What is he doing here?

"What? How?" Nellie's eyes looked Elijah over, "Are you real?"

"Yes, I'm real." He crouched down in front of her, glancing at Bronywyn before his gaze returned to Nellie's. "What happened, Nellie?"

"What happened? They have kidnapped me, that's what happened."

A look of concern crossed over Elijah's face as he stood up and marched over to Bronywyn. They whispered furiously; their conversation too quiet for Nellie to hear more than snippets of their words.

"... tripped..." Bronywyn gesticulated furiously.

"How?" Elijah growled, his eyes flashing with some emotion as he looked back at Nellie.

"... ran away... mother..."

"... sight..." Elijah ran his hands through his hair, his shoulders tense as he rubbed the back of his neck. He kept glancing between Nellie and Bronywyn, indecision clear on his face.

".... Doesn't understand the danger." Turning her head to look at Nellie, Bronywyn huffed. "Nellie here is having trouble understanding that we saved her from a possibly terrible fate in the capital."

"Stop it." Nellie said, raising her chin and staring at the two of them. "Stop talking about me like I'm not here. I am a real person and I can hear you. If there's something you'd like to know, Elijah, ask me."

Long beats of silence passed as no one spoke.

"Nothing?" Nellie's jaw clenched. "I have a question for you, Elijah. Why does it look like you're... well acquainted with my kidnapper?"

"Nell-bell..." Elijah whispered in that low, deep voice of his. He crouched down next to her, his large hands fiddling with his tunic.

The sound of her childhood nickname sent a jolt through Nellie. She grimaced, her blood rushing to her face. "Don't you Nell-bell me. Something is wrong here. I can feel it. So spare me the use of my nickname and tell me."

Elijah groaned, running a hand through his hair. His face looked pained as he studied her. "I just..."

Nellie felt the tips of her ears turn red as she glared at her former friend. "Elijah. Why are you here? Where is everyone else? The Protectors, Dion, the other citizens? What is going on?"

"It's a long story," he said.

Huffing, Nellie turned away from Elijah as she crossed her arms. Twisting, she stared at the warrior. The sudden movement sent a flash of pain running through Nellie's ankle. "Tell me exactly what is going on."

The warrior let out a long breath, rubbing her hand over her face before she responded.

"You're right, Eleanor. You deserve the truth." Bronywyn sighed, "We'll try to explain everything as best we can."

"You'd better do more than try." Nellie clenched her fists at her sides, her breath coming quickly as she looked between Elijah and Bronywyn. Any goodwill that had existed between Bronywyn and herself had officially dissipated.

At the warrior's direction, Elijah scooped Nellie up and carried her to another small clearing filled with half a dozen wooden stumps set in a semi-circle. He gently placed her on the stump, clearly taking care not to jostle her injured ankle. The same blue-green grass covered the ground, its long tendrils poking through the bandage on Nellie's foot.

Determined not to show weakness, Nellie simply glared at Elijah. Undeterred, he took the seat next to her and they sat in silence. Even seated, he was so big. Nellie was just shy of six feet tall, but sitting next to Elijah made her look short. His legs stretched out far ahead of him as he sat on the log next to her, mulling over his words.

Huffing, Nellie looked about the clearing. From her vantage point on the log, Nellie could see an empty table made from a fallen log at one end of the clearing, set about two hundred feet away from the stumps.

Eventually, Bronywyn came and took up a seat a few logs away from Nellie.

"Well?" Nellie said curtly, looking between the two others, "let's hear it."

Chapter Nineteen

"Elijah, why don't you start?" Bronywyn murmured as she pulled a dagger from a hidden sheath. "I have a feeling this might come better from you."

"Good idea," Nellie's former friend murmured, "I know this is going to be a lot to take in, but I need you to listen with an open mind. Can you do that for me? Please?"

"I'll try my best, Elijah," she replied, her eyes narrowing. "But I give you no guarantees."

"Thank you. That's all I ask. Do you remember my Sequencing three years ago?"

Nellie nodded. Of course, she remembered. Elijah had been under Guardian Clarence as well, and they had been close friends. After Elijah had been Sequenced and sent to Ion to train as an Engineer, they had given Guardian Clarence a newly turned three-year-old boy named Victor to fill the vacated spot.

"I'm glad you remembered that." The corner of Elijah's lips tilted up ever-so-slightly. "After my Sequencing Ceremony, I left the next day for

Ion. Just like your journey to Deavita, Protectors rode with us and an Official escorted us to Ion. However, unlike your journey, we arrived relatively unscathed and my training began. The Master Engineer I was working under was kind and fair and I learned a lot."

Out of the corner of her eye, Nellie saw Bronywyn cross her arms as a huff came from her lips. Elijah glared at the warrior before he turned back to Nellie.

"For the first few months, everything went as expected. I trained under various Engineers as we worked on a variety of new projects. We were designing plans for new buildings and working alongside the Builders to make them a reality. I really thought the Source had known exactly what I needed when She Sequenced me. For a time, I was happy."

"While I'm thrilled to know that you were happy," Nellie said, her fists clenching and unclenching at her sides, "this still doesn't explain the situation at hand. What is going on? How do you know my kidnappers?"

"Patience, Nellie," Elijah said, running his hands through his hair. "I'm getting there. A few months after my apprenticeship had begun, they sent me to Deavita with my Engineering Master to help design a new building for the Queen. I felt so honoured. When we first arrived in Deavita, everything seemed to go so well. The Master Engineer I was training with lived in a large home and he and his wife invited me to stay with him. They fed me and I slept in a guest bedroom, enjoying the life of a First in Deavita. Everything seemed amazing. But then, I began noticing that some things were off."

"What things?"

"There were people disappearing from the capital." Elijah hung his head, rubbing his temples. "At first, it appeared random. There were whispers of re-Sequencings and of some people going missing, but I hadn't seen any evidence of it. To be honest, I just chalked it up to tales the

Servers shared around their work. Interesting, but likely not based on reality."

The sound of birds chirping filled the clearing as Elijah fell silent, rubbing his hand over his face.

"Nellie," his voice cracked. She watched as tears ran down his cheeks. She felt her heart fracture slightly at the sight. "There was a young Healer that I had met in Ion. Her name was Isadora, and she was amazing."

"Was? What happened to her, Elijah?"

"We had courted in Ion. Isadora was born and raised there, and she took me under her wing when I moved there. She showed me so many things during my first few months in the city. By chance, we were both summoned to Deavita around the same time. The timing couldn't have been better. We were ecstatic, having made plans to marry once my apprenticeship was over. She had even looked for a residence for the two of us in Deavita. We were happy, Nell-bell. That is, until she vanished. One day, Isadora was working in a House of Healing, and the next day when I went to pick her up after her shift, she was gone."

Eyes wide, Nellie gasped. "Gone?"

Elijah's Adam's apple bobbed as he swallowed roughly, his voice thick with emotion. "I asked everyone at the House of Healing and none of the other Healers could tell me what happened to her. No one had seen her at all that day. That made little sense. Isadora loved her work as a Healer. She went to work every day, excited about what was to come. I knew something was wrong. I asked about her all over the capital, and no one knew where she was. No one had seen her and I couldn't find a single person who could tell me what happened to her."

Standing up, Elijah paced the clearing as he rubbed the muscles on the back of his neck. His shoulders were tense and his jaw was pressed in a hard line. Tears slipped down Nellie's face as she watched him. She hadn't forgotten her anger, but she felt it shift and make room for sadness. With each step he took, his footsteps made deep impressions in the blue-green grass. Soon, all the grass in the clearing was flat.

"I searched for Isadora for three months. I looked for her all around Deavita, searching unspeakably horrible places to find her. That's how I met Bronywyn, through some connections I had made while looking for Isadora."

Elijah stopped talking and took a deep breath, his shoulders shaking. His tears darkened his tawny cheeks, dampening his gray tunic.

"Bronywyn," he croaked, "I-I can't. I thought I could, but I can't."

The warrior stood up and hugged Elijah. The intimacy of the act surprised Nellie. Bronywyn turned and took Elijah's place next to Nellie on the log.

"When I met Elijah, and he told me about Isadora, he confirmed our worst fears. We had suspected that Healers were going missing from the Capital for some time, but we lacked solid evidence of this happening."

"We?" Nellie questioned.

"Yes, we. We have gone by many names over the years, but most people know us as the Subversives. Our singular objective is to save the Sequenced and released Tiarny from the stranglehold the Sequencing has placed on its people."

Nellie chewed on her bottom lip, processing the information.

"I'm sorry," Nellie replied, frowning. "This is a lot to take in. This group, the Subversives, you're trying to help save people? And Isadora? What happened to her? Why did you kidnap me? You still haven't answered my question."

Elijah walked over to Nellie's other side and sat down. He put his head in his hands, drawing in a shuddering breath, his voice wavering "S-she didn't make it. We only found out a few weeks ago that the Royal Protectors had taken her all those months ago. She was being held in the dungeon under the Palace. They tortured, starved, and beat her until it was too much for her frail body. She was tiny, my Isadora. Barely five feet tall and thin, with beautiful cat eyes. She had long black hair that fell straight down her back. She was amazing. And they... they killed her. They murdered my love. She died in a place that she should never have been."

On the last word, Elijah's voice broke. The tears that had been running down his cheeks became sobs that wracked through his entire body. Tears blurred Nellie's vision as she mourned for the woman she would never have the chance to meet. Out of the corner of her eye, she saw Bronywyn take a seat on the other side of Elijah and stroke his back, her hand running in small circles as he sobbed.

The three of them sat on the fallen stumps, grieving for Isadora. Nellie wrapped her arms around Elijah, holding her friend as he grieved for his lost love. His grief was palpable, spreading throughout the clearing like clouds on a rainy day. There was a heaviness in the air as Elijah lamented the life that was lost and the future he could have had. As Elijah, Nellie, and Bronywyn lamented, Bronywyn's personal guard stood watch, monitoring the trees beyond the clearing.

After a time, Bronywyn stood up and turned to Elijah.

"I'm so sorry for your loss, brother. All of us are mourning alongside you."

Bronywyn bowed low to Elijah and touched the index and middle fingers of her right hand to her brows. Nellie raised her brows, recognizing the gesture as a sign of respect usually kept for Officials and Elders in the community. Elijah lifted his right fist to his chest in a sign of acknowledgment, his head bowed low. Nellie copied Bronywyn's gesture, dipping her head as the last of her tears ran down her cheeks.

"Thank you." Elijah's eyes had a haunted look about them. "Hopefully we can stop anyone else from suffering a similar fate."

He shifted on the stump and glanced at Nellie. He caught her hand and waited until she looked him in the eye.

"Nell-bell," he said. "When I heard they would be Sequencing a new Healer from Liantis, I knew I had to do something. I didn't know it would be you, but I would never want someone to suffer the same fate as Isadora. There must be a reason that the Royal Protectors are going after Healers. First, they went after Isadora, and now Axel as well? The Subversives barely got him out of the prison in one piece. Something is happening and we need to figure out what is going on. We don't know why the Royal Protectors are going after Healers, but we had to spare you Isadora's fate."

Nellie nodded, but her eyes were blank. She was still trying to process all the information. This was a lot for anyone to take in.

"Okay," she said. "That makes sense." Nellie looked between Elijah and Bronywyn. "Can you tell me where we are? Why are the trees so green?"

Smiling, Bronywyn nodded.

"That, Eleanor, we can do."

Chapter Twenty

"You are at the headquarters of the Subversives." Bronywyn said, gesturing to the land surrounding the group. "The keep, otherwise known as The Haven, is our central hub. There were special magics placed on the land long ago, spells that were cast to keep The Haven concealed from prying eyes. The people responsible imbued the land with their powers, ensuring it would remain lush no matter what happened to the rest of Tiarny."

The Haven.

Nellie was certain she had never heard of such a place before. It definitely didn't appear on the maps of Tiarny she had to memorize when she was a ward.

"When Elijah sent word through our messenger network that a new Healer was being Sequenced in Liantis, we knew we had to save you. Elijah has been working as a man on the inside for the Subversives ever since Isadora disappeared. He spent months making connections among powerful Officials and learned about the upcoming Sequencing."

Nellie's gaze flew to Elijah, her brows furrowed as she listened.

"I know you may disapprove of our methods, Eleanor, but we had to get you out. We know that the Royal Protectors are taking Healers, but we don't know why." Bronywyn said.

Nellie looked sharply between Bronywyn and Elijah.

"What about all the men who died when you rescued me?" She said, visions of blood-soaked ground flashing before her eyes. "I was there. I saw the bloodshed. It was horrifying."

Bronywyn shifted in place, her imposing face stony.

"Each of those men gave their lives to save you. They knew death was a possibility when they left The Haven, but they did it for the greater good. Each one of them died knowing that they were giving their lives for the future of Tiarny. They died heroes."

Nellie was having a hard time understanding all of this. She stared at Bronywyn as her heart began pounding. Sweat poured down the back of her neck as she struggled to breathe.

Seeming to sense the shift in Nellie's demeanor, Elijah shifted closer to Nellie. He gently took Nellie's hand in his, rubbing his thumb over the back of her hand. His hands were so large that his thumb covered half of her entire palm. The warmth and the gentleness of his touch pulled Nellie back to the present, allowing her to breathe her way through the panic.

Elijah's brown eyes were heavy with sorrow as he kept rubbing his thumb in slow circles on her hand.

"As soon as I saw you come out in that black tunic, Nell-bell, I knew I'd do anything to save you," he said. "You're one of my closest friends and I just... I couldn't... I don't want to lose anyone else."

Unlike Bronywyn, Elijah didn't have the luxury of being able to mask his emotions. He wore them all on his face. Devastation was clear on his face as he spoke about the role he had played in her abduction. Fear, sadness and worry all flitted over his expression as he gazed at her. Nellie knew Elijah had good intentions.

That meant something. It did.

Nellie just wasn't sure if it was enough.

As the sun was setting, Bronywyn led the group back into the Haven. For the first time, Nellie was happy she had been unconscious when the Subversives had abducted her. She would not have willingly gone down a hatch into darkness and knowing what she did of the rebels, it sounded like she wouldn't have had much of a choice in the matter. While Nellie might not have approved of their actions, their motivations were clear. They truly believed they saved Nellie from the same fate as Isadora and Axel.

Nellie admitted to herself, their evidence was compelling. She wasn't sure if she believed the Sequenced were as dangerous as Bronywyn and Elijah claimed, but she couldn't deny the truth of what she had seen in Axel's abused body.

Elijah carried Nellie down the stairs back into the keep, eventually bringing her back to the same room she was in before. The next few days passed by relatively peacefully.

Nellie rested in the room, as either Bronywyn or Elijah came and brought her food three times a day. Someone took care of washing Nellie's clothes and they brought water into the room for her so she could freshen up. Bronywyn had even had Solange Wymark, the Haven's resident Healer, come and look at Nellie's ankle. Nellie had sighed in relief when Solange had confirmed that her ankle wasn't broken, but simply sprained.

Solange appeared to be about thirty-five years old. She was an average-height with long, blue hair the colour of the sky that fell in soft waves down her back as she moved, rippling like water. Her skin was a pale white, almost translucent. Her eyes were brown, but she always wore a pair of glasses with thick black rims.

Nellie had never seen glasses before, and their complexity intrigued her. The third day after she had met Solange, she learned the Healer had been working in Deavita, before she escaped in 741 Years after Inception.

"I've been living in the Haven for seven years," Solange had said as she wrapped a fresh bandage around Nellie's ankle. "They took myself and my husband Rafael in after we had to escape Deavita."

When Nellie had asked what caused them to flee the capital, Solange had said she wasn't ready to share. "It's not that I don't want to, Eleanor, but just that... It's too fresh. Maybe one day, I'll be able to tell you."

Elijah brought Nellie a few books to pass the time, and she soon lost herself in the stories he brought her. The desire to leave The Haven was still strong in her mind, but Nellie knew she couldn't go anywhere with an injured ankle. Not for the first time, she cursed her clumsiness.

By the fifth day, Nellie was getting restless. Her ankle felt well enough that she hobbled around the room on it, using a crutch that Solange had brought with her the day before. Deciding that she had had enough of staying in the room, Nellie creaked open the door and looked out. She let out a sigh of relief as she realized the hallway was empty. Grabbing her crutch, Nellie shuffled out down the corridor. The intricacies of the keep never ceased to amaze her, and she looked around at the building that she now knew was completely underground.

Her hand on the walls, Nellie followed the twisting corridor. She heard the muffled sounds of conversation coming from ahead of her and she quickly shuffled the opposite way. For a time, the only sound filling the hallways was that of her crutch on the floor as she moved along at the speed of a turtle.

They had built The Haven like a maze, and soon Nellie's eyes widened as she looked around her. She rubbed her temples, trying to remember where she came from.

Perhaps leaving my room unattended wasn't the best idea I've ever had.

Turning around, Nellie attempted to retrace her steps.

I definitely turned left here... or was it right? Groaning, she slumped down against the wall as she massaged her injured foot and tried to mentally retrace her steps. The sound of footsteps and conversation filled the hallway, and it grew louder by the second. Nellie struggled to push herself back up, urging her feet to move faster. She had just begun to walk back down the hall when she ran into a large chest. Her eyes flicked up, and she stifled a groan as she looked into Elijah's brown eyes.

"Going for a walk, Nell-bell?" The corners of his lips turned up as he looked down at her.

"Of course," Nellie said as primly as she could. "You know what they say. Exercise is important, and all that." She waved a hand dismissively, and Elijah laughed.

"Well, I'm glad I ran into you- literally. I was just about to come ask you if you wanted to join Bronywyn and I for lunch, since Solange has given her all-clear for you to be out and about. But I suppose you already figured that out, didn't you?"

Nellie considered his offer for a moment before nodding. Smiling, Elijah offered her his arm. Together, they walked down a few more hallways before they came to what Elijah called a meeting room. Nellie had long since given up hope of trying to find her own way back to her room and was grateful that he had found her.

The first thing that hit Nellie was the aroma of delicious food. Her stomach grumbled as she walked into the room.

"Hungry?" Elijah grinned. "There's lots here. Bronywyn had them bring enough food to feed an army."

"I'd say," Nellie muttered under her breath. Her eyes took in the platters of bread and butter, bowls filled with spiced beans and quinoa, along with a large jug filled with a strange tea.

Elijah pulled out a chair for Nellie, gesturing for her to sit. Once she had gotten settled, Bronywyn walked in, followed by her pair of guards. They stood with their backs against the wall, calmly observing everything.

"What are you waiting for?" Bronywyn said, "let's eat."

Nellie eyed Bronywyn out of the corner of her eye. The green-haired warrior seemed much more at ease than she had the last few times Nellie had seen her. Elijah poured a cup of what he called *kalif* for Nellie. She lifted it to her lips and sipped. Instantly, she choked at the intense flavour that filled her mouth. Her eyes watered as she tried to keep the liquid down.

"What-what is this?"

Laughing, Elijah took a swig of his own cup before replying, "this is kalif. It's made by steeping the root of a purple flower that bears the same name. You might have noticed it in the clearing?"

Frowning, Nellie pushed the cup away. The cup scraped across the table; the sound making her flinch. She picked up a piece of flatbread covered in a strange jelly. Swallowing, she reached for a glass of water. "I think I'll stick with this, thank you. Kalif definitely seems like it's an... acquired taste. You know what I do like, though? This jelly." She smacked her lips. "It's spicy and sweet at the same time. What is *this*?"

She looked at Elijah for answers, but it was Bronywyn who replied.

"This, Eleanor, is *lonama* jelly. It's a fruit that grows on the other side of the Forest of Resim. The berry is bright red with dark blue seeds and when cooked, it develops the flavours you're tasting. Not only are the berries delicious, but their leaves have medicinal qualities."

"Interesting," Nellie mumbled as she stuffed more flatbread loaded with lonama jelly in her mouth.

"Lonama plants are extremely rare," the warrior said, "so we pick the entire plant whenever we find them."

Nellie was so enamoured with the exquisite flavour that it took her a moment to process everything she heard. She hadn't tasted food this good since... she didn't even know when. After the rains stopped coming, eating became more of a chore and less of something done to delight in flavours. She used to love food, but over the past few years, she had eaten simply to survive.

Nellie's brows furrowed as she replayed Bronywyn's words in her mind. "Hold up. Did you say the other side of the Forest of Resim? That's not possible. Everyone knows the forest stretches on forever."

Elijah shook his head, his eyes tinged with sadness. He put down his cup of kalif before drawing in a long breath.

"No, Nellie. It isn't. They lied to us. They taught us that Tiarny is the only country left on this planet, that the Source saved us and only us. But it's not true. This is just another one of the many lies that the Sequenced told us. For a long time, I believed the same thing."

Nellie stared at Elijah, her jaw hanging open.

"I know it's a lot to take in, but it's true. I've seen the land beyond the Forest with my own two eyes. The Sequenced aren't what they seem. They're liars and murderers."

Nellie pulled away from Elijah, her chair creaking as she slid it backwards on the floor. Her hands gripped the armrests. Expectant silence filled the room as all the occupants turned their gaze to Nellie. She could feel blood rushing to her face as she tried to ground herself.

Inhale.

Exhale.

Repeat.

Rubbing her temples, Nellie lifted her gaze to Elijah's.

"If the Sequenced and all they believe in are so bad, Elijah, why are you still working with them? I was there on the Queen's Road. I know you were friendly with Dion, a Sequenced Official. Explain that to me."

At the mention of Dion, Elijah's expression fell. His face contorted, and he looked as though he was going to say something before Bronywyn stopped him with a glare that spoke volumes.

"Not yet, Elijah." Her voice was strong and business-like, all features of lightheartedness firmly wiped away. Her warrior-mask was firmly back in place.

Not yet? Not yet what? Why is there always something else I am not privy to?

"No, Bronywyn." Elijah stood up, looming over Nellie and Bronywyn. Nellie instinctively shrunk back as Elijah gritted his teeth. His words echoed through the room. "I have deferred to your judgment so many times in the past week. We abducted Nellie, we held her here without adequate explanation, and now you want me to lie to her again? That's the line. I'm drawing it in the sand."

He clenched his fists at his side as he looked at Bronywyn. "I will not do it. She deserves to know the truth."

"Elijah," Bronywyn cautioned, holding her hand up as she slowly inched her chair back. "We need to be careful."

"We've been careful, Bronywyn," he said sharply. "The rest of the convoy has already made it to Deavita. Word came in yesterday. You know this. We have no reason to hide it anymore."

The rest? Does that mean everyone survived the attack?

Nellie watched from her seat as tension filled the room. Bronywyn and Elijah stared at each other, unmoving. Bronywyn's guards simply watched the altercation from a distance, seeming to wait for a signal from their leader.

"Elijah," Nellie whispered. "What are you doing?"

"Nellie," he stooped down and whispered in her ear. His voice was deep and despite the tension in the room, Nellie felt shivers running down her back.

"I need to show you something. Please don't fight me on this. You need to see this."

Sighing, Nellie rubbed the back of her neck as she stared at the man she had once called friend. She contemplated his words for a moment before nodding.

"I'll go with you, but this is *my* decision."

"Fine," Bronywyn sighed. She nodded at her guards, who opened the door and stepped aside.

"This was your idea, Elijah. Lead the way."

Nellie followed Elijah down a hallway and through a dark passageway. Between his arm and her crutch, she was walking almost normally. Nellie could hear insects skittering on the ground and she saw spiderwebs hanging between the sconces on the wall. She instinctively moved closer to Elijah as they walked.

For someone who had insisted on this descent into darkness, Nellie thought Elijah was being oddly quiet. He seemed to be stuck in his own thoughts, his breathing the only sound coming from his direction. He had barely uttered two words since they left the meeting room.

The more they walked, the fewer doors they saw. Finally, they turned down a corridor with a singular door at the end of the passageway. Bronywyn marched right past them, moving with the confidence of someone who had taken this path many times before.

"Come on Eleanor," she said. "You made it this far, you might as well keep going."

Nellie followed Bronywyn, her grip tightening on Elijah's arm as darkness engulfed them. The only light came from a taper that was resting beside the door. Once again, the darkness sucked away all sense of time.

This is the most disconcerting feeling I've ever had. Who would have thought I'd be missing the hourly tolling of the bells in Liantis? Certainly not me.

Life in Tiarny was dictated by time. Wards needed to be at the warding centre by seven bells so their parents could get to their Sequenced positions on time. They ate lunch promptly at twelve bells. Parents collected their wards at the eighteenth bell and took them straight home.

It had been less than a fortnight since Nellie had last heard the tolling of the bells, but after having lived her entire life as a slave to time, she pined after the stability they had offered the citizens of Liantis.

The tunnels seemed to go on forever, and the lack of light made it easy to get lost in thought. Bronywyn's candle continued to flicker at the head of the group, casting eerily long shadows on the wall.

Just when Nellie thought she might not be able to take another step into the unending darkness, Bronywyn came to an abrupt stop in front of an unmarked door. There was a white-haired guard standing in front of the door, his back straight as he looked silently at the group. He was the same height as Nellie, but he gave off an imposing aura. The guard's gaze was sharp as he looked between Bronywyn and the rest of the group.

"Rafael," she said firmly. "We're here to see you-know-who."

The guard nodded, his hand on his sword as he pulled a key out of his pocket and gave it to Bronywyn.

"Here we are," the warrior said. Her eyes were sharp as she looked directly at Nellie. The flickering candlelight cast strange shadows on the woman's face. "No more lies. No more secrets."

Bronywyn turned on her heel, placing the large iron key in the lock. It groaned, then clicked as the door swung inwards.

"After you," Bronywyn said, extending her arm for Nellie to enter first.

Nellie shook her head and crossed her arms.

"No way am I going in there without you going first. How do I know it's not a trap?"

"Fine," Bronywyn huffed and stepped into the room. Spreading her arms wide, she spun around and looked at the group. "See? No traps. Come on in."

Nellie warily followed Bronywyn into the room, limping as she moved. It was small and dark, even compared to the hallway. She squinted, trying to see into the darkness. There was a figure sitting on a cot, staring directly at her. Nellie's mind went blank as she struggled to understand what she was looking at.

She turned, glaring accusingly at Elijah and Bronywyn before returning her gaze to the person before her.

"You?" Nellie's brows furrowed as she looked straight ahead. "What are *you* doing here?"

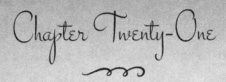

Chapter Twenty-One

S tanding in a tiny room in the middle of an underground building, Nellie stared at Dion. She didn't move as Bronywyn lit a few candles around the room, the space incrementally brighter then it had been a moment before.

Dion was here.

The Official who had haunted her dreams every night since her Sequencing. As Nellie had followed Bronywyn through the dark keep, she had wondered what could be so important that Elijah needed to show her. Dozens of thoughts had flown through her mind, but she never imagined they were leading her to Dion.

Of the five Officials who had presided over her Sequencing ceremony, Dion was the one that she couldn't seem to shake. Nellie saw his long robes and hooded face in her sleep, haunting her as the word "trouble" repeated over and over again in her mind.

There was something about his voice, the power in the way he spoke, the irritating way he said her name, that tormented her. She couldn't seem to escape him.

And now, here he was, in front of her.

Here.

In The Haven.

Apparently, *a prisoner?*

Nellie had grown accustomed to seeing Dion without his hood or long robes when they were riding atop the accursed horse together. Their two days together had been filled with painful muscles and mostly one-sided sarcastic comments.

She had become accustomed to the dark, piercing glare of his eyes. There was a strength and power that surrounded the infuriating man's every movement.

That was the Dion she had known.

The man standing in front of her was not the same one she had watched fighting the rebels. This new Dion was in a vulnerable state, looking more broken than he ever had before. The very air that surrounded him was dank with the scent of sweat and unwashed bodies, as though he hadn't left the room in several days.

Here, in the underground Haven, surrounded by rebels, Dion had definitely seen better days.

His long, silver tunic marking him as an Official was filthy. The color was barely visible, a thick layer of dust and grime covered it. The tunic itself was torn in several places, exposing the mahogany skin of his stomach. He still wore his black boots, but his dark blue, almost black pants had a hole in the thigh the size of Nellie's hand. Dirt covered the Official from head to toe.

As Nellie's gaze shifted upwards, she gasped, her hand flying over her mouth.

Dion's once elegant, unmarred face was now sporting a long, jagged cut that ran the length from above his left ear down his cheek, ending an inch from his chin. Nellie felt relieved to see that his beautiful obsidian eyes were untouched by the long, thin laceration.

Nellie took a step closer, her eyes glued to Dion's face. The wound itself still looked relatively fresh. It stood out from his face; the pinkness jarring against his mahogany skin. Nellie knew all about the danger of infections from her own experience with injuries. She felt relieved to see that the cut appeared to be healing. There weren't any visible signs of infection as she visually inspected the wound.

"Hello, Eleanor." Dion's once powerful voice came out in a hoarse whisper. For all the times he had said her name mockingly, it didn't seem to carry the same register of hatred right now as it usually did.

"Hi," she replied.

Hi? Nellie thought, her cheeks turning pink as her eyes never left Dion's face. *What's wrong with you, Nellie.*

Something was wrong. Something had changed.

Nellie was unsure what to make of this new, somewhat broken man standing in front of her. The terrifying Official from her Sequencing Ceremony was gone. The man standing in front of her looked fragmented, as though part of him was missing. Sadness, and something else, filled his eyes.

She barely registered the fact that her feet were moving until she stood directly in front of him. Her fingers rose and gently brushed the side of his wound. His cheek felt smooth, the laceration warm under her touch. As she ran her fingers down Dion's cheek, Nellie heard him inhale sharply, but he didn't pull away. Her gaze travelled upwards to his black eyes, his gaze piercing as he looked back at her. Time seemed to slow as they stared at each other, each one searching for something in the other's face. After a time, Nellie realized what she was doing.

What has come over me? This man tormented me for days and now I'm touching his face? Get a hold of yourself.

Shaking her head, Nellie pulled back her hand before turning towards Elijah and Bronywyn. Her green eyes were alight with flame as she spoke to them, her voice tight with anger.

"I need an explanation *right now,*" she said, her voice low as she glared at the two rebels. Her nostrils flared as she clenched her fists at her side. "What is happening? You said you were doing good things. How is this good? What happened to him?"

Nellie nodded towards Dion as she put her hands on her hips. Her blood rushed to her face, tinging the tips of her ears as she stared at Dion.

"How can you explain this? Jacinta said I wasn't a prisoner, but it certainly looks like you're holding him against his will. He needs medical attention! This wound could get infected. On top of that, he's an Official! Don't you think people will look for him? It has been what, more than a week? Has he been down here the whole time?"

Nellie's chest rose and fell rapidly as she stared at Dion, her ankle beginning to throb as she stood.

"Eleanor," Bronywyn said, taking a half-step towards her before seeming to think better of it, "take a breath. Calm down."

"Calm down?" Nellie repeated as she gesticulated. "Calm. Down. That's the opposite of what I'm going to do."

She rubbed her temples as she stood, her jaw set in a firm line as her face reddened. She could feel herself on the verge of another panic attack when, suddenly, Elijah came up behind her and laid a hand on her shoulder. She looked back, her head tilting as she glared at her former-friend.

"Nell-bell," he whispered, his eyes pleading with hers as he gestured to a set of wooden chairs tucked in the back corner of the room. "Please, sit down. You need to take care of yourself."

She collapsed on the proffered seating, elevating her injured ankle, and laid her head in her hands. Inhaling deeply, Nellie shut her eyes.

Concentrate. You can do this. Just focus on your breathing.

After a few minutes of meditative breathing, she felt her thoughts slipping into order. Once she felt as though her breathing was under control, she lifted her head and stared at her former friend.

"You," Nellie seethed. "You *knew* Dion was being held captive."

She hadn't asked a question, but he answered regardless.

"Yes. I knew." Elijah sighed, grimacing as he rubbed the back of his neck. "May I?" He gestured to the chair next to Nellie. She nodded, and he sat beside her, his backside barely making contact with the seat as he sat on the edge. "This wasn't the plan. We never planned to kidnap Dion..."

"But you planned to abduct me." Nellie interjected as she shot him a dirty look.

Elijah winced, having the decency to look ashamed. "Yes. We needed to get you away from the Sequenced. Going to the capital could have meant a death sentence for you. Just look at what happened to Isadora."

"So you've said." Her tone was harsh, her eyes blazing as she held Elijah's gaze. Her anger overshadowed the grief she felt for her friend's loss. "But how does *that* explain *this?*"

Nellie gestured towards Dion, who now sat on the edge of the bed. The mattress looked identical to the one Nellie had woken up on her first morning in The Haven. Dion sat hunched on the bed, his hands resting on his knees as he looked at Nellie, his expression stark. The candlelight kept flickering over the room, casting the Official's face in shadows and making the laceration on his face seem even more pronounced. His black eyes bored into hers. It was as though he was staring straight into Nellie's soul. Despite the distance separating them, she shivered under the weight of Dion's gaze.

If Nellie was honest with herself, the fact that he seemed to get past all of her defences and stare straight into her soul was disarming. Nellie had never met anyone like Dion. As she studied the deep laceration on his face, her eyes filled with tears.

The silence in the room was growing with every passing second. Minutes went by, Elijah and Bronywyn whispering in the corner while Nellie stared at them. The silence was growing oppressive and Nellie felt a heavy weight settle on her as they ignored her.

"Excuse me?" Nellie waved her hand. "Does anyone want to explain to me why Dion is here?"

"Eleanor," Dion spoke up from the cot. "I asked the same questions. Bronywyn and I have had many... heart-to-hearts over the past week."

Bronywyn nodded; her arms crossed as he watched Nellie.

"Do you remember when I gave you my dagger?" Dion asked.

"Of course, I remember." Nellie snapped. "That would be hard to forget as it happened right before they kidnapped me."

Dion snorted. "Always so spunky, Eleanor," he pronounced her name in that irritating tone of his. "Yes, that's right. As you know, I was fighting alongside the Protectors. Things seemed to go our way in the battle as most of the rebels had been taken care of or they had fled on foot."

"Killed, you mean." Nellie interjected, her eyes narrowing. "They weren't *taken care of.* The Protectors killed them. Those men lost their lives. It doesn't matter who they were. I watched as their blood seeped into the ground. They died that day."

"That's true," Dion avoided her gaze, looking at the floor. "I'm sorry for it. I have never enjoyed fighting, but sometimes it is a necessity in life. They were attacking us, Eleanor."

Nellie sighed as her stomach twisted in knots. The entire situation was infuriating, and it seemed like she was the only one who really felt the weight of the rebels' deaths.

Dion crouched down in front of Nellie, taking her hand in his. His hands were so much larger than hers, the callouses she had noticed earlier feeling rough against her skin.

"I'm sorry, Eleanor," he said, maintaining his crouched position. "I know they were husbands, fathers and sons. It brought me no joy to play a part in their deaths. Nonetheless, I did. I will carry the weight of every life that ends on my sword for the rest of my life."

Dion sighed, rubbing his free hand through his silky brown hair. The rest of the occupants of the room watched on in silence, listening to what he had to say.

"As the fighting was dying down," Dion continued, "I left the fighting to the Protectors to find you. However, when I got to the tree, I couldn't find you anywhere. I saw the dagger lying on the ground. I just knew you wouldn't leave it on purpose. In my panic, I searched the entire camp. All the other citizens and Protectors were accounted for, except for you and Elijah. We suffered no losses in the attack. The longer I searched, the more I was afraid for your well-being. Fear overcame me as I dreaded that the worst had happened."

Dion stroked Nellie's hand, his thumb running circles over the skin of her palm. His eyes had a haunted look as he looked at Nellie. "Visions flooded my mind. I saw you on your back, blood seeping out of you as you lay glossy eyed. I imagined someone dragging you off and assaulting you. The thought of coming across your mutilated body was ripe in my mind. I had to find you. The Source Herself charged me to look after you and I failed."

"I didn't think... I didn't think about what you must have thought when you found the dagger on the ground." Her chest constricted as her eyes swam with tears.

Oh, Source. What did all the people in Liantis think of the situation? What had Fay and her mother been told? Did someone tell them she was missing?

"My mother." Nellie choked out, her face paling. "Does she know? What must she think?"

"We don't know what the Sequenced are saying yet, Eleanor,"

Bronywyn said, "but we have spies who are looking for information. Rest assured, as soon as we know, we will tell you."

Nellie's lips trembled as she thought of her mother. "I need to get back to her. You don't understand. She needs me. If she thinks I'm hurt, it might break her. I'm the only thing she has."

Grimacing, Nellie pressed her hands to her cheeks, breathing in deeply.

"What happened next?" She asked. "What happened to your face?"

"When it became clear that you weren't in the camp, I picked up your trail fairly quickly and followed it at a distance. Your kidnappers moved quickly, but they didn't cover their tracks well. More and more rebels joined the one who had grabbed you. I stayed back, watching from behind a large oak tree. Things took a turn for the worse when they stopped in front of a strange tree-"

Bronywyn shifted from her post and began pacing the room.

"I think, Dion," Bronywyn said, her voice sharp, "that it may be best if I continue the tale from here. You see Eleanor, what the *Sequenced Official* came across was the use of one of our sacred portals. He was absolutely not supposed to see that."

Bronywyn glared at Elijah, her eyes steely as she stared at him. "This is your fault, you know. If you had paid more attention, we wouldn't be in this situation."

"Excuse me?" Nellie exclaimed. "What in the Source's holy name is a portal?"

Waving a hand in the air, Bronywyn ignored Nellie as she continued to berate the tall man. "If you had just looked around, Elijah, then maybe..."

"Am I invisible? Did I suddenly disappear from this room? What is a portal?" Nellie's voice was rising, her face turning red as she was once again ignored.

"Nellie," Elijah said, rubbing his hand on the back of his neck, "be calm."

"Calm. Calm. *Calm.*" Nellie laughed maniacally before she clenched her fists together tightly. "He uses words like *portal* and then tells me to be calm. I'll show you calm!"

She had really lost all pretence of composure by this point. She stood up, grabbing her crutch and, before she knew what she was doing, she stood directly in front of Elijah. Her ankle screamed in pain, but she ignored it as she looked at him. With her face no more than two inches away from his, she raised her index finger and pointed it at his face.

"I was *calm* when I was Sequenced. *Calm* when I was travelling. Source-knows, I was even *calm* when Jacinta and Bronywyn 'introduced' themselves to me. But now? Now I am not *calm.*" Her voice thundered throughout the room. Even Bronywyn seemed taken aback by Nellie's temper. "Tell me what a portal is or consider our friendship irrecoverably over. Forever. There will be nothing you can do to restore it."

Sighing, Elijah lifted both hands in supplication. "Okay."

"Okay?"

Elijah nodded. "Will you just please sit down? Your ankle must be throbbing."

Nodding, Nellie backed up and sat back in the seat, a moan escaping her as the pressure was taken off her foot. She glared at Elijah, willing him to continue.

"There used to be many portals all across the land," her soon-to-be former friend said, "but over the years they've disappeared along with the Subversive's ability to wield them properly."

Wield. Why does that word sound so familiar?

Nellie racked her brain for a moment before she suddenly remembered. Her hand went to her chest, some tension leaving her shoulders as she felt the bump of her pendant. She still hadn't taken it off once since her mother gave it to her the morning of her Sequencing.

"Wielders?" Nellie whispered.

She hadn't realized that she had spoken out loud until everyone stopped in the room. Silence covered the room like a thick blanket, choking out every sound except for everyone's breathing. Everyone stared straight at her.

Bronywyn's mouth gaped like a dying fish as she stared at Nellie.

Finally, the dark-green-haired warrior seemed to regain control of her body and whispered, not removing her eyes from Nellie's for even an instant. "What did you say?"

"I... um.... Wielders?" Nellie said, suddenly nervous. She twisted a lock of hair in her fingers as she looked around the room. Five pairs of eyes bored into her and she slouched backwards, wishing she could disappear.

"Where did you," Bronywyn said, moving to stand directly in front of Nellie, "a *Sequenced member of Tiarny*, a *First*, hear of the Wielders?"

Gulping, Nellie looked around the room, seeking an ally in what had suddenly become a room of wolves, all circling around the lamb looking for their next dinner.

Bronywyn was staring at her, the warrior's facial features sharp and dangerous. Her personal guards had shifted their stances. They stood shoulders and feet apart, their hands resting on the hilts of their swords as they stared at Nellie. Dion subtly shifted in front of Nellie, his body between her and the guards. Elijah stood against the wall, his hands tapping against his side the only sign he had heard her.

Sweat beaded on Nellie's forehead as she took a deep breath.

"The-the morning before my Sequencing took place, my mother told me a story about Wielders." She rubbed her temples, whispering. "It was just a story. I didn't believe her, I just thought it was something she had made up."

Bronywyn stepped forward and pulled Nellie to her feet, forcing Dion to step back from his crouched position, before speaking in a commanding voice. Nellie cried out, the sudden movement jarring her ankle.

"Not only is it not *just* a story that your mother made up," the warrior said, "but the Wielders are also *the* story. They are an integral part of the history of The Haven. It is their magic that holds this place together. That your mother, a Sequenced citizen, knows anything about the Wielders is extremely unusual and something we will have to delve deeper into. I need to know exactly what she told you."

Great. Yet another thing that I have *to do. Free will isn't much of a thing here in The Haven, is it?*

Nellie pulled Bronywyn's arm off her, looking at the woman in the eye. She stared, despite her desire to cower in the corner.

I need to regain some control. Somehow, I need to use this to my advantage.

"You want to know what my mother said?"

Bronywyn nodded, her jaw clenched so tightly Nellie thought she could hear teeth cracking.

"I'll tell you. Tomorrow. I need to go back to my room. My ankle is screaming and I have to rest."

She looked at Bronywyn and grabbed her crutch, which had fallen on the floor beside her. "Please, take me back to my room. Tomorrow, we can finish this."

Chapter Twenty-Two

T he next day, after a good night's sleep and a chance to clean her hair, Nellie found herself back in the same room. As soon as they had entered Dion's cell, she sat back down. She had come up with a plan last night and she was eager to see if it would help.

Remember, I have some leverage.

Bronywyn took up the same position as the day before, her back rigid against the wall as she crossed her arms and glowered at Nellie.

You can do this.

Inhaling deeply, Nellie broke the silence. "You want me to tell you what my mother said, Bronywyn? Why exactly should I tell you? You haven't exactly earned my trust."

The green-haired warrior pushed herself off the wall, coming to stand right in front of Nellie. "Look who grew a back-bone overnight. What are you going to do, Eleanor? You can't run from us again; your ankle is still in terrible shape."

Nellie had expected this. "You're right. I'm not going anywhere, at least until my ankle is fully healed. But Jacinta said that I should be treated as a guest, and I'm pretty sure threatening me *isn't* what she had in mind."

Dion laughed from his position on the bed, his gaze never leaving Nellie's. "I'm glad to see your fighting spirit is still alive, Eleanor."

Turning on her feet, Bronywyn glared at Dion. "Quiet, Official. This doesn't concern you right now."

"Actually," Nellie interjected, "it does. If you want me to tell you what my mother said to me, you're going to agree to move Dion out of this cell and into a *proper* room. If you don't, you will never know what I know."

Wide-eyed, Bronywyn stared at Nellie. "I didn't think you had it in you, Healer." She sighed. "Fine. Once we are done here, and I am satisfied you have told us everything, I'll ensure we make Dion more comfortable. Do we have a deal?"

"We do."

Satisfied, Nellie sat back and explained everything her mother had told her. Word for word, she shared the story of the Wielders, but she didn't tell them about the pendant. Somehow, it felt right to keep it a secret. It was hers and hers alone.

Once she had repeated the tale three times, Bronywyn seemed mollified.

Now, Nellie sat back in the wooden chair, her leg elevated as Elijah paced back and forth, his legs making quick work of the room. He could only go about five paces in either direction before he hit the wall and had to turn around. The candles were burning lower as time wore on and Nellie watched as the shadows followed Elijah. Nellie felt herself growing anxious just watching him pace.

"Elijah," she said, rubbing her temples, "what happened with the portal? Why is Dion here?"

Clearing his throat, Elijah unfolded his hands and rubbed them down the front of his tunic. He shifted on his feet, fidgeting for a few more moments before turning towards Nellie.

"Well," Elijah said, "as you know, I was travelling with the convoy from Liantis."

"Yes, Elijah." Nellie sighed. "I remember. We've been over this. You came with us to Liantis, travelled with us on route to Deavita, hid your true loyalties, betrayed us, and you got me kidnapped. Again, it's pretty hard to forget that awful moment of broken trust."

Elijah had the decency to look ashamed for his role in her kidnapping. He ran his hand through his hair before continuing to speak.

"Yes, well, I know. I'm sorry for the role I played, but we needed to keep you safe."

"Elijah." Bronywyn growled, grinding each syllable out between her teeth. Evidently, she was just as eager as Nellie to finish the tale and move onto alternative topics of discussion.

"Sorry, Bronywyn. I'll try to remain on point. Now, where was I?" Elijah mumbled to himself before continuing. "After the attack, the plan was always for me to leave the convoy and join the Subversives at our pre-arranged meeting point. We had always planned for me to get out of the Sequenced society once we had rescued the new Healer from Liantis. We didn't know it would be you, but after... after we got the news that Isadora had died, we knew the dangers were too high for me to remain."

Elijah closed his eyes and drew in a shuddering breath. He wiped away a tear before he spoke once more.

"I watched as Adrian took you through the portal. Just as I was about to go through it myself, Dion saw me and came barrelling through the trees."

Before Elijah could continue speaking, Dion jumped in and interrupted him. A vein popped out of the Official's neck as he spoke, his jaw clenched.

"Obviously, I didn't know that Elijah was working with the rebels, Eleanor, or I would never have approached him. I saw him from a distance and I thought he was in trouble. Worried as I was for his well-being, I rushed after him towards what I now know was a portal."

Bronywyn interjected, her eyes flashing. "A portal whose very existence *you* had no business knowing about," she said.

"Bronywyn. Dion." Elijah looked at both of them, holding up his hands in a sign of supplication. "Please. This is an argument for another time. The point is, Dion followed me and rushed into the path of the portal. The thing that you need to know about portals, Nellie, is that once you get too close, you can't stop them. They are essentially doors that open for a limited amount of time, regardless of who is around. This is the reason that they are so rarely used. I had been watching to ensure that Adrian had safely carried you through the portal when I heard a noise come from behind me. I saw Dion come rushing at me out of the corner of my eye, but I couldn't stop moving because I was too close to the portal's perimeter. As soon as his body hit mine, it pushed both of us through the portal and we ended up outside The Haven."

Nellie looked at everyone in the room, their faces reflecting the truth in Elijah's words. She stood up and rolled her shoulders. Grabbing her crutch, she hobbled over to Dion and gently touched his cheek before sighing.

"And his face, Elijah?" Nellie asked. "Did he somehow get this laceration by falling through the portal with you? You have ten seconds to explain how he got such a wicked cut on his face."

Bronywyn exhaled and rubbed her hand over her face before speaking.

"That, unfortunately, is my fault. When Dion fell through the portal, I recognized him instantly as a Sequenced Official. I was waiting on the other side of the portal for you to arrive. You understand, Eleanor, that we are a secret organization? It is imperative that The Haven remains a secret while we work to dismantle the Sequencing. We cannot have random Sequenced members of society running around."

Bronywyn glared at Dion, her face steely, before she continued.

"When people take a portal, it almost always renders them unconscious for a few moments. We believe that this is due to the effects of travelling a great geographical distance in a short period. Dion came through the portal unconscious, and I had planned on... dealing with him when he woke up faster than expected. I was going to end things quickly when he shifted. My dagger missed his neck and instead slid up his face. For a man who had recently been unconscious, he moved quickly. Fortunately, there were enough Subversives around who helped me subdue Dion before things... escalated further."

Before things escalated?

Nellie would consider a slash down the face to mean the situation had already escalated, but seeing as how Bronywyn just admitted to trying to kill Dion, Nellie could see how a laceration on his face seemed like minor damage to the fierce warrior.

Dion walked over from his position on the bed and sat next to Nellie. He shifted; their thighs lined up with each other. Startled at the sudden contact, Nellie's breath caught.

"Eleanor," Dion said. His voice was low, a trace of unexpected tenderness present in his tone. Nellie almost missed the snarky attitude Dion had during the ride. At least then she had known what to expect from him. "It really isn't their fault. Honestly, I probably would have tried to kill myself too if I had been in their shoes." He paused, a smirk dancing on his lips. "It's not like they succeeded, anyway."

"Is that it?" Nellie looked around. "You forgive them, Dion?"

He looked shocked, pulling back. "Well, no, but I understand. One warrior to another, I understand why Bronywyn did what she thought she had to do. Besides, after the plethora of... meetings they have subjected me to since I've arrived, I'm pretty sure Bronywyn is confident I'm not a threat to her. Isn't that right?"

The green-haired warrior nodded briefly. "We are confident that Dion is not an immediate risk to The Haven."

Dion put a hand to his heart and chuckled. "You flatter me, Bronywyn. You tried to kill me a week ago and now you're saying I'm not an immediate risk. Be careful, or I might think you like me."

Bronywyn huffed, but Nellie could have sworn she saw a tiny smile dancing on the warrior's lips. "I think we're done here, Eleanor. I'll have Elijah take you back to your room."

Nellie nodded, her gaze swinging to Elijah. Instead of helping her to her feet, Elijah scooped her up and swung her around. He carried her back to her room, her feet knocking against his arms as he moved. His chest was warm and Nellie felt safe for the first time in over a week. Elijah placed her on her bed and walked over to the door. Before he left, he turned and looked at Nellie. His eyes were heavy as he stared at her.

"Nell-bell. I hope... I hope you can forgive me."

Sighing, Nellie ran her fingers through her hair, mulling over her next words.

"Forgiveness requires a foundation of trust and time. For now, I accept you acted in a way that you thought was protecting me. And while I may not fully appreciate that, I understand why you did that."

"I'll take it," Elijah smiled softly before turning the knob. "I will build that foundation of trust. It's a promise."

Part Three

Chapter Twenty-Three

The next morning, Nellie woke up in her soft bed as the clanging sounds of the morning chimes rang through her room. Huffing, she grabbed her pillow and held it over her head, refusing the give in to their musical demands. She had just drifted back into a fitful sleep when a knock came from her door.

"Who is it?" She replied blearily, blinking as she removed her head from the safety of her pillow.

"It's me, Nell-bell." Elijah was standing on the other side of the door, his face barely visible through the tiny crack as he held it open. "I was wondering if you wanted to come for breakfast?"

Nellie groaned and pushed the pillow over her head. "No offense, Elijah, but I need a few days to myself. The past week has been a nightmare and I need to think. Please, leave me be."

A sigh came from the hallway before the sound of the door clicking shut echoed throughout the room. She closed her eyes, but the sound of retreating footsteps never came.

"I'll bring you some food, Nell-bell." Elijah sighed, his voice rough with emotion. "I just... I'm sorry. I'll ask Solange to come see you and leave you alone."

True to his word, Elijah stayed away from Nellie. He brought her food and water three times a day, leaving it outside the room on a tray. On the second day, Nellie had been sitting in an armchair and watched him as he lay the tray outside her door. His eyes had glistened, but he didn't say anything. Nellie had watched him walk away, his back hunched. His footsteps had echoed through the halls long after he had disappeared from sight.

Solange came twice daily to check on her, the Healer excitedly telling Nellie that her foot was healing quickly and she would soon be able to walk without the crutch. Bronywyn even came to check on Nellie once a day, claiming she was "just keeping an eye on things."

On the third day, Nellie worked up the courage to ask Bronywyn about Dion. "He's fine," Bronywyn replied, waving her hand through the air as she turned to leave Nellie's room. "As you requested, we had him moved to more comfortable accommodations. Solange has been looking after him and Mother is convinced of his innocence. We believe he didn't knowingly follow Elijah to The Haven."

Nellie sighed, her lips turning up slightly as she rubbed her temples. "That's good. Thank you, Bronywyn."

The warrior nodded curtly, turning once more to leave.

"Wait." Nellie nibbled on her bottom lip before she drew in a breath. "Bronywyn, I-I still need to leave."

Bronywyn's brows furrowed. "After everything you've been told, you want to go?"

Nellie gulped, nodding her head. "I do."

Shaking her head, Bronywyn stared at Nellie for a long moment. A beat of silence passed, then two. "I'm sorry, Eleanor. We can't let you."

"So I'm to be a prisoner, then?" Nellie's voice was sharp as she stared at the warrior.

"You are an honoured guest."

"A guest who is unable to leave."

"But still a guest."

Bronywyn turned and closed the door, slamming it shut so hard that the entire wall rattled with the impact. Nellie stared at the door, her mouth set in a hard line, as hours passed by.

I will get out of here. If it's the last thing I do, I will get leave. I'm coming, Mother. I promise.

After spending the entire day thinking of ways to escape, Nellie collapsed on her bed in exhaustion. Her plans were nothing more than scraps of ideas and she still had no good way to get out of the Haven. Sleep evaded her that night, and she tossed and turned in her bed.

The next morning, Nellie awoke to the sound of shuffling outside her door. She inched her way to the door, forgoing her crutch in an effort to build strength back in her ankle. She threw open the door, her brows rising as she took in the sight of the green-haired warrior holding out a pale purple dress the colour of lilacs. There was also a small bag dangling from her wrist.

"Here." Bronywyn grunted as she held out the dress. "This is for you. It belongs to my partner, Cecelia. She's your height, so it should fit. I also brought you some charcoal toothpaste and a toothbrush. I thought it might help you be more comfortable."

Nellie's eyes widened as she looked between the proffered items and back at Bronywyn. Her brows furrowed as she tried to think of what to say. "Thank you?"

Bronywyn curtly nodded. "You're welcome. I was...thinking about our conversation yesterday and thought you might feel differently about your stay here if you have the chance to see more of the keep."

Nodding, Nellie took the dress out of Bronywyn's outstretched hands and shut the door. She practically ripped off her black tunic and leggings, happy to leave them in a heap on the floor. They were covered in wrinkles. Despite Nellie's best efforts to remain clean over the past two weeks, they bore evidence of being worn for an extended period. As she slipped the lilac dress over her head, tucking in the pendant and feeling it swing between her breasts, Nellie wondered about Bronywyn's partner Cecelia. *She must put up with a lot, being with Bronywyn.*

Bronywyn was easily the scariest person Nellie had ever met. Having slipped on the dress, she took a moment to admire her reflection in the full-length mirror hanging on the back of the door. The woman in the mirror stared back at her with haunting green eyes that contrasted with her midnight blue hair. Cecelia's dress stretched thin over Nellie's frame, flowing at the hips. The slits allowed for effortless movement, which Nellie tested by lunging from one side to the next. Running her fingers over the fabric, she admired the soft material as it hugged her form.

No wonder Bronywyn prefers these dresses over tunics. They allow so much movement.

"Eleanor, if you're not out the door in two minutes, we won't make it in time for breakfast."

Sighing, Nellie ran her fingers down the dress one more time and grabbed her crutch before she pulled open the door. Her stomach grumbling, she followed Bronywyn and her guards down the dark hallways with no complaint.

She was getting used to the darkness in the winding tunnels. The eating area wasn't far from Nellie's room; the group arrived in just a few minutes.

Next to the fluffy pillows on her bed, Nellie thought the cafeteria was the best thing she had seen in a long time. She had never been extremely thin, like Fay, and had always enjoyed eating. The stress of the past few weeks had only emphasized her need to eat delicious food. Luckily for her, it seemed that The Haven's residents were of the same mind. She gasped as she entered the room, an exquisite aroma filling her senses the moment the door opened.

Wide-eyed, Nellie turned in a slow semi-circle as she took in the space. The space was large with pale blue walls. There weren't any windows, of course, but flickering candlelight illuminated the space. There were sconces bolted to the walls, as well as long tapers set in the middle of each table. She counted eight long wooden tables that were scattered throughout the chamber, each set with a dozen chairs in various seating arrangements. The air carried an intoxicating aroma, smelling of freshly baked bread and spices.

Unlike the eating area in the warding centre, there was a disorderly quality in the cafeteria. Warmth filled Nellie's chest, her eyes crinkling as she looked about the room.

The buzz in the air was electric.

People were talking and laughing in small groups as children ran back and forth alongside the tables. The raucous laughter of the youth running around accented the sound of cutlery hitting against plates and bowls.

Watching on in amazement, Nellie giggled as she noticed a small toddler with terra-cotta skin darting from one table to the other, evading grabbing hands by diving under seats. Wide-eyed, Nellie turned to Bronywyn, "I've never seen such unadulterated joy before."

She could have sworn a smile tugged at the warrior's lips before Bronywyn quickly turned, waving at someone in the back of the room.

"Ulric, why don't you bring Eleanor over there so she can eat?" The green-haired warrior gestured to a table in the far corner of the large room.

Nellie followed her gaze, relief filling her as she caught sight of Dion and Elijah sitting side-by-side at a table. A guard, the same one who had opened Dion's cell door for Bronywyn, stood a few feet behind Dion, the man's back against the wall as he observed the room.

After a moment, his name came to Nellie. Rafael. He didn't appear to be too concerned with Dion's presence, his posture was relaxed as he nursed a mug of something warm in his hands.

Forgetting all about Bronywyn, Nellie hurried as fast as she could over to the table. The two men had been engaged in conversation, but they both stopped talking as she approached.

"Good morning, Nellie," Elijah said, standing up and pulling out a chair beside him. She saw a flicker of uncertainty cross his eyes as he stared at her. "Would you like to sit here?" There was an awkwardness between them that hadn't existed before, and she wasn't sure what to make of it.

"I would, thank you." Nellie studied Elijah's face for a moment before easing herself into the chair, lifting her ankle and placing it on the empty chair beside Dion. "How are you feeling, Dion?"

"I'm doing... Okay. Thank you. The Healer has been taking good care of me."

She had been. The cut was a light pink now, standing out from Dion's face but free of any signs of infection.

"I'm glad to hear that, Dion." A smile tugged at Nellie's lips as she leaned back in her seat, taking in the chaos that surrounded her. Mothers were yelling after their children while teenagers ran around, trying to wrangle the younglings back into place. Nellie had never seen such unchecked behaviour before. Fingering the scar on her left arm, she grimaced as the children ran back and forth. Out of the corner of her eye, she noticed Dion get up and head into the kitchen. His guard followed at a distance, but didn't appear too concerned.

The moment Dion stepped away from the table, Elijah leaned over and placed his hand flat on the table next to Nellie's. She stared at it.

"Nell-bell, I-I'm sorry. I know I said it the other day, but I just... I want you to know how sorry I am." Nellie looked up at Elijah. His shoulders were dropping and heavy shadows lay beneath his eyes.. "I hope that in time, you can forgive me."

"Elijah, it's... it's too soon. I don't know. But I'm trying." She inched her hand over, the edge of her pinky touching his thumb. "I've been thinking a lot during the past few days. I'll never forget the way you looked after me as a ward. Do you remember when Guardian Clarence said I couldn't eat for a day and you slipped me some bread that evening?"

"Do I remember? Of course, I remember." Elijah sat up straight, his eyes blazing as he stared at Nellie. Gone was the downcast man from a moment ago. "Nellie, that was wrong of them. They should never have done that. Their 'punishments' are cruel. I'm sorry I couldn't save you from them."

"That wasn't your job, Elijah. Besides, you couldn't have done anything to help me without getting yourself in trouble."

At that moment, Dion returned to the table carrying bowls full of delicious-smelling red beans and rice. He set them on the table with a flourish, smirking as he bowed before re-taking his seat. The group ate in silence for a few minutes, enjoying the meal as the noise in the cafeteria grew louder and louder.

Having finished her food, Nellie leaned back in her chair. She had a cup of water in her hand and was raising it to her lips as she gestured to the room.

"This is-" Before Nellie could finish, a small pale-faced girl with her long blond hair tied up in two pigtails ran behind Dion, laughing. She couldn't have been more than three or four years old. Her legs pumped as her too-big burnt-orange tunic dragged on the ground behind her. It was being held up by a rope tied around her middle, the ends of the belt flying behind her as she ran. Laughing as she circled the table, the young girl bumped into Nellie's arm, sloshing the liquid from the cup onto the borrowed dress. Nellie gasped at the shock of impact and grabbed a napkin to blot up the liquid.

"Oh no, mwiss," the child said, her lip quivering as tears filled her wide blue eyes. She was missing two of her front teeth, giving her an adorable smile and causing all of her words to come out with a slight lisp. "I so sorry. Pwease mwiss, dowat be angwy wit me," the girl said. Her voice was timid as she grabbed onto Nellie's hand, squeezing tightly. "It was awwident."

"It's okay, child." Nellie said, patting the girl's hand. "I'm not upset at all. It's just a dress. I have a *brief* history of clumsiness myself."

The sound of the men guffawing in the background filled the air as Nellie tried to comfort the little girl. She glared at them before turning her gaze back to the child. The corners of her mouth quirked up as she looked at the young girl.

"I promise, it's okay."

"You not mad, mwiss?"

Nellie shook her head.

"No, dear. I'm not angry."

The little girl's face reflected her shock as she blurted out, "But my Momma says you the Sequwenced wady and I muss stay away becwause the Sequwenced huwt her and they wanna huwt me two."

Nellie's mouth fell open, her brows knitting as she looked at the child. *What? Why would I hurt this young girl?*

Just as Nellie was trying to formulate a response, a bedraggled woman ran up to the table. Her face was just as pale as the young child's and her sandy blond hair was drawn up into a messy bun that sat askew on top of her head. There were wisps of her hair flying all over the place as she flew after the child.

The woman appeared to be a few years older than Nellie. Her long face spoke of sleepless nights, while her brown teeth conveyed a significant lack of nutrition when she was a child. The woman's ocean blue eyes were wide as she looked between the young child, clearly her daughter, and Nellie.

"Oh my goodness," the exhausted woman said, breathing deeply as she put a hand on her chest. "Mazie, don't you ever run away like that again."

The frazzled mother stared at the trio sitting at the table with fear in her wide, blue eyes.

"Elijah, sir, miss, I am so sorry." She looked at each person as she spoke, her grip on the child so tight that her knuckles turned white. Nellie couldn't move her eyes from the woman's gaze, shocked at the fear she saw in her eyes. "Please don't mind Mazie. She forgets her manners. Please don't take her away from me."

"Like I said to Mazie, it's fine," Nellie said, nodding her head while trying to force a reassuring smile on her face. She wasn't sure if it was working, but she had to try. "Really, it is."

The frantic woman nodded, terror flashing in her eyes, before she grabbed Mazie's arm and pulled her away forcefully. Nellie could hear her scolding the child as they moved.

What did she think I was going to do?

Nellie watched them leave the cafeteria, her gaze never leaving them. Handing Nellie a cup of kalif, Elijah whispered softly, glancing back and forth between Dion and Nellie.

"Nell-bell, the people here... they've lost a lot of things to the Sequenced. Most of these children you see running around have never seen the light of day. They were born here in The Haven and they've never left."

"Is that why they're so pale?" Nellie looked around and studied the faces of The Haven's residents. As with all residents of Tiarny, there were a multitude of hair and skin colours, sizes and shapes. That wasn't unusual at all. But now that Elijah had mentioned it, Nellie couldn't ignore the fact that almost all of them looked extremely pale and lacked the typical markers of exposure to the sun.

He nodded, rubbing the back of his neck. "Sequenced society isn't safe for the Subversives. Leaving the safety of The Haven is dangerous and not something most people do willingly."

"Hmmm," Nellie reflected as she sipped the kalif. She grimaced at the strong taste. "I suppose that explains part of the woman's aversion."

Dion was silent during this exchange, nursing his own mug of kalif while he surveyed the room. Nellie watched as his brows raised, something catching his eye behind her. Twisting around in her seat, she saw a small child sitting at a table across the cafeteria. A piece of leather pulled his curly brown hair away from his face, highlighting his terra-cotta skin as it reflected the light of the sconces hanging on the wall. That wasn't what drew her attention. The child was wearing an oversized tunic with the right sleeve pinned up under his elbow, empty space where his right hand should have been.

Although Nellie looked away, she found her gaze returning to the small child repeatedly. In all of her life, she had only ever seen people whose bodies looked.... Well, they looked like those of the Source and the Goddesses. She hadn't even known people could exist with deformities.

"Elijah," she said, frowning. "What happened to him?"

Elijah's brows drew together as he followed her gaze. "This is Mateo. His story is one of strength and resilience. Dion, seeing as how your... stay with us had been interesting so far, I'm guessing you haven't met him either as well?"

Dion nodded and mumbled something under his breath about how his "stay" felt a lot like "captivity". He didn't seem too worked up about it, but evidently his position as a less-than-honoured guest had been getting to him.

"Would you like to meet Mateo, Nellie?" Elijah asked in that soft voice of his. His eyes were searching her face.

"Yes, I'd like that." She said.

Elijah nodded, a look of approval shining in his eyes as he rose from the table. "I'll go talk to him now and see if he's willing to share his story with you. You understand, surely, that we would never force residents of The Haven to share their stories?"

"Of course, I understand." Nellie shook her head and smiled at Elijah. She knew it was rude to stare and pulled her gaze away from the boy. "I'd love to get to know him if he's willing to speak with us."

Nodding once, Elijah walked over to Mateo. The child was engaged in conversation with a wrinkled old man who was carrying a stack of books in his arms.

Who is *that? I'd love to meet him, whoever he is.*

"Do you think there's a library here, Dion?" Nellie leaned across the table to ask him.

"Hmm? Oh. Probably? You'll have to ask Elijah." Dion appeared distracted as he looked around the cafeteria.

Nellie made a mental note to ask Elijah later about the man carrying the books.

In Tiarny, the Officials controlled access to all forms of books and pamphlets, regardless of the subject. Wards had to ask their Guardians for permission to read books. Nellie had always loved to read but had found the literature made available to her disappointing. There were only so

213

many times one could read a recounting of the Sacred Solstice during the Year of Inception before it became boring.

A few minutes later, Elijah came walking back over to the table with the young boy in tow. Gesturing towards Nellie and Dion, Elijah introduced him to them.

"Mateo, this is Eleanor and Dion. They're our guests and they were hoping to meet you."

Nellie stood up and reached out her hand to greet Mateo. He looked taken aback for a moment, but then grabbed her proffered hand with his left arm and shook it enthusiastically.

"Hello Mateo," Nellie said, her voice soft. "It's very nice to meet you. Would you like to sit with us?" She gestured at the table, smiling.

Mateo grinned, his smile wide and full of teeth.

"Thank you, miss," he said, "I'd love to!"

Nellie laughed.

"Please Mateo, call me Nellie."

"Nel-lie." Mateo said her name slowly, testing it out on his lips, moving the syllables around on his tongue. "Nellie. I like your name!"

The young boy seemed to find her name amusing, as he suddenly broke into a fit of laughter. The mirth quickly became contagious and spread throughout the room. Nellie, Dion and Elijah all giggled alongside the young child.

When the laughter had finally subsided, Mateo sat at the table next to Nellie. He looked at Dion and reached out his arm across the table as though to touch Dion's face.

"Sir, your face. What happened?"

Dion looked taken aback at the question, his face contorting as he ran his fingers over his cheek. He quickly recovered and smiled softly at Mateo before answering in his deep voice.

"I fell through a portal and landed in the wrong spot, my friend. "

Mateo's eyes went wide with shock at Dion's admission. Nellie had never seen Dion around children before and it pleasantly surprised her to note that his usually gruff persona was nowhere in sight. He actually seemed to enjoy the child's attention, which was certainly not something Nellie had expected to see.

"Wow, sir." Awe filled Mateo's voice as he spoke to Dion. "I have never seen a portal, but I'd sure like to one day."

The child's eagerness was contagious, a smile touching the corners of Nellie's mouth.

"I really like your scar," he said. "I think it makes you look dis... dis... disguished."

Elijah chuckled, running his thumb and index finger over his chin. "I think you mean distinguished."

Grinning, Mateo nodded. "Yes, sir." He smiled, whispering the word to himself before he said it out loud. "Distinguished! I like you, sir."

Dion chucked as a smile danced on his lips.

"I like you too, Mateo."

Just then, Nellie felt a hand on her shoulder. She jumped before she realized it was Bronywyn. The warrior stood tall, looking over the group. "Eleanor, I have some things to attend to. Will you be alright if Elijah takes over as your guide for the day?"

A moment of silence passed as Nellie considered before nodding her agreement. Seemingly satisfied, Bronywyn marched off as the group sat in silence. A moment passed before Dion turned towards Mateo.

"Elijah here mentioned you may have a story to share with us?"

Nellie leaned over, placing her hand on Mateo's smaller one.

"We'd love to hear it if you're willing to share it with us," she said. "But please, don't feel pressured to share."

Mateo grinned, his teeth on full display. "Oh, Miss Nellie. I would love to tell you my story."

Chapter Twenty-Four

For the next hour, Mateo sat with the unlikely trio at their table in the underground Haven and shared his tale. It was all that Nellie could do to sit and listen to the child. Mateo's words lacked emotion as he painted a tale so appalling that Nellie didn't know how he survived, let alone appeared to be thriving in The Haven.

Speaking in a matter-of-voice that comes from the retelling of stories over and over again, Mateo explained he had never met his birth parents. "I don't know where they were Sequenced, what city they came from or even if they were Firsts, Seconds or Thirds. Most of what I know is what Miss Priscilla, my adoptive mother, could tell me. She told me that when she first saw me, I was barely the size of her forearm. The first time she saw me, she said she cried and hugged me tight. Miss Priscilla loves me, yes she does."

Tears welled up in Nellie's eyes as she listened to Mateo. She pulled him onto her lap, squeezing him tightly. Her tears soon soaked his curly brown hair.

"How did you come here, Mateo?" She asked.

"Miss Priscilla told me they found me in the wild. She said I was just hours old. Some Subversives had been patrolling near a portal when they heard a whining sound coming from under a large tree. I still have the blue tunic that I was wrapped in."

Drawing in a shuddering breath, Nellie wiped tears from her eyes.

"What happened then?"

"The rebels found me near the portal and brought me home. They think I was left because I look different. But everyone here treats me like everyone else."

Nellie made a mental note to ask Elijah more about the portals at a later time, but this was clearly not the time for that.

Looking across the table, the two men were sitting with identical tear marks running down their faces. Elijah's head was in his hands as he listened to Mateo, while Dion sat unmoving as he stared at Nellie. The group sat still as the statues in the Source's Temples. Even Rafael, who hadn't moved from his position against the wall, had tears in his eyes.

"Miss Priscilla took me in and raised me ever since. She had her own baby, and she fed us both. She is my momma now." Mateo said proudly.

When the curly-haired boy came to the end of his tale, everyone around the table sat in horrified silence. Nellie opened her mouth, trying to find something to say, but words escaped her. She hugged Mateo to her chest, revelling in the human contact.

How could anyone throw away a baby?

How could the Source allow that?

Mateo's story was so horrifying, so unlike anything Nellie had ever heard. If she hadn't had the proof sitting on her lap, she would have brushed the story off as outlandish and untrue. Nellie had never heard of anyone in Tiarny ever being born crippled. But how could she deny the evidence sitting right in front of her?

Eventually, Mateo broke the silence as he let out an enormous yawn, his mouth opening wide as he stretched. Just like that, the spell was broken. Everyone shifted in their seats, stretching out their muscles as they wiped dried tears from their faces. Mateo stretched his left arm high and wiggled it around before he turned and gave Nellie a one-armed hug.

"Miss Nellie." Mateo whispered, squeezing her neck. "I like you."

Nellie's voice cracked as she squeezed the young child. "Oh Mateo. I like you too."

With that, Mateo hopped off Nellie's lap and waved at the men before he skipped out of the room. Nellie watched Mateo bound out the door before she turned back to the table and lay her head in her hands. Terrible sobs wracked through her body as she tried to come to grips with everything she had just heard. After a few moments, she heard a chair sliding against the floor before she felt warmth settle beside her. Looking up, Nellie saw Dion had moved and was now seated on her right-hand side, his thigh pressing up against hers. The warmth of his body was comforting as Nellie wept.

"How can..." Nellie stuttered, forcing the words past her lips, "How could anyone do that? Abandoning a newborn? What kind of blackened hearts did his parents have?"

Breathing heavily as she rubbed her temples, Nellie's eyes suddenly flew to Dion's face. His black eyes had filled with tears, just like hers, when hearing Mateo's story. He appeared just as shaken by the story.

But.

Nellie knew Dion had lived in Deavita. He was an Official, and an important one at that.

Had he known about this?

Seeming to sense her inner turmoil, the man in question reached over and took Nellie's hand in his. His large hand engulfed her long, thin fingers, as he wrapped her hand up in his. Dion looked at her with so much intensity that her breath caught in her throat.

"Dion," Nellie whispered, her words barely audible. "Did you know?"

She didn't need to elaborate. He understood what she meant.

"No, Eleanor," he said. At the sound of those three syllables on his lips, Nellie shuddered as relief wracked her body. "This, today, this is the first time I've ever met anyone like Mateo."

"Do you swear you didn't know?"

"I swear to you on my life, I have never, ever, taken part in anything having to do with babies. I had heard rumours of things like this happening, but I've never actually seen evidence of it happening." Dion shifted in his seat, fidgeting with his tunic. "Believe me Eleanor, I never would have done anything this... this horrific."

"Elijah, is-is this something that happens a lot? What would have happened to Mateo if the patrols hadn't found him?"

A second ticked by, then another, as silence filled the room.

"He would have died," Elijah whispered, the horror of his words reflected in the depths of his eyes. "We still don't know how his birth parents knew to drop him off near the portal. We don't know if it was an accident or if someone knew we'd find him. Knowledge of the portals is limited and few people know they exist. It's not as though they have signs on them that say *portal here*."

Nellie felt her inner walls completely crumble. There was so much death lately, so much pain. She had never witnessed much death before her Sequencing, but now it surrounded her on all sides. The rebels who had died during the attack, Isadora, and the nameless babies she was now sure had existed.

She shuddered as she felt herself completely fall apart. Her shoulders shook with the weight of her tears, her sorrow flowing out of her in rivulets of tears. They fell on her dress, turning the pale purple fabric into a much deeper violet. She reached for a napkin as she tried to calm her breathing. There was so much pain. How could so much pain exist in the world?

Nellie lost track of time as they sat huddled in the cafeteria. People came and went as she mourned the loss of so many lives. Nellie didn't know what time it was, but it must have been the afternoon by now. She felt so tired. She was emotionally drained.

Still, something was nudging her at the back of her mind. A question that had been forming for hours, but she couldn't quite put her finger on it. Something to do with the portal...

"Elijah, Dion." Nellie hiccupped as the tears slowly came to a stop. Her voice was raspy as she tried to form words. "I still have one big question. What do the portals look like? You said they weren't obvious if you didn't know what to look for."

Dion crossed his arms over his chest, rubbing them as he looked ahead. "I can't speak for all portals, but the one I followed Elijah through was a tree. Or at least, it appeared to be a tree. Its leaves were burnt-orange and from afar, it appeared to be on fire."

Why does that sound so familiar?

Something was nagging at Nellie's mind, but she couldn't quite figure out what it was. The rest of the day went by in a whirlwind of introductions before Nellie collapsed in her bed right after dinner.

Nightmares haunted her as she slept, tossing and turning in the enormous bed. The comfort of a deep, dreamless sleep escaped her as she tried to rest.

Something was calling for her in the distance, summoning her, but she couldn't figure out what it was.

All she knew was that this thing, this connection, was the key that she was looking for.

Chapter Twenty-Five

The morning after she met Mateo, she had a very long and unproductive meeting with Jacinta. To Nellie's dismay, the leader of the Subversives had determined it was far too dangerous for her to leave The Haven. They wouldn't allow her to go to the Surface, in case the wrong people saw her. Her unusual position as a kidnapped "guest" remained.

Later that day, Nellie had been complaining to Dion and Elijah over lunch when Bronywyn had stopped by their table. Nellie had dropped her fork, eyes widening as she realized the warrior had likely overheard her comments.

"Eleanor, I'm going to be leaving for a few days to go to the Surface. I'd ask for your assurance that you will not try to run away again. Ulric will be staying in The Haven, but I'm sure he would rather not have to keep you under lock and key until I return."

"Is that really necessary, Bronywyn?" Elijah sighed.

"It is." Bronywyn glared at Elijah. "Well, Eleanor?"

"I'll be good," Nellie mumbled around the food in her mouth. "I don't think I could find my way out of here if I tried."

Seemingly content with Nellie's response, Bronywyn had left. True to her word, Nellie did not try to escape while the warrior was gone. She did, however, walk all throughout the Haven and try to make sense of the endless corridors. She only got completely lost twice, something she was proud of. Ulric, who had been following her at a distance, had to help her back to her room both times.

In an effort to help her feel more comfortable, Jacinta had ensured that she was supplied with an entire wardrobe of the strange dresses that Bronywyn favoured.

Despite wanting to hate everything about the Haven, Nellie found she enjoyed the freedom they provided. The Haven was much warmer than she was used to, so she was extremely grateful for the light fabric of the dresses. It had taken her a few days to get used to showing her bare arms, but the ease of mobility made up for the lack of modesty.

Upon Bronywyn's return four days later, she held a meeting in what Nellie had learned was Jacinta's office. Everyone sat back in the large wooden chairs, candlelight flickering over their faces as they listened.

"I'm afraid we have some bad news. The Firsts in Deavita are still running constant search parties for Nellie and Dion. They have accounted for everyone except the three of you in the convoy from Liantis. We noted three separate parties of Royal Protectors patrolling the Surface. There are constant stops on the Queen's Road. It's proving to be extremely dangerous right now."

"They're looking for Nellie and Dion? What about me?" Elijah asked, his brows furrowed.

"From the sounds of things, you've been presumed him dead, Elijah." Bronwyn spoke without emotion, her eyes sharp as she sipped her kalif.

"That's a little insulting." Elijah's face contorted as he rubbed the back of his neck.

"Look at it this way, now you don't need to work as a double agent."

"That's true." A brief look of relief crossed Elijah's face, although Nellie still saw a haunted look in his eyes.

With each day that passed, Nellie's heart ached for home. Despite her repeated pleas, Jacinta refused to allow her to leave. "You can't leave, Eleanor. I'm sorry, but it's not safe."

When Nellie brought up her mother, Jacinta simply tapped her chin as she thought for a moment. "What if you wrote her some letters? We can't send them, but it might help you feel more comfortable."

Despite having scoffed initially at the idea of the letters, later that same evening, Nellie penned a letter on a spare piece of paper she had found in her bedroom.

Dear Mother,

I've been here for eleven days now. They still won't let me leave.

I know you'll never receive these unless I give them to you myself, but Mother, I miss you so much. I think you'd like this place, The Haven. It's completely underground. Can you believe that? I can't believe how much I miss the sun. I know, I know. I can hear you now, talking about how I always complained about it. But now that it's gone... I just wish I still felt the kiss of sunlight on my cheeks.

Kisses, Nellie.

Mother,

It's been sixteen days. I'm still here.

Today, Dion and I explored a bit. They've seemed to realize he won't kill everyone on sight, so they're relaxing their hold on him.

The man is infuriating, Mother. One moment he is all sarcasm and wit, and the next, he says something endearing. His guard, Rafael, seems really nice. I don't know his story, but I think you'd like him. His wife is the Healer here. She cared for my ankle. Did I tell you about that? I tried to run away, but then I slipped and twisted it. Don't worry though, it's all healed now.

I miss you.

Love, Nellie.

~

Days became weeks, and still Nellie remained in the Haven.

~

Dearest Mother,

It's been twenty-nine days and I'm still in The Haven. I'm really getting the hang of things here. There aren't any bells here, but there are chimes that ring throughout the entire keep thirty minutes before each meal. They serve as time-keepers, since, of course, we can't see the sun. I have my own room with the softest pillows around. Every morning, I go to the rest area to plait my hair. It's enormous! There is a huge mirror that spans an entire wall.

After we wake up, we break our fast in the cafeteria. It's this large room that is always filled with chatter. Guardian Clarence would hate it. They eat much of the same food here as we always did. Usually, breakfast is hard bread made from oats with red or black beans. My favourite is when we have eggs, though. But Mother. You would love the food. It's amazing! They use so many spices. Maybe one day, I'll get to tell you about it face-to-face.

I've been helping in the kitchen after breakfast, scrubbing pans and learning how things are run. It feels good to help.

There's someone knocking at the door. I'd better run.

Love you to the moon and back,

Nellie.

After three full-moon cycles had passed since Nellie first entered The Haven, she was strolling through the hallways with Elijah and Dion when she halted. Although she still didn't fully trust Elijah, their friendship had come a long way in the past few weeks and things were finally feeling like they were mending.

"Elijah, where does the water come from? I've been trying to understand it, but I just can't seem to figure it out."

Elijah's face lit up when Nellie asked about the water, a grin spreading across his face as he bounced from one foot to the other. "Do you really want to see?"

"I do," Nellie said, a grin spreading across her face. The moment Nellie saw joy flit across her old friend's face, she knew she would do anything to bring back that expression. Far too often, he was sitting silently in a corner, his face heavy as he re-lived his memories of Isadora.

Nellie knew that grief was a massive weight to bear and only time could heal the wounds it caused. In life, there were moments of joy and others of devastating loss. Although she knew she couldn't erase Elijah's pain, Nellie delighted in the fact that she could pull him out of his grief for even the briefest of moments.

"Okay. Let's do this." Elijah pumped a fist in the air, practically vibrating with academic excitement.

"Right now?" Dion asked.

"Do you have anywhere else to be?" Elijah lifted his brows.

"I guess not. Lead on." Dion gestured down the hall.

For the next three hours, Elijah led Nellie, Dion and Rafael through The Haven. "The keep, you understand, wasn't built by a singular Builder. No, it's the product of collaboration by many Engineers and Builders over the years. As a result, the structure is massive, its hallways and tunnels running deep beneath the surface."

During their tour, Elijah led them through dozens of tunnels that led them deeper and deeper into the earth. He answered any and all questions that Nellie and Dion asked. Rafael silently walked behind them, his footsteps the only sign of his presence.

Eventually, they came to a stop in front of a large wooden door that had an intricate carving of a water droplet etched into it. The engraving was massive, about the size of Nellie's head.

There were two guards standing in front of the door, backs straight and arms at their side as they stood at attention. Upon seeing Elijah, the guards bowed and moved back, allowing the group access to the area.

Once Elijah had pushed open the door, he stood back and grinned. Nellie and Dion stood still in the doorway, their eyes wide and mouths open in shock as they stood bathed in a strange blue light.

Nellie gasped as her eyes adjusted to the light, the sound of her voice shattering the fragile silence of the chamber. The blue glow was coming from thousands of crystals that covered the walls and ceiling of the cavern. The stalactites were shimmering as they emitted low blue and purple lights. Captivated, Nellie stepped into the chamber and touched one of them. The crystal was cool to the touch; the surface smooth like glass. Dion followed Nellie into the chamber, his footfalls reverent as he moved behind her. Nellie had never imagined that anything like this ever existed. Far inside the enormous chamber was a deep, blue pool of water that stretched as far as the eye could see.

Although the ceiling of the cavern couldn't have been over twelve feet high, the chamber was magnificent.

"What... how?" Nellie stuttered, her eyes never leaving the lake. She bent down and put her finger in the water, the liquid a cool kiss on her skin.

"This lake stretches for miles underground." Elijah reverently touched a crystal. "The Haven's engineers built the keep around the lake. The water it provides is the life source for all the residents. There are hundreds of rivers and streams that run to and from the lake, threading throughout the land nearby."

"Does everyone know about this?"

Elijah shook his head. "Not exactly. Most people know it exists, but they don't know where it is. This is one of The Haven's greatest resources. It is under guard every hour of the day."

The tour of the underground lake had only increased Nellie's appreciation for water. Unlike in the rest of Tiarny, there weren't strict regulations in The Haven surrounding water. However, there was an unspoken understanding between the residents that if they wasted the precious resource, rules would be imposed upon them.

Nellie had witnessed residents of The Haven drinking their cups to the dregs. They used minimal amounts of water when brushing their teeth and washing their hair. They were careful with water.

Staring at the underground lake, Nellie wondered to herself what would happen if someone in The Haven wasted water.

Chapter Twenty-Six

Ο ne day, about a week after Elijah had shown her the underground lake, Nellie was scrubbing away at a particularly unruly pan after breakfast when she overheard heavy footsteps coming up from behind her. The scent of soap and sweat was thick in the air, the kitchen humid and sticky. The ovens made the heat unbearable at times, although today it wasn't too bad. Humming to herself, Nellie started when she heard a voice come from behind her that chilled her to the bone.

"Matthias Fernbriar," the stranger shouted. Nellie paled at the sound, goosebumps peppering her flesh. This voice haunted her nightmares. "Someone has reported you for wasting a precious resource. You need to come with me for questioning."

Nellie told herself not to turn around, to keep facing the sink, but she couldn't help herself. Curiosity overcame her, and she shifted. She stared at the man Elijah had called "Adrian". She would know that voice anywhere. He was the one who had kidnapped her at spear-point and brought her to The Haven. Her blood ran cold as she looked up at the man towering over her. He was built like a warrior, his sandy blond hair standing out from his pale skin, the sunburn on his face marking him as a Surface walker.

Nellie pushed herself against the sink, willing herself to fold up as small as possible to get out from under the imposing warrior's piercing gaze. The man's aura was dangerous and something about him unsettled her. Thankfully, his gaze swept over Nellie.

"There you are." A smirk settled on Adrian's face as he marched to the back of the kitchen towards his target. The man he was looking for appeared to be in his fourth decade of life. He had warm, brown skin and a balding head. When Nellie had first started helping in the kitchen, he had kindly shown her around and helped her find something to do.

"Wait." Nellie put up her hand as she stepped into Adrian's path. "Where are you taking Matthias?"

Adrian scoffed at Nellie, his tone dripping with condescension. "Little lady, that is none of your concern. Now, step out of my way, or I'll make you move."

Before she could reply, Matthias looked at her with furrowed brows. He shook his head. "Don't, Nellie. It's not worth it."

Sighing, she stepped aside. Her eyes followed Adrian as he pushed Matthias out of the room. The large man glared at the rest of the people in the kitchen before following Matthias out. Silence filled the kitchen as the muffled sounds of argument soon came from beyond the door. By the time Nellie had opened the kitchen door, the cafeteria was empty. She couldn't find Matthias anywhere.

Once she finished in the kitchens, Nellie almost always spent an hour or two in The Haven's library. She had learned The Haven housed an extensive collection of books, including hundreds of pieces of literature that were written in the Common Tongue. A lover of the written word, Nellie had quickly befriended The Haven's resident librarian, a wizened old man named Tomas.

Tomas was pale, as was the norm in The Haven, and his wrinkled face and hands spoke of many decades of life. He spent nearly all his time in the library, organizing and sorting the hundreds of books found in The Haven.

The first day that Nellie had discovered The Haven's underground library during what was becoming her daily quest to explore the keep in hopes of finding an exit, she had entered the cavernous room and stopped short. Whatever she had been expecting, it certainly wasn't what she found.

The walls of the enormous room stretched high, higher than Nellie had thought possible for an underground cavern. They had to be at least three to four stories tall. Bookshelves lined the walls, brimming with books in all shapes and sizes. The library smelled of earth and grass, with a faint scent of vanilla that wafted through the space.

Nellie had gotten used to the fact that The Haven was lit with candles, but upon entering the library, she stopped short. There wasn't a candle to be seen in The Haven's library. Instead, there were the same strange luminescent crystals adorning the walls that she had noticed in the underground pool. These crystals emitted a soft blue and pink glow throughout the room, bathing the books in their cool light. Nellie thought if she stood still, she could hear a hum coming from the crystals themselves. The first time she had entered the library, Tomas had greeted her at the door.

"I don't get many visitors here, dear. It's a delight to meet you."

When Nellie had asked Tomas about the crystals, he had snorted. "Firelight and books don't mix, Eleanor. I have expressly forbidden candles from entering my precious library."

The room was teeming with books. Bookshelves covered the walls, overflowing with precious tomes. Piles of books covered on the few chairs and tables throughout the space, their excess overflowing into heaps on the ground. Of all the spaces Nellie had seen in The Haven, this one spoke the most to her heart. She loved books and could not believe the enormous collection found in this most unlikely of places.

Tomas had explained to Nellie that the cavern housing the library was part of the same underground lake that she had seen earlier. They had discovered the enormous cavern three decades ago as they were expanding the keep, and Tomas had claimed it as the perfect sanctuary for his books. He hadn't had to do much to the space. The crystals lighting the room were part of the network of naturally occurring caverns deep in the ground. Nellie had never seen anything like it and soon took to spending time in the library every chance she got.

Unlike most of the residents of The Haven, Tomas wore a tunic marking him as a Sequenced Scholar. It stood out to Nellie, as she had gotten used to seeing most women wearing the sleeveless, slitted dresses while men typically wore armour or plain brown tunics with leggings.

Nellie and Tomas quickly became friends. The decades separating them didn't matter, as they found common ground in their love for literature. There weren't many Haven residents who spent time in the library. It quickly became Nellie's refuge, the place where her status as a Sequenced *guest* didn't matter. Tomas was an amazing person to talk to. He listened intently, offering wisdom and counsel without prejudice. Nellie soon considered Tomas a close friend and confidant.

It became routine for the two of them to share a cup of kalif in the morning as they discussed literature and anything else that came to mind. Nellie was finding the drink bothered her less and less each time she drank it. Some of her favourite stories had been of Tomas's partner Felix.

"He was my light. Everything good in my life came from him, young

Eleanor. If you ever find someone like that, you hold on for dear life. My Felix, he made everything better for me. With him, I knew I could get through anything."

"Was?"

"He went to be with the Source two years ago." Tomas's eyes had filled with tears. "I will be forever grateful that we had all the time together that we did. Don't you waste a second of your life, my dear. One day, you will look back and wondering where it all went."

One day, she had asked Tomas how he ended up in The Haven.

"I'd love to tell you that, my dear." He smiled softly. "You remind me of someone I knew long ago... she loved stories too."

As the librarian poured their ritualistic cups of kalif, Nellie had cleared off two chairs and sat as Tomas took them back in time.

"I was born and raised in Deavita. My Sequencing took place 688 Years after Inception. I was Sequenced as a Scholar, which was perfect for me. My love of literature meant that I fit in with the other Scholars easily. Scholars are Firsts, as you know, but we lived such a secluded life that we never really took part in any of the activities other Firsts did. I finished my apprenticeship, working as a Scholar in the Queen's Library for many years. That's where Felix and I met, you know. He was a Server, working as a cleaner in the Library. The moment we laid eyes on each other; we were smitten. It was love at first sight."

Nellie had sighed, placing her hands over her heart as Tomas spoke of his husband. "That's so romantic. Maybe one day, I'll have a story like that too."

"Maybe you will, dear. We couldn't be open about our affections in Deavita, since he was a Third, and me, a First."

Frowning, Nellie gazed at the old man. "That's so sad."

Humming his agreement, Tomas continued. "It was. I worked in the Library for a decade after my Sequencing, sorting books, searching for important information when needed and keeping a written account of the Queen's Reign." He rubbed the back of his neck, his glazing over as he spoke of the past.

"Everything had been going so well until the day that a Royal Protector marched into the library. She came bearing terrible news. The Queen had issued a Royal Decree demanding that I destroy all books that were over fifty years old."

Gasping, Nellie's hand flew to her mouth. "No." She had crossed her legs underneath herself as she sat unmoving in the hard-backed chair. She stared at the old man intently, unable to do anything but listen to him speak.

"Yes, it's true," he nodded emphatically. "The moment the Royal Protector informed me of the decree, I knew I could not go through with it. I would never defile written works by feeding them into the fiery depths."

"Of course," Nellie breathed. "I wouldn't expect anything less of you. But what did you do?"

"Fire is a fickle master," Tomas patiently explained to Nellie in his low, soft voice. "It has a hunger that is never satisfied. It takes, and it takes, and it takes, giving heat in return. But my dear, sometimes the cost you have to pay for that heat is too high."

Nellie nodded, her eyes filled with tears. "Far too high," she agreed.

"For the next two days, Felix and I siphoned off as many books as we could from the Library in two days before disappearing ourselves. The order from the Queen went against everything I had ever sworn to do. I had made some contacts with the Subversives a few years prior to receiving the Queen's decree, but had hoped to never have to use them. I sent dozens of books with my contacts before Felix and I fled the capital. That night, we were carrying as many books as our arms and backs could bear."

"Were you... were you scared?" Nellie's green eyes were wide as she stared at the elderly librarian, imagining the small man laden with books as he fled the Royal Protectors.

Tomas chuckled, his wrinkled hands reaching out to hold hers. "My dear Eleanor, terrified doesn't even begin to describe what I was feeling. I had never done anything so petrifying in my entire life. My life was meant to be lived in the library, learning, reading and teaching. This was so far outside of my comfort zone; I had no idea what I was doing. But in life, if you know something is the right thing to do, even if it terrifies you, you must do it. Protecting knowledge is one of the most honourable things a person can ever do. Even if I had paid the price of that protection with my life, I would have died knowing I gave my soul for something worthwhile."

Sitting on that hard-backed chair listening to Tomas explain that he would have given his life for the books he saved, Nellie was in awe. Tears ran down her cheeks as she listened to the old man reverently speak about the books he had saved. Tomas had lived a life of prosperity as a Sequenced Scholar, working in the Queen's libraries, and yet he gave it all up to protect knowledge. Where many others would see a frail old man, Nellie saw a man who risked everything for what he believed was right.

If something like this were to happen to me, Nellie had thought later that day, *would I be brave enough to act as Tomas did? Please Source, let that be the case.*

Nellie made it a priority to visit the library every morning. It was a less frequented part of The Haven, and few of the residents seemed to appreciate, or even know, of the library's existence. It was a shame, for Tomas's wisdom seemed to know no bounds. He always had something to add or advice to give, no matter Nellie's questions.

Tomas quickly became one of Nellie's favourite people in The Haven, his presence a calming balm on her rising anxiety about being trapped in this keep with no chance of escape. She went to the library every chance she got.

One day, a few weeks after she discovered the library, Nellie had been bending down to pick up a book when she felt her pendant shift out of her dress and slide free. Gasping, she quickly adjusted it and slipped it back under her clothing. She looked around, but was relieved when Tomas's head was bent over a book at his desk, clearly caught up in whatever he was reading.

After that, Nellie took extra care to make sure her pendant was firmly tucked into her underthings wherever she went throughout The Haven. Most people still ignored her, but not Tomas. There were a few times when she caught him looking at her strangely, as though he wanted to ask her something, but he never did. The library and its keeper soon became a safe haven for Nellie. And she needed one, badly.

There was still no hope of returning to the Surface. No matter how many times Nellie asked, Jacinta continued to refuse her freedom.

Nightmares plagued Nellie and she would often wake in the middle of the night, grabbing a book to read instead of falling back into the clutches of her dreams. One of the few places Nellie found peace was in the library. Little did she know, the peace would not be long-lasting.

Chapter Twenty-Seven

~~~

T he Haven ran like a well-oiled machine. Every resident of the keep had a job, a role they filled to maintain the underground residence. Privately, Nellie thought the system was very similar to the Sequencing, but she never dared voice the thought out loud. Besides working in the kitchen, Jacinta had assigned Nellie to work and train with Solange as soon as her ankle was healed.

Once she started training as a Healer, Nellie's day fell into a pleasant, but busy, routine. She would remain in the library with Tomas until the second chime rang, warning everyone that the mid-day meal would begin soon. After the meal, Nellie went to the infirmary with Solange.

Like the library, the infirmary wasn't lit with sconces but with the crystals Nellie now associated with rooms and caverns that existed deep within The Haven. Unlike the other rooms, the infirmary's crystals all glowed a brilliant green. It was shocking to see at first, but soon the room became as familiar to Nellie as her bedroom in Liantis.

Solange was one of the few Healers in The Haven and as such, her services were always in high demand. Not only did she know the typical potions and ointments, oils, and rubs for healing, but she also acted as the resident midwife for any expectant mothers.

On one of Nellie's first days in the infirmary, she had asked Solange about the monthly birth control. She had last received her shot the day before her Sequencing, and it had been just under a month since she had left Liantis.

"Do you have those here?" Nellie had flushed, her fingers fiddling with her dress as she asked Solange.

"Of course. The shots are not mandatory, but residents can request contraception. It is up to them whether they want them. If not, we have other, less invasive forms of contraception available."

"Really?" Inclining her head, Nellie tried to process this new information. "I'd like to keep using them for now. With everything going on with me, I just don't feel like I have the time or energy to deal with monthlies."

"Not a problem, Eleanor. Everyone has a choice in the Haven."

Choice. That was new and something that took some getting used to.

Solange was extremely busy, and she had welcomed Nellie's help with open arms. A few days after Nellie had begun, Solange had confided with Nellie as they hurried along a dark corridor.

"You know, Eleanor, I've been working alone for so long. As soon as Jacinta had told me we had another Healer in the keep, I demanded that you be allowed to work with me. I have so much to teach you about herbs, tending minor cuts and specific oils used to help people feel better."

Most of the injuries and ailments suffered by The Haven's inhabitants were minor, but each time Nellie healed someone, she felt her soul sing. Healing came easily to Nellie. Her hands moved quickly and seemed to know exactly what needed to be done.

Finally, Nellie had a place where she was both needed and wanted.

Dear Mother,

It's been sixty-seven days since I entered The Haven. They seem to trust me, but still won't let me leave. I miss you deeply. I'm training under a Healer here named Solange. She is studious and so kind. She's been teaching me so much and I feel honored to be learning from her.

I'm a good Healer. I never thought I would say that. Solange even thinks I might be able to become a great Healer one day, if I keep up my studies. Finally, it feels like I'm not a burden. Before you say anything, I know Guardian Clarence always felt like I was a chore, and you can't deny that it was harder for you to take care of me when the rains stopped falling. Don't blame yourself.

Here, when I'm working with Solange, people respect me. Yesterday, I accidentally dropped a needle into my mug of kalif (this horribly strong drink that grows on you), but the patient just laughed as I re-sterilized it. Mother, I think I might be happy as a Healer.

Tomorrow, we are going to be attending a birth. I can't wait to tell you all about it.

Love,
Nellie.

One day, about five full-moon cycles after she had first come to The Haven, Nellie waved goodbye to Dion before she walked to the small infirmary after lunch. Under her arms, she held a book that Tomas had recommended, *The History of the Healing Arts in Tiarny.*

"As soon as I pulled this book, I knew it would be perfect for you." Tomas had said, tucking it into Nellie's arms that morning. His lips had tilted up, his eyes a soft glow as he studied her. "You know, Felix and I never had children but if we could have had a family, we would have loved to have a daughter like you."

The statement had blown Nellie away. She had stammered for a few minutes, before placing her hand overtop Tomas' withered one. "Thank you," she had replied earnestly. "I never knew Felix, but for him to be such a good husband to you, I am sure he was a great man."

Tomas had nodded, a faraway look in his eyes. "He was," he murmured.

Soon after, Nellie had hurried to meet Dion for lunch. The entire time she had walked away from the library, she couldn't help but feel so grateful for Tomas. For some inexplicable reason, she felt attached to him to.

He didn't see her as a Healer or a "guest" of The Haven, but as another lover of literature.

Even though they had only known each other for a short period of time, Nellie knew that she would always consider Tomas a life-long friend.

She had begun reading the book on her walk from the cafeteria and had found it fascinating. It was a fount of knowledge, full of history that she had never learned.

Nellie almost always met Solange in the infirmary, although sometimes the blue-haired Healer would send a messenger to ask her to meet in another part of The Haven. That day, she had received no such message, so she was walking to the infirmary with her book in one hand and a fresh mug of hot kalif in the other. Lost in thought, Nellie was mulling over the contents of her book as she walked. Her eyebrows flew up when she opened the door to the infirmary, seeing not one, but two people deep in conversation.

She recognized Solange's sky-blue hair right away. As always, it was hanging in loose waves down her back, ending right before her tailbone. She could see that the older woman was deep in conversation with someone, but Nellie couldn't tell who it was right away. Clearing her throat, Nellie called out from the doorway. "Um, hello? Is this a good time, Solange?"

The older Healer turned and smiled at Nellie before grabbing the arm of the man standing in front of her.

"It's perfect timing," Solange said, giving the arm a tug. "Eleanor, this is Axel. I believe you have met him before?"

Of course. Nellie barely recognized the Healer who had almost died at the hands of the Royal Protectors. The last time she had seen him, he had been all skin and bones. Now that about two and a half months had passed, his flesh had filled out. As a whole, Axel looked much healthier, although shadows still haunted the man's brown eyes. His skin was a shade paler than even those born into The Haven.

Nellie waved at the man, a tiny smile dancing on her lips.

"Hello, Axel. I'm glad to see you're up and about."

At that, the man in question grimaced a little. "I am definitely doing better, thank you Eleanor. I was finally feeling well enough today to go in search of the infirmary. I thought it only fitting to offer my services to Solange, seeing as how she has been spending almost every morning tending to my own wounds when I could not do so."

"Ah, so you're the mystery patient."

Axel's cheeks reddened. "I suppose I am. Solange has been looking after me, and I am so appreciative of it."

Solange looked between Nellie and Axel, a wide grin bursting forth from her lips. She was practically bouncing on the balls of her feet.

"Axel," Solange addressed the man as she walked over to the shelf where she stored medical supplies, "I don't want you to overdo it, but I certainly am happy to have you here. Eleanor is still in training, but she soaks up everything I can throw at her. To be honest with you, she's one of the most brilliant Healers I've ever come across."

Really?

Nellie preened at the compliment. She had never been good at anything, let alone called "brilliant".

"Thank you so much Solange." Nellie grinned as she put down her kalif on a side table and went over to help the older Healer with the supplies. "You've been such an outstanding teacher, it's really all because of you."

Axel stood up straight, his shoulders going back as he stretched his arms to the ceiling before he settled into a comfortable standing position. The man walked over to the medicine cabinet and whispered conspiratorially to Nellie. "I, for one, am tired of convalescing. I'd love to work with the two of you."

Solange grinned, her eyes sparkling as she looked between the two younger Healers. "We'd love to have you, Axel. Your own considerable knowledge of healing would be a boon to Eleanor's training."

Nellie's eyes widened with excitement.

"Oh, I'd love that too," she said excitedly. "I've learned so much from Solange in such a short amount of time. I am eager to learn anything you have to offer me as well."

Axel agreed, and so it was decided. The three of them became a team in The Haven. Solange imparted her vast amount of healing knowledge to Axel and Nellie, and Axel shared with Nellie all the techniques he had learned in the capital.

Nellie loved learning from the other two Healers. They had so much wisdom and experience. Solange and Axel never laughed at her questions. They always took the time to answer them as thoroughly as possible, showing her new techniques for healing as they worked in tandem. Every time Nellie learned something new, she felt more alive than she ever had before.

For the first time, she felt at home in The Haven.

∾

Nellie worked with the Healers until the third chime of the day. After a quick dinner in the cafeteria, she would spend the rest of the evening with Dion. One evening, they followed the haunting sounds of music through the hallways to a large common room.

Nellie had grabbed onto Dion's sleeve the moment they entered the room. All eyes swung to them, but she didn't even care.

"Dion, there's so much music. It's so beautiful." Nellie's eyes had widened as she looked about the room.

"Sometimes I forget, Eleanor, that you aren't from Deavita." Dion smirked, but there wasn't anything cruel in the expression. "If you love music, life as a First there will suit you. There's a symphony I think you would love."

"A symphony?"

"It's... think of it as something like this, but much bigger in an auditorium built for music. There is a massive Music Hall in Deavita. I'll take you there sometime."

There were people playing on makeshift drums while others sang and clapped along to the beat. Nellie even saw a person playing an instrument that she later learned was called a *lyra*. She had never seen anything like it. The lyra was about two feet long and they crafted it out of wood. The base was oblong with a long neck protruding from one end of the instrument. It was hollow, with five long strings that ran up the front of the instrument to the top of its neck. When the musicians plucked its strings, the lyra produced a haunting melody. Nellie couldn't get the sound out of her head. It was beautiful.

Listening to the musicians after a long day of work in The Haven became a favourite pastime of Nellie's. She would often meet up with Dion after she spent the day healing a variety of cuts and bruises, broken arms and lacerated feet. Most injuries weren't severe, but there were over five hundred residents of The Haven, so there was always something to deal with.

When they met in the evenings, Nellie and Dion would often trade stories of how their days had gone. She had nearly made him throw up after her colourful description of the birth she had attended earlier in the day.

Surprisingly, the more time Nellie spent with Dion, the less his abrasive attitude bothered her. She even looked forward to his company in the evening.

Rafael still accompanied Dion throughout the keep. However, the longer the Official remained in The Haven, the more the Subversives seemed to trust him. For all the niceties, however, both Nellie and Dion were feeling the effects of their captivity. For as lovely of a place The Haven was, it was still a cage. Even with Tomas and Solange, Nellie still felt alone.

She missed the sun, the heat of its rays and even the endless blue sky.

One day, Axel and Nellie were working together in the infirmary while Solange was attending an important meeting. They were categorizing medicinal herbs, and the infirmary was filled with the scent of oils and the sound of glass jars clinking together.

Closing the lid on yet another jar, Nellie had turned to Axel.

"Do you miss it?"

"The capital?"

Nellie nodded.

"Not at all. To be honest, I'll be happy if I never leave The Haven again."

That had been the first, and last, time that Nellie had expressed her feelings of entrapment to Axel. However, as often happens with emotions that are repressed, they were bound to erupt at the worst possible moment.

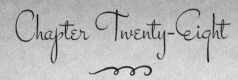

Chapter Twenty-Eight

One day, about three months after first coming to The Haven, Nellie, Elijah and Dion were all summoned to Jacinta's office. Standing outside the meeting room, the trio stared at each other.

"Do you know why we were called here?" Nellie whispered, glancing around.

"I have no idea," Dion replied.

"I'm not sure either," Elijah said as he ran his fingers through his hair. "It might have something to do with me leaving, though."

"What?" Nellie and Dion spoke at the same time.

"You're leaving?" Nellie's eyes were pleading as she looked at Elijah. "Take me with you. I need to get out of here."

Before Elijah could reply, the door to Jacinta's office swung open. "That's not his decision to make, is it?" Nellie groaned as she looked at Bronywyn. The warrior hadn't warmed up to Nellie over the past three months, and the feeling was mutual. Bronywyn held the door open as she gestured inside. "Why don't you come in?"

Once everyone was seated, Nellie looked at Jacinta. The elderly woman was seated once more at the head of the table, her back straight and unseeing eyes alert. Nellie had been meeting with Jacinta on a weekly basis, and the woman never ceased to amaze her.

Bronywyn cleared her throat. "Right. Since you heard Elijah is leaving, let's begin there. It's true that he and I are going to the Surface. We received some important information and we have to leave."

Nellie raised her chin, looking at the fierce warrior. "I want to come. No, I need to leave. I've been here long enough, surely the danger has passed."

Bronywyn smirked. "The danger has passed? The last time you were on the Surface, you turned your ankle in the middle of the forest. What was your plan, by the way? What would you have done when night fell?"

Grinding her teeth, Nellie glared at Bronywyn. "Obviously, I didn't think that through. But nonetheless, here we are. If you're leaving, I want to come with you. Let me and Dion leave. *Please.*"

Sighing, Bronywyn shifted and bent her head, whispering with Jacinta. After a few minutes, she sat back with a smirk on her face.

Jacinta cleared her throat, "unfortunately, Eleanor, we cannot let you and Dion leave. I'm sorry, but it isn't safe. You will both remain here as our guests until we deem things safer." Jacinta folded her hands in front of her, her unseeing eyes firm. "Elijah and Bronywyn will leave tomorrow, and we will revisit this issue upon their return."

"But..." Nellie interjected.

"This decision is *final*. We didn't summon you here to discuss this, but rather to talk about how things are going. Eleanor, Solange and Bronywyn tell me you've been flourishing in the infirmary. Is that right?"

"Yes, that's right."

"Good. Now Dion. Let's talk about you. Rafael tells me you have been restless."

Dion snorted; his jaw clenched as he looked at the leader of the Subversives. He ran a hand down his cheek, rubbing the scar on his face. Nellie felt a pang run through her as she watched him. "That's one way to put it. I, too, would like to put in my two cents. Eleanor and I should be allowed to leave."

"It's not happening, Dion." Bronywyn sneered. "Now drop it and listen to what my mother has to say to you."

Jacinta put a hand on Bronywyn's arm. "Enough. What I was saying, young man, is that we have a proposition for you. Elijah has been training our youths in hand-to-hand combat, but since he's leaving, we don't want them to go without help. I thought you might want to step in and train them?"

Dion rubbed his shoulders as he surveyed the room. "I suppose that's better than doing nothing."

Smiling, Jacinta brushed her palms together. "Then it's settled. You may go."

Shutting her eyes, Jacinta leaned back in her chair, dismissing everyone with a wave of her hand.

One exceptionally warm afternoon, when Solange had an emergency to attend to on the Surface, Nellie went to The Haven's gym with Dion instead of going to the infirmary. Nellie sat on the sidelines, her chin resting on her hand as she watched Dion teach. He moved like a dancer, deflecting blows with his arms, all the while manoeuvring around his opponents with ease. He seemed to anticipate everything his opponents would do before they even realized it themselves.

Not only did Dion train the youth, but he seemed genuinely interested in them. He patiently answered their questions about his life outside of The Haven. His candid responses surprised Nellie, since the infuriating man had been so cagey with her on the road. If nothing else, being away from Sequenced society had definitely softened Dion's attitude towards Nellie. The Official was still sarcastic, but the overall tone of his voice had lessened in severity.

Nellie wasn't sure how she felt about the shift, but with Elijah gone and being trapped in The Haven together, she and Dion ended up spending a lot of time together.

Once the youths had left for the day, Nellie watched as Dion drank an entire cup of water in one big gulp. Wringing her hands together, she took a deep breath and walked over to him.

"Will you teach me?"

Dion turned and stared at Nellie, his dark eyes reflecting the candlelight.

"To defend myself." Nellie rushed through her words, not wanting to lose her confidence. "After everything that has happened, I want to know that I can take care of myself, you know?"

Tilting his head to one side, Dion surveyed Nellie for a long moment. His eyes seemed to search her face. Finally, his lips turned up in a smile and he nodded. "You've got a deal. Let's do it. Every night after dinner sound good?"

"That sounds great."

"Perfect. We'll begin today."

"What? Now?"

Dion smirked. "Now. Unless you weren't serious?"

"No. I was serious. Let's do this."

For the next two hours, Dion led Nellie through a series of warmups and exercises.

"I don't understand why I have to do this," she complained while planking on the floor. "How will this help me with an enemy?"

"This will help, Eleanor, because it will allow you to strengthen your core." Dion was standing to the side, his arms crossed as he watched Nellie.

She scoffed. "Easy for you to say. You're not doing it. I'd like to see you try."

A gleam entered Dion's eye as he dropped next to her. "Challenge accepted. I bet you I can hold this longer than you."

Nellie tried to beat him. She really did. Sweat was pouring down her face by the time she collapsed on the floor.

"How long was that?" She panted.

"Two minutes." Dion said, laughing. "Don't worry, you'll get there."

Nellie groaned, but they kept working at it every evening. Her muscles were screaming, but she noticed that her body was becoming more toned after every session.

"Hand-to-hand combat," Dion had explained one evening after a particularly tough training session that left them both panting, "isn't about winning. It isn't really even about fighting. It's about being able to stand up for yourself in the face of danger and feeling confident in your abilities."

Nellie often replayed Dion's words in her mind as she practiced the moves he taught her late into the night. Soon, she came to look forward to these training sessions more than anything in her day.

Dear Mother,

It's been one hundred and seven days since I first entered the Haven. They still won't let me go. I miss the sun more than anything else. The warmth, the way it brightens everything up. Everything is so dark here.

Dion's been training me. Besides the Healers, Dion has become one of my only friends in The Haven, other than Rafael and Tomas. Remember him? He's the old librarian.

Dion's patience is astounding, Mother. I never thought him capable of such a thing, but he is both kind and compassionate to me. Don't tell him I said that, though, he'll never let me live it down. I'm getting stronger, too. One day, I'll show you everything he's taught me. I promise. He still pushes my buttons. He refuses to stop calling me 'Eleanor', despite my constant remarks against it.

Most of the other residents of The Haven avoid us. I don't really blame them. Half of them are scared of what we represent and the other half hate us for being Firsts.

I'll let you in on a secret, Mother.

Sometimes, I forget I'm a prisoner. It almost feels like home here.

Almost.

I will come back. I promise you.

Love,

Nellie.

∽

The worst day of Nellie's life took place about five months after she entered The Haven. On that fateful day, she woke up well before the first chime struck, her recurring nightmare having plagued her all night as she tossed and turned.

After breakfast that day, Nellie stumbled into the kitchen, rubbing her eyes. "Morning," she said to Matthias, who was already washing pans. The day after he had been taken for questioning about wasting water, he had returned, a haunted look in his eyes. He didn't have any bruises that she could see, but Nellie knew that the lack of physical evidence didn't mean nothing had happened. Matthias hadn't yet confided in her what had happened to him, but she knew that once day, he would.

"Mhmm." Matthias twisted slightly, nodding in Nellie's direction in greeting. She grabbed a pan and started scrubbing, her movements stiff as she tried to focus on the work at hand.

Visions of her nightmare kept flashing before her eyes as she worked, causing her focus to slip. Nellie was almost done with the pan when suddenly, her hand slipped and scalding hot water suddenly cascaded down the back of her right hand, spilling over onto her thigh. Nellie screamed, the pan clattering on the floor as the water rushed down her skin.

Luckily, she had her medical kit on her. Nellie quickly applied some medicinal balm containing aloe and pot marigold to her reddened skin. It tinged the skin of her palm a pale green, but the stinging of the burn quickly evaporated.

Groaning as she wrapped her hand and thigh in a bandage, Nellie realized she didn't have enough time to go to the library before lunch. She had just finished reading a collection of tales that spoke of foreign lands where there were flying dragons, winged pixies, and even people who could move their bodies from one place to the next with only a thought. Nellie had found the book so fantastical that she had devoured it all in one day and had nothing left to read.

Swallowing her disappointment, Nellie hurried back to her room for a fresh gown. She rushed through the halls that had become as familiar to her as the streets in Liantis. Breathless, Nellie had just sat down for lunch when Axel came barrelling into the cafeteria.

"Come quickly, Eleanor." He spoke in a huff, his hands landing on his knees as he panted for breath. Sweat dripped down his face, glimmering in the light emitted by the sconces. His eyes were wide, darting back and forth as he stared at Nellie. She had not seen Axel look this frightened since the first day she met him.

"Grab your kit," Axel said hurriedly. "There's an emergency and Solange needs our help right away."

Downing her glass of water in one gulp, Nellie pushed in her chair and raced after the other Healer. Her lunch forgotten, she raced after Axel, their path taking them past the infirmary and deep into The Haven. As they ran through the darkened corridors, the reality of where they were headed dawned on Nellie.

"No," she cried, her lungs burning with effort. "No. No." Nellie gasped as she ran, her hair flying behind her as she moved through the halls. They ran past surprised residents of The Haven, who quickly plastered themselves against the wall as they ran past. "No. It wouldn't be fair. Not him."

Too soon, Axel came skidding to a stop in front of the library door. Nellie moaned as hot tears rushed to her eyes before she brushed them away.

Be strong, Nellie. The Source chose you for a reason.
You can handle this.
You need to handle this.

Nellie gripped the doorknob as she breathed in a shallow breath, her lips quivering as she exhaled before she opened the door. Blinking as her eyes adjusted to the crystal lighting, Nellie stepped into the nightmare that awaited her on the other side.

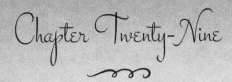

Chapter Twenty-Nine

She felt a strange sense of calm overtake her as she walked into the dimly lit room. It was as though someone had severed her soul from her body. There were two Nellies now.

One, a frightened eighteen-year-old with midnight blue hair who loved books and friends. As she stood in the doorway of the room lit not by firelight but by glowing blue and pink crystals, Nellie could see this young woman as though she were standing right in front of her. With a shock, she realized who she was looking at.

This... apparition was her soul.

The Nellie that was often buried under sarcasm and wit, the one that loved her mother and Fay and longed for the easygoing days of her wardship. Soul-Nellie's hair was dishevelled, her lack of composure evidence of her race through The Haven. Her light grey dress was full of wrinkles and one shoulder was slowly slipping off her frame. Soul-Nellie's emerald green eyes were enormous as tears poured out of them. Her mouth stood agape and her shoulders shook as she took in the scene in front of her.

Nellie felt a deep well of pity swell up inside of her as she watched this version of herself. It was with detached interest that she watched as her soul crumpled in the doorway, screaming in agony, crying out repeatedly as she beheld the terrible sight in front of her.

This Nellie was a wreck.

This Nellie was useless.

The other version of herself was emotionless, stoic even, as she assessed the situation. She needed to act quickly if she would have any hope of rectifying it. Nellie breathed in deeply and shook her head, shoving down each emotion as it arose. She did not have time for emotions right now. She needed to work.

The scene in front of Nellie was horrific. Tomas was on his back, his eyes glazed over as his legs lay at unnatural angles. She could see the white glimmer of bone peaking through his right leg, as she watched detached, assessing the situation.

Somewhere inside of herself, Nellie knew she would have nightmares about this moment for the rest of her life. A pool of blood gathered on the once-white carpet underneath the librarian. The scent of iron wafted through the air, staining the once-pleasant scent of the library.

Solange crouched next to the elderly man, holding his hand as she stroked his fingers. There were books scattered all around Tomas, their spines flayed open as though they were birds in flight.

The rest of the room disappeared from sight as Nellie focused on the injured man. She let out a sigh of relief when his chest moved, although the movements were far and few between. Swallowing hard, Nellie crouched down beside Tomas and took his free hand in hers. He had always been pale, but now his skin had an almost paper-like quality to it.

Nellie had never seen an injury this bad before in The Haven. Until that point, the worst thing she had seen was childbirth. While messy, that was normal, and Solange had been well-equipped to deal with any complications that might have arisen.

She vaguely remembered witnessing a horrific accident in Liantis when she was eight years old. A new building had been under construction, a training centre for new Tutors, when a Builder had fallen off his scaffold onto the packed dirt far beneath. Nellie remembered the sound of screams echoing through Liantis when the man had gone to be with the Source later that night.

The dead man's wife had shrieked long into the night; her wails being carried by the wind to the ears of all the residents of Liantis. The widow had mourned for days until the Protectors took her away. When Nellie had asked her mother about the wailing woman, Maude had shushed her before stating in a low voice that the widow had been Re-Sequenced. That was the last they had ever heard of her.

Lost in the pull of the past, it took Nellie a moment to realize that Solange was calling her name. Shaking her head, she pulled her eyes from Tomas's face to look at Solange. The older woman adjusted her glasses, running her hand through her sky-blue hair before looking at Nellie. Solange's face was grim, her mouth set in a straight line as she slowly shook her head back and forth.

No. No. Why Tomas?

Nellie felt her grip on herself slipping, giving way to her emotions as she stared at Tomas. Shaking, she pushed all of them deeper down inside of herself. Shuddering, Nellie clenched her jaw and counted to three before looking at Solange.

"What happened?" Nellie gently stroked Tomas' wrinkled face. She almost burst into tears when his grip on her hand tightened. Inhaling deeply, she wiped a hand on her brow. "Solange. Please. Tell me what happened."

Tears streaked down the older woman's face, fogging up her glasses as she lifted her head and looked at Nellie. Her sky-blue hair was falling over her face, creating a curtain as she looked at Nellie.

"Oh, Eleanor," she murmured. "I wasn't here when it happened, so I don't know for certain. What I know, Eleanor, is that this isn't good." The older woman paused for a moment to wipe the tears running down her cheeks. This was the first time Nellie had seen her cry, and she felt her heart break even more in the moment.

Nothing good ever comes to those who associate with me. Nellie thought grimly, her eyes on Tomas's face.

"I was sorting out my newest herbs when young Leo ran to get me from the infirmary. He told me that Tomas had fallen. I rushed over here as quickly as I could and this is what I found."

"Fallen?" Nellie echoed the Healer's words, shock roiling through her. "You mean he climbed the ladder to get to the top shelves? But they're thirty feet high!"

Solange nodded. "It appears that way. What I don't understand is why he was climbing the ladder in the first place? He knows better than that."

Nellie was trying to understand the same thing when the librarian suddenly groaned and shifted underneath her hands. She gasped as his eyes flew open. The movement stirred Solange into action, who quickly began barking orders.

"Tomas. Don't you move an inch. It isn't safe."

The old man opened his mouth, but no words came out. He reached out a hand towards Nellie's chest, as though trying to touch her. His hand fell to the ground, the fingers grasping at empty air.

"It's okay, Tomas." Solange wiped his brow with a cool cloth. "You're in shock. I'm here with Eleanor. Axel went back to the infirmary to get a stretcher. We're going to take care of you."

The librarian's enormous eyes stared at Nellie, blinking slowly as though he was beseeching her to understand some hidden message.

"Shhh. It is going to be okay." Nellie whispered as she slowly stroked his hand. "You silly old man," she said, forcing a tiny smile on her face, "what were you doing climbing the ladder? You should have waited for me; I would have helped."

Nellie felt a sudden pang in her chest as she remembered she had planned on being in the library earlier in the day, but because of the burns, she hadn't had the time to come here.

Maybe if I had been more careful, this never would have happened.

As quickly as the thought came to her, Nellie pushed it aside. She was slightly conscious that somewhere deep inside of her, her soul was cracking at the sight of her friend lying prone on the floor in a state of collapse, but she did not have the time or ability to focus on that right now. She pushed aside all emotions to focus on what she needed to get done.

"Solange?" Nellie spoke, her voice low but filled with urgency. She watched with wide eyes as the blue-haired Healer dug through her medicinal kit. "Is there nothing we can do while waiting for Axel to return?"

Solange sighed as she looked at Nellie, her brown eyes filled with pain.

"Unfortunately, not. I don't know..." Solange's voice cracked. "Come talk to me a moment?" She gestured to a spot a few feet away from Tomas's prostrate body.

Nellie looked at the old man, who smiled at her and squeezed her hand slightly.

"I'll just be right over there, Tomas. Don't you worry, I will not leave you."

As Nellie stood up from her crouched position on the ground, she carefully stepped backwards, avoiding the old man.

"Eleanor." Solange put her hand on Nellie's shoulder as she whispered in her ear. "I know you get along really well with Tomas. That's why I had Axel get you. This injury is extremely serious. He fell from the top shelves. It's honestly a miracle he is still alert right now."

Nellie had realized as much, but knowing something and hearing it come out of her mentor's mouth in such a matter-of-fact manner were two different things. She looked at the older Healer with a look of absolute horror in her eyes.

"Eleanor, listen to me. Tomas has lost too much blood. I'm not sure that he will survive if we move him."

"What... What can we do? We can't just leave him here!" Nellie was trying to whisper, but her voice was becoming more frantic by the second.

This could not be happening.

Not now, not to the one person who welcomed Nellie with open arms regardless of her Sequenced status.

Not to Tomas, rescuer of books and keeper of knowledge.

Solange shook her head, pity and sadness in her brown eyes. She pushed her glasses up on her nose, breathing in deeply. The sound of footsteps in the hallway rang through the library and before they could say another word, the library door banged open as Axel came bursting into the library with Dion and Rafael on his heels. Nellie watched as they carried the stretcher into the library. It was about six feet long, with stiff white fabric that was suspended between two wooden poles.

Sighing, Nellie rubbed her temples as she watched them carefully place the stretcher on the ground. They maneuvered around the pile of books, taking care not to step on Tomas as they moved. She felt a bit of her anxiety ease upon seeing Dion. She wasn't alone in this any longer.

Nellie darted away from Solange, who began speaking in low tones with Rafael, and took back up her position beside Tomas. She leaned over him to speak in his ear.

"It's okay, Tomas." Nellie whispered, squeezing the old man's hands. His eyes had shut while she had been speaking with Solange. "It's going to be okay now. Axel and Dion are here and they're going to help you. Just hold on." The only sign that the librarian had heard her was that his hand slowly tightened around Nellie's. Tears rushed to her eyes as she tried to keep her emotions at bay.

"Hurry, please." Nellie looked between Axel and Dion, her eyes pleading with them. "I don't think we have much longer. He has lost so much strength already."

The men placed the stretcher on the floor and moved it as close to Tomas as they could without touching him. Rafael and Solange rushed over, but before anyone could move, Tomas suddenly began speaking. Everyone froze, eyes glued to the elderly Scholar.

"Eleanor," he murmured, his voice so low and raspy that Nellie had to move her ear right next to his mouth to hear her. "No. I can't. I..."

"What do you mean?" Nellie tried to infuse lightheartedness into her voice, but her words came out sounding robotic, emotionless instead. "You silly old man, you can do this. We just need to get you to the infirmary and Solange will fix you right up."

Her voice cracked on the last word; a solitary tear slipped down her cheek.

"Don't be daft, dear." A trace of a smile flickered on Tomas's chapped lips. "You know as well as I do I will meet the Source by the end of the day."

"No," Nellie whispered, shaking her head back and forth. "Don't say that. I need you."

"You are much stronger than you think, Eleanor. I know you can do this. My Felix is waiting for me. I want to go to him. Now, I need you to do something for me."

Tomas's grip on Nellie's hand tightened suddenly, a wave of strength flooding his body.

"Okay." Her voice shook. "What do you need? I'll do anything and then, will you let us take you back to the infirmary?"

"I need you to find me a book, Eleanor. It's bright red with a silver border. The title-" Tomas broke off as a violent cough suddenly overcame him. The old man's shoulders shook as he coughed up a mass of red blood.

"Eleanor." Solange hissed from behind Nellie. "We need to move him now."

"No, Solange." Tomas spoke firmly, his eyes fixed on Nellie. "I will say this here. Eleanor, you need to find the book. The fate of the world depends on you. *The Biographical Works of Queen Francesca.* You must... promise... me."

Nellie felt herself lose her grip on the emotions she had kept tamped down. She choked out a strangled "I promise" before Tomas took one last shuddering breath. His eyes glazed over, staring at the shelves filled with his beloved books, never to move again.

The horrifying sound of screaming filled every corner of the library, permeating all of Nellie's senses. It went on and on, never ceasing. All other sounds stopped as the screams continued. After a moment, she was struck with the realization that the sound was coming from her own mouth. She couldn't move, let alone stop as her screams echoed throughout the entire Haven. She was vaguely aware of someone forcing a sickly sweet liquid down her throat before mercifully, the screaming stopped and everything went black.

Chapter Thirty

Several hours later, Nellie woke up in her own room, her head foggy. Groggily, she sat up in her bed and looked around.

Was it a dream?

Before she could get her hopes up, her eyes adjusted to the darkness of the room. There was a solitary sconce lit near the door, casting shadows on the walls. Dion's enormous frame was scrunched up into a much smaller wooden chair.

Nellie shifted on the bed, the sheets crinkling under her, as she realized she desperately had to use the restroom. She flung the coverlet off herself before swinging her legs onto the floor. The moment her bare feet hit the hardwood, Dion's jet-black eyes flew open and met Nellie's. He moved to unravel himself and came to stand in front of her.

"Tomas?" Nellie's voice cracked.

Dion shook his head. His eyes filled with tears.

"No." She sobbed, bunching the comforter in her fists as tears soaked her dress once more.

It was real.

Tomas was dead.

Nellie cried out, her hand flying over her mouth in shock as an enormous wave of grief flooded her.

How could Tomas have died? What was the point of such a senseless death?

Just yesterday, Nellie had been laughing with Tomas in the library as he recommended new books for her to read. Just yesterday, he was alive.

Ever since her Sequencing, it felt as though things were being taken from her at every turn. She lost her mother, her friends, her home and even her freedom.

"Eleanor." Dion's deep voice was low as he spoke to her, his obsidian eyes darting from hers to her cracked lips and below. Nellie followed his gaze, taking in the extremely wrinkled dress that hung off her body.

The Official touched Nellie's chin gently, drawing her eyes to his. His touch was soft, sending shivers down her spine as she looked at him with tear-filled eyes. "I'm going to run to get you something to eat and drink. Will you be okay without me for a moment?"

Okay? Nothing will ever be okay again.

She didn't say that, though. She just nodded mutely and padded down the darkened hallway to the restroom while Dion went to get her some food. Once she had relieved herself, she shuffled back to her room and crawled into bed. She lay her head on the pillows and just waited for Dion to come back. Nellie had thought that being kidnapped had been the worst thing that had ever happened to her, but she was wrong. At least there had been meaning behind her abduction.

Even Dion's presence in The Haven had a purpose, however convoluted it may have been.

But this?

Where was the meaning of this?

Nellie lost track of time, barely eating or drinking, as she mourned the sudden loss of Tomas. Dion never left her side, sleeping in that tiny chair and eating small bits of food. The few times she was alert, she tried to speak, but her mouth was so dry and her sorrow was so devastating that she could barely get a few words out before she descended back into the well of grief. It felt as though everything had fallen in on itself.

Nellie struggled to find a reason to wake up.

Life was fickle.

This was the conclusion she had reached. She felt stuck in a seemingly endless cycle of exhaustion. She lacked energy to do anything more than take care of her basic needs. If Dion hadn't been looking after her, she wasn't sure if she would have accomplished even that.

She slept her days away, losing all track of time.

As she slumbered, Nellie had the same dream repeatedly. She would see a large burnt-orange tree in the distance. It wasn't in a forest, surrounded by its coniferous peers. Instead, the tree stood sentry all alone, surrounded by a field of grain. No matter how far she ran, she could never reach it. She could hear the tree summoning her by name, calling her, telling her to seek the truth.

Sometimes Nellie would feel a shadow in her dreams beseeching her to pay attention. Without fail, she would lose the vision as soon as she woke up, sweaty and wrapped in her sheets. No matter how hard she tried, she could not recall it.

Deep in her soul, she knew this was a dream of consequence and she vowed to find out its significance.

Chapter Thirty-One

Time no longer had meaning. Nellie wasn't sure if it was days or weeks that were going by. All she knew was that Tomas had died and nothing mattered.

Dion kept his vigil by her side, leaving only long enough to take care of his own needs. One day, she awoke from the same dream to the sound of two familiar voices speaking in the hallway outside her door. She looked around, but Dion wasn't in the room.

That's odd.

Struck by a sudden desire to find out what was going on, Nellie decided to investigate the voices outside her room. Her muscles protesting, she swung her legs out of bed and stood up.

Her legs wobbled; her muscles were not used to carrying her weight after so many days spent lying in bed. The ankle she had twisted all those months ago throbbed. She smoothed over her worn nightgown as she stood on trembling legs. Shivers racked her body, causing her feet to curl and goosebumps to stand out on her arms. Shivering, she wrapped a turquoise throw around her shoulders, her body swaying with the effort of moving.

After a moment, she found enough strength to walk to the nightstand and pick up the taper left for her in case of emergencies. She held onto the wall, using the sconce to light it. With trembling hands, Nellie gripped the taper and hobbled to the door. Two figures stood in the hallway; voices hushed as they engaged in a serious conversation. The moment the door creaked against the wooden floor, the pair turned in union towards her.

"Ah, Eleanor. Just the person we came to see." Bronywyn was standing in front of Nellie, the woman appearing as much of a warrior as the first time she had met her. The rebel wore her dark-green hair in a series of intricate braids that ran down her back, twisting together like vines on a wall. Bronywyn was wearing her traditional dress, although in addition to the usual daggers on her thighs, she also had a long sword hanging from a scabbard on her hip. She looked every bit the terrifying warrior Nellie knew she was.

"Nellie, I came as soon as I heard." Looking around Bronywyn, Nellie gasped. Elijah was standing in the hallway, his tunic still covered in dust and grime. He must have come straight from the Surface to see her. The moment they made eye-contact, Elijah crossed the distance between them and pulled her into a tight hug.

"I am so sorry," he whispered, rubbing her back. "I wish I had been here for you."

At the reminder of Tomas's horrible death, Nellie sucked in a deep breath.

"Oh Lijah. It was awful." Nellie wept into his chest, her hands gripping the dirty material, seeking comfort. She was vaguely aware she was sobbing into a dirty tunic, but she overlooked the dust that covered Elijah's clothes for the comfort of an old friend's embrace.

Tears poured out of her, drenching Elijah. He murmured soft nothings into the crown of her head as she wept for Tomas. Finally, she pulled her head back and drew in a deep breath.

"Won't you come into my humble abode?" Nellie let out a raspy laugh at her attempt at humour as she opened the door and gestured for them to enter the room. There was only one chair, so Nellie sat with her back against the headboard as Bronywyn took Dion's regular spot in the chair. Elijah looked around the dimly lit room before he perched on the edge of the bed.

Silence filled the air as everyone looked at each other. Nellie raised a hand to her head, feeling a jumble of tangles in the place of her usual long, silky hair. She couldn't even remember the last time she had bathed, although the smell in the room led her to believe it had been quite a while. Colour rushed to her cheeks, her face burning as she sat on the bed.

Elijah's gaze followed her hand to her hair. A tiny smile touched his lips. "I thought I looked worse for wear after having been on the Surface, Nell-bell, but it looks like you might have me beat." Coming from anyone else, Elijah's implications might have insulted Nellie, but she felt a strange sense of comfort at being acknowledged and accepted by her friend.

She looked down at herself, grimacing. "I suppose I do look a mess, don't I?"

Elijah hummed as he rubbed the back of his neck. "Do you remember when you fell into the mud puddle after the torrential rainstorm when we were wards and Guardian Clarence threatened to have you whipped if you touched anything with your muddy hands?"

Nellie grinned at the memory.

"Of course," she said. "How could I forget?"

"Well," Elijah said, a smile on his face, "I think he would faint if he saw you today. He would take one look at you and say, 'Eleanor Merrick. You go clean up right now. You are a disappointment to the Source by looking like something that rolled right out of a pig-sty.'"

Nellie snorted out a laugh before her eyes went wide and she covered her mouth with her hand. She had never thought she could laugh again, not after she watched Tomas die in her arms. As quickly as the feeling of laughter had set upon her, it slipped away. Her hand fell away from her mouth as she collapsed against the bed. *How can anything feel right ever again?*

Bronywyn coughed from the chair and stood up. She wore an expression of irritation on her face, as though this entire situation was beneath her.

"Well, as touching as this all is, I'm going to go check in with my mother. Elijah, meet me later to debrief? Perhaps the next time I see you, Nellie, you'll look a little more alive."

Ouch. She's just as sharp as ever. At least that hasn't changed.

As much as the warrior's comment hurt, Nellie couldn't help but acknowledge the truth in her statement. She had been lying in bed for days, and it was evident by the way her hair had tangles running throughout. Frankly, she smelled like a dead horse and she needed to take a few moments to compose herself. Her mouth tasted like sour apples and her hair desperately needed a washing.

Elijah nodded, but kept his eyes on Nellie. "Not a problem, Bronywyn. I'll be here for a while yet. Nellie needs me."

Nellie drew in her breath as she watched Bronywyn leave.

"Lijah... I need to clean up."

"Hmm." Elijah let out a non-committal sound of agreement that sounded like a cross between a laugh and a huff. "You probably do. Why don't you do that and I'll hunt down some food?"

At the mention of food, her stomach rumbled loudly. She had barely eaten since Tomas died and the lack of nutrition in her body was definitely getting to her.

"Good idea," she said. "Maybe you can find some of those delicious lentils?"

For the first time in days, she was actually hungry.

Having agreed to meet back shortly, they split up. Nellie hobbled to the ladies' restroom, her arms laden with a clean dress, her toothbrush and toothpaste, as well as soap for her hair. The walk to the restroom took her much longer than normal, her muscles still stiff from her bed rest. Mercifully, the door opened to reveal an empty room.

Once she deposited her belongings on the counter, Nellie braced the edge and stared at herself in the large mirror. She didn't recognize the reflection looking back at her. Her eyes were enormous, with dark shadows underneath them. Her face was taunt, her once-curvy body reflecting her lack of nutrition. She swore to herself that she would find a way back to the woman she had been.

Finally, Nellie emerged from the chamber. She had quickly braided her now-clean hair before flinging it over one shoulder, the damp hair leaving wet marks on her dress. She didn't mind, though. She felt more alive in these moments than she had since Tomas's death. The water from the bath had pulled her from her grief-induced trance, and she was ready to tackle whatever lay ahead.

Back in her room, Nellie sat on her bed. While she was out, some kind soul had been in the room and had replaced all the sheets and bedding. They had even brought in some specially scented candles. Curious, she sniffed at one candle, careful not to light herself or her hair on fire. The scent was incredible, the aroma of evergreen trees and vanilla intermingling, and filling the room with a pleasant scent.

Oh, how she wished she could see trees right now. She hadn't known how much she enjoyed life on the Surface until the Subversives had ripped it away from her.

Shaking her thoughts away from the Surface, she arranged her dress to make sure she covered her legs. The women who lived in The Haven were far less concerned with their modesty than those who lived on the Surface, but Nellie still couldn't bring herself to shake the confines of her upbringing.

Soon after she returned to her room, Elijah came in carrying a large wooden tray. Not only did the tray hold a bowl full of the spiced lentils that she loved, but there were pieces of flatbread peppered with sesame seeds on the top, a bowl of refreshing chutney and even some cooling yogurt. He placed the tray on the bed, retaking his seat on the edge of the bed.

Without Bronywyn in the room, the air seemed a lot calmer. They ate in silence, gorging themselves on the delicious food. Finally, they both sat back, their stomachs pleasantly full.

Nellie looked at her friend, noticing that he had taken the time to change before he returned to her room. He had traded in his dusty tunic for a clean one, but he hadn't shaved. Stubble graced his face, adding an air of aloofness to his overall appearance. Nellie found she didn't mind it at all. She took in a deep breath, steadying herself on the bed before she spoke.

"Okay, Elijah." Her voice was weak, betraying the exhaustion that still ran rampant throughout her body. "Out with it. How long"

"How long?" He echoed her words, a look of confusion crossing his face briefly before he seemed to realize what she was asking. "How long was I gone?"

Nellie nodded, her hands subconsciously running down her damp braid. She was full of nerves, and she could see that he wasn't sure how to answer her question.

"Just tell me," she said. "Please. I've... I don't know how long it's been since Tomas died and I feel like I lost part of myself that day." Nellie looked over at Elijah, her eyes pleading with him. "I don't know how to explain it, but I feel like I need to understand everything that happened if I'm ever going to be myself again."

"Nellie, I'll do my best to help. You know me, I would never stand in your way of anything. Especially not this." Elijah sighed, standing up and running his hand through his curly black hair. "I've been on the Surface for the past three months. As soon as we heard what happened to Tomas, we dropped everything to come back. If I had known something like this would happen, I never would have left you alone."

Nellie's mouth was dry as she tried to form words.

Three months. That means half a year has passed since I last saw my mother.

The thought was too much for Nellie to handle. She missed her mother more and more each day. She had never imagined that being away from her would feel this terrible. Tears began running down her cheeks as she tried to understand everything that was happening.

Elijah shifted closer, but she shook her head. "No, I'm okay. Just give me a minute."

Nodding, he sat back down on the edge of the bed and watched her. Grabbing the cup of water she kept on the nightstand, Nellie drank every drop of the life-giving liquid before shifting her glance to her old friend. He hadn't moved, his body as still as a statue on the edge of her bed.

"So, it's been about two weeks, I suppose." Nellie shook her head. How could two weeks feel like an instant *and* an eternity? "Did I miss... did they cremate him?"

In Tiarny, it was a tradition to cremate most bodies after they met the Source. Typically, the Gravediggers gave the family an urn with the deceased's ashes after the cremation, but Nellie knew Tomas didn't have any kin left in The Haven. She had always thought the term Gravedigger was a misnomer, since the only people who received actual graves were Firsts who lived in Deavita.

"Bronywyn said they did." Elijah shifted on the bed to hold one of Nellie's hands. His voice was low and deep as his eyes searched Nellie's for... something. There was a tension between them that hadn't been there before. "Can you tell me what happened?"

Nellie knew she should pull her hand away, but she just couldn't make herself do it. All she had been feeling lately was sadness and exhaustion. Now, finally, Elijah was making her feel something else. And she needed that feeling more than anything in the world.

"Where do I start?" Nellie muttered, trying to sort all the events of the past few weeks in her mind. She didn't realize she had spoken the words aloud until Elijah responded.

"How about at the beginning? The messenger who came to get us had little information that he could share, so I'd appreciate anything you can tell me."

"I guess that's as good of a place as any."

And so, Nellie told Elijah the events that lead up to Tomas's death. She told him about the exhaustion she had been feeling and the resulting burn she suffered. When she got to the part about missing her regular library visit, she burst into tears once more. Elijah moved closer to her and put his left arm over her shoulder. He held her as she wept for the librarian, his right hand gently rubbing circles on her leg as she wept.

"It's okay, Nellie." Elijah whispered into her hair, his hands continuing their mindless movements. "It's not your fault."

Nellie's shoulders shook as she sobbed. "But... you... don't... understand." She choked out the words that were little more than whispers, clutching Elijah's hand like a life preserver in the ocean of her grief. "It is my fault. If I had only gone to the library in the morning like I normally do, Tomas would never have been climbing the shelves. If it wasn't for me, he would still be alive today."

"Nellie." Elijah spoke softly, his voice deep and husky. Each word reverberated through her as they sat next to each other on her bed. "Look at me, Eleanor."

At the sound of her full name, she drew in a breath. In all the years they had known each other, he so rarely used her full name. She shifted slightly on the bed so she could see his face. Elijah's eyes were glistening with tears, his eyes filled with tenderness. He put his finger on her chin, gently drawing her face to his.

"It is not your fault, Eleanor." He was whispering now, his voice husky.

How come when Dion says my name like that, it grates against my every nerve, but the way Elijah said my name feels so different?

Suddenly, Nellie froze as she realized just how close the two of them were. The air electrified between them, every spot where their bodies touched danced with electricity. She breathed in a shallow breath as she looked up into his eyes. He towered over her, his dark skin glowing in the flickering light of the scented candles.

If Nellie moved at all, she knew her lips would find themselves on top of Elijah's. It wasn't as though she has never kissed anyone in her life. There had been boys before, of course. Not many, but she had gotten to know a few of the other wards back in Liantis. Her first kiss had been nothing remarkable, a peck on the lips with a boy named Marcus. It had been quick and dry and didn't really make Nellie care for the boy or kissing in general. Since that first time, she had kissed a few other boys, but none of them had ever made her feel like she did at that moment. Sitting next to Elijah as she cried her heart out, Nellie felt more comfortable than she ever had before.

The air was thick with tension as Nellie shifted her gaze up from his lips to his wide, unmoving eyes. They stared at her, watching her every movement. She had never noticed that Elijah's eyes weren't completely brown but had golden flecks studded throughout, giving his eyes the appearance of having shards of sunlight woven into them. The intensity and affection in his gaze caused her breath to hitch in her throat. Nellie felt as though she could see into his soul.

"Eleanor," Elijah murmured, his hand still touching her chin. She was aware of every place their bodies came into contact. "We don't have to-"

At that moment, Nellie decided. She wanted this.

"Lijah." Nellie whispered; her voice thick. "Let me make a choice, for once."

A flicker of emotion crossed Elijah's face at the reminder that Nellie never had freedom. Before he could say anything, she made her choice.

"Elijah," she said huskily, her hand rising to touch his face gently. "Can I kiss you?"

His eyes searched hers, the kindness in them threatening to overwhelm her. "Yes," he whispered.

She crossed the distance between them, the inch feeling like a mile. The moment their lips met; the room seemed to fade away. Elijah's lips were both warmth and softness, his touch reverent as they explored each other hesitantly. This was leaps and bounds from anything she had experienced before.

Everything disappeared as the kiss deepened. The flickering light from the sconces, the feeling of the wooden headboard behind Nellie's back, the scent of the evergreen candles all faded away. The only thing Nellie could focus on was this kiss.

The sensation was like nothing she had ever felt before. It was as if Elijah was a beam of sunlight that had broken through the darkness that had surrounded Nellie for the past few weeks. Every moment that his lips stayed on hers, she felt a little more like herself.

Time itself seemed to realize the importance of the moment, as everything slowed to a crawl. What began as a tentative touch of the lips deepened into something more.

Nellie's hand moved to cup Elijah's neck, pulling loose the ribbon that was holding back his long, black curls. They came tumbling down around them and she giggled against his lips. She felt him smile before his lips moved against hers once more.

Nellie didn't know how long they spent in that position before she heard the door swinging open. They flew apart at the sound, barely an inch between them, before they saw who was standing in the doorway.

Chapter Thirty-Two

"Hello Elijah. What a *surprise* to see you here."

Dion stood in the doorway, his voice dripping with something that seemed like irritation as his eyes swept over the room. His mouth was tight, his lips tilted downwards as he glared at them.

The tension in the room was thick.

There was a sudden shift in the air that thoroughly confused Nellie. She didn't have time to investigate it further because, at that same moment, Elijah all but leapt off the bed. The mattress shifted to adjust for the change in weight and she fell back, her head landing on the pillows before she could catch herself.

Nellie blinked, and Elijah was standing in front of Dion. The two men glared at each other, tension rolling off of them in waves. They were engaged in some strange staring contest, which she didn't understand. They had better things to do than stare each other down.

Nellie shifted from her seated position, sliding off the bed and adjusting her dress so it fell to the floor.

"Dion, where did you go? What's going on?"

Both men turned and looked at her, their faces reflecting a level of hostility that Nellie didn't have time to unpack.

The Official glared at Elijah before his gaze shifted to hers, his eyes softening as he studied her every feature.

"Eleanor," he said her name in that exasperating tone of his. "I'm sorry I wasn't here when you woke up. Jacinta called me away as soon as Bronywyn, Cecelia and Elijah returned from the Surface and because of my..." Dion coughed before continuing, "Interesting position as a *guest* of The Haven, I wasn't able to refuse."

Nellie nodded her head in understanding. At least she could claim that the Subversives wanted her there, despite her desperate and continuous pleas to let her leave. She could not say the same about Dion. He was, by all accounts, an unwanted guest being held against his will.

Dion continued, irritation lacing his words, mingling with some other emotion she couldn't quite put her finger on. "Elijah and Bronywyn had said they would stay with you while I spoke to Jacinta, so imagine my surprise when I returned and found Bronywyn had disappeared and Elijah was... not talking to you."

Nellie's eyes widened at the implication that she had been doing something illicit with Elijah. Her fingers flew up to touch her swollen lips before she realized what a telling sign that would be.

"Dion, Nellie was just about to go over what happened in the library with me." Elijah crossed his arms as he stared at the Official. "I don't think I heard the whole story yet. Why don't we move to the common room? We can finish that discussion there."

Elijah has always been the peacemaker.

Nellie's lips tilted up as she saw Elijah fitting right back into the role he had always held in her life. She wasn't sure when it had happened, but as she searched her heart for anger towards him regarding his role in her kidnapping, she found it was all gone. Somewhere along the way, she had forgiven him for his role in her abduction.

Besides, Nellie thought. *If I hadn't come to The Haven, maybe I never would have learned about how dangerous the Sequenced are. I certainly would never have met Mateo, Tomas, Jacinta, Bronywyn, or any of the other amazing people I've encountered since the rebels brought me here.*

Not that she was happy that the Subversives had kidnapped her. She wasn't developing some strange captor-appreciation syndrome. It was that the world was a lot bigger than the Sequenced had made it out to be. And that was perhaps their biggest sin of all. They trapped people in their Sequenced occupations and stole their freedom of choice.

"That's a great idea." Dion still seemed annoyed, but some of the tension had left his posture as he headed first out the door.

Elijah held the door open, sharing a look with Nellie before they left.

"Are you okay?" He whispered.

She nodded, and Elijah's shoulders relaxed as he followed her out the door.

The walk to the common room had only taken ten minutes, although it had felt much longer as silence filled the corridors. The only sound had been that of their shoes marching on the wooden floor as the two men glared at each other.

Nellie's shoulders were tense when they arrived, although some of it left her when she saw the space was empty. Even though it was midday, it wasn't unusual to find a few of The Haven's inhabitants taking a break in the common room.

The room had an inviting atmosphere and was one of Nellie's favourite places in The Haven. It was large and lined with a few worn couches. There were blankets thrown over the various pieces of furniture and rugs strewn across the floor. It was lit with the same crystals that were found in the library, their ambient lighting adding to the overall calming effect of the chamber.

Sighing, Nellie sat down and crossed her legs under herself as she pulled a lime green blanket onto her lap. Tucking it around herself, she looked up to see the two men sitting on the couch across from Nellie, each as far away from the other as possible. Dion's back was as straight as a board as he sat staring at Elijah, while the man in question spread his legs and leaned back as though he hadn't a care in the world. Despite his attempt to portray ease, Elijah's facial expressions betrayed his true feelings. His jaw was clenched in a firm line, his brows furrowed as he stared at Dion. Elijah's eyes were fiercely dark as glared at Dion.

Nellie sat gawking at the two men, wondering if they even remembered her presence in the room. The tension between the two of them was so intense, the air felt like thick mud after a rainstorm. Finally, she grew impatient with the two of them and threw a lumpy navy-blue pillow at them. Her aim was terrible, and it landed in the middle of the couch with a thump. Both men tore their gazes away from each other and stared at Nellie.

"What was that for, Eleanor?" Dion's voice was low and deep as he spoke. Shivers ran down Nellie's back at the emotion running through Dion's eyes. He appeared tense, but there was a hint of a smile gracing his lips.

Elijah seemed perturbed by the interruption of the inane staring contest. He crossed his arms and began glaring at Nellie instead of Dion.

She sat up straight, the back of the armchair digging into her spine as her gaze swung between the two of them.

"What do you think? Whatever issues the two of you have, they need to go away now. I barely had the energy to walk here, let alone to play mediator to whatever weirdness you have going on."

"Issues?" Dion repeated, his voice sharp with ire. "We have a lot of those. For starters, Elijah and his *people* are holding us captive here."

"You would know about that, wouldn't you, Dion?" Elijah spat back at him. "After all, you worked high up in the Sequenced government as an Official. Surely you knew they were holding Healers captive?"

"We've already gone over this Elijah." Dion ground out his words. "I did not know they were taking Healers. If I had, I would have..."

"You would have what? What would you have done?"

Dion sighed and rubbed his hands over his face. The room was silent, hostility thick in the air as the two men glared at each other. Finally, Dion exhaled before he replied, his voice thick with emotion.

"You're right."

Elijah's mouth fell open. "I'm sorry, what?"

"You. Are. Right." Dion muttered. "I didn't know, but I am not sure that even if I had known, I would have done anything. And that is my eternal shame." He dropped his head into his hands, rubbing his palms over his eyes. Nellie had been watching the exchange silently, but now she sat up.

"Dion." Nellie murmured his name, her voice barely audible, but somehow, he still heard her. "You can't blame yourself for something that you didn't know was happening. But now that you know, you can help. We still need to figure out why the Royal Protectors are taking Healers. I think that Tomas might have known something about that. He tried to tell me something right before he died."

"What?" Elijah looked up at that, his eyes flashing. "What did he say?"

Nellie breathed in deeply and looked at the floor, her eyes watering as she recalled the day. "He was lying on his back, books strewn out all around him, when he looked me in the eye." She paused, wiping her eyes as a few tears escaped down her cheeks. She looked up to see both Elijah and Dion sitting on the edge of the couch, rapt with attention.

Her brows knitted, Nellie rubbed her temples. "He said... he said the fate of the world depended on me finding a book. It sounded like the ramblings of an old man. Maybe in those last moments he lost his sanity?"

"I don't know, Nell-bell. What book did he tell you to find? Maybe the clues lie within." Elijah looked at Nellie, his shoulders angled away from Dion.

Groaning, Nellie closed her eyes and pulled herself back to that awful day. She felt the wave of grief roll over her, but this time, she held fast, riding it out to reach her memory. "He said I needed to find a biographical work. It sounded like nothing I've ever read before..."

The memory began slipping from her mind when suddenly, she gasped. Her emerald green eyes flew open as she whispered, "I remember. *The Biographical Works of Queen Francesca.* Have either of you heard of that?"

For the first time since they entered the common room, Dion and Elijah looked at each other. They shared a glance, each shaking their heads before facing Nellie once more.

"I'm sorry, Eleanor, I haven't," Dion said.

Nellie buried her head in her hands. "What good is the title of one book? Finding something based on a title is like looking for a needle in a haystack."

"Nell-bell, don't give up. Tomas believed in you." Elijah stood up from the couch, threading a hand through his hair. "Let's go find that book. I don't know everything about literature, but I'd hazard a guess that we can find it in the library."

At those words, Dion raised himself off the couch. His muscles rippled as he pushed himself up, his every movement noticeable as he moved. All the training with the youths had certainly helped him maintain his physique. Elijah seemed to ignore the other man, keeping his gaze firmly on Nellie.

Dion took a step towards Nellie before glancing back at Elijah.

"Look, whatever's going on, let's put it aside for her sake." His voice was firm, unwavering, as he gestured towards her.

Elijah's brows drew together, his nostrils flaring as he studied Dion. "I'll do it if you will," he said finally.

"It's a deal."

The two men clasped hands, shaking once, before turning towards the door. "Are you coming, Eleanor?" Dion spoke to Nellie as he followed Elijah out into the hallway.

Shaking her head, Nellie stood up and followed the men. She would never understand the mysterious way these creatures functioned.

"Alright boys," she said softly. "Let's go solve a mystery and give Tomas's death some meaning."

Chapter Thirty-Three

~∞~

Nellie looked around the library with sadness. The last time she had been in here, Tomas had been lying on the floor, dying. Someone had clearly been in here since then. They had picked all the books up from the floor, swept the room and righted all the furniture that had overturned in the chaos. Somehow, Nellie had thought that the room would be different after everything that happened, but it didn't. The crystals still glowed softly, the room smelled faintly of books and vanilla, and papers were still strewn over Tomas's desk.

Who would take over as librarian now? The thought suddenly struck Nellie, her heart clenching at the thought of Tomas's hard work going undone now that he had died. As Nellie took in the room, Dion and Elijah began searching through stacks. The two men had separated as soon as they walked into the room, as though they couldn't stand to be too near each other at the moment.

"Why did you ask this of me, Tomas? Of all the things you could have said on your deathbed, why this?" Nellie muttered as she sifted through the items on Tomas's desk.

Soon, the only sound filling the air in the library was that of paper shifting and books being moved. Nellie focused on her task, as everything else faded away. Minutes passed by.

As Nellie got to the end of the items on Tomas's desk, she was about to move when she felt a hand land on her shoulder.

"Eleanor."

The corner of Nellie's mouth turned up at the sound of Solange's soft voice.

"It's so good to see you out of bed. We've missed you," the older Healer said.

Nellie turned around, her face breaking into a genuine smile as she saw the sky-blue-haired Healer standing in front of her. She glanced over Solange's shoulder, seeing Rafael talking with Elijah.

"Solange. It's so good to see you. How are you?" Nellie pulled her mentor into a hug, relishing the warmth of the woman's body. She looked the same as always. Her blue hair was falling in waves down her back, a sharp contrast to the slitted black dress she wore. Unlike Bronywyn, Solange didn't carry any daggers, but she had her medicinal bag slung over her shoulder.

"I'm okay, thank you. I've missed you, Nellie." Solange said. "Both Axel and I do. It's not the same in the infirmary without you. I checked on you daily, you know."

"Thank you, Solange, that means a lot to me."

Solange looked beyond Nellie's shoulder at Dion before she leaned in conspiratorially, waggling her eyebrows.

"You know, Eleanor. That man was so protective of you, he wouldn't let you out of his sight while you were recovering after Tomas's death. It was impressive. In all my years as a Healer, rarely have I seen a partner so attentive."

Blood rushed to Nellie's face, the tips of her ears reddening as she stared wide-eyed at her mentor.

"Oh no, Dion and I, we're not, it's not, there's nothing..."

Solange giggled and patted Nellie's arm. "It's okay, dear. You may not be ready to see it yet."

Nellie felt as though she was about to combust into flames as mortification overtook her.

Dion and I? Solange is observant, to be sure, but the man hates me. And I hate him too. Don't I?

Before she could go any further down this rabbit hole, a triumphant shout came from the corner of the library.

"I found it!" Dion leapt up from his position in the library's corner. Crouched in the back of the library, the Official had been scouring through piles and piles of old books in search of the missing biography.

Elijah grumbled something about wishing *he* had been the one to find the book, but there was no malice in his voice. Nellie rushed over to Dion's side to see the book, her eyes widening when she looked at what he held.

"*This* is what Tomas wanted me to find?"

Dion held a small book in his hands. It was perhaps four inches wide and six inches tall. The cover was a deep red, resembling the colour of spilled blood. There was elegant gold writing scrawled on the spine. It was nothing like the block writing that adorned most of the books in Tiarny. This writing looked like artwork, the letters all flowing into each other, looping in giant swirls as they created words.

The book itself was ancient. Yellowed pages stuck out of the spine, standing in stark contrast to the blood-red ribbon sticking out of the bottom.

As Dion turned the book over in his hand, Nellie noticed that there was a tree embossed on the cover. Its roots ran deep into the ground while its branches stretched high into the sky, as though it was reaching for something. Something about it reminded her of the four goddesses she had seen on the corners of the Temple in Liantis.

I've seen this tree before. Nellie thought suddenly. *I know it. Maybe this will finally shed some light on its importance.*

None of the others seemed to notice the tree, however, as they were all caught up in the inspection of two dates embossed on the bottom of the back cover.

"530-562 Years After Inception," Solange read the dates out loud, wonder threading through her voice. "I've never seen anything this old. I was aware Tomas had saved some books, but I didn't know anything still existed from this time period."

Silence filled the cavernous library as the five pairs of eyes stared at the small tome.

Nellie leaned over, reading the title as Dion held the book outstretched in his hands. She knew without looking that Elijah was standing behind her.

"*The Biographical Works of Queen Francesca*". Nellie looked around at the strange group gathered about. "Well," she said, "should we read it?"

Amid murmurs of agreement, Nellie reverently took the book out of Dion's grasp and carried it back to Tomas' desk. Her stomach was in knots, anxiety roiling through her body. Somehow, the librarian's old desk felt like the right place to read it. He had died searching for this book, and now Nellie held it in her hands.

What was so important that you couldn't wait for me, Tomas?

The rest of the group dragged chairs over, forming a circle around the large mahogany desk. The library was lit better than most of The Haven because of the crystals scattered throughout. Nellie didn't even need to squint as she flipped open the ancient book. What she saw on the first page left her speechless.

Chapter Thirty-Four

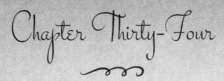

Nellie's green eyes were wide as she stared at the book. There wasn't any writing on the first page. Instead, Nellie was staring at a sketch of a pendant that looked remarkably similar to the one that she wore around her neck.

Her mouth opened and closed as she looked at the two-hundred-year-old text, wondering how an image of her necklace ended up in the book. Her finger stretched out, tracing the lines of the pendant absentmindedly as she tried to understand what was happening.

Nellie looked up from her thoughts to see that everyone was staring at her.

"Eleanor," Dion spoke, his brows furrowed as he took charge of the situation. "What is it? Do you recognize this pendant?"

Suddenly, Nellie felt mirth rising in her. She laughed at Dion's statement. It wasn't a quiet laugh, but one that shook her entire body as she tried to contain the hilarity. Everyone stared at her as though she were mad. And perhaps she was.

"I'm sorry. I know it's not funny, it's just... do... I... recognize... it?"

Nellie spoke the words between fits of laughter and gasping for air. "Yes Dion, I recognize it."

Nellie reached under her dress and pulled out the pendant she had worn since the morning of her Sequencing.

It was as though all the air had disappeared from the room. Nellie heard a chorus of gasps as she sat in her chair, giggling as she fingered the chain that hung around her neck.

Elijah's eyes were wide as they darted between the book and the pendant. His mouth kept opening and closing, resembling that of a dying fish.

Rafael stood behind Solange, hands on her shoulders, as he watched. His eyes weren't on Nellie at all, but rather on his wife. She sat stoically; her eyes frozen on the book.

"How did you... Eleanor, what does this mean?" Dion asked as he rubbed his shoulders.

Nellie groaned, her head falling in her hands. "Honestly, I have no idea. This is as big of a shock to me as it is to all of you."

"Nellie," Elijah finally spoke, his eyes wide. "How did Tomas know about this book? Did he know you had this pendant?"

"I don't know how he would have. I always hid it under my dresses. It's not like I wouldn't have noticed if it had slipped out. Here's what I do know though..."

For the next few minutes, Nellie shared everything with the group that she knew about the pendant. That her mother had gifted it to her on the morning of the Sequencing with the implication that the pendant was important. Upon reaching the end of her tale, she sat back with an enormous sigh.

"I still don't know what it means." Nellie said as she rubbed her eyes. " Please, if anyone has any insight, this all feels so important, somehow."

Solange broke out of her stupor and leaned forward. "Can I see the pendant, Eleanor? I'd like to examine it."

Nellie reluctantly lifted the pendant off her head. "Please be careful. It's the only thing I have left of my mother." She placed the pendant in her mentor's hand before moving to sit beside her.

Solange hummed to herself as she looked at the necklace, turning it this way and that as she examined the piece of jewellery. Her eyes sparkled as she studied it, seeming to have figured something out.

"Eleanor, pass me the book, please."

Nellie did as Solange asked. It was always a pleasure to watch her mentor work, and this was no exception. Solange hemmed and hawed for a few minutes before she sat back, clearly pleased with herself.

"This tree, does it have any significance to you, Eleanor?"

Shaking her head, Nellie was about to reply "no", before she halted.

"My dreams," she gasped as memories of dozens of forgotten dreams suddenly poured into her mind. They came rushing in as a wave, flooding Nellie's senses. "Oh Source, the dreams." Nellie grabbed her head with both hands, groaning, "the dreams."

Dion and Elijah looked at each other in confusion.

"What dreams, Eleanor?" Dion asked quietly.

Nellie wanted to answer him, but she struggled to breathe with all the new information. This was too much. Her lungs were on fire, her heart beating too quickly as she struggled to get air. Gasping, Nellie looked at Solange. The Healer jumped into action, rubbing Nellie's back and encouraging her to focus on her breathing.

In and out.

Inhale.

Exhale.

Repeat.

The blue-haired Healer ordered Dion to fetch a glass of water while she sent Elijah to find a blanket to wrap Nellie in. Soon, the men returned and after a few minutes had passed, Nellie felt more like herself. Her fingers kept running over the tree embossed on the cover, tracing its lines as she breathed.

Nellie's breathing had returned to normal; Solange returned the pendant to her. A sigh of relief left her the moment she slipped it back over her neck, her entire body relaxing as the necklace rested in its rightful place on her chest.

Never again, she vowed to the pendant. *You won't leave my neck again.*

Her breathing under control and her pendant back where it belonged, Nellie took a deep breath and a drink of the chilled water before she spoke. Her voice was soft, the words quiet. Everyone was silent, watching her from their seats.

"I've been having dreams. Well, they're nightmares, really. This tree, it's been calling to me for months." Nellie shook her head, trying to shake the memories of the nightmare from her mind. "I don't know how to explain it. I just know that this tree is important."

Solange handed Nellie another cup of water.

"Drink this, please. It appears the tree from your dreams is the same as the one on your pendant and on the cover of the book. Perhaps the answers lie within?"

"What kind of answers might a biography of an ancient Queen have for me?" Nellie questioned.

"I don't know, Eleanor. But we have to find out. For Tomas." Her mentor's voice was grave, her eyes troubled with the memory of Tomas' death.

"For Tomas." Each person in the room echoed the sentiment, grief joining their voices together.

It turned out that a biographical work of a Queen's life was just as boring as it seemed. Most of the entries involved detailed descriptions of complaints brought before the Queen, problems she had solved and petitions she heard. Dion was yawning after the first page, and Elijah soon followed suit. Even Solange seemed to be having trouble staying alert as Nellie read page after page of the biography out loud, looking for any answers.

She soon grew frustrated with the book itself.

"Ugh." Nellie groaned, standing up and stretching. "Other than the image of the pendant on the front page, it appears this is completely useless."

By this time, Elijah had fallen asleep in his chair. His legs were spread in front of him, stretching his body to its full extent before falling asleep. His mouth hung open, exposing a mouthful of bright white teeth as he slept. A string of saliva hung from his mouth, hanging precariously above his shirt. Dion appeared as though he was about to follow suit, but when Nellie stood up, his jet-black eyes flickered open.

"Eleanor." Dion whispered, reaching over to pull Nellie in for a hug. "I have a good feeling about this. Let's just try a few more pages and see if we can find anything of importance."

Nellie sighed, rubbing her hands over her face. Dion *would* be logical. "You're right. Of course, you're right. Tomas wouldn't want me to give up."

Flopping back down in the chair, Nellie picked the book up and kept reading in her head. Page after page, the biography covered the same menial events. She was about to give up for good when she noticed an entry from the year 546.

That's odd, she thought. *My mother mentioned that year as well.*

Nellie skimmed the paragraph before she let out a whoop of excitement. Her shout startled Elijah, who yelled as he woke up.

"What? What's going on? Is Nellie hurt?" He spoke in a rush, his eyes wide as they took in the scene in front of him. After a moment, the tall man's posture softened, his arms dangling at his sides.

"I'm fine, Lijah."

Dion stood up and stretched his arms behind his head, his arms nearly knocking into a crystal perched on a nearby wall. The Official settled back into his chair, his hands resting on his knees as he looked at Nellie. "Well, Eleanor?"

"Are you going to share? We would all love to know what you found." Solange had been sorting her medicinal herbs while Nellie had been reading, but she had put them away as soon as Nellie had cried out.

"Right," Nellie grinned as she looked each person in the eye, excitement flooding her senses for the first time since Tomas had died. "I was reading this passage when I remembered something my mother had told me. When my mother gave me the pendant, she mentioned something about a Purge in passing. I didn't mention it before because-"

Elijah stood up then, interrupting Nellie. "Wait. Purge? Are you sure that's what she said?"

Nellie nodded.

"I need to get Bronywyn. She needs to hear this. Our mission involved the Purge, but we didn't find what we were looking for. Hold that thought."

The tall man raced out of the library faster than Nellie had ever seen him run. A few minutes later, Elijah returned to the chamber with Bronywyn and her personal guards on his tail. The warrior wasn't even out of breath, but the red tint on her cheeks betrayed the speed with which she had run to the library. She dismissed her guards with a wave before she came to stand before Nellie.

"What's this I hear about the Purge?" Bronywyn's voice was as sharp as ever as she glared at Nellie.

"As I was saying before Elijah ran off, my mother mentioned something about the Purge when she told me about the Wielders and gave me this pendant." Nellie gestured to the pendant hanging on top of her dress. "I was reading through this book looking for clues from Tomas when I stumbled across the word and-"

Before Nellie could say another word, Bronywyn moved forward and yanked on the book, trying to pull it out of Nellie's hands. Perturbed by the audacity, Nellie swatted the warrior away.

"That's mine," she said. As soon as she laid claim to the book, she knew it in her heart to be true. The book and the pendant belonged together. The pendant felt *right* as it hung off her neck, and the book carried the same sense of belonging. Nellie couldn't explain it, but they were hers.

Bronywyn took a step back and scowled at Nellie, but she didn't move to take the book from her again. Huffing, she sat on the arm of a chair and crossed her arms over her chest. "What was so important that Elijah had to come running for me?"

Having won the battle for the book, Nellie smiled softly as she sat back down. She thumbed through the pages, landing on the spot she had found. Clearing her throat, she read out loud.

546 Years after Inception - The Sacred Solstice

The Queen successfully purged the country of the Wielders today. It was fitting that today, of all days, the Wielders were finally dealt with. The Purge is complete. The Sequencing is saved.

The Majestic Queen Francesca found the last remaining Wielder, a

Healer by the name of Margarite Ann Barlowe, guilty of Wielding the elements. Her Majesty, having interceded with the Source on the Wielder's behalf, graciously commuted the traitor's sentence from execution to Re-Sequencing.

Upon hearing the Royal Decree, the Royal Protectors removed the Wielder from the Queen's sight immediately. They took her to the Oblitus Mountains to be Re-Sequenced.

The Queen has purged the country of Wielders.

The Purging is complete.

Tiarny is safe.

Long live the Queen.

Nellie closed the book and looked around the room. There were five pairs of eyes focused on her.

"That's it?" Elijah asked. "Was there more?"

Nellie shook her head. "No, it speaks about some goats that were sold at the market and the treatment of some Builders who had a grievance against some Firsts later that year. There was nothing else that I could find about the Purge or Wielders. I'm not even sure if it's important except for the fact that Tomas was so insistent that I find this book."

Elijah exchanged a glance with Bronywyn before he stood up. "I think it's very important. You have the pendant and the book here, and they obviously sought you out. Bronywyn, I think the prophecy is finally coming to fruition."

"Prophecy?" Nellie spoke at the same time as Solange and Dion. "What prophecy?"

Bronywyn groaned, shaking her head.

"I can't explain it all right now. But I think Elijah's right. There's only one problem, Elijah. If you're right and this is the key, we can't keep her here."

"You're right." Her friend was pacing now as he rubbed the back of his neck, his long legs making easy strides across the library. "We would have to go to Deavita. The prophecy is clear about that. Are you sure?"

Nellie stood up, standing in between Elijah and Bronywyn.

"Excuse me?" She said, "I'm not going anywhere until someone explains to me what is going on. Right now. Or I'm taking *my* pendant and *my* book back to *my* room."

"Shall I tell her, Elijah, or will you?" Bronywyn said, her foot tapping impatiently on the floor.

"Go ahead, Bronywyn," Elijah replied. "I know you're itching to get going."

"Very well. Eleanor. There is an ancient prophecy that has been passed down through the Subversives for the past two hundred years. It states that there will be a moment in time where things seem to be at their worst. At that time, someone will be Sequenced who will be able to Wield the elements once more. It is only by finding this Wielder and harnessing the power of the three talismans that they will restore the balance in Tiarny."

Nellie's jaw hit the ground as she stared at Bronywyn.

"I believe, Eleanor, that your pendant and the book are two of the three talismans needed to restore the balance. We've been told they marked the talismans with a symbol that would be recognizable as soon as we brought the talismans together. Evidently, the tree is the binding symbol on all three talismans. We don't know where the third one is specifically, but we know it is in the capital. We must go there to retrieve it."

"Wait." Nellie held up a hand, looking between Elijah and Bronywyn.

Disbelief rang through her voice. "You believe I am this.... Wielder? Why? I've never done anything like this before in my life."

Bronywyn sighed, running her fingers through her hair. "It's hard to explain, Eleanor. The Subversives have been around for a long time and we have extensive records. We know all Wielders were Sequenced as Healers. We don't know why or what exactly that means, but we know we've been waiting for a Healer. The prophecy spoke of you."

"And Tomas? How did he factor into this?" Crossing her arms, Nellie stared at Bronywyn.

"I'm not sure, Eleanor. He was a very wise old man, and chances are, maybe he read about the Purge in one of the historical documents he kept. The only reason we know about this is that the Subversives have kept its memory alive. It certainly isn't something that Guardians are teaching wards about."

"No, they most certainly are not." Shaking her head, Nellie groaned. "He must have known something to direct me to this book. I just wish... I wish he had waited for me."

"His death isn't your fault, Eleanor." Dion spoke quietly, his gaze piercing. "You did not cause this. But this," he gestured to the book, "is something you can do. A way to honour his memory."

Nellie nodded, her eyes staring at Dion. He always seemed to be able to look right into her soul.

Bronywyn huffed. "This is all well and good, but we need to make a plan. We must leave for Deavita as soon as possible."

Dion stepped forward; his arms folded as he studied the warrior. "Do you believe this to be true?"

Bronywyn nodded, her expression grim.

"And going to the capital is the only way for this... prophecy... to be fulfilled?" Dion's black eyes flashed as he glared at Bronywyn. This was the man Nellie had first met in the Sequencing Ceremony. Even Bronywyn shrunk back as the Official spoke.

"It is," she said. "I'm certain of it."

Dion tilted his head, examining the warrior for a moment before turning to Elijah. "And you? Do you believe this too?"

Elijah nodded; his expression sombre.

Sighing, Dion turned towards Nellie, coming up to stand beside her behind the large desk.

"Eleanor," he lowered his voice, whispering so softly only she could hear him. "They're telling the truth. I don't know how to explain it, but I've always been able to tell these types of things. I think we have to go to Deavita."

Nellie looked at each person in the room as she stood up to her full height. She never would have imagined this scenario the morning of her Sequencing Ceremony. If she followed down this path, it would irrevocably change her life. If the prophecy was correct, she may never have had a chance at normalcy, anyway.

Breathing deeply, Nellie closed her eyes and counted to three, sending a prayer to the Source for safety and well-being. She straightened her dress and drew back her shoulders, her head held high. The pendant was warm against her skin, imbuing her with strength. Nellie's voice resonated through the room.

"Well then. It looks like I'm getting my way after all. Let's go to the capital."

Chapter Thirty-Five

"Perfect. I'm going to inform Mother what we have learned. I'll be back shortly so we can plan." Bronywyn practically ran out of the library, Ulric following close behind her. The moment the warrior left the library, Nellie watched, speechless, as Dion and Elijah began yet another staring contest. She stared at them, trying to find words to say, when she felt a hand on her shoulder.

"We're coming with you." Solange whispered in Nellie's ear as she pulled her into a hug. "Raf and I. It's the right thing to do."

"What?" Nellie drew back, her eyes searching her mentor's face. "But you haven't left The Haven in over seven years."

"That's exactly why we need to go. Rafael and I have some connections in the capital that may be of use to you." Solange glanced over to her husband, the two of them engaging in the type of silent conversation that only people who had been together for a long time could achieve. "It's already decided. We're going to help you. You can't fight us on this."

True to their word, after a month of planning, Solange and Rafael accompanied the rest of the group to the Surface. The bright light was blinding, and Nellie winced when she came out the hatch. "I don't remember the sun being this bright ever before."

"It gets easier once your eyes get used to being outside again," Elijah said.

"I sure hope so." Nellie replied, shielding her eyes to the brilliant sunlight. Begrudgingly, she had to admit Elijah was right. Her lips tilted up as she fingered the pendant, her book clutched in her left hand. She gazed around the clearing, taking in the bright blue sky and the lush grass. Even in the midst of the resting season, it was beautiful.

One step closer to home.

From the clearing, it took an hour to walk to the nearest portal. Bronywyn and Elijah had tried to prepare Nellie for what she would experience when she went through, but no amount of planning could account for what actually happened.

Elijah was the first to approach the portal, dagger in his hand, while the rest of the group waited behind. "It may not be safe," Bronywyn explained. The warrior wasn't wearing her usual dress, but instead the tunic of a Protector. "It's safer this way, to wear the clothing of the Sequenced. Everyone needs to be careful. The portal should let us out near the Queen's Road in Dariani and it's usually deserted, but you just never know."

Nellie had watched, gripping the small red book, as Elijah got close to the tree with the burnt orange leaves. As soon as he got close to the tree, he suddenly just... disappeared.

"Is it always like that?" She asked Bronywyn, eyes wide as her mind struggled to comprehend what she just saw.

"It is." The warrior confirmed. "This is why we guard the portal near The Haven so closely."

Even now, there were three Subversive guards standing back, patrolling the area as the group went through the portal. After Elijah,

Solange and Rafael walked up to the portal hand in hand. Nellie watched as they murmured something too low to hear, embracing each other in a way that made even Bronywyn blush, before they disappeared together into the portal.

"Okay, Eleanor, it's your turn. Remember, you'll be unconscious for a few minutes after you go through the portal and that's okay. It's expected. Elijah will be there waiting for you. Dion and I will be right behind you."

Dion grimaced at Nellie. Earlier that day, Bronywyn had been adamant that they would still be keeping an eye on him, despite the fact that he had been with them in The Haven for the past seven months.

Rolling his eyes, Dion had reluctantly agreed. "One day, Bronywyn, you'll trust me."

"Maybe so, Official, but that day isn't today."

Just before she walked towards the tree, Nellie turned back to look at Dion. His eyes followed her every movement, the jagged scar on his cheek stark in the midday sun. "Eleanor," he murmured. "Be safe."

Be safe.

"I'll do my best, Dion."

Turning around, Nellie stood still as she stared at the tree, willing her mind to comprehend what she was about to do.

The sooner you do this, the sooner you can re-unite the talismans and go home.

Inhaling deeply, she gulped before shutting her eyes.

One.

Two.

Three.

She opened her eyes, clutching her book to her chest. The pendant warmed against her skin, seeming to encourage her forward.

When she was close enough to reach out a hand and touch one of the burnt orange leaves, Nellie jolted as she felt a tearing sensation ripple through her stomach. Before she could say anything, she fell into blackness as pain radiated through her entire body. It felt as though she was being ripped apart at the seams. Her temples throbbed, her very skin felt like it was being flayed off her bones.

When Nellie thought she couldn't stand another second of the agony ripping through her, it disappeared completely. Nellie groaned, her body aching, as she felt something soft beneath her palms. She opened her eyes, the midday sun blinding her as she looked around. She was... on the ground surrounded by Solange and Rafael.

Nellie pushed herself up and looked at her surroundings. They were in front of yet another tree that matched the one they had just walked through, although this tree was in a grove of evergreens. Pine needles covered the ground, sticking to her hands as she pushed herself off the ground. Just as Nellie rose to her feet, she saw Elijah coming around a tree. He gripped his dagger, his brows furrowed. "Nellie? I thought you went in the portal after me."

"I-I did. I came after Solange and Rafael."

"Then how are you awake? You should be unconscious for at least a minute after that."

"I don't know."

Suddenly, Bronywyn and Dion landed on the pine needles in front of the tree. Somehow, the portal's magic ensured that people didn't land on top of each other, but placed them almost gently onto the ground beside one another. They too, were unconscious and lying there as Solange and Rafael came to.

Ten minutes later, the group was once again alert and conscious as they huddled in a circle near the evergreen trees.

"Maybe it's the pendant?" Bronywyn mused. "She was already unconscious last time she went through the portal, so we can't be sure. We could have her try again..."

"No." Nellie interjected, her voice firm. "I am not a guinea pig to be used for your amusement. Whatever kept me from passing out will have to remain a mystery for now. I've waited for months to get to the Surface. Now that I'm here, let's get going."

A few hours later, the group had arrived on foot to the abandoned two-bedroom wattle and daub hut that Bronywyn's scouts had marked as a safe-house. A large, circular fence surrounded the property, with a gate at one end.

"They must have had goats or horses here at one time," Bronywyn said, "but they don't anymore. The land used to belong to a Farmer, but my scouts tell me the man and his family were relocated after the rains stopped falling."

The portal had spat them out close to Dariani, and they were far enough from Deavita that even the special irrigation systems the Engineers had created weren't able to save this part of the land. Nellie's stomach had been grumbling by the time they walked up to the hut and she had almost cried when she saw the supplies of food and water that the scouts had left.

The next day, Nellie had stared open-mouthed when Bronywyn had returned from a scouting mission leading a very large black horse into the yard. "This is Midnight," the warrior said while petting the horse's mane, a soft smile on her face. "She will be perfect."

The perfect way to kill me, Nellie had thought morosely. Looking up at the massive creature, Nellie's palms were clammy as she realized that she would have to learn how to guide this creature on her own. She felt herself losing control of her breathing when she felt a warm presence come up behind her.

"Eleanor," Dion said softly, "it's okay. I'll teach you. You'll be a master horsewoman in no time."

"Hmmm." Nellie made a noncommittal sound as she stared at the horse. "Remind me why I agreed to this plan again?" She looked over her shoulder at Dion.

"Because it's the best way to get into the capital. Right before we go in, we'll acquire another horse for me. And the sooner we get to Deavita, —"

"The sooner I can get back to Liantis." Nellie finished his sentence for him.

Dion smirked, a twinkle in his eye. He stiffened, and before Nellie could ask what was wrong, she heard footsteps approaching.

"You aren't the only master horseman here, Dion." Elijah said as he walked towards them, his arms full of wood for the fire. "I'd be happy to help you learn how to ride Midnight, Nell-bell."

"Well...." Nellie drew out the word, looking between the two men. "I suppose you can both teach me?" She shrugged. "If you two can deal with being around each other, that is. Besides, the sooner I figure this thing out, the sooner we can get out of here."

Placing a large hand on Nellie's shoulder, Dion glared at Elijah. "I'll put aside my differences if he agrees to do the same."

Elijah bristled; his jaw clenched as he stared over Nellie's head at Dion. "This is for Nellie. For her, I'd do anything."

Hands on her hips, Nellie stared between the two men. "Fine. It's settled. Elijah can teach me today, and Dion, you can teach me tomorrow."

"Eleanor—" Dion said but Nellie held up her hand.

"Don't you *Eleanor* me. You agreed, so deal with it." She glared at him until he backed away, hands up.

It turned out that letting Elijah teach Nellie meant that Dion spent most of the next hour leaning against the hut, his arms crossed as he watched Elijah teaching her how to saddle the horse. Nellie felt the weight of his stare as she moved around Midnight, buckling the saddle and getting used to the horse.

After an hour had passed, Solange seemed to have taken pity on Dion, for she came outside and beckoned the Official to join her. Nellie was too far away to hear everything they were saying, but she heard the words "distraction" and "help" come out of her mentor's mouth.

Seeming to relax once Dion was inside the hut, Elijah helped her on the large animal, his voice low. "Shoulders back, Nell-bell. Relax. The horse can feel if you're anxious. Just breathe. Midnight isn't out to get you. Look ahead, don't look down."

"Okay. I can do this." Nellie breathed in deeply, shifting her hips as she settled into the saddle. She leaned forward, patting the horse's mane. "Please be kind to me, Midnight."

The moment Elijah let go of the reins and stepped back, Nellie felt her mind go blank. She froze, staring straight ahead, as the horse shifted underneath her. Gulping, she looked down at Elijah as a drop of sweat rolled down her forehead. Her hands were clammy as she gripped the reins. "Elijah," she whispered as her pulse quickened, "I looked down. I looked down, and it's really far. I don't think I can do this."

Seeming to sense her panic, Midnight whinnied and stamped her front hoof on the ground. Dust billowed up all around them, temporarily blinding Nellie. Whimpering, she gripped the horse's reins. "Stop, please stop." Tears began to run from her eyes as Midnight ignored her pleas and began to gallop around the property. Unsure of what to do, Nellie held onto the reins for dear life as she wept.

"Dion! Elijah! Help!" She screamed as Midnight ran a circle around the hut, the horse's hoofbeats ringing in her ears.

Oh Source, I just knew I would die on the back of a horse. I knew it. No plan is worth this.

"Nellie! You need to tighten your grip around the horse." Elijah was yelling, his voice frantic as he ran after the horse. He was breathless, his voice betraying his nerves as he followed them.

"What?" Tears clouded Nellie's vision, making it difficult to see. "I don't know how to stop, Elijah!"

Nellie heard Elijah screaming. He sounded like he was in front of them now. Somewhere in the back of her mind, she realized he must have circled the hut from the other direction. "Woah, Midnight. Woah. Nellie, you need to squeeze your legs and pull gently on the reins."

Sobbing, she did as Elijah asked. Miraculously, Midnight slowed down. Before the horse came to a full-stop, she swung her feet out of the saddle. She threw herself to the ground, her shoulder banging up against the side of the hut as she landed back on the ground. Elijah ran over to her, grabbing the reins before tying them to a nearby tree. He hurried back over to her.

"Nellie, are you okay?"

"Am I okay?" She sobbed. "No, I am not okay. The horse almost killed me, Elijah. I am definitely not okay." Nellie rubbed her shoulder, the muscles throbbing where she hit the hut.

"Eleanor!" Dion yelled as he came running out of the hut. Solange and Rafael were on his tail as he rounded the corner. His eyes filled with fury as he looked between Nellie, still seated on the ground, and the horse. "This is what you call teaching her to ride, Elijah?"

Dion clenched his fists, his dark hair stuck to his face in the afternoon heat. He took a step forward, his anger radiating off him in waves, as he glared at Elijah. "You were supposed to protect her."

Elijah scowled; his jaw clenched as his lips drew back in a snarl. "I did protect her. The horse stopped, obviously."

"You should have taught her how to stop before letting go of the reins. You are insane. Your actions could have gotten her killed!" Dion's voice rumbled through the air, as he approached Elijah.

Oh Source. They're going to fight.

Groaning, Nellie pulled herself to her feet, her hands in the air as she shifted to stand between the two of them. "Stop. *Please.* This is not going to fix anything."

"Eleanor," Dion growled. "He almost got you killed."

"But I'm still alive, Dion." Nellie took a step closer to Dion, putting her hand on his forearm. "Please, don't do anything stupid. We need Elijah for the plan."

"I suppose you're right, Eleanor." Dion said, sighing. "But I'm taking over your lessons now. The last thing we need is for you to have another accident. You might not be so lucky next time. The sooner you learn how to ride, the sooner we can leave this Source-forsaken hovel and get back to Deavita."

Chapter Thirty-Six

"Don't put your foot there Eleanor, you'll fall off again if you do that." Dion said as he watched Nellie atop Midnight, his hands on his hips.

Gritting her teeth, Nellie groaned. "I know, Dion." Her grip on the reins tightened, her fingers stiffening as she shifted in the saddle. Her entire body protested the movement, her muscles groaning as she shifted.

Midnight whinnied, her hooves stirring up the dust of the Queen's Road. A week had passed since what Nellie had taken to calling the *incident* in her mind. Dion and Elijah avoided each other as much as possible, which was saying something, since the hovel was rather small. Elijah and Bronywyn had spent most of the week with their heads huddled around the only table, discussing the various plans and contingencies they had put into place.

Sighing, Dion ran his hand through his hair. His shoulders were tense, his body looking ready for battle as he stood in the middle of the dusty field. "Okay, Eleanor. Let's go over the plan one more time. The only reason Bronywyn agreed to let us out of her sight at all is that you promised you'd stick to it."

Stroking the pendant that lay under her tunic, Nellie grimaced as she looked down. "I know, Dion. It's all anyone can talk about. Elijah can't come into the city because they think he's dead, so it's just the two of us. He's going to stay at a safe-house on the outskirts of Deavita with Solange and Rafael, and we'll meet up with them as soon as it's safe. I listened to all of you arguing for days in The Haven before you all agreed to the plan."

"Yes, and now that Bronywyn has agreed to it, she needs us to actually follow it through," he said.

"That's right, I do." Bronywyn's melodious voice came from the grove of trees off the Queen's Road. Nellie glanced over, her eyes catching on the warrior's dark hair as she stood between a pair of enormous evergreens, making her seem as though she was one with the forest. "Just because I'm not coming into the capital with you, Eleanor, doesn't mean that the plan is any less important. After all—"

"You're going to be connecting with the other sects of the Subversives throughout Tiarny while we are in the capital." Nellie sighed, patting the horse's mane. "I remember. For our cover story to work, I need to know how to ride because we'll be showing up in Deavita on two horses."

"Yes. What are the best lies made of?" Bronywyn queried from her position by the trees.

"Portions of the truth." Nellie rubbed her temples, clutching the reins with one hand. "I remember."

Seemingly appeased, Bronywyn walked away, pulling herself over the fence before walking into the fields. She had been doing this all week, and no matter how many times Nellie asked, Bronywyn wouldn't tell her where she was going.

"Speaking of riding, Eleanor, let's see what you can do." Dion had the gall to *wink* at her, as though the sight of her on a horse was amusing. He had relaxed quite a bit over the past week, making sure to teach Nellie everything he knew about horses before she even attempted to get back on Midnight. Her second time on the horse had gone much better, although Dion had insisted on holding the reins the entire time for fear of repeating the same incident.

They had been outside every single day this week for hours at a time, sometimes while Solange and Rafael watched, other times, all alone. Elijah always seemed to disappear during Nellie's training sessions. Finally, though, it seemed that she was gaining some confidence.

Rolling her eyes in Dion's direction, Nellie squeezed her thighs and encouraged the horse into a trot. She inhaled, focusing on her breathing as the black steed began to move. "Okay Midnight, let's see if we can stay together this time."

Rubbing her left shoulder as she gripped the reins with one hand, Nellie grimaced as she fingered the bruise that had bloomed after her fall.

Don't fall off. That's your only goal.

Inhale

Focus.

Exhale

You can do this.

Repeat.

As Midnight trotted around the hovel, Nellie tried to remember everything she had been told about riding horses in the past few days.

"Eleanor," Dion ground out through clenched teeth after Midnight passed him a third time. He was tapping his foot on the ground, rubbing the back of his neck as he watched her. "What is the plan?"

She circled the horse around, encouraging Midnight to stop right beside Dion. The man didn't move, not even as the horse came to stand less than a foot from him. She sighed, handing the reins to Dion before she hopped off the horse. She landed on the ground, feet straight, and didn't even wobble once. Grinning, Nellie laughed. "I did it, I actually did it." Spinning in a circle, she patted Midnight's flank. "Good girl. Thank you for not killing me."

"You did well." A hint of a smile danced on Dion's face.

"Wow, Dion. Did it hurt you to compliment me?" She smirked up at him, her eyes twinkling.

"It kind of did. Now, Eleanor, the plan?" Dion raised a brow, but she could see him suppressing laughter.

"Okay, fine." Nellie sighed, crossing her arms in front of her chest. "For the hundredth time. Almost eight months ago, after the rebel attack, you and I got separated from the rest of the convoy. We were taken by the rebels and they brought us into the Forest of Resim."

"And then?"

"And then they kept us captive for months. We stayed quiet, gaining their trust while we learned about them. We lived in near-darkness, the light of the leaves making it impossible to see much of anything. Finally, we were able to steal two horses from them and escape in the middle of the night. With the Source's Blessing, we made it out of the Forest unscathed, and raced as fast as we could up the Queen's Road to the capital."

"That's right." Nodding, Dion led Midnight to her trough. "I think, Eleanor, that it's time."

Two days later, Nellie and Dion stood in front of the wattle and daub hovel, their horses laden with packs. Bronywyn had acquired Pearl, the white steed that was currently sniffing around the yard, through what she had said were "less-than-reputable means' ' the day before.

She looked at the group, a lump in her throat forming as she pulled Solange into a hug. "I'm going to miss you so much," she whispered.

"I know, Eleanor. But it's okay. We're going to travel by night and we should be right behind the two of you. Do you remember where to meet us?"

Nellie nodded, swallowing her tears. "Yes. The Fare and Spigot. It's a pub on the outskirts of town, in the districts usually inhabited by Thirds. Once there, we should ask for Lucinda or Abram."

Solange smiled. "That's right. They'll be able to help you, won't they, Rafael?"

The white-haired man nodded. "They sure will. I'll make sure of it."

Elijah cleared his throat, stepping forward. "I'll be staying with Solange and Rafael, but I'll make contact as soon as possible. Bronywyn and I think we might have a way to get me into the city without anyone noticing. Nellie, promise me you'll be careful. Just... be careful."

"I promise, Elijah." Nellie smiled softly at her old friend. He shifted on his feet, his face reddening slightly. "Nell-bell, can I... can I hug you?"

"Of course." She replied instantly. Elijah's arms were warm as he enveloped her. "Nellie, I'm so sorry for what happened with Midnight, I just—"

"Lijah. It's okay. I forgive you."

He sighed, giving her a final squeeze before releasing her. "Thank you. I promise, I'll see you as soon as possible."

Nellie looked at Bronywyn, who had her arms crossed as she stood back from the group. "Don't think you're going to get a hug from me, Eleanor."

"I wouldn't dream of it, Bronywyn."

"Good. You should arrive in Deavita in four days. Your saddlebags are well packed with food and water. Make sure you don't stray off the Queen's Road, just to be safe."

Nodding, Nellie turned towards Dion. He was holding the reins of the horses, his obsidian eyes trained on her as she moved. "Are you ready, Eleanor?"

Breathing in deeply, she closed her eyes momentarily before nodding. "As ready as I'll ever be."

"Then let's go." Dion lifted her onto Midnight, his hands lingering for a moment on her hips as she settled into the saddle. His touch was warm, sending tingles down her spine. He mounted Pearl with ease, as though he was one with the steed. Dion nodded towards the group, his head dipping. "We'll see you all soon. Ready, Eleanor?"

Biting her lip, Nellie grabbed the pendant and turned it over in her hand. She smiled, its warmth radiating throughout her body.

"Let's go, Dion. Deavita awaits."

TO BE CONTINUED...

THANK YOU SO MUCH FOR READING SEQUENCED!

DID YOU KNOW THERE IS A BONUS CHAPTER? TO READ THE SEQUENCING FROM DION'S PERSPECTIVE, CLICK HERE TO SIGN UP TO MY NEWSLETTER AND STAY UP TO DATE WITH MY BOOKS.

IF THE LINK DOESN'T WORK, GO TO: https://www.elaynargallea. com/bonus-content

Keep reading for a sneak peek at Rise of the Subversives

OUT NOW!

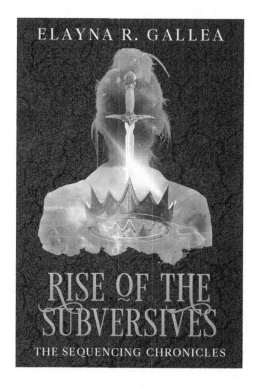

The outskirts of Deavita

"This is it, Eleanor. Are you ready?" Dion's voice rumbled as he rode up behind Nellie. Dust flew in the air as the dry earth crumbled under their horses' hooves.

"Mhmm," she mumbled as she sat astride her horse, Midnight. Her mouth was agape, her eyes wide as she stared straight ahead. "It's just... more. So much bigger than I thought."

Nestled in the enormous valley below them was the beginning of a massive cityscape. Nellie tried to count the buildings, but she soon realized the futility of the exercise. Her grip on Midnight's reins tightened as she swept her eyes over the horizon.

"Eleanor?" Dion glanced at her, concern evident in his voice. He reached over, leaning off his white horse to place a hand on her shoulder.

She jolted at the touch that sent jitters down her arm. "I... Deavita is so much larger than I ever thought it was. It makes Liantis look like a poor little shantytown." Nellie stared at the city, her eyes unable to comprehend the vast amount of infrastructure in front of her. "How are we ever going to find the talisman in a city this size?"

"We will, Eleanor," he said confidently. "The pendant and the book found you, and I'm sure the third one will as well."

"I hope so," she sighed, her gaze never leaving the capital as Midnight shifted under her. "I can't believe the size of this city. There must be thousands upon thousands of people who live here. It's nothing like Liantis."

As a non-committal hum left Dion's lips, Nellie looked over at him. He sat tall on Pearl, his hands hanging lazily as he held the reins, his obsidian eyes sweeping the horizon. "I suppose it is quite different, isn't it? Just wait until you see the Palace."

Shivers ran through her at the mention of the Queen's residence. Before they had left the small hut where they'd been staying, Nellie's mentor Solange had told Nellie about her unfortunate experience with the Queen's Hand in Deavita.

"I think I'll be just fine if I never see the Palace, Dion," Nellie said, shaking her head.

With a swing of his legs, Dion dismounted from his horse and held out his hand. "Let's take a walk, Eleanor."

"What, now? But we're so close." Disbelief was apparent in her voice as she stared at him.

"I want to show you something. Please."

Please.

Intrigued, Nellie hopped off Midnight and followed Dion off the Queen's Road. Dust billowed up around them as they walked, the parched earth screaming for water after over four years without rain. Nellie unhooked the jug of the life-giving liquid they had brought with them, watering the horses before tying their reins to a nearby branch.

By the time she had secured the knot, she turned around to find Dion standing right behind her. "What did you want to show me?" Nellie asked, her voice soft as she looked up at Dion. The scar he had received almost eight months ago from Bronywyn had faded, the jagged line that ran down his cheek a bright pink in the sunlight. It was a stark reminder that they had been kept against their will for over six months.

"Come here," he said, tilting his head and gesturing to a spot not too far away.

She followed him, glancing back to make sure the horses were okay. Pearl was munching on some blades of grass that she had found near the tree, while Midnight simply stood and watched them.

Dion stood on the crest of the hill, his gaze intent as he looked into the valley below. To the east, far off on the horizon, Nellie could see the beginnings of the Forest of Resim.

The trees were completely black, their bark and leaves absorbing all light, and even now, the far-away forest seemed to absorb the brilliant sunlight shining down from the bright blue sky. In front of them, there was what appeared to be a large stone ring that encircled the capital, the sunlight glimmering off the wall.

"There, do you see that, Eleanor?" Dion pointed towards the city, his arm outstretched towards the buildings on the eastern side. "That tall, pale grey building over there?"

Nellie had to squint, but finally, she saw the structure Dion was referring to. It had to be at least four stories tall, towering over the rest of the infrastructure in the area. "I do," she breathed. "What is it?"

"That is my home," he said, shifting on his feet. "Or at least, it was. I don't know if it still is."

Wide-eyed, Nellie shifted to look at Dion. Never, not once in the past eight months, had he ever referred to his life in Deavita or exactly what he did as a Sequenced Official.

"That massive building is *your* home? As in, you live there? All by yourself? You could fit an entire army of wards and Guardians in that building." Raising a brow, she stared at him, placing a hand on her hip. "What kind of Official are you?"

Dion laughed, the sound reverberating through Nellie as they stood side-by-side. "Let's just say the kind that even most other Firsts might be jealous of."

"I'll say," Nellie groused. Even from here, his home looked enormous. It was nothing like the small townhouse she had shared with her mother back in Liantis. "We had nothing like this back home."

Dion glanced at Nellie, the breeze causing his silky brown hair to blow in his eyes. He brushed it aside, clearing his throat as he rubbed the back of his neck. "You're a First now, Eleanor. You need to get used to things like this. Remember, the plan depends on us blending back in."

She sighed, shaking her plaited hair as blue-black tendrils floated into her face. "I remember. We've gone over the plan countless times since we came back to the Surface. It's imperative we find the final talisman, and in order to do that, we need to get into the capital."

Right before Nellie and Dion had left the little wattle and daub hut where they had been staying, Bronywyn had received word from an acquaintance of hers who ran a sect of the Subversives out of Ion. She had come running inside the hut just as Dion and Nellie had been packing their saddlebags.

"Oscar just sent this note," Bronywyn had said breathlessly, her hands clutching a small, crumpled piece of paper. "His pigeon was just here."

"Pigeon?" Nellie had asked, her brows raised. "I've never heard of a pigeon being able to deliver messages before."

"Carrier birds are one of the most reliable methods of communication used by the Subversives." Bronywyn puffed out her chest. "For centuries, we have trained pigeons to fly undetected throughout Tiarny."

"Oh." Nellie had replied, shrugging. "That's... unexpected. I never thought we could use birds for that."

"We can," Bronywyn nodded emphatically. "I sent Oscar a message when I got Midnight. We're lucky he could get back to us in time. He says he thinks the third talisman is likely to be found in a building with restricted access in Deavita."

A scuttle of fear had run across Nellie's back as she clutched the pendant. She hadn't bothered to hide it, since they all knew she carried it. "Did you tell him about my necklace and book?" She had asked, indignant. "If so, you had no right."

Dion had turned to Bronywyn, his obsidian eyes flashing. "She's right, Bronywyn." He growled. "Did you endanger us by sending this message?"

Bronywyn had taken a step back, her hands raised in the air. "No, I only told Oscar we found the other two talismans. Do you take me for a fool? Of course, I didn't say anything that would reveal your identities. Nellie is far too important to us."

Dion had narrowed his eyes at the warrior, but he hadn't said anything else.

In the four days since they had left the small hovel, Nellie had been searching the bright, endlessly blue sky for any signs of birds flying above. She didn't see anything out of the ordinary.

As they stood on the hilltop, Dion shifted, running his hand through his hair. The scent of lush grass and fresh rain wafted over her as they stood gazing over the capital. Nellie felt her chest tighten as she realized how close they were. His arm brushed hers as he turned, his eyes dark as he studied her face. He lifted a hand, gently tucking a wayward strand of loose hair behind her ear. "Eleanor," he said gruffly. "There's something—"

Before he could finish the sentence, they both jolted as the sound of hoofbeats filled the air. Nellie looked up, blood draining from her face, as four imposing horsemen clad in blood-red tunics crested the hill.

"Halt," one of the Royal Protectors called out, his hair the colour of the sun. "What is your business in Deavita?"

Gulping, Nellie looked at the guards. They sat as still as statues on their horses, their expressions hard as they stared down at them. Nellie was grateful she had hidden the pendant underneath her Healer's tunic this morning after we woke up. Her palms grew sweaty, and she had to remind herself to be the picture of relaxation as she stood, unmoving.

Breathe, Nellie. You prepared for this. Remember the plan.

Before she could reply, Dion stepped forward. His gaze was steely, his eyes cold as he stared at the Royal Protectors.

"My name is Dion Marchmont," he said firmly. His voice was like iron, hard and unfaltering.

Nellie raised a brow. "I thought—"

Dion twisted and glared at Nellie. She took a step back at the sight of his dark eyes. They were devoid of the warmth that had just been there a moment ago. The change was so sudden, Nellie was wondering if he had ever been showing her any kindness at all.

"Eleanor, *not now*," he hissed, clenching a fist at his side. Turning back to the guards, he continued, "I can assure you that you want to treat us with respect."

One of the Royal Protectors shifted on his horse, his gaze travelling up and down them. Nellie knew they must look a sight, covered in dust and grime from the road they had travelled. They had tried to keep clean, but hygienic practices were difficult enough to maintain on the road even when water was in good supply.

In the middle of a four-year drought?

It was nearly impossible.

"Is that so?" The blond Protector said, his voice nasally as he looked down on them. "And why is that?"

Dion glared at the man. Nellie took a step back. Gone was the man that she had come to know over the past eight months. In his place was the cold Official who had been at her Sequencing. His posture was rigid, the very aura emanating from him demanding respect.

A dark, mirthless laugh escaped Dion. "Because I am not just any Official. I am cousin to the Queen."

Want to know more about Solange and Rafael?

Their story is covered in The Runaway Healer. Click the picture to read now.

Acknowledgments

This book wouldn't be possible without so many people. First and foremost, I want to thank my husband, Aaron. You are amazing, my love, and you know that I would never have done this on my own. You make me strong and courageous. Thank you for believing in me and being my biggest cheerleader. I love you.

To my two amazing children, Britanny and Jack. You are both incredible and we love you so much. No matter what you choose to do in life, I know you will succeed. God bless, my loves.

To my writer's group. Daniela A. Mera and K.G. Myro. There aren't enough words in the English language to express the extent of my appreciation of both of you. I know this book would have never come into being without your constant encouragement. I am so grateful for everything you ladies have taught me. Thank you for putting up with the multiple drafts and edits this book has gone through. I love our weekly meetings and cannot wait to see what we all do next.

To my alpha, beta and ARC readers. Thank you! You have been amazing and this book wouldn't be what it is today without you.

To my family, thank you so much for encouraging my love of reading. Without that, this would never have happened.

To BookTok and AuthorTok. My word, what fantastic communities. I am so appreciative of all the people I have met on the platform.

To you, the reader. A book is a baby, and I am so grateful that you took the time to read mine. I hope you enjoyed it as I did writing it! I hope you'll come back for more.

Also by Elayna R. Gallea

The Sequencing Chronicles:

The Runaway Healer

Rise of the Subversives

The Wielder of Prophecy (04.05.2022)

Romancing Aranthium:

Opposite Ends of the Sea

About the Author

Elayna R. Gallea lives in beautiful New Brunswick, Canada with her husband and two children. They live in the land of snow and forests, near the lovely Saint John River. When Elayna isn't reading or writing, she can be found teaching French online to her amazing students.

Made in the USA
Coppell, TX
30 April 2022

77244245R10188